Suzanne Wright lives in England with her husband and two children. When she's not spending time with her family, she's writing, reading or doing her version of housework – sweeping the house with a look.

She's worked in a pharmaceutical company, at a Disney Store, at a primary school as a voluntary teaching assistant, at the RSPCA and has a First Class Honours degree in Psychology and Identity Studies.

As to her interests, she enjoys reading, writing, reading, writing (sort of eat, sleep, write, repeat), spending time with her family, movie nights with her sisters and playing with her two Bengal kittens.

To connect with Suzanne online:

Website: http://www.suzannewright.co.uk
Facebook: https://www.facebook.com/
suzannewrightfanpage

ALSO BY SUZANNE WRIGHT:

The Dark in You

Burn
Blaze
Ashes
Embers
Shadows
Omens
Fallen
Reaper
Hunted
Viper
Legion

The Devil's Cradle

The Wicked In Me
The Nightmare in Him
The Monsters We Are

BLACK WILLOW WITCH

Suzanne Wright

PIATKUS

PIATKUS

First published in Great Britain in 2025 by Piatkus

1 3 5 7 9 10 8 6 4 2

Copyright © Suzanne Wright, 2025

The moral right of the author has been asserted.

All characters and events in this publication, other than those
clearly in the public domain, are fictitious and any resemblance
to real persons, living or dead, is purely coincidental.

A CIP catalogue record for this book
is available from the British Library.

ISBN: 978-0-34944-642-4

Typeset in Goudy by M Rules

Printed and bound in Great Britain by
Clays Ltd, Elcograf S.p.A.

Papers used by Piatkus are from well-managed forests
and other responsible sources.

MIX
Paper | Supporting
responsible forestry
FSC
www.fsc.org FSC® C104740

Piatkus
An imprint of
Little, Brown Book Group
Carmelite House
50 Victoria Embankment
London EC4Y 0DZ

The authorised representative
in the EEA is
Hachette Ireland
8 Castlecourt Centre
Dublin 15, D15 XTP3, Ireland
(email: info@hbgi.ie)

An Hachette UK Company
www.hachette.co.uk

www.littlebrown.co.uk

For Sophie

PROLOGUE

◦◦◦

Emberlyn, age seven

Her heart beating superfast, Emberlyn sprinted up the hill. Her leg muscles burned, but she didn't stop.

So close. They were so close. Running. Panting. Laughing.

They were always laughing. Always whispering and pointing and saying mean stuff to her at school.

Every day they came at her. Shoulders shoved into hers. Feet tripped her up. Stuff got tossed at her head. Hands 'accidentally' knocked her pens off the table. And always, *always*, they'd laugh and call her 'pathetic'.

Sometimes, other kids in her class laughed along. It made her feel small, embarrassed and alone.

Emberlyn had told her teacher about it. He'd promised to 'have a word' with Tyra and her four flying monkeys. But if he had talked to them – and maybe he hadn't, since Tyra was the daughter of his High Priestess – it hadn't made a difference.

Then, just yesterday during recess, Tyra had pushed her so hard that she'd fallen into a puddle that had left her with a cold, wet butt.

And again, they'd laughed.

'You might as well stop, freak!' yelled Sera, Tyra's cousin. 'There's nowhere to go!'

Well there was *somewhere*, but Emberlyn wouldn't be heading into Bloodhill Forest. Not many did – the bullies behind her had nothing on the creatures that roamed it. She just wanted to reach the top of the hill. So she ran and ran and ran, never looking back; worried she'd otherwise trip. But she sensed that they were gaining on her.

She'd known that they would track her down after school today – they'd been angry that she'd talked to the principal again. Not that it had helped. They'd denied everything, and it was her word against theirs. Emberlyn's word meant nothing to the coven.

Why?

Because she wasn't part of it, much like her grandmother – a woman they both feared and resented. Okay, so they were right in claiming Millicent was 'into some pretty dark stuff' and that she wasn't the nicest person in the world. But that shouldn't mean that the coven could be mean to Emberlyn because of it.

When she'd told her grandmother about yesterday's puddle incident, Millicent's advice had been simple: *If someone pushes you, you push them back harder. A lot harder.*

So that's what Emberlyn would do.

Finally reaching the top of the hill, she came to a stop, raspy breaths bursting in and out of her. She turned on shaky legs, watching as the bullies skidded to a halt.

Tyra smirked, shoving her red braid over her shoulder. 'Aw, did the little freak run out of steam? How sad.' She paused, trying to catch her breath. 'I'd dare you to go cry to your mommy and daddy . . . but you can't, can you?'

A round of giggles went up, and Emberlyn felt her ears go red.

'I heard my parents talking about yours,' said Sera. 'It isn't true that your dad got asked to leave town, you know. He cheated on your mom and then left with his side piece.'

Emberlyn *did* know. Her grandmother had told her all about how she'd cursed that 'lying, cheating, son of a bitch'.

'Your mom just couldn't hack it, could she?' taunted Tyra. 'She let herself fade away, not caring that the only person you'd then have would be that psycho you live with. No offense, Ames,' she added, sliding her gaze to Emberlyn's *very own cousin*.

He only grinned. 'None taken. My Grams *is* a total psycho – everyone knows that.'

He may think that, but he was super nice to Millicent, the two-faced ass.

Tyra planted her hands on her hips. 'You got nothing to say, orphan?'

'Yes.' Emberlyn smiled sweetly. 'I just wanted to say "thank you".'

Tyra's brows snapped together. 'For what?'

'For letting me lure you out here, where no one'll hear you scream.' Emberlyn raised her hands and, calling on the lessons that Millicent had given her, sent out her magick in glittering, rippling streams that whirled around and settled on the grass.

Thorny vines sprouted out of the circle of magick ... then snakes ... spiders ... cockroaches ... toads.

The kids screamed and tried running away but hit an invisible barrier. Trapped, they called to their own magick, *zapping* the creatures, but it didn't help. Vines, serpents, insects and toads climbed up their bodies – pricking, biting, stinging.

Two girls started to cry. Sera shrieked like a banshee. Ames fell to the ground, screaming, 'Get off! Get off!' at the creatures. As for Tyra ... she begged Emberlyn to make it stop.

Emberlyn snapped her hands closed, balling them into fists. Like that, the magick settled and the creatures disappeared.

The bullies nervously peeked around, only going quiet when they saw that the hill was clear. Ames awkwardly stood, his knees buckling.

Glaring at them, Emberlyn warned, 'If there has to be a next time, I won't make them disappear so fast ... if at all.'

Eyeing her like they'd never seen her before, they backed up a few steps and then ran off.

Taking a deep breath, Emberlyn lowered her arms back to her sides. Hearing a rustle of grass behind her, she whirled. Her grandmother stood there in one of her black robes, her long gray hair its usual scraggly mess.

'Not bad, girl, not bad,' said Millicent, staring down at her through pale-hazel eyes that she'd passed onto Emberlyn. Eyes that people called eerie. 'The little fuckers sure had it coming,' she added, anger in every word.

'You weren't mad yesterday when I told you what they'd done.' Millicent hadn't even looked away from the book she'd been reading on soul stealing.

Millicent frowned. 'Girl, I was majorly pissed. I came close to infesting their homes with every bug you can think of. But the coven needs to see that you can fight your own battles.'

'And you were curious to see what I'd do,' Emberlyn sensed.

Millicent grinned. 'Something like that. You know, they only pick on you because they fear you and they're jealous of your potential. They sense that your magick is strong, so they want to make you feel weak. Others from the coven will try to do the same.' Her face darkened. 'Don't let them. Not now, not ever. If they or anyone else comes at you, you make them wish they hadn't. Be the biggest, baddest witch in town so no one ever dares bully you again.'

CHAPTER ONE

❦

Twenty years later

'Wait!'

The word sliced through the air, causing everyone at the gravesite to pause. It was Emberlyn's aunt who'd spoken, her blue eyes wide, her arms stretched out.

Gill licked her lips. 'Did anyone check the casket? Just to be sure she hasn't ... you know ... come back?'

Not one person snickered. In fact, some shifted uncomfortably at the thought. If any witch could have found a way to cheat death, it would have been Millicent Vautier.

She had not been well liked at Chilgrave, nor had she made any attempt to be. All Millicent had been interested in was acquiring more power. There were no forms of magick she hadn't dabbled in, no spells she'd shied away from. She'd had not one problem casting curses, sacrificing animals, invoking demons, working with dark deities or any such shit.

Given the risks that Millicent had consistently taken and the depths of magick she'd explored, Emberlyn considered it an absolute miracle that her grandmother had died a peaceful death – falling into an eternal slumber while taking a nap on a park bench on a warmish March day.

The threads of grief wrapped tight around her heart contracted as she recalled hearing news of Millicent's passing. It had been a dark day for Emberlyn, who'd loved the woman fiercely regardless of her … proclivities.

The High Priestess Reena cleared her throat. 'Maybe we *should* take a look.'

Three of Emberlyn's relatives stepped out of the nearby cluster of mourners.

Not really 'part' of the family, Emberlyn stood off to the side with her best friends, Paisley and Kage. The twins were her only *real* friends, to be truthful.

As people cautiously approached the coffin like it was a ticking bomb, Emberlyn idly swept her gaze over the charmingly gothic cemetery. It was perched on a slight hill, so the lines of headstones were a little higgledy-piggledy. Most of the tablets were granite, but others were concrete and marble – and all in various hues with lawns and flowerbeds. Sun-bleached statues and carvings and other monuments were sporadically placed here and there.

The cemetery's charm was woven throughout the entire town. Surrounded by lush forests that stretched for miles upon miles, Chilgrave was a patchwork of buildings from various eras … and it had once been home to both the first witch and the first werewolf.

There were lots of theories as to how Lilith Vautier – Emberlyn's ancestor – had come to be a witch. Similarly, there were many stories explaining how her lover, Lupin Stone, had become a werewolf. No one knew the 'hows' of it for sure.

Whatever the case, fascinated enough by the fictional stories of preternatural creatures, the couple had sought – and found – a way to become them. Lilith had shared her power with some of her townspeople. Likewise, Lupin had subjected others to the Change, creating more just like him. The coven's children were subsequently born witches, just as the clan's offspring were born werewolves. A grave inheritance indeed.

And so here in this town lived the descendants of the original coven and the original clan. It meant they were stronger and more powerful than average witches and werewolves.

Hearing a creak, Emberlyn looked to see her Uncle Dez awkwardly opening the casket. She couldn't see the interior from this angle, but going by the looks of relief that graced the faces of her relatives, she would imagine that it did still contain a corpse. Then their expressions once again crumpled with fake grief.

Paisley leaned into her, sighing. 'They already know they were named in the will,' she whispered. 'Why are they pretending to give a damn that she's gone?'

Someone in the crowd snorted. Probably a werewolf. Their hearing was exceptional.

'They're all about appearances,' Emberlyn reminded her, keeping her voice ultra-low.

On her other side, Kage hummed his agreement. 'I'm betting they'll break out the champagne and party poppers later.'

Quite possibly. Neither of Millicent's living children had had much time for her. They'd detached themselves from her when young and moved in with their father, mortified by how she'd become a lone practitioner who'd trodden a sinister path.

It was only Emberlyn's mother Avery who'd stayed with her as a child. Millicent had had little to do with the raising of Gill and Dez. Little to do with anyone but Avery and then, later, Emberlyn.

Over the years, Emberlyn had absorbed all that Millicent had taught her. She'd explored different forms of magick. She'd encountered the many deities her grandmother had conjured. And she'd taken Millicent's advice: Emberlyn had become the biggest, baddest – yes, she did know that wasn't a real word – witch that she'd needed to be in order to keep threats at bay.

But it meant that Emberlyn wasn't popular among the other witchy folk. Apparently, she made people nervous. Especially when she smiled. So she smiled *a lot.*

Now that the casket was set to rights, Reena continued reading aloud the blessing. Emberlyn found her gaze shifting to the nearby white tablet adorned with an elegantly pointed arch and ornate tracery. *Avery Vautier, loving mother of Emberlyn.*

Emberlyn swallowed hard, her gut twisting as she failed to pull up an image of her mother's face. She couldn't do that anymore. Couldn't remember much about Avery. The memories that Emberlyn did have of her mother were so vague they were dreamlike.

'I know I used to whine about how I could never go to funerals, but … yeah, I don't know why I whined,' said Kage. Before becoming a werewolf – something that had suppressed his magickal abilities – the once-clairvoyant-witch had had to avoid graveyards. 'It's super dull.'

Emberlyn felt a frown tug at her brow. 'What did you expect? Dancing and drum-beating?'

He shrugged, plucking at his short, russet-brown hair. 'I don't know. Maybe some "Safe travels" messages. A *We'll miss you* banner. A few goodbye gifts.'

'We're mourning her death, not sending her off on a cruise.'

Paisley snorted, mirth dancing in the same moss-green eyes she shared with her twin. Her long hair was slightly darker than his, but it was just as thick. While she was a little over five feet tall, Kage had a longer, leaner build.

'On a more interesting topic,' Paisley began, 'who do you think your grandmother left the manor to?'

Emberlyn puffed out a breath. 'No idea.'

Normally, copies of wills would be posted to beneficiaries. But Millicent had always had her own way of doing things. She'd drawn up the will herself and given it to her attorney, along with a list of her beneficiaries and strict instructions that the will be read aloud after her funeral. She'd also insisted that it be read aloud by Reena – which was weird, since Millicent hadn't been part of the coven for a very long time.

No one had been able to peek at the will because she'd spelled the envelope closed. Only a prick of blood from Emberlyn – someone Millicent had evidently felt confident wouldn't disrespect her wishes – would open it. Reena had 'suggested' that Emberlyn could do this beforehand, but she'd firmly refused.

Emberlyn knew why the High Priestess was eager to see the will. Reena wanted to speed along the purchase of the manor. She had been trying to get her hands on it for years, but Millicent would never sell, insisting that it should remain with the Vautier line.

Reena disagreed.

The High Priestess had big plans – it was talk of the town. She not only meant to take over the manor, she also planned to build houses on the expansive stretch of land attached to it. Money had already exchanged hands between her and a construction company run by a werewolf clan.

Either Gill or Dez would inherit the manor, and both were willing to sell it to Reena. As such, she likely would have already started transferring her possessions to the place if she'd been able to get inside. People were having a little trouble with that right now.

'Gill is awful sure the manor will be hers,' said Kage.

Yes, Gill and her husband had even urged their daughter Mari to give up her apartment, promising she could have their current home when they moved into one of the soon-to-be built houses. 'But so is Dez.'

Dez had actually been taunting his ex-wife about how she could have been a very rich woman if only she hadn't divorced him, because Reena would pay him a ridiculous amount of money to finally be the Lady of Black Willow Manor. Or, as most would more simply term it, Black Willow Witch.

'Knowing Millicent, she left everything to her cat,' muttered Emberlyn. 'Although … she wasn't quite as evil to Mari, so maybe she left the manor to her.'

'Maybe,' said Paisley. 'But there's something smug about Dez's idiot son. Like he knows something we don't. Ames made it his mission to serve her over the past six months. Do you think maybe she was so grateful that she decided to leave him everything?'

Emberlyn frowned. 'She hated that asshole. She *called* him "that asshole".' Ames hadn't whatsoever 'grown up'.

'She hated everyone,' said Paisley. 'You most of all.'

Emberlyn's frown deepened. 'Nah, she hated him *way* more.'

'All your birthday cards were addressed to, "My biggest disappointment".'

'Not over the last few years.'

'No, they said, "To whom it may concern". Face it, she hated you most.'

Emberlyn sighed, Millicent's voice drifting into her head …

'Why do you have to be so damn awkward, Emberlyn? You have so much potential; could access so much more power. The price isn't that high. Would it really be so awful to sell slivers of your soul?'

Uh, *yeah*.

But her grandmother hadn't seen it that way. She hadn't understood why Emberlyn didn't harbor the same hunger for power that had taunted her, or why Emberlyn wouldn't join her in devoting herself so fully to the craft that she had no real life.

After Emberlyn left home at eighteen, Millicent had contacted her very rarely over the years. It had been even rarer for her to return Emberlyn's calls or answer the door when she visited. But Emberlyn hadn't taken it *too* personally – Millicent was like that with everyone.

A particularly loud sob burst out of Gill, who all but stuffed her face into a tissue.

Unreal.

'If your grandmother's here watching this performance, she'll be wanting to dish out a few bitch slaps,' said Paisley.

Most likely. 'Millicent claimed she'd never go to her own funeral. Said it's tacky.'

A soft motorized hum sounded as the casket was slowly lowered to the ground. The backs of Emberlyn's eyes stung with unshed tears. Dammit, she'd thought that she was all cried out at this point.

Some wouldn't understand how she could have loved a woman such as Millicent. It was true that she hadn't been kind or affectionate or loving. But she'd fed, clothed, sheltered and mentored Emberlyn. More, Millicent had made her strong; had ensured that Emberlyn never let others convince her that she was anything else.

It helped to know that her grandmother's soul wasn't totally gone, it was merely somewhere else now. A realm where only those who'd passed on could go.

A sniffle popped out of Emberlyn before she could stop it.

Paisley put a hand on her back. 'You okay?'

'It's just allergies,' Emberlyn lied.

Finally, the motorized hum switched off. The fake weeping coming from her relatives kicked up a notch. No one tossed any soil or flowers on the casket, as if wary of doing anything that might disturb and 'wake' the corpse.

'Come on, let's go,' she urged the twins.

The three of them joined the other mourners in making their way down the hill, Emberlyn's high heels giving her no issues – she'd mastered the art of walking in them long ago.

As they reached her car, Emberlyn tugged her keys out of her black leather purse and—

'Quick warning,' Kage whispered, 'the Reeds are on their way over.'

Emberlyn tensed at the mention of her old in-laws. *Shit.* Hearing their footfalls behind her, she turned a little woodenly to face them.

Claris flashed her a weak smile, clutching the bottom of her dark braid. 'We just wanted to say that we're sorry for your loss.'

His arm curled around his mate's shoulders, his burly figure all but swallowing hers, Colton said, 'Michael would be here for you if he could be. And maybe one day he will.'

He looked so much like Michael – the same wide-set brown eyes, same strong nose, same chin dimple, same tawny hair – that it had once hurt to look at him. Not so much nowadays, though.

Emberlyn gave them a wan smile. 'Thank you.'

They each dipped their chin and then walked away.

A breath easing out of her, she turned to the twins. 'I never know what to say to them.' She just felt so awkward around them now.

'They're only so nice to you because they think it'll make you feel guilty about moving on from Michael,' said Kage. 'Don't forget how they initially reacted.'

There had been yelling. Crying. A lot of *howcouldyous.*

Shoving that scene out of her mind, Emberlyn opened the driver's door. 'Let's go get this will reading over with.' She slid into the car.

Kage went to hop into the front passenger seat, but Paisley beat him to it, so he slid onto the back row.

Clicking on her seatbelt, Paisley said, 'I'm still surprised that your grandmother left me and Kage something. We weren't related to her.'

Emberlyn dumped her purse on the floor behind her seat. 'No, but she loved annoying people. Said it fed her magick. And Gill, Dez and the others are peeved that she left something to non-relatives.' Emberlyn gunned the engine. 'Makes me wonder if there's anyone else outside the family line who she'd included in her will for funsies.'

Driving to Reena's home, Emberlyn couldn't stop her thoughts from drifting back to Michael. Unlike his parents, she had no belief that he'd return one day.

There had been a time when she'd used magick to try to track him; when she'd joined regular search parties or even launched her own. But she had eventually accepted that he was lost.

Unlike shifters, werewolves didn't have fated mates. They could claim people *as* their mates, but no preternatural link formed. It was no different from two witches handfasting.

She'd started dating Michael in high school. He'd claimed her a year after they'd graduated. They'd moved in together, started to build a life ... but things had gone wrong. Horribly wrong.

His parents intellectually knew that there was nothing else for her to do but consider the mating null and void – all people did in her situation. Emberlyn got why they didn't feel good about it, though.

Finally, they neared the *Welcome to Bellcrest* sign.

There were four neighborhoods in Chilgrave; some separated by large wooded areas, some so expansive their boundaries 'bumped' that of other neighborhoods. Bellcrest, filled with Georgian-style homes, was occupied by the majority of the coven.

Each of the three werewolf clans resided at the other neighborhoods – Ashwood, Cedargrove and Elmsbrook. But witches who were mated to a werewolf sometimes lived among their clan, and vice versa.

Emberlyn had lived in Bellcrest as a kid with her parents. Her years spent at Millicent's manor had situated her just beyond the border of Bellcrest. Emberlyn hadn't returned to the neighborhood at eighteen, not feeling inclined to rejoin the coven. Instead, she'd moved to the center of the town where the schools, stores and other businesses were located – it was considered neutral territory. Of course, she'd moved in with Michael at Cedargrove when they mated . . . only to return to her apartment in neutral territory after everything fell apart.

Though Chilgrave was reasonably small, anything a person could need would be available here. Which was good because it was hours away from civilization. The town couldn't be found unless one knew where to look.

Even if any outsiders *did* manage to stumble upon it, they wouldn't stay long. There was no cell phone service. No internet. No cable TV.

Personally, she couldn't imagine having a cell phone. How did anyone get to read a book in peace? Or play the '*I didn't know you'd tried calling*' game when they wanted to dodge someone? How draining would it be to feel that you always needed to have something interesting to post on social media sites?

Fair play to them for living in that lane. Emberlyn never could.

'There's Mom and Dad,' said Paisley, waving at the couple through the window.

Kage didn't bother, keeping his gaze straight ahead.

'Any progress with your parents?' Emberlyn asked him.

'Nope,' he replied. 'I'm enjoying the silent treatment while it lasts. They'll soon be up in my shit, raving about how I'll regret my choice one day. My only regret is not going through the Change sooner.' His werewolf-lover had bitten him during sex a few months ago. Instead of using antivenom, he'd let the Change take him.

It did not surprise Emberlyn that Ethel and Thad Sanders were unhappy about their son's decision. They didn't have anything against werewolves *per se*, but they were among the few who considered wolves to be inferior to witches.

'You don't miss being able to talk to the dead?' she asked Kage.

'Fuck, no. I never got a minute's peace, and I was tired of helping them cross over. How hard can it be to walk into a goddamn light? It's not like you can miss it. *It's a light.*'

Paisley tossed him a haughty sniff over her shoulder. 'I still can't *believe* you took the Change when you know I've been considering it for years. You've—' She gasped as he splattered a teeny fly against the window with his hand. 'You didn't have to kill it.'

He wiped his palm on his pants. 'I don't like flies. I don't like insects *period*.'

'You need to have more respect for nature,' Paisley reprimanded. 'Your problem is that you can't appreciate the beauty in anything. You should be more like me. There's no hate in my heart. Only peace and love—'

'And pure bullshit. You despise lots of stuff and lots of people. Including me.'

'Why would you ever think that?'

'Because you told me. Told me every day since you learned to speak.'

Emberlyn inwardly sighed. Neither of the twins were the type to hug, kiss or exchange kind words. Their love language was full of cursing and put-downs and teasing I-hate-yous. They had an airtight bond, but both went out of their way to irritate the other – a childhood habit they'd decided not to shake off, for whatever reason.

'Enough, we're here – you can squabble more later.' Emberlyn pulled up outside Reena's home. 'The others beat us to it,' she noted as she cut the engine, seeing a number of cars parked here.

'Of course they did.' Paisley unclipped her seatbelt. 'They're eager to find out who Millicent chose to be her main heir.'

More than likely.

'I think Emberlyn's right and that she left it all to Lucie,' Kage chipped in, referring to Millicent's cat.

Also more than likely.

Exiting the car, the three of them strode up to the front door of the beautiful Georgian home. It was Reena's husband who opened it. Ward was a strong witch, but not *very*. Female Chilgrave witches were more powerful by nature, so the coven had always been matriarchal. When a High Priestess handfasted, she rarely allowed her partner to rule alongside her. Most of the time, there was, essentially, only one 'Alpha' in the arrangement.

The asocial Ward didn't smile their way or even say hello. He merely waved them inside, closed the door and then led them through to the spacious parlor.

Inside, Reena sat in a turquoise velvet chair, her posture as regal as always. She was powerful. Charismatic. A good leader. And quite possibly responsible for the false rumors that Emberlyn had traded slivers of her soul for health, beauty and success.

Such a darling.

Well, she still held Tyra's 'childhood traumatic incident' against Emberlyn. As did Sera's mother, Penelope ... and just about everyone else. Ha.

There were two matching sofas in the room, one of which had been claimed by Gill, her husband Hank and their daughter Mari. The other sofa was empty. Dez and Ames stood before the grand fireplace, their hands clasped behind their backs.

All aside from Reena looked casual, smug and eager. Their grins cooled when Emberlyn strolled inside.

'Afternoon all,' she greeted brightly.

Reena's mouth hitched up half-heartedly. 'Ah, you're here.' The envelope containing Millicent's will on her lap, she gestured at the free sofa. 'Do sit.'

Emberlyn and the twins lowered themselves onto the couch. As she and Paisley placed their purses on the floor, Emberlyn didn't miss how her family cast her friends snotty looks. They were clearly still annoyed that the twins had been included in the will.

'I'm just waiting for one more person, and then we can get started,' Reena added.

Kage cast Emberlyn a quick glance. 'What person?' he asked in a whisper.

Emberlyn gave a slight shrug.

Her relatives chatted among themselves as they waited, pointedly ignoring Emberlyn and the twins. Blonde, blue-eyed and curvy, Gill and Mari so closely resembled each other that they looked like the exact same person at different stages of life. There was no sign of the ginger-haired, gray-eyed Hank in his daughter.

Dez and Ames were both handsome in a pretty way – small nose, small chin, naturally possessing very little facial hair. But whereas Dez was blue-eyed with ash-blond hair, Ames had his mother's brown eyes and dark hair.

Everyone quieted when the doorbell rang. Ward exchanged a look with his wife and then disappeared from the room. Moments later, his muffled voice came from the hallway, along with two sets of footfalls. When he reentered the room, Emberlyn looked at the tall figure behind him—

And her gaze collided with steely honeydew-green eyes that always held an animal alertness. Her belly promptly did a slow roll.

Ripper. Alpha of a werewolf clan. A direct descendant of Lupin and a she-wolf he'd dallied with during one of his and Lilith's 'breaks'.

Ripper's presence alone put people on notice, so there was an instant *shift* in the atmosphere. Muscles tightened. Backs straightened. The air turned static.

There was not one thing subtle about Jax 'Ripper' Stone. Dominance boldly rolled off him. Raw, gritty and unpolished, he took 'rugged masculinity' to an entirely new level.

He was totally badass in that hunter-gatherer, mountain-man, could-survive-any-conditions way. He made her think of a grizzly – burly and gruff with the unruffled calm of an apex predator whom you just *knew* could explode into violence in a mere second. Beneath it all ran a vein of hardcore brutal sexuality that promised all sorts of pleasure.

What he *wasn't*, and never had been, was a friend of Millicent. So why she would make him a beneficiary of her will, Emberlyn had no idea.

She studied the reactions of her relatives. They were tense, seeming equally surprised and confused.

'*He's* on the list of beneficiaries?' Dez asked Reena.

'He is, yes.' Reena fluidly rose to her feet as she tucked a stray strand of auburn hair behind her ear. 'Good afternoon, Ripper. It's a pleasure to have you here.'

He only inclined his head, his face its usual stony mask.

'Please sit,' she said, indicating a spare armchair.

As he stalked further into the room, Emberlyn couldn't help but *look*. Tall and broad, he was built like a tank. Everything about his body language – his strong eye-contact, upright posture, slow and purposeful walk – spoke of a person who knew he was a danger to all those around him. He engendered the kind of respect and fear that cleared him a path.

Vicious scars sliced through either side of his scalp, leaving stripes in his short black hair. A dark scruff peppered his well-defined jaw and the strip of skin above his full mouth.

Tribal tattoos peeked out of sleeves and collars, crisscrossing over yet more savage scars that spoke of the hard life he'd led and the multiple fights he'd partaken in.

Not that those scars meant he'd *lost* said fights. Far from it. When Ripper attacked, it wasn't pretty. Wasn't merciful. Wasn't quick.

Given how brutal and gory the results would be, Emberlyn could see why some had nicknamed him Jax the Ripper ... which had eventually been shortened to Ripper.

He sank into the empty chair, which placed him more or less directly opposite her.

She forced her eyes away from him, not interested in being caught staring. Her body had always gotten a little giddy around him. Okay, *very* giddy. A tingling sexual awareness always peppered the air between them when they were up close. And it sucked to be so unshakably drawn to someone when nothing would ever come of it.

Witches were totally off his menu – it was pretty understandable, given his past. Also, he was caught up in some kind of weird love triangle.

'Now that everyone's here, we can get started.' Reena turned her attention to Emberlyn. 'As you know, I need your blood to open the envelope. Ward, get me a thin needle.'

'Not necessary,' Emberlyn told her, lifting her hand up. She released a thread of magick, let it 'prick' her finger, and then sent the little droplet floating through the air to land on the envelope.

Reena's face tightened in that way it always did when Emberlyn did something that the High Priestess either hadn't learned to do or simply couldn't.

Reena tore open the envelope. 'I've said it before, yes, but Ward and I are very sorry for your loss,' she said to Emberlyn and her relatives. 'Millicent . . . she might not have been beloved by many, but she will be missed. In a way.'

The High Priestess pulled out the papers, and her brow creased. 'Ah, there is a letter attached. She would like me to read it aloud before moving onto the will.

> To my nearest, dearest and miscellaneous. I will write no words to ease your grief because I know you will feel none. I was not a good wife, mother, sibling or grandmother. I devoted every ounce of myself to my craft.
>
> It would be a lie to claim I have any regrets — I have seen, achieved and experienced so much through my quest for power; I would wish none of it away. In other words, feel no guilt at not experiencing any pain at my passing. There is no need to be sad for me in any case. I have never feared death. It is but another adventure for the soul, and I have ever been the adventurer.

Clearing her throat, Reena moved on to the will itself.

> My darling Gill, knowing how much you love Black Willow Manor, I have bequeathed to you the antique dollhouse replica. May it bring you much joy.

Gill spluttered, leaning forward. 'I'm sorry, what?'

Reena paused, her brow pinched. 'Um . . .'

'A dollhouse? She left me *a dollhouse?*'

Emberlyn barely managed to hold back a chuckle. She heard a sound come from Kage that sounded like a strangled snort.

'Keep going,' urged Dez, visibly excited . . . as if having concluded that the manor was definitely his. 'Some of us have somewhere to be.'

Even as Gill spluttered again, Reena looked back down at the will and read,

> To my handsome son, Desmond, I leave my truck. It doesn't run anymore, but I'm sure someone somewhere could fix it.

Oh, God. Emberlyn didn't dare look at either of the twins, knowing she'd otherwise burst out laughing.

Dez did a long blink. 'She . . . are you serious?'

Kage leaned into Emberlyn. 'She's left everything to the cat, I'm telling ya.'

'I am merely reading what it says,' said Reena.

> Ames, to you I bequeath my chessboard — it's the perfect game for sneaky fu . . . people who think to outmaneuver their grandmother. By the way, I do appreciate you wiping my ass that one time.

Paisley dipped her head as she audibly choked on a giggle.

Ames's cheeks flushed with anger. 'This is a joke,' he bit off. 'It's obviously a joke.'

Reena hurried on,

> Mari, the dragonfly brooch you stole from me and keep in your jewelry box is now rightfully yours. P.S. I don't know why you thought I wouldn't know that it was you who'd taken it.

Mari's jaw dropped. 'She *knew*? But . . . she never said anything.'

Probably because she'd concluded that Mari had done it for attention. Millicent wasn't in the business of giving anyone anything they wanted.

Kage, my Ouija board awaits you. Use it soon. We can stay in touch.

Tickled by that, Emberlyn nudged him. 'Now you can talk to the dead again.'

'Well, ain't that great,' he deadpanned.

Paisley, my Aztec coin collection now belongs to you. Don't spend it all at once.

The brunette's lips curved in genuine delight. 'Awesome.'

Emberlyn, my collection of voodoo dolls is now yours. You may also have your mother's pearl earrings if you take care of Lucie. Don't disappoint her as you have done me.

Emberlyn rolled her eyes at the latter sentence. As for the dolls and earrings? It was more than she'd hoped for. She'd wanted the earrings since she was a child, but Millicent had rarely gifted people anything . . . as if to do any good deeds would diminish her power.

'This can't be right,' Gill adamantly stated. 'It *can't*. Or it's an old will, I don't know, but this is all wrong. She swore the house would be mine!'

'She also swore it would be mine,' Dez curtly remarked. 'Said that though she couldn't regret treading down her chosen path, she did wish I hadn't suffered for it. Said—'

'That she wanted to soothe the wound by leaving you the manor as an apology?' asked Gill.

His gaze sharpened. 'Soothe the wound, yes. She said the same to you?'

Sighing, Gill nodded. 'More fool us for thinking she meant any of it.'

Mari sat back, putting a hand to her forehead. 'Oh my God, she really did hate us all, didn't she? I used to think that it was an act; an effort to hide that she had a soft underbelly.'

Hank put a hand over hers. 'No, sweetheart, she hated everyone. What else does the will state, Reena?'

Rubbing at her wrist, the High Priestess went on,

Jax Stone, to you I bequeath both the land that once belonged to your clan—

She cut herself off, her face darkening. 'No, that isn't possible. Millicent can't do that.'

Ripper fluidly straightened in his seat, his entire being practically perking up in interest.

The jaws of Emberlyn's paternal family all but hit the floor, as did that of Ward.

Emberlyn grinned. Millicent had clearly been aware of Reena's plans – perhaps through gossip, perhaps because she'd always 'known' certain things – and she'd taken moves to ensure that the land she'd loved couldn't be turned into an upper-class neighborhood for the coven.

'No,' Reena repeated, staring down at the will, 'no, the land wasn't hers to give away! It is part of Bellcrest!'

'It lies beyond the border, actually,' Ripper corrected, his voice deep, thick and rumbly – pure vocal testosterone. 'It belonged to the Vautier line, not to the coven.'

The corners of Reena's eyes tightened. 'It comes with the manor.'

'No,' Ripper objected. 'It was originally my clan's land. It was purchased by a Vautier witch who hadn't wanted the house to be so close to werewolf territory; she'd wanted more space. Our clan has been trying to get it back for years, but no one would ever give it up. Until now.'

Reena shook her head hard, the will crumpling in her hand.

'What else did she leave me?' he asked.

Reena blinked. 'What?'

'You didn't finish your sentence. It read, "I bequeath *both*", as if there's more.'

A little flustered, she flicked her gaze back to the papers in her hand.

Jax Stone, to you I bequeath both the land that once belonged to your clan and . . .

She trailed off, her brow creasing.

And my granddaughter, Emberlyn.

Oh, that *hag*.

Ripper looked at Emberlyn, his brows inching up.

She flapped a dismissive hand. 'Just ignore that last part.'

'This whole thing is ridiculous,' Dez proclaimed. 'You don't bequeath people in wills, and you can't dole out land like it's candy. Reena, what about the manor, the money, everything else? Whoever owns the building can probably contest this.'

Reena looked back down at the will so fast it must have hurt her neck. She pointed to the bottom of the sheet. 'Well, she added here: "'The rest of all I own, my small fortune included, will belong to the new owner of Black Willow Manor. By new owner, I mean whoever manages to get inside it.'"

Gill's lips parted in enraged shock. 'She didn't. She did *not* pull that archaic bullshit tradition out of her ass!'

Emberlyn exchanged amused looks with the twins. It had once been tradition for the manor to go to whichever of the Vautier beneficiaries it 'chose'. Every piece of material used to construct it had been imbued with sentient magick, so the house had an 'awareness'.

It would be interesting to see which of them it chose.

'What about my coin collection?' asked Paisley. 'How do I get it?'

Again, Reena consulted the will. 'According to this, she placed it in a storage facility for you, along with the other items stated in the will.' Her gaze cut to Emberlyn. 'Except for the earrings. She left those in the manor. So if you want them . . .'

Realization dawning on her, Emberlyn inwardly sighed as she finished, 'I'll have to get inside.' *Motherfucker.*

Paisley looked at her. 'See, I *told* you she hated you most.'

CHAPTER TWO

✑

Well, it looked as though her friend was right. Because however this played out, it would be painful for Emberlyn in some way.

She'd never get her hands on those earrings via one of her relatives. Those sly, greedy, arrogant asses wouldn't give her *shit*. Which left her no choice but to go to the manor if she wanted her mom's earrings.

One of two things would then happen.

Either the house would magickly strike to keep her out – and yeah, there'd be bruises as a result. Or it would bid her entrance . . . which would mean that it had 'chosen' her to be its new owner.

Emberlyn *loved* the manor. She would snap up the opportunity to live there again. But to do so would earn her the wrath of her family, Reena, and probably also the werewolf clan, who thought they'd be making a shit-ton of money by building all those houses for the coven.

Kage's eyes danced. 'You know that Millicent will be looking up at you right now, laughing her ass off, right?'

Emberlyn swiped her tongue over her teeth. 'Yeah. Yeah, I do.'

'This is unbelievable,' Gill breathed. 'Absolutely unbelievable.'

None of the amusement that Emberlyn could feel rolling from the twins could be seen on the faces of her relatives. As they eyed Emberlyn, all appeared a mix of furious and worried.

They *should* be worried. The manor's magick fed on power, and she had plenty of that.

She found her eyes drifting to Ripper ... only to realize that he was staring at her. There was nothing to read in his expression, though.

'It isn't necessary for you to put yourself through the bother of attempting to gain entrance to the manor, Emberlyn,' Gill told her, all kindness. 'Whichever one of us it chooses will pass your mother's earrings to you, along with Lucie.'

Emberlyn snorted. 'No, you won't. You'll keep the cat and claim you can't find the earrings; that Grams must have tossed them out or buried them somewhere to mess with me.'

Gill hiked up an offended brow. 'You think me that petty?'

'Totally.'

'You're judging me by Millicent's standards. *She* was the petty one. I was not close to Avery, but I would never begrudge her daughter a pair of her earrings.'

'If my mother wanted you to have the house, Emberlyn, she would have left it to you,' Dez cut in. 'She might have raised you, but she didn't care for you. You weren't family to her, you were her protégée. One she loathed because, though she did a good job of corrupting you and your magick, you never lived up to her standards. Which you shouldn't take personally, because nobody did.'

It hadn't been about standards, but whatever. '"Corrupted" isn't a word I would use.'

Gill scoffed. 'You might look pure class at all times with your glossy hair and manicured nails and stylish clothes; might be all manners and grace and stuff. But there's no hiding the crone within. It comes out somehow. With you, it's in the eyes.'

Mari's nod was hard and curt. 'Just because you don't wear tatty black clothes and robes and have scruffy long hair like Grams did doesn't mean you aren't like her.'

'And you're always smiling,' Dez tossed out, his brows drawn together. 'What has anyone who was raised by Millicent got to fucking smile about?'

'She wanted to mold you into another version of her, and she did,' Ames spat. 'The difference between you and her is that she wore her evil on the outside.'

Emberlyn gave an uncaring shrug. 'What any of you think about me is irrelevant. The manor will choose whom it chooses. Which may or may not be me. You can't forbid me from attempting to enter it to play the odds. And you won't,' she firmly stated, her voice hard.

Reena sighed, long and loud. 'She's right, we have no choice here but to follow tradition – any Vautier witch can attempt to enter the manor.'

Gill's eyes widened. 'But she shouldn't be allowed to do this! She's not really family.'

'And she hardly had anything to do with Millicent at the end!' Dez burst out.

It wasn't for the lack of trying. 'None of you did. Aside from Ames. And my guess is that she only allowed him to visit so she could fuck with him.' Emberlyn looked at Ames. 'She told you that she'd made you her main heir, didn't she? That you'd inherit everything?'

He averted his gaze, cricking his neck.

Dez scowled down at his son. 'You never told us that.'

Ames spluttered. 'She made me promise not to. Said she'd

know if I went back on my word. And she was super clear that she didn't want Emberlyn to inherit *anything*. I'm shocked she left her the dolls, earrings and cat.'

'She said the same to me about Emberlyn,' Mari piped up. 'And although she didn't tell me I'd get the house, she *hinted* at it. Said stuff like how I'd make a good lady of the manor one day. What about you, Emberlyn?'

'I never asked; she never said,' Emberlyn replied. 'I figured she'd leave everything to your mom and Dez.'

'She *should* have,' Gill insisted. 'It's our birthright. She might not have made you false promises, but she'll have taken magickal measures to make sure that you don't get inside the manor. By leaving the earrings in there, she ensured you'd never get them.'

'No, she ensured I'd have to *try* to get them,' Emberlyn said. 'And I am going to try.'

Gill hissed and then turned to her High Priestess. 'But Reena, she—'

'Enough, Gill,' ordered Reena. 'May I remind you that though I was asked to read the will aloud, I am not the executor – Millicent's lawyer is. You are complaining to the wrong person. If you are set on preventing Emberlyn from trying to enter the manor, you must take it up with him. But I think you know it will amount to nothing.

'Your mother did not state that Emberlyn could not partake in this – in fact, Millicent all but dared her to try to gain entrance to the manor. He will not favor your wishes over that of his client.' Reena rose to her feet. 'Let's get this done. Ripper, I am sorry that you were dragged into Millicent's games. She was cruel to have done that. The land—'

'Is mine,' he finished, his tone non-negotiable. Standing upright, he pinned her with a serious look. 'I'm not giving it up.'

Reena pressed her lips tight together. 'You're not thinking

clearly. I have already signed a contract with Carver,' she said, referring to another werewolf Alpha. 'I paid him a small deposit, not the amount in full, but he practically spent the rest of it in his mind. He won't like hearing that the money will not be his.'

No, he wouldn't. Because Carver was a gambling addict with far too many debts.

'Not my issue,' said Ripper with a lazy, uncaring shrug. 'You shouldn't have gone ahead with plans that you had no guarantee you could follow through on.'

Reena's cheeks went red. 'None of us could have foreseen what Millicent would do.'

'Maybe you should have. It isn't exactly strange, given her character, that she'd take this one last opportunity to stir some shit.'

He had a point there.

'We *will* be contesting the will,' Dez told him. 'The land won't be yours.'

'Seems to me that it already is.' Ripper gave Emberlyn one last – and again unreadable – look before prowling out of the room.

Reena cursed beneath her breath and marched out, Ward trailing after her. Emberlyn's relatives fell into step behind them.

Taking up the rear with the twins, Emberlyn said to them, 'I was not expecting Millicent to leave the land to Ripper. And yet, it doesn't surprise me that she did.'

'She also left him *you*,' Kage reminded her.

'As a joke. When Michael first hinted at claiming me, she tried talking me out of it; said I'd be a fool to let a man own me. I told her that no man ever would, mate or not.'

'So she "gave" you to a guy, thinking it'd rile you up,' said Paisley.

'Exactly.'

Outside the house, everyone hopped into their respective cars and drove through the neighborhood, past its outskirts and up the hill on which Black Willow Manor stood.

Emberlyn smiled as it came into sight. The tall building was magnificent. Regal. Timeless. Elegant.

Painted in both red and black, the house had a wraparound timber porch, elaborately carved doors, stained-glass bay windows, a steep gabled roof, beautiful decorative trim and grand towers and turrets.

To its left was a huge-ass black willow tree – hence the manor's name. Beyond the tree was a spacious plot of land that bled into the thick forest … but not a plot big enough to build new homes on. On its right, however, was a *huge* stretch of sparsely forested land. Land that now belonged to Ripper.

Pulling up outside the house, Emberlyn felt her smile kick up. Growing up there had been no easy ride, but it had been the only place that had felt like a true *home*.

As she slid out of the car, her gaze flicked to one of the other parked vehicles – a truck against which Ripper and a member of his clan leaned. Apparently they'd decided to see who the manor would choose.

Ripper's eyes clashed with hers again, but she turned away, her focus now on entering the house in front of her.

Like the other witches, she stopped several feet from the front yard's gate. From there, she could feel the buzz of the manor's defensive magick in the air. If it read anyone as a physical threat to its owner, it wouldn't allow them to get to the front door. As it currently had no owner, they were all vulnerable to an attack.

Reena and Ward stepped away from the group, basically making it clear to the manor that they had no intention of attempting entry.

Dez rolled his shoulders. 'I'll go first.'

Gill's brow pinched. 'I'll go first.'

As the two siblings quibbled, Emberlyn turned to the twins and whispered, 'Out of all of them, Gill's got the best chance at winning the manor's favor.'

Kage nodded curtly. 'She's stronger than the others. Mari's the least likely to be chosen.'

'Stop being difficult, I'm the oldest!' Gill heatedly reminded her brother. 'That means I should go first.'

'Fuck this shit,' muttered Ames. He rushed toward the manor at top speed, sprinting along the path and jogging up the stone steps—

Hit by an invisible force, he zoomed backwards, his legs kicking.

Everyone else skidded to the side, watching as he landed hard on his back with a pained grunt.

Emberlyn whistled low. That had to hurt.

Dez hovered over him, grimacing. 'Son, are you okay?'

'Fine,' was the wheezed reply.

Busy smirking smugly at her nephew, Gill didn't notice Mari dart toward the house until she heard the fast footfalls.

Mari took the porch steps two at a time—

Her body jerked so forcefully it folded in on itself as she went soaring backwards.

Hank looked as if he'd try to catch his daughter but then seemed to think better of it. He moved out of the way and winced as she hit the ground with a thud.

Paisley snickered. 'That was a "Hell, no" from the manor, wasn't it?'

'Looked like it,' said Emberlyn.

'I'm done with this idiocy,' Gill proclaimed, helping Mari to her feet. She then blew out a breath. 'Here I go.'

Gill didn't run. She walked. Her pace leisurely, she strolled up the path with her chin tipped up, her posture all arrogance ... like the house was hers for the taking. She climbed the stairs, reached out to grab the porch frame—

And her head snapped back as if she'd received an uppercut.

She staggered, slipped and toppled down the stairs, falling to her back with an ungraceful flop.

Hank winced. 'You okay, honey?'

'*Of course I'm not okay,*' Gill gritted out, rolling onto her stomach.

Inching up his chin, Dez straightened the lapels of his jacket. 'My turn.' Like his sister, he walked calmly toward the house and – not even bothering to help her stand – paused at the base of the steps. He then stretched his arms out at his sides and began to chant ritual words that were very familiar.

Kage wrinkled his nose. 'Why is he blessing the house? What exactly does he think that will do?'

Emberlyn pursed her lips. 'He may be hoping that he can neutralize the defensive magick.'

'Ah,' said Kage. 'Yeah, that won't work.'

'I know.' Such magick wasn't dark merely because it was aggressive.

Finished with the blessing, Dez lowered his arms to his sides and then cautiously ascended the stairs. Pausing at the top, he slowly reached out, his fingers splayed. He jolted as his head violently whipped to the side. He teetered on the top step for a painfully long moment and then went tumbling down the stairs, landing in an awkward heap with his legs all but thrown over his head.

Now back on her feet, Gill sniffed down at him. 'A blessing?' she scoffed. 'Really?' Focusing once more on the house, she said, 'I've had enough of this.' She lashed out with blast after blast of magick, pummeling the defensive power.

Power that batted away the blasts, sending them right back at her.

Gill's body jerked with each hit, her face creased in pain.

Notching up his chin pompously, Dez launched his own attack, flaying the defensive power, cursing when his hits bounded back on him.

Emberlyn shook her head. 'This is a total shit show.'

'An entertaining shit show,' Paisley remarked.

Ames, apparently deciding not to learn from his father's mistake, copied Dez's move – his own blasts much more intense. So intense that when they moments later rushed at him, he didn't have a chance to dodge. They whacked him so hard he flew back.

Mari, her face a mask of '*I will be the one to do this*' determination, slammed up her hands and hurled waves of magick at the house . . . only to have them crash back into her.

Rubbing at various parts of their bodies, the four defeated witches gathered together, their expressions a blend of aggravation and helplessness.

Reena let out a sound that was something between a growl and a scoff. The woman could probably feel all her plans falling to pieces around her.

Emberlyn raised a hand. 'Okay, now me.'

Dez glowered at her. 'The manor won't let you in. Millicent must have cast an additional spell; something to keep people out. *No one* is going to get inside until we can figure out what spell it is.'

'There's no spell,' Emberlyn told him, approaching the gate.

'There *has* to be,' Gill insisted. 'And since she wouldn't want you to claim the house, you can bet your ass she'll have taken extra measures to ensure that you never do. The spell would react even worse to you than it did us.'

Ignoring her, Emberlyn didn't walk to the steps, she paused

halfway up the path. She sent out just a few ribbons of magick; watching as the glittering dust drifted toward the manor and then gently brushed over the translucent defensive barrier. An offering. A gift. An introduction.

The sentient power studied hers, tasted it and she felt the *click* of recognition. It remembered her magick. Remembered *her*.

It didn't reject her offering, which she took as a very good sign. She walked a little closer, chanting as she let her magick roll out in a rush of more glittering dust. That dust became thousands of moths – some black, some silver, some dark teal.

Wings fluttered as they streamed toward the manor, parting to surround the defensive barrier. Not attack it, not intimidate it, *tempt* it with the promise of more power.

Sentient magick was like a predatory pack animal – it could do just fine on its own, but it knew there was strength in numbers and preferred to not be solitary. Emberlyn was giving it a promise of power, of protection, of a partnership.

She kept on chanting, and the moths swirled around the mansion uber-fast – some clockwise, some anticlockwise. Inside the insect-tornado, electricity buzzed.

Then the defensive power reached outwards and clashed into her magick. Welcomed it. *Connected* to it.

She closed her fists, ending the chant. The moths rose above the manor and then disappeared down chimneys.

Inside the house, lights switched on and off, curtains flapped and the stained-glass windows seemed to bulge outward.

Then the magick settled, and one of the front doors slowly swung open in invitation.

Delight curled Emberlyn's lips, and she metaphorically rubbed her hands in glee.

She heard a distinct feminine curse come from far behind her. *Reena*. Ha.

'Why?' asked Dez. 'Why didn't it attack you?'

Easy. 'I wasn't rude,' she replied, facing him.

He stared at her numbly. 'Rude?'

Emberlyn swept her gaze over her family. 'You came with no offer of goodwill. You weren't respectful of the manor's boundaries. You didn't politely introduce yourself. You just boldly tried to *take*. And bashing the barrier was pure bad form.' She cocked her head. 'Do you know nothing about sentient-magick etiquette?'

Emberlyn looked at the twins, who both wore huge grins, and gestured for them to follow as she advanced up the path.

'What do you mean, an offer of goodwill?' Gill called out. 'What did you give it?'

Halting halfway up the porch stairs, Emberlyn peered down at her. 'Power, no strings attached.'

Gill's eyes narrowed. 'You manipulated the manor into accepting you?'

'It wasn't manipulation, it was common decency,' Emberlyn corrected. 'You all threw yourselves at the spell not only physically but magickly. Which is a lot like trying to kick down a person's front door. And yet, you *expected* entry; intended to claim ownership of the place. You can't own sentient magick. Really, you should know this stuff.'

Snickering, Paisley scurried past her and into the manor with her brother in tow.

Emberlyn was about to follow them, but Gill notched up her chin and said, 'There was no need for courteousness on our part. We're Vautier witches. The manor belongs to our line. It is our *right* to take it.'

'The manor won't accept a Vautier witch just because of their ancestry.' Emberlyn looked at Reena, who, her face pinched, her hands fisted, her body wooden, stared back at her. 'Let me be clear that I won't be relinquishing it to you. It's my home now. I intend to keep it that way.'

Reena's eyelids lowered. 'It should not have chosen you; should not have skipped a generation.'

'This manor is deserving of someone with status,' Ward declared. 'A High Priestess, just like Lilith.'

'You did something other than give it a gift,' Ames accused.

Emberlyn smiled. 'Oh, you mean the part where I promised it my first born?'

Gasps sounded.

She rolled her eyes. 'Kidding, kidding. I didn't *need* to do anything else. The manor could have rejected my offering. Or kept it but rejected *me*. It did neither. But that's not because I did anything dark.'

'I will not stand for this,' Gill bit off, magick crackling around her hands.

Oh, she thought to take Emberlyn on? Novel.

'You've got this, Mom,' said Mari. 'Those on the benevolent path always win.'

The benevolent path? *Dear Lord*.

Reena strode forward. 'Stand aside, Gill. I will deal with this.'

Emberlyn couldn't help but smile. 'You want to come at me? Really?' Laughing, she whipped up her arm and shot a stream of magick high. A black cloud ominously roiled in the sky like a swirling dark bruise. A lightning fork stabbed downward, sharp and bright.

With curses and alarmed squeaks, the other witches backpedaled.

Thunder boomed, loud and aggressive. A wind rapidly built up, whipping the willow branches back and forth, making her dress flap and her hair flutter.

Then Emberlyn brought her arm back down, and it all stopped.

She waited a few seconds before speaking. 'You're strong, Reena, but trying to "deal with this" won't end well for you.'

Licking his lips, Ward backed away even further. 'You're just like her. Millicent.'

Emberlyn felt her mouth curve. 'Hmm, maybe a little. Just a smidgeon.'

'She made you into her,' said Reena, a slight shake to her voice.

Emberlyn waved a hand. 'No, silly. Millicent *liked* being a singular being. She was never going to want a mini-me. But she had wanted me to join her in embracing the darkness – that much is true.'

'And you did,' snarked Gill.

'Nope. What I embraced is reality. You all use terms like "the benevolent path" and "the malevolent path". They don't exist. *No one* always uses magick for good, just as no one always uses it for bad. I follow my own path using my own moral compass – we all do. I'm willing to own it aloud, unlike any of you.'

Feeling eyes on her, Emberlyn looked to see Ripper watching her somewhat speculatively. Turning away, she stepped onto the porch and advanced into the house, which kindly closed the door behind her.

CHAPTER THREE

❧

'Now *that* was impressive,' said Kerr.

'It was,' Ripper conceded. Reluctantly. Because he quite frankly begrudged that *any* witch would have the ability to make him feel impressed.

He had no personal beef with Emberlyn Vautier. He barely knew her. She'd never done harm to him or his clan. But he'd known a witch like her once – one who'd used magick to exact revenge. And she'd fucked with the lives of so many, including his.

Kerr glanced at the witches stood near their cars talking rapidly while jerkily gesticulating. 'If their shock is anything to go by, Emberlyn hasn't shown them exactly what she's capable of before now. Either that or they were sure "the benevolent path" would prevail,' he added with an eye roll.

Ripper hummed, sliding his gaze back to the manor. 'They underestimated her. And she let them until now.' It was cunning, really. And an indication that she'd felt absolutely no need to prove herself to them.

'Which sets her apart from Millicent. That woman made sure everyone knew exactly what she had in her magickal arsenal. Emberlyn showed the coven just enough to make them wary of crossing her.'

And they had been wary. Yet, her family had tossed a lot of shit at her today. She hadn't flinched under the weight of their disapproval, insults or accusations – not here, not at Reena's house. In fact, Emberlyn hadn't appeared in the least bit fazed. She'd regarded them with a bored disappointment, as a teacher would unruly children. And when they'd thought to attack her, she'd fucking laughed.

It had almost made Ripper smile. Almost. Not much did that.

'Makes you wonder if she even showed the full extent of what she can do just now,' said Kerr.

It did. Especially when Ripper took into account something that Millicent had once said to him when he'd purchased a potion from her . . .

'The coven talks like my Emberlyn is evil. Pfft. She's no angel – I couldn't have abided an angel; I would have drowned her at some point. Truth is that girl has the ability to commit every magickal heinous act you can imagine. But she has a code; lines she won't cross. Unless you push or corner her – then she has few limits. That doesn't make her evil, it makes her ruthless.'

You would never imagine, at a glance, that such ruthlessness existed within Emberlyn. She was elegance and poise and style. Friendly but slightly aloof, like a cat. Forever dressed in silk or cashmere or satin or other refined clothing, she looked like she belonged in a goddamn fashion magazine. She never had a hair out of place or a slump in her shoulders.

But if you got close enough, you could sense that there was more to her. Emberlyn's presence hummed with a charged, quietly fierce warning. Like the air a dominant wolf gave off that calmly asserted its power. It had caught his attention from their first up-close encounter.

Not that he hadn't noticed her before then. A guy didn't *not* notice a woman who looked like her.

Emberlyn Vautier was ... unusual. Unearthly. Hauntingly beautiful.

Slender and average height, she had glossy iridescent hair that made him think of a raven's wing. Her facial features were as delicate as her curves. Except for her mouth – it wasn't delicate, it was carnal. Her eyes were an ethereally pale hazel that he'd heard some describe as eerie.

They weren't spooky. They were fucking bewitching.

There was a little scratch in her voice that tickled your awareness and dug in hooks to keep your attention. *Everything* about her snared a man's attention.

Compelling. In a word, she was compelling. And it galled the ever-loving shit out of him that he couldn't be immune to it.

For a while, he'd been able to combat it by holding the image of her in his mind as a one-dimensional wicked witch. But that had become impossible after Michael vanished – she'd been lost back then, her eyes shadowed by pain and panic.

She wasn't lost anymore.

She was also his new neighbor. And now that Millicent was gone, he might have to visit Emberlyn often. Because, according to the old woman, her granddaughter was the only living witch who could create the elixir he needed.

Whether she'd *agree* to create it, he didn't know. Nor could he know what kind of price tag she'd put on it if she was willing to help him.

A howl rang out somewhere in the distance – one filled with turmoil.

Ripper sighed. 'Seems like Logan took my advice to shift and go for a run.' He'd recognize his brother's howl anywhere. 'I didn't think he would.' Logan had been entirely too pissed.

'*Stop being a selfish fucking asshole – or do you want to have to watch CeCe one day get claimed by another wolf? Because that's what'll happen if we don't do it first, Rip.*'

'Instead of getting calmer as the weeks have gone on, he's gotten more wound up,' Kerr remarked. 'It's a good sign.'

Ripper frowned. 'Is it?'

'Yeah. He's getting angrier because he's finally facing that you're not going to change your mind. He feels CeCe slipping away. And hey, I sympathize with him. But the sooner he accepts reality the better.'

Ripper rubbed at the back of his head. 'I should never have agreed to share her with Logan that night.'

'You couldn't have known what would happen.'

'No, but it's fucked everything up.' It was never good for two brothers to want the same woman. Neither he nor Logan had said it out loud; neither wanting to do something that might lead to a situation that hurt the other.

Three weeks ago, they'd been drinking heavily and – influenced by the beer he'd downed and the call of the full moon – Ripper had agreed to share her with his brother just once.

Worst fucking decision ever.

Because CeCe wasn't content for them all to go back to being platonic friends. On the contrary, she had proposed that they enter an official triad.

Triads weren't uncommon among werewolves. But although Logan was willing, Ripper was not. CeCe was adamant that she couldn't choose between them – it was both or neither. And since Ripper wouldn't change his mind, Logan was pissed at him.

'You're not the one who jacked everything up,' Kerr upheld.

'You recently gave them the greenlight to pursue a relationship, saying you'd support it. It's CeCe who's the problem, claiming it ain't fair of her to be with Logan when she also loves you. How is it unfair when he'd be well aware of the situation?'

Shrugging, Ripper scraped a hand over his jaw. 'She went on and on about how she knew it'd hurt me to see them together and that she wouldn't be able to handle it. I assured her that she was wrong. I mean, would I like it? No. But I wouldn't stand in the way of my brother's happiness, either. Telling her that I'd be good with it just pissed her off, though.'

'Because she doesn't want you to be okay with it.'

'Yeah, I get that. But I'm fucking sick of Logan making me out to be the bad guy here. The person standing between him and what he most wants is CeCe herself.'

'Which is what I pointed out to him yesterday. He mumbled something under his breath and walked away. My opinion? I don't think he's mad at you because you won't agree to a triad. I think he's mad at you because she's insisting on having you both. It isn't your fault, no, but he can't help resenting you for it. What guy would want to feel that he's not enough for the woman he loves?'

Ripper let out a long breath. 'I don't see what else I can do at this point. I've talked to both of them, I made my stance on the triad thing clear, and I promised I'll support them if they go ahead with a relationship. But somehow, I still come off as the bastard in this scenario.'

Hearing a car engine come to life, Ripper looked to where the witches once stood. 'Looks like they're leaving.'

'This won't be the end of it, though,' said Kerr. 'They'd all reached agreements between themselves before Millicent passed, thinking they had a decent idea of what the will would state. They're gonna give Emberlyn trouble.'

Probably. 'I doubt it will get them anywhere.' The woman didn't appear to give one single measly fuck – which he begrudgingly respected. More, she didn't strike him as someone who'd break. Even at her most vulnerable, when Michael had done a disappearing act, she'd radiated strength and self-assurance. 'Millicent left her to me in her will.'

Kerr's head whipped to face him. 'What?' he asked, the word coming out on a chuckle. 'You're serious?'

Ripper frowned at him. 'Has there ever been a single time in my life that I've told a joke?'

'Well, no, but it just doesn't make sense. Unless she was hinting at you making Emberlyn an ally. It actually might be a good idea,' Kerr mused. 'It's like with Millicent – you didn't approve of her, but you knew it was smart to stay on her good side. I think the same applies to Emberlyn. Especially when you're going to need her to make those elixirs for you.'

True. And if Ripper held out an olive branch and suggested an alliance, she might be less likely to try to contest the will and reclaim the land.

'Also, as of today, you'll both be dealing with the same problems from the same people,' Kerr added. 'Makes sense to team up. You two don't need to be on opposite sides of the fence just because of your personal feelings about witches in general.'

'It's not about witches in general. I don't like the coven because they rally around their own instead of making them face consequences, and I don't like witches who use magick to avenge slights.'

He'd heard of Emberlyn's many 'exploits'. She'd infested homes with toads, turned pool water to blood, covered cars in slugs, given people the hiccups for twenty-four hours straight, and even once somehow blocked every toilet in Bellcrest.

Okay, yeah, some of it had been amusing. And yeah, he could

understand why she'd been driven to make her point. It was no different from him showing his claws to those who thought to challenge him. She'd done darker deeds, such as lumbering people with chronic hip pain and making their teeth rot and fall out one by one. But, to be fair, she could probably have done a lot worse – if the demonstration she'd just made was anything to go by, at least.

Only witches had been victims – she seemed to have no issue with werewolves. And, aside from when she'd been a child herself, no kids were ever harmed. But it still made her a wild card, and Ripper wasn't comfortable having those in his life.

'Still, an alliance would be good,' Kerr persisted. 'I don't know for sure that she'll be up for it, but you can at least run the idea by her, can't you?'

Undecided, Ripper twisted his mouth.

'Talk to her. Feel her out. See what vibe you get from her.'

Ripper exhaled heavily. 'You know, I originally thought that Millicent left Emberlyn to me in the will because she wanted others to assume that her granddaughter would be under my protection so they'd leave her be.'

'But ... ?'

'But after seeing Emberlyn's little show of power just now, I don't think Millicent was too concerned about her safety. I think she was hoping that Emberlyn wouldn't get pushed into a corner.'

Again, Millicent's words echoed in Ripper's mind ... *That girl has the ability to commit every magickal heinous act you can imagine.*

Kerr turned to him, his brow creased. 'You're saying Millicent created a monster, regretted it at the end, and took measures to help prevent that monster from losing it?'

Ripper shook his head. 'No. I'm saying Millicent created a

monster, relished that fact and wanted Emberlyn to have allies just in case she destroyed half the fucking coven.'

'Oh.'

'Yeah. Oh.'

CHAPTER FOUR

⌘

Feeling the familiar 'vibe' of the manor settle over her, Emberlyn let out a long breath. It was like having a warm, weighted blanket tucked around you. Nostalgia crashed down on her in the best way.

'I missed this place.' She could see the glitter of her magick everywhere; it was still in the process of saturating the walls and flooring.

Kage and Paisley were glancing around the grand entrance hall, their expressions awed.

'I always wanted to come inside, but my parents made me promise to only go as far as the porch,' said Paisley.

Kage nodded. 'I think they were worried that Millicent would sacrifice us in a ritual or shove us into another dimension, never to be seen again.'

Snorting, Emberlyn placed her purse on a circular table and brushed her fingers over a plant that rested on it. While Emberlyn doubted that Millicent would have harmed the twins, the old woman would have delighted in scaring them for the fun factor.

Much as the twins' parents Ethel and Thad weren't fond of Emberlyn, they hadn't protested the friendship for two reasons. One, Paisley was weak in magickal terms, and they knew that Emberlyn protected her. Two, the twins weren't very popular among the coven either, purely because Chilgrave witches tended to consider multiple births a bad omen.

Still, Emberlyn hadn't been welcome at the twins' home, and their parents hadn't wanted them to come here, so there'd been no sleepovers or tea parties. Restrictions had been put on their friendship, and yet it had survived and remained strong.

'I just *knew* that the manor would let you in,' said Paisley, smirking.

Kage frowned at her. 'No, you didn't. You *hoped* it would.'

Paisley's brow lazily lifted. 'Is there much difference?'

'Yes.'

Emberlyn's heels clicked along the parquet flooring as they walked further inside. 'I never thought I'd live here again. I thought Grams would stick with tradition and pass the place along to one of her children. It never occurred to me that she'd do anything different.'

'She might have left it to either Gill or Dez if it weren't for their plans to give it up,' said Paisley, using her heel to smooth out a slight kink in the rug. 'Speaking of those plans ... Want me to come stay here with you for a few weeks?'

Surprised by the offer, Emberlyn tilted her head. 'Stay here?'

'You having this place has put a halt on *many* people's plans,' Paisley pointed out. 'They're likely gonna want you out of here. It might be better if you're not alone.'

Touched, Emberlyn gently waved her offer away. 'I'll be fine.' Plus, she didn't want to drag her friend into this issue.

'Uh, Em,' Kage began, pointing at a sheet of paper that had been tacked to the grandfather clock. 'You might want to take a look at this.'

Frowning, Emberlyn strode over to what turned out to be a letter. She recognized the handwriting as Millicent's. It read,

Emberlyn, if you thought I wouldn't know that the manor would choose you then you're a fool. It's meant to be yours. A disappointment or not, you're currently the strongest of the Vautier line. And the manor should only ever belong to someone who will love, treasure and protect it.

I'm well aware you'll now have some fires to put out, but you can handle it. Still, take what aid the wolf offers — it'll make things run smoother.

P.S. They'll answer to you now.

P. P. S. Do reconsider trading pieces of your soul for power — I promise you won't miss them.

Emberlyn did a slow blink. 'She knew. She wrote this note because she knew how things would play out. No, she *maneuvered* things into playing out this way.'

'What did she mean "they'll answer to you now"?' asked Kage. 'Who's "they"?'

'You don't want to know,' Emberlyn mumbled. 'As for the wolf she mentioned . . . she's talking about Ripper. She didn't only leave the land to him so that Reena couldn't have houses built on it, she did it so that I'd have an entire clan of werewolves for neighbors.'

Paisley nodded. 'It makes you less vulnerable. It also means that anyone desperately wanting the land needs to go to *him*, not you.'

Kage bit his lip. 'I can't go as far as to say she loved you, Em. Sociopaths don't experience love – and Millicent was a sociopath for sure. But she valued you in her way. And I think leaving you to Ripper was an attempt to protect you.'

Emberlyn frowned. 'He's not going to take that seriously.' *She* wasn't taking it seriously.

'Of course he won't,' Kage agreed. 'But your family might. That would be good because people are reluctant to do anything that might poke at Ripper.'

'She's dragged him into one hell of a messy situation,' Emberlyn muttered. 'I'm sure he's *thrilled* about that part.' Ripper wasn't stupid; he'd surely see that Millicent had used him.

'Going by how intent he seems on keeping the land, I don't think he'll hold it against her, so he shouldn't give you problems,' said Paisley.

'Others will, though,' Kage tacked on. 'It doesn't matter that all you have is the manor. Reena will still want it.'

Emberlyn nodded. It had once been Lilith's home, and she'd woven much of her magick into these walls. That made it a huge prize.

Kage rubbed at his nape. 'If Millicent wanted you to have it, why didn't she just leave it to you in her will?'

Emberlyn sighed. 'Millicent never did things the easy way. Plus, she was all about making people "prove" themselves *to* themselves.'

'The earrings were a lure, then,' he said. 'A way to ensure you tried to gain entrance to the manor. Leaving you the cat was extra insurance.'

'Yup. I don't think she wanted me to have the manor merely because I'm the strongest of our line. I think it was because she knew I wouldn't sell it. She was resolute that Reena's plans wouldn't come to fruition. And she was mad enough with the rest of the family for being willing to sell it that she kidded each of them into thinking they'd be her sole heir and that I'd end up with nothing.' Emberlyn sighed again. 'She really put the "wicked" in "wicked witch".'

Paisley snickered. 'I always liked that about her.'

Funnily enough, so had Emberlyn. Millicent had been unashamedly herself, and there was something admirable about it.

Paisley clasped her hands together as if in prayer. 'On a less serious note, can I take a look around? I've always been curious about this place.'

'Go for it,' Emberlyn invited. 'Better yet, I'll give you a tour.'

As she led the twins through the first floor, lamps turned on by themselves. Fires roared to life in the hearths. The overall temperature adjusted, becoming not too cold nor too warm.

It was the manor's way of taking care of its owner.

As they walked, Emberlyn ran her hands over the rich fabrics of the sofas, the ornate fireplace mantels, the intricately detailed woodwork and the smooth surfaces of the stunning antiques. She drank in the nostalgic sights of the patterned wallpapers, lush drapery, opulent rugs, interesting artwork, gilded wainscotting and the chandeliers hanging from the high ceilings.

There was an abundance of large-scaled rooms throughout the manor, including the living area, parlor, study, dining room, kitchen, utility space, music room, two-floored library and multiple bedrooms with en suites. The rich color schemes of each room featured reds, blues, greens, black and even pomegranate.

Weirdly, though . . . 'None of her personal touches are around. No altars, no jar spells, no broom, no nothing.'

Kage blinked. 'Huh. Could the manor have put them away somehow to make room for *your* witchy touches?'

Emberlyn pursed her lips. 'Maybe. Though I wouldn't have thought so.' Shrugging it off for now, she asked, 'Ready to see the first floor?'

'Are we not gonna look at the basement?' asked Paisley.

'Nope,' Emberlyn replied simply, smoothing her hand along the banister as she ascended the winding staircase.

Paisley followed. 'And you're not going to explain why?'

'Nope.'

'You're only making me more eager to check it out.'

Emberlyn snorted. 'It won't let you in, anyway.'

'Wait, what?'

As they reached the landing, she turned to the twins. 'This house ... it's special, but not always in warm and fuzzy ways. Some parts of it are better left unexplored, trust me on that. Now, come on, I want to go see my old bedroom. I left a few things behind, like furnishings and stuff. I hope they're not in a crumpled heap on the floor.'

After a long walk down a hallway, Emberlyn arrived at her destination. She swung open the door. And sighed, her shoulders slumping. It was empty. Nothing that had once remained of her room was here. 'Millicent probably burned it all,' she mumbled.

'Uh ... Emberlyn?'

The odd note in Paisley's tone had Emberlyn snapping her gaze to her friend. 'What is it?'

Paisley didn't look at her, but focused on the end of the hallway. 'We ain't alone.'

'*What?*' Kage tracked his sister's gaze, swore beneath his breath and then pointedly looked away. 'I don't see dead people, I don't see dead people, I don't see dead people.'

'You're *totally* seeing a dead person.'

Peering down the hallway, Emberlyn noticed a partly transparent dark-haired woman in an old-fashioned blue gown, pointing at a certain door. She smiled. 'Don't worry, that's just Betty. She's one of the nice ones.'

'*Nice* ones?' repeated Kage. 'So there are bad ones? Hey, you never said this place was haunted.'

'Because it isn't,' Emberlyn told him. 'Mostly. Some ghosts do hang around, but none are bad. It's the *others* that you have to watch out for.'

'Expand,' he urged.

'Millicent summoned many dark entities. Whenever Betty told me to hide, I'd know that Millicent was up to something *not* so good. I'd head straight to my room, and the house's magick would keep any entities out. Though they left shortly after being summoned, some were able to return via whatever rip she made in the veil between our realm and theirs.'

As they began walking down the hall toward Betty, the spirit faded from sight.

'So this house, amazing though it is, wasn't always a safe place to be for you growing up,' Kage surmised.

Stopping in front of the last door in the hall, Emberlyn confirmed, 'No, it wasn't.'

'What is this room?' asked Paisley.

'The master.' Emberlyn twisted the knob, pushed open the door and stepped inside. She double-blinked, caught off-guard.

'Ooh, I love all the different shades of deep purple with splashes of teal,' said Paisley as she pushed past her. 'It gives the room a moody, witchy look. Totally. Adoring. The vibe.'

'Look, there's a reading nook built into the turret,' Kage said to his sister. 'My God, the woman had a *lot* of books.'

Paisley gasped in delight. 'Aw, there's a little velvet footstool and built-in sofa in the nook – I could sit here for hours and just *be*. Oh, and those silk drapes are fabulous.'

'They are,' Emberlyn said absently, skimming her fingers over the weathered French dresser. It was constructed of the same rose wood as that of the nightstand, wardrobe, four poster bed and dressing table.

Moving further into the room, she ran her gaze over the

nearby shelf. A gold candlestick stood either end of it, bordering a collection of crystals, stones and ornaments.

Kage sank onto the chaise longue that was propped up against the foot of the bed. 'Your grandmother had good taste.'

Emberlyn lightly fingered the pearl earrings sitting on a gold trinket dish on the nightstand. 'This is my stuff.'

'What?' he asked, smoothing a hand over the elegant lacy bedding.

'This is my stuff. All of it. The furnishings and knickknacks, I mean.'

Paisley turned away from the ornate cheval mirror. 'You're saying Millicent moved your things in here?'

'No doubt using magick, yes.' Emberlyn let her gaze touch on the glass-art lamp that she'd wanted to take with her when she moved out. Millicent had refused to allow it. *It belongs to the house, not you,* she'd said.

Kage sat up. 'That's crazy. And confusing. Unless she knew her time was almost up.'

'By the looks of it, she did.'

'Maybe she foresaw it,' Paisley suggested.

'Could be the case.'

Kage rose from the chaise longue. 'What do you think she did with all her own stuff?'

'She probably relocated most of it, if not all, to the spooky spare room. It's the one place I'm highly unlikely to go, and even in death she'd want her things left untouched.' Emberlyn shuddered just thinking about the room.

Kage twisted his mouth. 'For her to have kept everything from your old bedroom all these years, she'd either known very early on that you'd one day be living here again, or she'd hoped you would.'

Emberlyn nodded. 'It would appear so.'

Paisley shyly raised a hand. 'Since you're moving in here, can I have your apartment?'

Emberlyn felt her lips curve. 'Sure.'

Her friend gave a little clap. 'Yay! My journey to work just got *much* shorter.'

It had, since Emberlyn lived above her place of business – which also happened to be where Paisley worked, along with a couple of others. Those 'others' were currently holding the fort. 'I won't be able to pack all of my stuff tonight, but I can pack the basics and go on a quick grocery shop so I have clothes and essentials to keep me going.'

'Can I use the bathroom first?' asked Paisley.

Emberlyn pointed at a door. 'The en suite is right through there.'

Kage jabbed his thumb behind him. 'Can I keep nosing around?'

'Sure.' Once the twins had walked off, Emberlyn sank onto the turret's sofa. Which was right when she heard a feline chirp.

She looked up to see a black cat lounging atop the wardrobe. 'Hey, Lucie.' Emberlyn made cooing noises, trying to lure her down, but she didn't move. 'All right, be like that.'

Not all witches had a familiar. They didn't always seek you out. Emberlyn could still remember the day Lucie had turned up at the manor. When her grandmother had welcomed the feline with a grin, Emberlyn had originally thought Millicent meant to use her in some sort of ritual sacrifice. On the contrary, she'd taken care of Lucie in a way she hadn't others.

Though, much as she'd generally left Emberlyn to her own devices, there had been times when Millicent spent what she considered 'quality time' with her. Their activities had included things like graverobbing, jinxing land, planting forbidden herbs and temporarily turning the lake to blood just to fuck with people.

While many were wrong in branding her Millicent's double, there were some traits she'd picked up from her grandmother. Emberlyn wasn't concerned with what others thought of her; didn't look to them for acceptance, approval or validation. And fulfilling their expectations was nowhere on her list of things to do. Plus, yes, she was equally vengeful and more than a little ruthless.

But she differed from her grandmother in one very distinct way: in connecting with her magick, Emberlyn embraced all parts of herself – the good, the bad, the ugly. Millicent had only ever embraced the latter two.

Hearing a howl ring out in the distance, Emberlyn looked out of the window, feeling her skin pebble. And, yet again, she found her thoughts sliding to Michael.

To what might have become of him.

Grabbing one of the fringed pillows beside her, Emberlyn hugged it to her. As descendants of the original werewolf, Chilgrave werewolves were quite different from those found in other parts of the world. Well built, with shaggy black hair and red eyes, they looked somewhere between a black shuck and a hellhound.

They also had three forms: the human, the wolf and the In-between.

In the latter form, they were a beast that was both man and wolf. They'd be ruled by their animal instincts, their humanity buried deep. Various things could cause the transformation, such as overwhelming emotions or full moons.

Generally, the transformation was only temporary. They'd be human again before the night was over. But certain things could hamper that – grief, pain, guilt, a need to escape, on and on it went. And so they'd turn Rabid.

Like Michael had.

He'd done as other Rabid had before and after him – he'd fled to Bloodhill. Many Rabid inhabited the seemingly endless forested area that bordered the town. They were savage and had zero control over their lust to kill.

Some occasionally came into town, particularly on full moons, so there was a curfew at such times. They'd otherwise attack, mindless in their thirst for blood and violence.

People didn't kill them unless necessary. They aimed to capture them, where possible. Because the Rabid could 'come back' from that state. But not always. It generally depended on how long they'd been that way.

Given that the Rabid were prone to turn on each other, Emberlyn didn't even know if Michael was still alive. But he was gone either way, really – he'd been Rabid too long, his mental processes would be permanently affected.

People in her position typically declared their mating null and void – breaking the mating tie, as the saying went – after five years. Though she'd moved out of the home they'd shared twelve months ago, she'd waited the extra year before making it all official. She'd also dipped her toe in the dating pool. That hadn't resulted in more than a brief fling or two. But it was something.

Once again, a distant howl rang out. Maybe it was one of Ripper's wolves – they were no doubt thrilled to have their land back.

His clan was definitely the toughest of the three. *Seriously* tough. Driving through Ashwood, where the majority of the clan lived . . . it was like entering a movie set for lumberjack porn.

Genuinely, they were badass. You could send a few out into the wilderness and they'd likely build you a village. And they did what the other clans and the coven wouldn't – they braved Bloodhill to hunt meat for the town. Meat they sold at their butcher's shop.

They also ran the brewery, tattoo studio, blacksmiths, diner, mechanic shop, a bar, a restaurant and a landscaping business.

All things considered, they would make great neighbors. Especially to someone with her current problems. Providing that their Alpha didn't intend to be a dick to her, of course.

She didn't see why he would, really. There were no frills with Ripper – he was blunt and to the point, but he wasn't an asshole needlessly. And she hadn't done anything to him.

The witch who'd targeted his clan all those years ago, though? *She'd* caused an epically bad situation. As such, Emberlyn could totally understand if he'd keep his distance from her. Especially since she'd cultivated an image of herself that wouldn't exactly endear her to people. He'd have no reason to assume that not all the rumors about her were true.

She didn't need people to like or approve of her, she just wanted them to leave her be. If he'd extend that courtesy to her, she'd appreciate it. She had enough drama coming from other angles.

On that note, thanks for this, Grams. Thanks a fucking lot.

CHAPTER FIVE

❧

Sipping her freshly made cup of tea the next morning, Emberlyn tossed her spoon into the sink. She'd slept like the dead last night, which she figured was partly due to her having given the entire house a spiritual cleansing beforehand to rid it of negative energies.

Okay, so she hadn't cleansed the *entire* manor. She'd left out the spooky spare room and basement. Those were her no-go areas, and for good reason.

She'd already chowed down a bagel, so she would be heading to work soon. She'd also take some time to go to her apartment and pack the rest of her things.

The majority of the coven's businesses partially, if not mostly, tended to the needs and wants of witches. Something Emberlyn thought was particularly short-sighted. When three-quarters of the town's population were werewolves, it made sense to launch a business that would provide an in-demand service for them.

Hence why she'd started Vautier Laundry Hub.

Werewolves were always fighting. More often than not, it was for the rush of it. They even had a bareknuckle fighting ring for such purposes. Then there were minor disputes that escalated into brawls, one-to-one challenges, group fights or even – though it was rare – battles with other clans.

As such, their clothing was regularly stained with blood, dirt and sweat. More, such clothing was often also damaged – whether during violent incidents or the need to shift very quickly. So Emberlyn's hub not only laundered clothing, it also offered supplemental services such as repairing tears or reattaching buttons.

The place had *a lot* of customers. Especially since she'd incorporated a little magick, positively guaranteeing that their clothes would return in perfect condition, smelling of whatever scent they'd chosen, and would be soft enough to accommodate their slight skin sensitivity.

As a small add-on service, she even sold werewolf-specific potions at the hub – some sped up the healing process, some were straight-up energy shots, others aided in fighting the moon's pull. On and on it went.

At one point, the coven had started their own launderette, thinking to cash in on this niche they'd either previously ignored or simply hadn't seen. But they hadn't managed to lure Emberlyn's customers away, and they hadn't liked how their electricity kept cutting off, their machines kept breaking or their front door kept sticking.

Yes, she'd had something to do with it.

And yes, the other witches had known that. They just hadn't had the balls to confront her over it. Instead, they'd closed down their launderette.

Right then, a knock came at the front door. Emberlyn felt her brow crease. It could be Paisley, but she doubted it – her friend wasn't an early riser.

Whoever it was, the manor didn't consider them a physical threat to Emberlyn, or they wouldn't have made it this far. Which didn't mean that it wasn't one of her relatives – they weren't likely to try punching her or anything.

Her pretty porcelain cup in hand, Emberlyn walked down the hallway. When she pulled open the door, her pulse did a little skip. On the porch stood a tower of deliciousness wearing a faded dark tee, worn gray denim jeans and black leather boots.

She blinked in surprise. 'Ripper.' It was a wonder that her voice came out even. Because, up close, this werewolf had a way of making her hormones feel faint.

She had a weakness for this guy. Her defenses crumbled in the presence of all that raw male power. Making it harder to fight the attraction, her magick never failed to stir around his apex-predator energy.

He stared at her, holding himself with an unnatural stillness that made her think of an animal ready to pounce. Tension sparked in the air, live and hotly sexual – always did when they stood so close. And she found herself thinking it was a crying shame that he was so wrapped up in another woman.

What would it be like, she wondered, to love someone who loved you ... but who also loved your brother? Would you pray that that brother moved on so that you'd be free to pursue her? Would you alternate from feeling love to anger to resentment? Would you want to let her go, or would you spend your time hoping she'd one day choose you?

At that moment, his gaze roamed over Emberlyn – from her lightly made-up face to her loose curls, ivory pencil dress, silver triple-moon anklet and ivory high heels. His eyes snagged hers again, heat simmering in their depths. 'You always look like that first thing in the morning?' he asked, a little gravel in his voice, sounding so ... put out.

And right then, she made an informed and very mature decision.

She was going to fuck with him.

'Not until after I've masturbated, showered and smoothed oil all over my skin.'

His jaw clenched, and a muscle in his cheek ticked.

Hiding a smile, she took a sip of her tea. He was *way* too serious. 'Can I help you with something?'

He planted his feet. 'We should talk.' A firm statement littered with intent.

'Okay.' Was Emberlyn going to invite him in? Uh, no. Werewolf social 'rules' were different; you had to be careful to speak their language.

You didn't let them into your home. You didn't feed them. You didn't let them leave their possessions in your house. Otherwise, you basically indicated that they could have rights where you were concerned if they wanted to claim them. And if you gave an inch with a werewolf, they'd take a mile.

He crossed his arms over his packed-with-muscle chest. 'First of all, I've got to know if you're going to contest the will and try to claim the land.'

'Nope.'

'Just nope?'

She propped her hip against the doorjamb. 'Just nope.'

He narrowed his eyes, skeptical. 'Why not?'

'One, I don't need it. Two, it rightfully belongs to you anyway. Three, I wouldn't disrespect my grandmother's last wishes. Though you should probably be aware that she only left it to you as part of a strategy.'

'Strategy?'

'She left me a note, making it clear she'd wanted me to have the manor. Partly because she knew I was the only Vautier who wouldn't sell it. She also knew I'd be subsequently facing all sorts of problems. You owning most of the land beside the manor limits those problems for me.'

He grunted. 'I don't care why she did it so long as I get to keep possession of the land.'

'As I said, I have no interest in taking it from you. But there are those who'll try,' Emberlyn warned.

He dismissed that with a look, evidently unconcerned. 'If that happens, I'll deal with it.'

Emberlyn didn't doubt it. He was a wolf who knew how to get shit done. The kind you'd look at and think, *He could handle it.* Given all he'd endured and pushed through, you'd likely be right.

He took two smooth steps forward, making her pulse hiccup. 'As for another reason I'm here . . . you're probably not aware of this, but I had an arrangement with your grandmother.'

'An arrangement?'

'She made a certain elixir for me on a monthly basis.'

Emberlyn felt her head twitch to the side. 'What sort of elixir?'

'The sort that aids a werewolf in fighting the pull of the moon, but higher strength than that of typical potions.'

'Ah.' Full moons called to werewolves; called to them to shift, run, mate. Some would spend time as a wolf. Some would spend the night fucking. Some would do a little of both.

The problem? It was very easy for werewolves to change into their In-between forms on full moons. Potions could help them fight it so they could instead enjoy the evening.

While all werewolves were susceptible to its pull, it was far worse for Ripper. At the age of eleven, he'd done as Michael had – he'd turned Rabid and fled to Bloodhill. He'd also done what Michael *hadn't* done.

He'd come back.

Mere days after his fifteenth birthday, he'd stumbled into town while in a Rabid state. Members of his clan had captured him and – with the help of magick – snapped him out of it. No one had expected him to be *himself* again, though.

Anyone who spent four years or more like that were 'lost'. They breathed, they ate, they slept. But they were an echo of the person they'd once been.

Not Ripper.

Although he'd come back from that Rabid state, he wasn't the same. He'd always been lethal and rough around the edges. But never so stoic and serious; never humming with the uncivilized air he now had.

Emberlyn pushed off the doorjamb. 'What did Millicent insist on in return?'

'My blood to use in her spells.'

Made sense. The blood of an Alpha werewolf, particularly one from Lupin's line, would be potent.

'She told me that if anything ever happened to her I should go to you; that you could recreate the elixir. She said the ritual can be found in her book of shadows.'

Huh. Millicent hadn't mentioned any of this to Emberlyn. 'I'm fine with making the elixir available for you. But I don't want your blood in return. Just the same five-dollar fee as that of a standard-strength elixir.' It wouldn't require additional ingredients, just stronger magick. 'That work for you?'

He eyed her intently for several moments. 'It works.'

'Do you have an elixir for tonight?' There'd be a full moon later.

He gave a curt nod. 'I have one left.'

'Come to me some time before the next full moon and I'll make you more.' Emberlyn expected him to leave then. He didn't. He lingered. And something in his expression told her . . . 'You have a question.'

'More of a proposal, really.' He swiped his tongue over his front teeth. 'We don't know each other well and we've never been anything close to friends, but I don't see why we can't be allies.'

Surprise fluttered in her chest. 'You don't need me as an ally. Politically speaking, I don't bring a lot to the table.' She wouldn't have thought that he'd want to associate with any witch beyond a buyer-customer thing in any case.

'But we both have the same enemies right now, don't we?'

True. 'You want us to present a united front?'

'There's strength in numbers.'

Indeed, but it would place her under his protection. And while Alpha werewolves were no doubt a delight in bed, they could be troublesome creatures. Nosy. Meddlesome. Prone to swooping in and taking control.

Emberlyn was a person who moved to the beat of their own drum. She didn't like people trying to coddle her, tread over her independence or interfere with her choices.

But then, she couldn't picture Ripper caring much about what she was doing or fussing over her safety. And she could do with some good connections right now. It might help keep the coven and Carver off her back. She could deal with them, she just didn't want to *have* to.

Ripper, well, he was the ultimate protector and defender. Dangerous. Loyal. Dependable. That made him a very good deterrent.

Also, she respected him, because it took some strength for a person who'd been through what he'd endured to stand in front of her now – whole and healthy.

Emberlyn nodded. 'I'll agree to it.'

'Allies, then?' He held out his hand.

She looked down at his open calloused palm, surprised.

Werewolves didn't accept or initiate touch easily. You had to wait for them to invite it.

She placed her hand in his, choosing to ignore the zap of static that shot up her arm. 'Allies.'

His eyes darkened in a way that told her he'd felt that zap as well. 'Good.' He slowly released her hand. 'I know you probably have to head to work but, as the boundaries of our territory now touch, we should settle a few things.'

Her palm tingling from the skin-to-skin contact, she almost rubbed it against her thigh. 'Such as?'

'I took a walk along the territorial line. It cuts through one of your grandmother's gardens. Some weird cluster of plants.'

'Oh, her Poison Patch.' Emberlyn hadn't realized that it didn't fall within the line.

'If you want the other half dug up and replanted on your side of the metaphorical fence, I'll get my wolves to do it while they're tidying our landscape – so long as you don't care that they're on your land.'

She would have asked why he'd do her such a favor, but she supposed it was more that he wanted the garden out of his way. And, well, they *were* allies now.

'I don't mind.' She took another sip of her tea. 'They should be careful, though. Some of those plants aren't friendly. They snap. Sting. Bite. That sort of thing. And they're all toxic.' Millicent had doted on them like they were her children.

'I don't want any magickal surprises. Is there a chance Millicent laid any traps on the land for trespassers?'

Emberlyn hadn't considered that before but, knowing her grandmother . . . 'She might have. Want me to come take a look?'

'It'd be appreciated.'

Emberlyn drained her cup and then placed it on the porch table. 'Let's go, then.'

They descended the steps together and strode down the path. Though their bodies didn't touch, it felt as though they did on account of the static buzz of energy he was giving off. She suspected it was due to the fact that there'd be a full moon tonight.

They exited the front yard and then circled around to the unfenced land on the right of the manor. It was a pretty sight, complete with various trees – hawthorn, apple, hazel, blackthorn.

'How are your heels not sinking into the soil?' asked Ripper, a slight gruff note to his voice.

She smiled. 'Magick.' The wild grass brushed over her feet as she followed him to where one of his wolves stood.

Said wolf curved his mouth. 'Hi, Emberlyn,' he greeted, his deep-brown eyes smiling.

She felt her lips hike up. 'Morning.' She liked Kerr. Tall and burly with unkempt russet hair, he was a good guy. One of the Watchers.

There wasn't a police force at Chilgrave. The town had what was basically a crisis unit. Anyone could be a Watcher. They protected, safeguarded, resolved issues and enforced laws.

Ripper wore authority, so he was an obvious choice for a Watcher. He hadn't accepted the position when offered it, though. He would hunt, put out metaphorical clan fires, lead search parties and all that jazz. But he mostly focused on his clan.

Kerr's smile dimmed. 'It must be weird being in that house with no Millicent plodding around.'

'Not as much as you might think. A lot of the time, she was in the basement or her study, so I was mostly left to my own devices.'

Both males frowned at that, seeming surprised.

'Anyway, let's check that she left no magickal landmines.' Chanting low, Emberlyn let out a thin rope of glittering magick motes that snaked along the grass, searching. 'Don't worry, my magick won't damage your land or set off any traps; only locate them, if there are any.'

'What you did yesterday ... that was pretty impressive,' Kerr praised. 'I don't think I've seen you use magick before. I mean, I've knocked back plenty of your potions, but I bought them from your laundry hub. I never saw you create them.'

'It's a pretty boring process to witness, so you didn't miss out.'

'I hear Millicent left you to Ripper in her will.'

Emberlyn narrowed her eyes at the taunting note in Kerr's tone. 'She did it to needle me. I once told her that no man would ever own me.'

'Ah,' said Kerr. 'So, you allied with our clan now?'

'I am. And, yes, it means you can all come to me when you need magickal advice or intervention if you wish to.' Feeling her magick *tug* at her, she looked over to see the glittering rope circling a spot on the ground. 'Hmm, we have something.'

They flanked her as she stalked over to the spot. 'You're going to have to stand back,' Emberlyn warned, reining in her magick to change its intention. The magick motes blended, twisted, spiraled and then poured into the ground. Soil parted until an object came into view.

Squatting, she felt her brow pinch. It was a glass jar filled with several things, including rusty nails, glass shards, red pepper and pieces of rotten meat.

She hovered her hand above it; felt the negative energy scrape at her palm as she read the spell's intention. 'Huh.'

Ripper moved closer – which was annoying, since his feral energy stirred up every drop of power she possessed. 'What?'

Emberlyn sprinkled some magick down onto the jar, letting the glittering motes slip through the loose seams of the spell to dissolve the negative energy. 'This is not Millicent's work.'

'You're sure?'

'Positive. Can one of you grab me a leaf from the butterbur plant over there?'

'Uh, yeah,' replied Kerr, who then melted away.

Ripper shifted even closer to her. 'How do you know it's not your grandmother's work?'

'It's sloppy,' she replied. 'Spells are meandering loops of interlacing magick. Think knitted items. You don't want holes, snags or pulls. This spell here? The pattern is slightly uneven, the edges weren't bound and there are dropped stitches. All this not only weakens the spell, it also leaves it vulnerable to being undone.'

Kerr returned with a large, roughly heart-shaped leaf. 'Here.'

'Thanks,' she said, taking it from him.

Ripper squatted beside her. 'Do you know what kind of spell this is?'

Resisting the urge to frown at him for coming so close, she replied, 'I do. Which is another reason I'm sure Millicent had no hand in this. She'd never poison the land.'

His brows flew together. 'Poison it?'

'This is a curse jar.' Although the spell had dissipated, Emberlyn wasn't about to touch something that had so much ill intent attached to it, so she curved the leaf around it before lifting it out of the soil. 'Somebody wanted to cause damage to the land. This jar has been active for at least a month, so you may see some signs of degradation. Patches of dead grass. Bare shrubs. Brittle tree bark.'

Ripper's gaze sharpened, a very low growl vibrating in his chest. 'There are a few spots like that,' he said, his voice rough in a way that made her nipples pay attention. 'Who the fuck would want to curse the land?'

'The coven wants to build on it, so it wouldn't have been them,' Kerr commented.

'Not necessarily,' said Emberlyn, standing upright. 'They could have thought that if they made this area look barren and ugly, she'd choose to sell it.' The jar was placed in the ground months before she died.

Ripper hummed, slowly straightening to his full height. 'Maybe. The other clans wouldn't care what happened to it, so they wouldn't have had one of their witches do it. No one from ours would ever damage it. And you say it wasn't Millicent.'

'Don't get me wrong, she was spiteful enough to destroy the land so that it'd be useless to the coven,' Emberlyn conceded, using magick to push the soil back into the hole. 'But they would have healed it eventually, so that wouldn't have been enough for her. And she'd have had no reason to harm the area if she'd planned on giving it to you. I can understand if you'd consider me a possible suspect, but I have more self-respect than to perform such poor spell work. There are far easier ways to poison land, anyway. If I'd done this, the area would look like a marsh by now.'

Ripper's eyes flitted over her face. 'I believe you.' He flicked a look at the jar. 'I thought the coven didn't approve of casting curses.'

'It's like I said yesterday, nobody uses magick for good all the time.' The coven's rebel faction came to mind.

'Think there might be other jars buried around here?'

'I doubt it, because there'd be more evidence of degradation. One jar is enough to afflict land with several sporadic areas of decay. But I'll check.' Emberlyn sent her magick out to search the area once more but, thankfully, found no additional curse jars.

'Now that you've dug that up, will the land heal?'

She felt her nose wrinkle. 'Not for a while. I can inject some healing energy into the earth if you want. Call it payment for your clan replanting half of Millicent's Poison Patch on my side of the invisible fence.' At Ripper's nod, Emberlyn wrapped the leaf tight around the jar and then gave it to him. 'Do *not* touch the jar.'

His raised brow said he didn't appreciate her tone.

'You're Kerr's Alpha, not mine.'

Kerr snorted at that, which earned him a glare from Ripper.

She crouched down and planted both palms on the ground, fingers splayed. She chanted again, releasing her magick into the earth – stirring it, greeting it, blessing it, healing it.

Grass rustled. Shrubs tremored. Flowers bloomed. Tree branches creaked.

Done, she brushed one palm against the other to wipe off dirt as she stood. 'It might take a day or two for the damage to completely disappear, depending on its severity, but it will heal.'

Ripper inclined his head in thanks. He went to speak but then stopped, his head tipping to the side as if picking up a sound. 'You have a visitor.'

'I do?' It was ten seconds or so later that she heard the faint rumbling of an engine in the distance. 'It would appear you're right.'

CHAPTER SIX

◆

Ripper tensed when Reena's car came into sight moments later. It would have been smarter of the woman to have given Emberlyn time to calm down before turning up here. But the High Priestess had plans to put in motion, so he supposed she couldn't afford to procrastinate.

Emberlyn exhaled heavily. 'Well, this has taken a piss all over my morning mood.'

Kerr snorted. 'Want us to make her leave?'

'Nah, I'd rather get this over with. She'll just turn up at the hub otherwise.' Emberlyn looked from him to Ripper. 'Not sure if you want her to know about the curse jar yet. But if not, keep it out of sight. You both hang back while I talk to her.'

Ripper couldn't help but bristle.

She shot him a severe look. 'We're allies now, yes, but I'm a solitary witch who lives alone on a goddamn hill and will not be seen to hide behind anyone. If I did, I'd look weak. You backing me up as my ally is one thing. Being my voice is another.'

Ripper clenched his jaw. He got what she was saying. He did. She was, in a sense, a lone Alpha. She needed to show she could not only defend her own territory but that she didn't need other people to do it for her.

But stand back the whole time and twiddle his thumbs? It wasn't in his nature.

Ripper took a stalking step closer to her. Her magick dusted his senses, smelling of vanilla and pink pepper. Her pupils dilated – a sight that made his lower stomach clench.

'All right,' he said. 'But I have to be seen to make my own statement so that she takes our being allies seriously. Which means if she stays too long, I come over there and make it clear I don't like it. That won't be me taking over or speaking for you – you don't need that from me. It'll be me ensuring she knows you have backup should you need it.'

Emberlyn twisted her mouth, her gaze pensive. 'I'm not so self-reliant that I don't see we *both* need to give a little here, so fine. This situation is about more than just me anyway – we're both on Reena's radar.'

He blinked, a little surprised she hadn't argued.

'But we won't always be, and it just occurred to me that you might then no longer consider us allies – it wouldn't benefit you anymore. If that's the case, so be it. I won't come for you as a result. *Unless* you cross me.' She leaned toward him, her gaze boring into his. 'So don't cross me.' With that, she spun on her heel and walked off.

Kerr blew out a long breath. 'She's intense. I like her.'

'Intense' worked. Ripper couldn't quite believe she'd threatened him. He couldn't recall anyone doing it during the entirety of his adulthood. But, as he'd noted before, Emberlyn was an Alpha in her own right. She'd show no fear.

'She clearly doesn't trust easily,' he said, not following her but moving to a position where he'd have a full view of the front of the house so he could better monitor the upcoming encounter. He'd hear everything just fine from here.

'Why would she? From what I can tell, there've been few people in her life she could trust,' said Kerr.

'True.' Ripper held the jar out to him. 'Stuff this in your jacket pocket.'

Kerr did so, his gaze on the car that had finally pulled up outside the manor. Emberlyn stood outside her gate, her arms folded.

Reena slipped out of the car, hauling a bulky bag with her. Catching sight of him and Kerr, she did the slightest double-take, her lips flattening. But then she redirected her attention to Emberlyn and cleared her throat. 'My behavior last night was uncalled for. I apologize. I'm just here to talk and to give you these.' She offered the bag to Emberlyn. 'The dolls left to you by your grandmother.'

Emberlyn took the bag, her expression blank. 'Thank you.'

Reena cast a look at the porch. 'Could we perhaps sit?'

Emberlyn tipped her head toward the house, indicating for Reena to follow, and then strode up the path.

That walk. It was effortless grace with a touch of sensuality. She wore heels like she'd been born for it and, Christ, if he didn't want to—

Ripper pushed the explicit thought right out of his head before it could take root.

Emberlyn placed the bag on the porch table and smoothly lowered herself onto one of the rockers, regal as any queen.

Reena took the other rocker, a tired sigh easing out of her. 'I have quite the predicament on my hands here. I made promises to people. Promises of new homes, more space, a few stores, new jobs and even a children's park for the little ones.'

'So I heard,' said Emberlyn, crossing one slim leg over the other.

'Then you can imagine just how many unhappy people are looking to me for assurances, alternatives and reimbursements.' Reena looked up at the manor. 'I realize this was your home for a long time, Emberlyn, but you're one person. One. The coven . . . We're talking hundreds of disappointed people.'

A *caw* sounded as a crow soared down and settled on the porch rail.

Reena gave it the side-eye, clearing her throat.

Without lifting her arm from the armrest, Emberlyn raised a finger. 'First of all, that you'd expect me to put the wants and needs of *your* coven before me – a person most of them refer to as "the devil's witch", in case you've forgotten – is pure and total lunacy. Secondly, whether or not I live at the manor has no impact on them. It's the land you need. I don't have it. It belongs to Ripper now.'

'As the owner of the manor, you could contest the will,' Reena reminded her.

'I'm not going to. I would never disrespect my grandmother's last wishes, especially when those wishes were fair. It's wolf-clan territory. In their position, you'd want back land that rightfully belonged to the coven.'

'Since when do you care what's fair?' Reena snarked.

'When haven't I?'

'You have misused magick many times; attacked many of my coven, even as a child.'

One of Emberlyn's brows slowly winged up. 'Oh, you mean the gang of bullies who thought I'd make an easy target? A group led by *your* daughter? If you had dealt with them – because yes, I eventually discovered that my teacher *did* talk to you about it – instead of dismissing it, I wouldn't have had to.

And let's be frank, I could have hurt them much, much worse than I did.'

Ripper felt his brows lift at the latter. None of the rumors had mentioned that Reena had been informed of the bullying and declined to intervene.

'It should be noted,' Emberlyn continued, 'that a lot of things you've held me accountable for were actually committed by the rebellious faction in your coven that you insist on swearing doesn't exist.'

Ripper had heard some rumors about that as well.

'Because it doesn't, you just like to shift blame.'

Emberlyn frowned. 'I've never, not once, denied anything that I've done. Why would I, when it was always in an effort to make a point?'

'And you've been making "points" since you were too young to use even a whisper of aggressive magick. You haven't only hurt people. You've caused damage to countless pieces of property. Like the swimming pools, for example. What did they ever do to you? What so earned them your wrath that you turned the water to blood?'

Another crow swooped down out of nowhere. It, too, perched itself on the rail.

Reena cast both birds a wary look.

'The pools had done me no harm,' Emberlyn replied, her words coming slow and calm. *Too* calm. An emotion that wasn't present in her eyes – they were dark, hard. 'But the owners of those pools? Each one *laughed* on hearing that Michael turned Rabid; said that being mated to me had fucked him up. And they chatted that shit *knowing* I could hear them.'

Ripper exchanged a surprised look with Kerr. He hadn't known that any of the coven had blamed her for what happened to Michael.

'You like to make out that I'm some sort of menace to society,' Emberlyn went on. 'I have largely kept to myself. A certain percentage of the coven has left me alone, and I have done them that same courtesy. But others didn't let me be, and so I dealt with them. It's not as if *you* would have done it on my behalf.'

'Magick should not be used to cause harm,' Reena clipped.

'Did you tell that to Tyra? Or to the fifty-two-year-old witch who tried hypnotizing me into going home with him when I was sixteen? Or to Sera, who tried magickly punching her way into my mind a few years ago?'

Ripper felt himself go stiffer with each angered word she spoke. He'd been very aware that a large chunk of the coven wasn't 'nice' to her, but he hadn't known that things had been quite that bad.

'I could go on and on, Reena,' she added, the small hairs around her face fluttering as magick crackled around her. 'All I did was make it clear that, contrary to what they believed, they don't have the right to come at me whenever they please, however they please. So do not. Fucking. Demonize me.'

Caws again split the air, and then two more crows appeared. One settled on the rail, but the other landed on Emberlyn's shoulder.

Either she was calling to them or they were responding to her distress – he couldn't tell which. But as it occurred to Reena right then that just a signal from Emberlyn could likely make those crows divebomb her, the High Priestess uneasily straightened in her seat.

'You're right,' Reena finally allowed. 'Ninety-nine percent of the time, you acted only in retaliation. It was unfair of me to imply otherwise. I'm simply frustrated. Carver is on my back, the coven isn't happy and the—'

'And the manor isn't finally in your possession,' Emberlyn finished.

Reena's nostrils flared. 'Millicent set this up so that you'd end up here, didn't she?'

'Maybe. Doesn't much matter.' Emberlyn raised her chin. 'I'm here. And I'm not leaving. *You* should, though.'

But the High Priestess didn't, her expression desperate. 'An entire coven is looking to you to put this right.'

Emberlyn lifted the shoulder on which the crow didn't sit. 'Where's the wrong? The manor was never intended for you.'

'Without it, I have no grounds to contest the will.'

'The land is rightfully Ripper's, just as this manor is rightfully mine. You might as well accept it and alter your plans.'

'*Cancel* them, you mean. That's what I'd have to do. I'd be letting down hundreds of witches, not to mention Carver. He's angry right now, and he's looking for someone to take it out on.'

There was a subtle threat there. So very, very subtle. But it put Ripper on edge.

Right. He was done hanging back. Emberlyn had had her say. Now he'd have his own. 'Come on,' he told Kerr.

As they made their approach, Emberlyn didn't react; she kept her eyes on the other witch as she said, 'Don't think to direct his anger at me. *You* made him promises, not me. If you want to extend Bellcrest so badly, do it in another direction.'

'I can't,' Reena bit off. 'The rest of the council won't agree to it. They don't want trees and plant life taken down unless necessary, and the rest of the land is needed for farming.'

'So talk to Ripper. Maybe he'd be willing to sell his portion to you.'

'*Sell* it?' Reena echoed, a hint of outrage in her voice. 'I'd be expected to purchase it?'

'He wouldn't give it to you for free. I realize that, being High Priestess, you're used to people making your life easier. But he's an Alpha werewolf. He's going to do what's best for his clan, not you. That said, he *may* sell you the land.'

'He'd ask for some outrageous price, knowing I'd never be able to afford it.'

'Ripper doesn't strike me as a person who'd play that type of game.'

'You're right, I wouldn't,' Ripper confirmed, pushing through the yard's gate.

Reena jerked in her seat and twisted to look at him.

'I also won't be parting with the land – not for any price,' he told her. 'So don't bother appealing to me with stories of disappointed families. I'm on the council.' As was Reena and the other two clan Alphas. 'I know you have plenty of housing at Bellcrest. Some homes are empty. Others underoccupied. You don't need to extend the neighborhood.'

Reena pressed her lips together. 'Maybe the plight of witches won't bother you, but what about Carver?'

Ripper ascended the porch steps. 'What about him?'

'Surely you care how his business fares. It will suffer if this project goes down the drain.'

'His construction business is doing just fine.' Which was a miracle, given his gambling habits. 'He doesn't need this project to keep it afloat.'

'But—'

'My answer is no. It will never be a different answer. Take Emberlyn's advice and accept the situation.'

Reena looked from him to her. 'You're both being unreasonable. My coven—'

'Is not my problem,' Ripper insisted. 'Nor is it Emberlyn's problem. So don't make a habit of turning up here appealing for her to change her mind. She gave you her answer – there's no need to go over it again.'

Reena's spine snapped straight. 'You cannot *tell* me not to come here. I am High Priestess, I govern Bellcrest.'

'The manor isn't part of Bellcrest, which you already know. Something you may not know is that Emberlyn and I are allies now – my clan has her back, and vice versa. So when I say that you're not to keep coming here, I mean *you're not to keep coming here*. I won't fucking overlook it.'

Her cheeks flushing, Reena balled up her hands.

'There's no point in pushing this,' Emberlyn told her. 'You've said your piece. We've said ours. Let's leave it at that.' She flicked her fingers toward Reena's car, and the engine came to life.

Her face hard, the High Priestess jerkily pushed out of her chair. 'Contact me if you change your mind.' She marched down the steps, flinching as the crows noisily flew off – their bodies only inches from the top of her head.

Ripper looked at Emberlyn. 'Will you?'

'What?' she asked, her gaze on the witch striding down the path.

'Change your mind.'

'No,' she replied, those striking pale-hazel orbs meeting his. 'Will you?'

'No.'

'Hey, voodoo dolls, cool,' said Kerr, looking inside the bag on the table. 'These were Millicent's?'

Emberlyn's lips kicked up a little bit as she stood upright. 'Yup. She made them.'

'Why would she leave you these in her will?' asked Kerr.

'I played with them when I was little.'

'You *played* with voodoo dolls?'

'She never told me they weren't normal dolls. I didn't know

any better. Didn't even realize she was teaching me how to make and use such dolls until I was older.'

Kerr's brow pinched. 'There's, uh, one of you.' He held up a doll that – going by the hair, eye color and classy outfit – was quite obviously meant to be Emberlyn. 'And its shoulder doesn't look good.'

Emberlyn grimaced. 'Every time I got a stabbing pain in my shoulder, I knew it was her. She'd do it when she wanted to talk to me about something. Most people just pick up the phone, but ... Anyway, where'd you put the curse jar? I'll dispose of it safely before I leave for work.'

'I got it,' Kerr told her, plucking it out of his pocket.

She took it, tucked it under her arm, grabbed her teacup and then nabbed the bag of dolls. 'Later, neighbors. Remember to warn the rest of your clan about the plants in the Poison Patch.' She went back into the manor, and the door swung shut behind her.

Kerr looked at him. 'Well, she going to make the elixir for you?'

Nodding, Ripper turned to the stairs. 'She's only going to charge the same fee she charges for those of normal strength. I had thought she'd charge more – I'm not exactly in a position to refuse.'

'Was this before or after she agreed to an alliance?'

'Before,' replied Ripper as they jogged down the steps.

'Did you have push her to agree to allying herself with our clan?'

'No, she saw the sense in it.'

'Not surprised. Really, she's no more a fan of the coven than you are. They wronged us by not properly holding Rosemary accountable for what she did, but that won't hold a candle to what they seem to have put Emberlyn through.'

Ripper grunted his agreement at the latter.

'It's good that you two are singing from the same hymn sheet.' Kerr lightly bumped his shoulder into Ripper's. 'Especially since you wanna hit that.'

Ripper frowned. 'The fuck?'

'You gonna tell me I'm wrong?'

He could. It'd be a damn lie, though. 'I need to head to the brewery. Get some wolves down here to fix the landscape.'

'And if they ask if she's off-limits, I can say no?'

Ripper found himself stopping dead near the end of the path. He ground his teeth, not liking the smirk Kerr wore. 'Cut the shit. I don't have time for it.'

'I'm just asking,' Kerr defended, all innocence. 'She's Crew's type. He'll want to know if he has the go-ahead to make a play.'

Stalking out of the small gate, Ripper let it slam back against Kerr's knees, the wolf's *oof* music to his ears. 'Don't piss me off more than you already have.'

'I don't think I can help it.'

'Try.'

CHAPTER SEVEN

✑

Parking at the curb outside the laundry hub, Emberlyn let out a long sigh. Her first morning at the manor had certainly been eventful, though not entirely negative. Reena's visit hadn't been fun, of course. But Emberlyn had collected some powerful allies, and it meant that she and Ripper could have the civility that she'd wanted.

Sliding out of the car, she took an idle look around. The street was a sleepy sight at such an early hour. There were many shops, including a hair salon, bookstore, clothing boutique, deli and flower shop. The storefronts all featured welcoming displays, planters and striped awnings. Benches, light posts and saplings were spread around.

She crossed to the hub's door, pushed it open and stepped into the reception area. It was warm, tidy and inviting. Fresh-white paint, sleek wood, marble flooring, good lighting. The wall-mounted TV was angled toward the plush seating and 'kids' corner'. Magazines and cup coasters rested on the coffee table.

Framed nature canvas prints adorned the walls. Posters, ads and flyers were pinned to the bulletin board. A potted dragon tree was tucked in a corner near the glossy white reception desk.

Stood behind the desk, Paisley smiled at her. 'Hey, how did your first night in your new home go?'

'Very well, thank you. My morning was weird, though.'

Paisley's brow dented. 'Weird, how?'

Rounding the desk, Emberlyn explained, 'In a very short space of time, I agreed to being allies with Ripper and had a visit from a very frustrated Reena.'

Paisley's lips parted. 'I can't decide which part I want to hear about first.'

Emberlyn shoved her purse under the desk out of the way. 'I'll start from the beginning.' She brought her friend up to speed, keeping it brief since customers would enter soon. She didn't mention the curse jar. It had been buried on Ripper's land, so whether he made it public knowledge was his business. If he made decisions regarding the manor, she'd want to kick him in the junk.

Paisley did a slow blink. 'Wow. I'm glad you said yes to being Ripper's ally – it's extra protection for you. I know you don't *need* it, but I like that you have it. Do you think Reena will heed his warning and let the situation lie?'

Emberlyn raked her teeth over her lower lip as she considered it. 'No, but I think she'll be careful how she goes about pushing this.' She inhaled deeply. 'Anyway, how was your morning?'

Paisley's eyes dulled. 'Not great. I had another fight with my mom. She doesn't like that I won't drop the idea of taking the Change. Says she can't "lose both her children". Like I'd be as good as dead.'

'Ah.' While a bite from a werewolf could put non-wolves through the Change, most witches would never do it due to the price tag for their kind.

'She went on and on about how I'd lose my connection with my magick. I know that already. But where's the big deal when my magick is weak anyway? Other witches in my position have taken the Change. Yes, it'll mean leaving the coven and joining the clan of whichever wolf turns me. But I can't say I'd miss being part of it.'

Knowing Ethel as well as she did, Emberlyn could easily guess . . . 'She threatened to disown you, didn't she?'

Paisley grimaced. 'Yes. Don't tell Kage, he'll flip, and that'll make things worse. I'm not close to my mom, but I wouldn't like to lose her. What do you think I should do?'

'I think you should do what you feel is best for you. Living to keep others happy . . . it's not living, it's people-pleasing. There shouldn't be conditions attached to a person's love for you.'

Paisley gave a hard nod. 'I'd like to join Ripper's clan. It has the best reputation. Shane's clan has its shit together now that he's Alpha, but it's not all the way there yet. And Carver's clan is . . . problematic.'

Yes, his wolves were fond of vandalizing, thieving, starting fights and flirting with the mates of other werewolves like it was their right. 'Plus, Kage is part of Ripper's clan.'

'So?'

'So he's your twin.'

'And?'

'And it'd surely be nicer for you both to be in the same clan.'

Paisley's nose wrinkled. 'I couldn't give a monkey's left tit what clan he belongs to. But, as you're allied with Ripper now, I'd feel safer being part of his. Do you think he'd agree to it?'

'First of all, it *will* make a difference to you to be in the same clan as your brother – no, don't deny it. Secondly, I don't know if my alliance with Ripper is going to be permanent, so only choose his clan if it would be your preferred option no matter the situation. Thirdly, I don't know what his vetting process is, so I can't say whether he'd agree to welcome you into his clan. But you could ask. You don't ask, you don't get.'

Hearing the door open, Emberlyn looked to see her other two laundry aides entering. 'Morning, girls.' The sisters Chrissie and Clementine were werewolves whose mom was a witch. A mating between a witch and a wolf never produced hybrids – only one or the other.

Chrissie blew out a breath. 'Sorry we're almost late. Clem's car wouldn't start again, so we had to walk.'

'That contraption hates me, I'm telling you,' Clem muttered. 'It operates just fine whenever I have a mechanic look at it. Other times, it acts like an ass.'

Chrissie sighed. 'It's a car, Clem, it can't hate you.'

'Wrong. So very, very wrong.' Clem marched to the back of the hub, her sister close behind her.

Paisley looked at Emberlyn, her eyes dancing. 'So, anyways, when are you heading upstairs to pack the rest of your stuff?'

'When we get a lull,' Emberlyn replied. 'It won't take me long, since I'm leaving the majority of the furniture behind for you. And I already got started on it yesterday, I just didn't take everything back to the manor with me.'

'Awesome. Because I'm packed and ready to move in once you're gone. My mom isn't pleased that I'll be living on neutral territory. But she does feel better knowing that you have wards all over it to keep intruders out.'

Just then, the front door once more opened. Emberlyn felt her lips curve at the middle-aged werewolf who strode in. 'Good morning, Mr Weaver.'

His default grin kicked up a notch. 'Morning, pretty witches.' He plonked his basket on the counter and blew a breath upward, making his unkempt salt-and-pepper hair flutter. 'You know what yesterday was?'

'What?' she asked.

'My fiftieth birthday, which means . . .'

'You now qualify for free delivery,' she finished. 'Happy belated birthday. Did you do anything fun?'

'At my age, you don't much celebrate it.' He took a complimentary mint from the bowl near the devil's ivy plant.

'We can also have your things collected, you know,' Emberlyn said, plucking a shirt out of his basket.

'But then I wouldn't have an excuse to come in and flirt with you, would I?'

She snorted. 'I suppose that's true.'

'Would you like tea or coffee?' Paisley asked him. 'Flirting is thirsty work.'

'I'll take a coffee. You know how I like it.' He gestured at the glass case built into the desk. 'I'll also take one of those potions that help with joint pain. These bones of mine ache something fierce at times.'

Werewolves generally suffered from pain in their joints as they aged, which wasn't surprising given the amount of shapeshifting they did. All the snapping and popping had to put a real strain on their bones over time.

Emberlyn swiped a tag and pen from beside the telephone. 'So, how's Mrs Weaver?'

As Mr Weaver talked about his mate, Emberlyn neatly wrote down the relevant details on the tag for his shirt – his name, the locations of stains, and that two buttons were missing and would need replacing.

She generally worked at the counter, tagging and inspecting clothes. Paisley would then sort the items according to the fabric and necessary treatment. Clem had a keen eye, so she'd apply magick-spiced solvents or other treatments to stains before passing them to Chrissie, who placed the items in the necessary machines. Once Emberlyn had sprinkled in a little magick, those machines would be switched on.

After the cycle, Clem would check the clothes for any stains or residue – something that very rarely happened. Paisley and/or Chrissie would then either steam, press or iron the clothes. Following that, Emberlyn would fold and bag them. It was a system that worked well.

Emberlyn kept the prices reasonable and provided discounts for customers who brought in more than a certain amount of clothes at a time, as well as special deals for their most frequent customers.

It wasn't a glamourous job. They were on their feet virtually all day. There was a whole lot of lifting, carrying, moving, organizing, cleaning, etc. A whole lot of talking, too, since customers liked to chat. But as a team they made it work, and there were aspects of it that they enjoyed. Also, a simple spell kept the place from being too hot and humid.

After Mr Weaver had left, Paisley sidled up to Emberlyn and said, 'I took it as a very good sign when you cut his nephew loose.'

Emberlyn felt her brow pinch. 'Uh, why?'

'It shows that you're *really* moving forward. I can see why you allowed said nephew into your bed six months ago. He's fun and hot and he doesn't do serious. You needed that then, because you weren't ready for more.'

'I'm still not.'

'I wouldn't say that. You're gun-shy when it comes to werewolves. I get it. But what happened to Michael isn't exceedingly common. The likelihood of you taking another mate who did the same thing is hyper-small. I've never heard of anyone who lost two mates to Bloodhill.'

Neither had Emberlyn, but stranger things had happened.

'I think you'd more easily date a witch. Maybe you should. It's easy to think of the coven as one entity, but there are plenty of people within it who don't agree with how you've been treated by the rest. Some guys in the coven are pretty decent; I've often heard them call you hot as hell.'

It was true that the coven as a whole weren't assholes to Emberlyn, but ... 'Witch or werewolf, I'm not looking for anything serious. Especially not now. My life has become super complicated overnight.'

'You got that right,' Paisley muttered.

'I'm going to head up and start packing in a few hours, when we have our usual lull. Don't forget we're closing early today.' They always did on full moons so as to ensure that they didn't miss the curfew.

'I won't.'

As Emberlyn had predicted, it didn't take her long to pack everything. Once done, she descended the stairs that led to the rear of the hub.

Ironing a tee, Chrissie looked from Emberlyn to the box she carried. 'Want me to help you haul down the rest?'

'No need; this is it,' Emberlyn told her.

Chrissie frowned. 'Everything you own is in here?'

'Well ... some of it is already at the manor. I moved it there yesterday.'

'Uh, okay. Want help unpacking or anything?'

'Thanks, but I'd rather do it myself. It's a witch thing. We nest.' Glancing at the wall clock, Emberlyn added, 'Okay, time for lunch.'

Overlooking the repositioned Poison Patch later on, Emberlyn had to concede that it looked good. She hadn't expected anything different, considering that Ripper's clan ran a very successful and highly regarded landscaping business.

Doing a U-turn, she swept her gaze over the yard, humming her approval. She hadn't unpacked everything yet. It had seemed best to start with her outdoor bits and bobs, since she would have to secure herself inside the house soon.

The little herb garden was cute and well tended. She'd added her magick into the earth to put her own 'touch' on it. Witch bells now hung from the doorknob. She'd hooked lanterns onto tree branches and hung fairy lights along the picket fence. Wind chimes dangled from the rear porch, and her favorite blanket was draped over the rocking chair there.

Satisfied, she followed full moon precautions – lured the cat into the house, ensured all outdoor trash cans were closed so as not to attract the Rabid, checked the motion sensor lights were on and then headed inside where she locked every window and door. Not that any beasts would bypass the manor's defensive barrier, but she didn't want Lucie getting outside. The damn cat was a daredevil who'd likely provoke a Rabid into chasing her.

The Rabid could spill into the town anytime, but it was more likely to happen on full moons. They became wilder. More aggressive. Were intent on hunting as much prey as they could find. It wasn't about eating for survival, it was about mindless killing.

Secure inside the house, Emberlyn went straight to the kitchen and over to the box she'd propped on the circular table there. She reached into it and pulled out another large box. And another. And another. On and on it went.

Unlike Chrissie, Paisley hadn't been surprised to see Emberlyn leave the hub carrying only one box. Her friend would have guessed that Emberlyn had bespelled it – making it essentially a bottomless carrier that would fit whatever she needed inside and also be light as a feather.

Emberlyn put her touches on the kitchen first. She added plants to the windowsill, placed dishware in cupboards, set her pestle and mortar on the counter, laid out her cookbook and set up her altar complete with a poppet – her little kitchen guardian.

A creak sounded to her right, and she watched as the door that led to the basement slightly edged open.

Her eyes narrowing, Emberlyn said, 'My answer is still no.' With a flick of her fingers, she sent out a magick 'hand' that closed the door.

Once she was done with the kitchen, she moved onto the other rooms on the first floor, laying out cushions, throws, candles, ornaments, incense burners, framed photos and other personal or merely fashionable touches.

The study was where she *really* went to town. It had been her grandmother's consultation room. If any customers came knocking, Millicent had brought them in here and prepared potions or whatever else they'd required – *if* she'd felt like it. Other times, she'd slammed the door in their face.

From here on out, it would be Emberlyn's consultation room.

She propped her cauldron on the altar where Millicent's own had once sat, imagining how it must have felt for her grandmother to remove all traces of herself from the room. Well, not *all* traces – she'd left her journals and book of shadows on the shelves among the ancient texts, grimoires, diaries and spell books that had belonged to past Vautier witches. Collectively, there was a whole lot of expert knowledge to be found in them.'

Hearing a feline chirp, Emberlyn looked to see Lucie slinking into the room. She crouched down and rubbed her thumb over her fingertips a few times as she coaxed the cat to her. As usual, Lucie took her sweet time – like Millicent, she moved at her own pace. After gracefully accepting a few strokes from Emberlyn, Lucie settled on a stool near the hearth and began licking her paw.

Switching her attention back to the task at hand, Emberlyn

spent over an hour in the study doing various things such as adding her own texts to the shelf, preparing the altar, cleaning the sink and fireplace, setting out her apothecary kit and filling the large trunk with empty jars, tarot cards and other such items.

When she was eventually finished and happy with the room's layout, she smiled to herself and walked out. Lucie followed her, sticking closely to her side as Emberlyn went back to unpacking.

It didn't take long to spread the rest of her things around the second floor. She also nosed around the attic, finding it no different than it had been the last time she'd—

A howl filled the air, long and loud.

But not *close* to the manor, thankfully.

Emberlyn looked out of the circular attic window. Through the stained glass, she was able to see that the moon was now full. She looked at Lucie, who sat a few feet away. 'Fingers crossed we don't have company tonight.'

CHAPTER EIGHT

❦

Around him, some of Ripper's clan members shifted right there in the clearing. Their shaggy fur black as night, they mingled in with the shadows, only their red eyes giving away their location. They scattered, weaving around the trees, yapping and howling.

His own muscles quivered with the urge to shift and run. The moon's energy spoke to his soul – an energy that was cold, electric and magnetic. *Too* magnetic for Ripper. Like it was tugging at his skin, threatening to remove it from his bones – an aftereffect of having spent years in a Rabid state.

As a child, he'd only felt compelled to *belong*. Every wolf did. It made their clan-bonds tight. But the period of time he'd spent Rabid had changed that for him.

He didn't properly remember those years – the snippets in his head were like those of a faded dream. The result, though? He didn't yearn to belong. He yearned to be free.

He hadn't told anyone, not even his brother, but at times Ripper had felt 'called' back to Bloodhill. He'd lost four and a half years of his adolescence – that was how it had felt when he'd come out of his Rabid state. At fifteen, he'd had to slot back into a life that had gone on without him and left him behind.

He hadn't known how to be 'normal', hadn't felt normal. He'd had no mental foothold. More, he'd felt like he didn't fit in his own skin.

The call to return to Bloodhill had been *so strong* he'd occasionally considered giving into it. It would have been easier to go back to that wild, primitive state where complex emotions didn't exist. The call felt much dimmer nowadays – the pull of the moon beating it by far.

Crew approached and nudged him, his blue-gray eyes lit with energy. 'You ready?'

Ripper only gave a curt nod.

Kerr wouldn't be running with them tonight. He'd found himself a female companion for the evening; had taunted Ripper with how he could do the same if only he'd let himself go to Black Willow Manor.

So Ripper had socked him in the gut.

He'd always had a certain image of Emberlyn in his head – her reputation preceded her, and rumors were aplenty. But having earlier realized there were things he hadn't known, having spent a little time in her company, he realized she wasn't quite what she seemed.

Still, he couldn't say *what* exactly she seemed; couldn't get a proper read on her. She only revealed the sides she wanted you to see. She didn't appear to mind being either misunderstood or underestimated. It was unusual for an Alpha personality.

She was unusual. And ... and he needed to stop thinking about her. She wasn't for him. Simple.

Peripheral movement snagged his attention. He looked to see

his brother approaching, his expression sober, his eyes dull, his wide shoulders stiff.

'We could be doing something else now, brother,' Logan clipped. 'Could be spending our evening with *our mate*. Instead, we're gonna have to burn off the moon's call by sprinting through the woods on all fluffy fours. That doesn't bother you?'

Ripper inwardly sighed. 'You really want to go over this again? What's the point? You know I won't change my mind.'

Logan's brown eyes flared. 'So you're good with someone else claiming her? Because that'll happen eventually. Right now, CeCe's giving you time to come round to the idea of a triad. She won't wait forever.'

Quite frankly done repeating himself, Ripper felt his jaw harden. 'Logan, I'm not going to "come round". This isn't something I'm ever gonna want.'

Logan stalked closer, his brows snapping together. 'You think *I* really want a triad? You think I want to share the woman I love with anyone? The truth is no, I don't. But I'll do whatever it takes to make sure I don't lose her. *You* won't, though, will you? Which shows you don't love CeCe anywhere near as much as I do.'

'You're probably right. But where's the sense in you being pissed at me? I'm not the one refusing to give you what you want because, as you've just admitted, what you want isn't even a triad – it's just for her to be yours.'

Crew leaned closer, scratching at his dark stubble. 'You might want to keep your voices down,' he began quietly, 'because she's just stepped out of the trees with her friends. *And* she's spotted you both.'

Ripper didn't let his gaze track her down, but his brother couldn't help but look.

Pain glinting in his eyes, Logan shoved a hand through his dirty blond hair. 'She's all I ever wanted, Rip. Sucks that she can't say the same about *only* me.' He stalked off, stripping as he went.

For Logan, it likely felt more 'unfair' because he'd wanted CeCe first. They'd grown close in the aftermath of the battle caused by Rosemary, which had resulted in the death of CeCe's parents as well. She'd been there for Logan while Ripper was Rabid, and she'd been one of the few people who hadn't treated Ripper differently when he came back. Who hadn't watched him, wary of what those years spent in Bloodhill might have done to him.

He'd grown to care about her, drawn by her confidence, her daring, her determination and her fierceness. But lately, he'd come to see the flip side of those qualities. Her belief in herself wouldn't let her consider that things wouldn't go her way. Her sense of daring made her push buttons she shouldn't push. Her obstinance meant she refused to back down. And her fierceness caused her to pursue her triad goal without fear.

Watching his brother dart into the woods in his wolf form, Ripper sensed CeCe sidling up to him.

'Is he okay?' she asked, her voice soft.

Ripper met her powder-blue gaze. 'You should ask him.'

Her pretty face fell at his hard tone. 'Don't give me the cold shoulder, Rip – I can't stand it.'

'I'm not being cold, I'm just not interested in talking more about all this. If you really care that he's hurting, if you really want to be with him, put him out of his misery.'

'But to do that would make *you* miserable.' She anxiously skimmed a hand over her brown curls. 'I don't want to come between you and Logan.'

She was already coming between them. She could have just accepted Ripper's initial refusal and dropped the whole thing. By dragging it out, she was not only keeping Logan's hopes alive, she was also ramping up his anger – an emotion he was directing at Ripper rather than her.

'I don't want to lose your friendship, Rip.'

'Then respect my choice and drop this triad bullshit.'

The corners of her eyes tightened. 'It isn't bullshit, it's a solution.'

'For you, yeah. Not for me. Not even for Logan – he'd go along with it to have you, but he'd never really be happy. The mating would eventually fall apart.'

She notched up her chin. 'I don't believe that, or I'd never have suggested it.'

'You *should* believe it because it's a fact. And even if you were right, it wouldn't make any difference – I'd still say no to a triad.'

She sighed. 'Look, I know you're possessive of me and you feel it would be hard to share me—'

'It isn't about possessiveness. I'm just not interested in what you're proposing.'

Her brows drew together. 'What do you have against triads?'

'Nothing at all. I just don't want to be in one. Either give a relationship with Logan a shot, or let's all go back to the way things were.'

She studied him carefully. 'Do you regret that night the three of us spent together?'

'Yeah, I do.'

She flinched. 'Ouch.'

He hadn't admitted it to hurt her; he'd done it in the hope that she'd finally get the message. 'Make a choice, CeCe – either take Logan for a mate, or we both go back to being simply friends with you. There's no other option on the table.' Ripper walked off before she could say more.

Keeping pace with him, Crew said, 'She's a good person. She is. She just never does well with being denied what she wants.'

Ripper rolled his shoulders. 'She needs to learn to deal with it, *fast*, because I'm not changing my mind.' Once he felt far enough away from her, he stripped and gave himself over to the shift – felt his bones reshape, his skin stretch, his jaw elongate, his claws slice out, his fur sprout, his vision change. It was over in milliseconds, and then he was on all fours.

Crew at his side, he ran.

Stood on the private dock of his lake house the following day, Ripper heard the rumbling of an engine. Tracking the sound, he saw a familiar truck approach and felt his mouth tighten. He'd expected a visit from Carver at some point. He'd thought the Alpha would turn up at one of the clan-run businesses, though, not boldly come to his home as if they were anything more than mere acquaintances.

Ripper had never liked the guy. Carver was all ease and charm and friendliness, but beneath it all he was a fucking snake. A person who did what it took to get his way. He'd push, nag, lie, conceal, steamroll, exaggerate his strength and skills – whatever.

It made him a good salesman at his car dealership. But it didn't make him a decent Alpha.

Carver didn't have a tight control over his clan. Worse, he didn't care. For him, it appeared to be a point of pride that his wolves were the 'bad boys' of the town.

No one else actually considered them 'bad boys', though. That was only Carver's assessment. In reality, they were just reckless and immature.

Reluctantly turning away from the view of the lake, Ripper stalked along the dock, the boards creaking beneath his boots. He weaved his way through the tall trees that framed his house, arriving at the small parking area just as Carver pulled up.

He wasn't alone.

His two sons had come along – one was riding shotgun, the other was in the middle of the rear passenger row. Both watched Ripper carefully. Neither would meet his gaze for more than a few seconds at a time, though.

Sunglasses concealing his eyes, Carver hopped out of his truck. 'I'll be two minutes,' he told them. He flashed Ripper a charismatic grin that pulled at his wiry beard – like his thick mussed hair, it was brown with little streaks of gray. 'I was hoping you'd be home.'

Ripper didn't greet him. He just folded his arms and waited.

Carver strutted toward him. Literally strutted. Like he could take on the world. Which he could not.

Thickset with a bloated stomach that spoke of his fondness for beer, he was a few inches shorter than Ripper and carried a lot less muscle. If a fight ever broke out between them, Carver would be overpowered by Ripper fairly quickly.

'I meant to come see you yesterday.' Carver removed his sunglasses and slipped them into the breast pocket of his flannel shirt. His amiable smile lit his deep-brown eyes, but there was also a glimmer of uncertainty there. 'I know you hate chitchat and dancing around shit, so I'll get straight down to it. You know why I'm here.'

Ripper inclined his head. 'It's an easy guess.'

'Reena was so sure the land would end up in her possession.'

'Yeah, I got that.'

Carver scratched at his sideburns. 'It never occurred to me that she'd be wrong. It's only right that a person's children inherit their belongings. Both Dez and Gill were clear to me that the land would be free to build on; that it would be sold to their High Priestess. A contract was drawn up. Money changed hands. Blueprints were—'

'Save your speech. I've told Reena, and now I'll tell you: I'm not giving up the land. It's mine,' Ripper firmly stated, no 'give' in his tone. 'It'll stay mine.'

Carver's lips flattened. 'You *have* land. You don't need more.'

'Same goes for you and Reena. But neither of you would give it up in my position.' They were both hypocrites.

'Maybe, but that don't matter much when it's not really yours to keep. I wasn't gonna say anything, but . . .' Trailing off, Carver hooked his thumbs through the waist loops of his jeans, but there was too much tension in his frame for the move to seem casual. 'Look, I'm gonna give you a friendly heads-up – there's a good chance you won't get to keep the land.'

'Is that right?'

'I heard all about Millicent's will, and I agree with Dez. The whole thing is weird as hell. She left a *person* to you, for shit's sake. He thinks that Millicent's sanity was suffering at the end. Makes sense to me. Her family didn't notice because they didn't have enough contact with her. But yeah, Millicent clearly didn't have all her faculties.'

Ripper's scalp prickled. 'That's the angle the coven's gonna go with, is it? Millicent wasn't in her right mind and so the conditions of the will should be overruled?' He ground his teeth, figuring he should have seen this coming.

'They're not wrong.'

'What they are is *pissed*. They'll try anything to have that will scrapped. And you're only supporting their argument because it suits you.'

Carver's brow creased. 'You're honestly telling me that the will didn't seem at all strange to you?'

'It was drawn up by Millicent Vautier. *Of course* it wasn't conventional. Nothing the woman did ever was. That doesn't mean her sanity wasn't intact. I bought potions regularly from her. She was *all* there, sharp as a tack right until the end.'

'Someone "sharp as a tack" doesn't think they can bequeath people in a will,' Carver countered.

'She was hinting at me claiming Emberlyn as an ally. Which I have. You'll have already heard about that.'

'And you think it's smart to be allied with the devil's witch? That's what the coven call her, you know. They've told me all kinds of stories.'

'Yeah, they do that. Turns out they extract important details first. I learned that for myself on hearing her and Reena talk yesterday.'

Movement in the corner of Ripper's eye plucked at his attention. He tracked it to see Crew casually striding toward them. He'd no doubt heard that Carver and his sons were on their way here so had come to ensure that Ripper had backup should he need it.

Carver gave the newcomer a quick chin tip before turning back to Ripper. 'After what happened with Rosemary, I wouldn't have thought you'd want to closely associate with a witch. Your parents would be alive if it weren't for Rosemary, and you wouldn't have spent years of your life Rabid.'

The reminder of what had occurred all those years ago made Ripper's jaw harden. 'None of which had anything to do with Emberlyn. Go home, Carver. I already made it clear that I won't be relinquishing ownership of the land. Continuing the conversation is pointless.'

Frustration rippled across Carver's face. 'I need to go ahead with this project, Ripper. I'll give you a percentage of the profits.'

'I don't want a percentage. I don't want anything except for you to let this go.' Ripper raised a palm when the wolf would have objected. 'You don't come here again, and you stay away from Emberlyn Vautier. We clear?'

Carver's mouth tightened. 'You made a mistake throwing your

lot in with her. She might say she's an ally, but she'll screw you over. She's a goddamn psycho.'

'All the more reason for you to leave her alone, wouldn't you say?'

'I'm telling you, she's not right in the head, and neither was her grandmother. Her family will prove Millicent wasn't sound of mind when she wrote that will. They'll get the conditions overturned, and you'll lose the land anyway. You might as well just give it up now so plans can go ahead as they should.'

'You're not listening to me. I don't like it when people don't listen to me.' Dropping his hands back to his sides, Ripper stepped right into his personal space. 'And I *really* don't like hearing you call someone under my protection "not right in the head".'

Carver's eyelids fluttered, his Adam's apple bobbing. 'I'm only telling you what I was told.'

'I don't need to hear anymore. All I need is for you to get into your truck and get the fuck away from here.'

His nostrils flaring, Carver flushed. 'Dammit, Ripper, things don't need to be this way.' But he tromped over to his vehicle and jumped inside. Moments later, he was speeding off.

'Did I hear right?' asked Crew. 'Millicent's family's planning to claim that she wasn't sound of mind and so her will should be declared invalid?'

'Yeah, you heard right.' Ripper sighed. 'Their little plot might even work. The conditions of the will don't exactly speak of someone whose thought processes were normal. But that *was* normal for Millicent. Still, it doesn't mean their lawyer won't manage to have it overturned.'

'The coven's lawyers are good, but so is Millicent's. He'll probably handle it.'

Ripper grunted in agreement. 'I'd hoped that they'd all back off once they realized that neither me nor Emberlyn were going to give in. Like I pointed out to Reena, she doesn't *need* the manor or the land. She just wants it.'

'Maybe Reena isn't behind this. Maybe it's Gill or Dez or both.'

'That's what I'm thinking. The way they speak about Emberlyn ... I used to think it was because they disapproved of the types of magick she dabbled in. But you know what I hear in their voices each time they talk to and of her? Resentment.'

'You think they're jealous that their niece is more powerful, or that Millicent raised her but not them?'

'Could be both, but I'm mostly leaning toward the first. It never occurred to them that the manor would end up in her hands, because Millicent told them she didn't want Emberlyn to inherit anything. They weren't prepared for this scenario, and they're scrambling to come up with a way to get the house from her.' He paused. 'I need to warn Emberlyn what they're planning. I don't want her blindsided by it.'

'I just saw her parking outside the Danvers' place.'

The Danvers, a mated couple from their clan, lived here in Ashwood. 'She was probably dropping off laundry.' She regularly did that for clients.

'She would be gone by the time you drove over there, but you could call their house now and ask to speak with her. She might not have left yet.'

'Only one way to find out.'

CHAPTER NINE

❧

'Thanks, Emberlyn, we really appreciate this.'

Folding the now empty laundry bag, Emberlyn smiled at Mrs Danvers. 'It's not a problem.'

Both the female werewolf and her mate were in their eighties, and the sweet couple didn't venture out much. Emberlyn regularly picked up and dropped off their laundry for them – a free service for customers past a certain age.

'Maybe not in your opinion,' said the she-wolf, 'but not a lot of businesses round here do home deliveries or pick-ups. They're not interested in making things easier for their customers, so don't think we don't appreciate that you do.'

'Well, it's always nice to be appreciated, so thank you.'

'Emberlyn?' Mr Danvers called out, his telephone receiver in hand. 'Our Alpha needs to speak to you. He was wondering if you could either wait here for him, meet him somewhere or drive to his home. He says it's important.'

Emberlyn blinked. Mostly at the option of her heading to

Ripper's house. She wouldn't have thought he'd extend such an offer, alliance or not.

'He said you'll want to hear this,' Mr Danvers added.

Hmm, her curiosity was officially peaked. 'I'll be passing the lake on my way out of Ashwood, so tell him I'll stop at his place.' She wouldn't say it aloud, but she wanted a little peek at it.

Minutes later, Emberlyn was driving down a narrow road approaching a large two-story house that had a mountain-modern feel. It was moody. Rustic. Earthy.

Both levels featured reflective floor-to-ceiling windows that allowed for a panoramic view of the lake. A sheltered seating area had been added to the flat roof as well as to the side of the house, where there was also a firepit.

Best of all, it overlooked a rocky shoreline, lush forest and the crystal clear-as-glass lake. Yellowy-orange beams of light from the gradually setting sun glittered off the water. A family of ducks floated along the surface. Geese could often be seen further along the shoreline's grass slope, but Emberlyn couldn't spot any here.

Ripper and Crew waited not far from the Alpha's truck, their eyes on her vehicle.

She parked her car, her gaze locking with Ripper's and . . . fuck her hormones. Fuck them sideways and longways and frontways. Because it absolutely was not fair that they insisted on melting at the sight of him. Didn't they have some pride? Didn't they have any wish to form some immunity to him?

As she slid out of the car, the warm air whispered over her, fresh and scented by flowers, water and dewy grass. It was quiet here, the only sounds the lapping of water, the distant calls of birds and the *shush* of greenery rustling with the gentle breeze.

She returned her attention to the two men opposite her and walked toward them.

Still and watchful, Ripper fixed his gaze on her with the

unshifting precision of a dangerous predator on the hunt. It was hard not to squirm under that kind of intense scrutiny.

'Nice place,' she told him. 'Great view.'

Ripper let out a grunt of what might have been thanks.

'Crew,' she greeted politely.

He grinned. 'Hey, Emberlyn. I was just heading out. I'll see you guys later.' He jogged into the forested area at the rear of the house, quickly disappearing from view.

She looked back at Ripper . . . to find his gaze skating down her beige cotton crop top, hint of belly, matching pants and strappy sandals.

At the growing need simmering in his eyes, her sexual bells started to ring-a-ding-ding-dong. More, her magick rose up, ever-attracted to his energy. She ruthlessly shoved it back down. But it wasn't quite as easy to get her hormones in line.

His eyes zipped back up, darkening as they stared right into hers, his unblinking gaze so damn *penetrating*. It wasn't only heat in his gaze. There was conflict. Like her, he was wrestling with this thing between them.

Good luck, dude.

She wasn't doing too well with it. His presence tugged at her. Like a magnet. The sexual pull was electrically charged. She was coming to the unfortunate conclusion that this chemistry wasn't going anywhere.

She cleared her throat. 'So, what's this super-important thing I need to hear?'

'Something you're not going to like,' he warned.

Just then, a droplet of water landed on her shoulder. She held up her palm, catching another droplet. It was starting to rain. Awesome.

He sighed at the sky. 'Let's go inside.' With that, he began prowling toward the house.

She blinked, stunned. Werewolves didn't easily let you into their home. You wanted to talk? They'd have a porch for that, or even a separate meeting house. 'Inside?'

He shot her a look over his shoulder. 'I want coffee. Need to go to the kitchen for that.'

Both confused and surprised at his gruff invitation, she nonetheless followed him up the narrow path. Werewolves operated differently. Their social language wasn't what you would always expect. To let you into their home was an indication that they were at ease with you and willing to allow a certain level of familiarity.

If they touched you of their own accord, it meant they felt unthreatened by you. If they sniffed you, they were 'logging' your scent into their inner database, enabling them to find you should they need to – which indicated a pinch of protectiveness.

Werewolves tended to attach, though there were different levels of attachment. If they fed you, it meant they felt protective and wanted to take care of you, which could be perfectly platonic. But . . . if they left their scent on you using the glands on their palms, it was an indication of possession – especially if they scent-marked your hair, neck or no-no places.

Any face nibbling or cheek rubbing were demonstrations of affection. If they touched your belly in front of others, it was a huge *back off* signal. As were bite marks, though the bites were never deep enough to break the skin.

Aside from their single and very businesslike handshake, Ripper hadn't ever touched her. So Emberlyn wouldn't have thought he'd feel at ease enough around her to be like, 'Hey, come on in.' He could have asked that she wait on his sheltered porch while he made coffee. Instead, here they both were walking into his house.

She glanced around. *Nice.* It was open, light and airy with exposed wooden beams and a lodge-like vibe.

She didn't dawdle; she stayed close behind Ripper as he walked further into the house. The color palette of warm beige, eggshell-white and taupe continued throughout, linking the rooms and adding to the open feel of the place.

Finally, they arrived at a sleek kitchen-stroke-dining room that provided plenty of seating. It was all dark woods and light-gray stone. Very masculine and contemporary.

'Coffee?' he offered as he pressed buttons on a machine.

Through his thin tee, Emberlyn could see the strong muscles in his back flexing and rippling. *Damn.* 'No, thanks.' She leaned back against the kitchen island, a little jealous of that machine right now – she couldn't help wanting those fingers to push *her* buttons. 'I'm more of a tea drinker.'

He let out a grunt.

'Yes, talking is hard.'

Pausing, he shot her a narrow-eyed look over his shoulder.

She gifted him a bright smile. 'So, you gonna tell me what inspired you to invite me here?'

Turning back to the machine, he set a cup beneath the dispenser. 'I had a visit from Carver. I got the impression he hasn't approached you.' There was a question there.

'He hasn't yet, no,' she confirmed.

'And he won't if he has any sense – I ordered him to stay away from you just now. He came to pressure me to relinquish the land to Reena.' As the coffee machine began whirring, Ripper turned to fully face her. 'He also informed me that your family is declaring that Millicent wasn't of sound mind when she wrote the will and so the conditions shouldn't be followed.'

Emberlyn felt her mouth tighten. 'Ah.' What little mother-fuckers they were.

Cupping the rim of the counter behind him, Ripper leaned back against it. 'I don't know if Reena is part of this. She could have decided to back off – either because she's letting it go or because she's fine with letting your family take all the risks. On the other hand, she could be running things from behind the scenes.'

Emberlyn ran her tongue along the inside of her lower lip. 'What does Carver intend to do?'

'There's nothing he physically can do. He supports your family's theory, but only because it suits him.'

'I should have considered they might go down this route, especially when they were hardly going to personally push you to cooperate – they can hide behind a lawyer.' Emberlyn was disappointed with herself for not expecting it.

The laws at Chilgrave were different. There were no trials, no juries, no judges. Members of the council supervised meetings where matters could be discussed while lawyers were present to guide the conversation and ensure that their clients' rights were protected.

'I regularly went to Millicent for potions,' said Ripper. 'Her mental state wasn't deteriorating.'

'No, it wasn't. But I'd struggle to prove that she was *ever* sane.' Emberlyn idly fingered the rose quartz pendant on her necklace. 'Still, I don't think them contesting the will could amount to anything. You have a rightful claim to the land regardless – it belonged to Lupin originally, and you're his descendant. I might not have been Millicent's daughter, but the manor *chose* me. It had the option of selecting either Gill or Dez. It didn't.'

'And if you're wrong? If they manage to get the conditions of the will overturned?'

'It won't change that the manor chose me. If Reena wants it, she'll have to take it from me by force – I won't give it up willingly.'

Ripper's gaze sharpened on hers. '*Could* she take it from you?'

Not a chance. 'What do you think?'

He stared at her for long moments, studious and pensive. 'I think I was wrong.'

'About what?'

'Wrong to believe that the majority of the coven is so against you because you operate outside their magickal rules and were mentored by Millicent. It's not so much that, is it? It's that you're a power. None are a real match for you, and they know it.'

True, but they were very good at making it sound as if Emberlyn had 'cheated'. She lifted a brow. 'Haven't you heard? I'm only so powerful because I made pacts with various evil deities.'

'If that were true, you would have caused death and destruction over the years. You've defended and avenged yourself, but you've never killed anyone. The coven villainizes you to justify their behavior. They'll believe whatever they need to believe to make that bullshit narrative fit.'

'So you're not all brawn,' she mused. 'Interesting.'

He responded to that with a droll look and then nabbed his cup, hard muscle bunching beneath the smooth tanned flesh of his arm. Would he notice if she took a quick bite? Probably. So sad.

'Ironic that they claim to abhor *you*, yet they'd defend someone like Rosemary,' he said. 'She should have been executed.'

'I have to agree.' The woman had used chaos magick to stir two Alpha males into fighting – and she'd done it on a full moon, knowing that a bloodbath could occur. And it had. The Alphas had morphed into their In-between forms and butchered one another. Their heartbroken mates had then taken their killing-rage out on each other.

And eleven-year-old Ripper, the son of one Alpha pair, had witnessed it all.

An experience that had overwhelmed him with so much dark emotion that he'd turned Rabid.

In his absence, his clan had demanded that Reena hand over Rosemary to be punished, but the High Priestess had insisted on dealing with the matter herself.

'Having your magick bound wouldn't be an easy ride – in fact, it'd be *torture* for a witch,' said Emberlyn. 'I suspect it's why Rosemary died. Some witches have withered away after being disconnected from their magick. But her actions called for a much worse punishment. She shouldn't have had the luxury of dying peacefully in her sleep.' She paused at the weird look on his face. 'What?'

Ripper sipped from his cup. 'Not evil, ruthless,' he said more to himself than to her.

'Hmm?'

'Millicent once told me that you weren't evil, just ruthless.' He tilted his head. 'Yesterday, you spoke to Reena of a time when her niece tried punching her way into your mind. I never heard about it.'

'There's a lot that isn't talked about.'

'What happened exactly?'

'Sera turned up at my apartment one day, wanting to apologize for the part she – along with Tyra, Ames and their friends – had played in trying to make me miserable when I was a kid. But it wasn't hard to sense that she wanted something from me. I eventually cut off her fake apology and told her to be upfront with me about why she was really there or to leave. She admitted that she wanted me to teach her a certain type of magick. I said no.'

'What kind of magick?'

'The kind that would enable her to invoke dark beings from other realms.' Even those within the coven who sneered at

Emberlyn still sought her out, looking for the kind of aid or advice that Reena would never grant.

He blinked. 'You could do that?'

'It's not as fun as it sounds.'

His brow knitted. 'It doesn't actually sound fun at all.'

To each their own. 'Millicent made it so. It was her way of teaching. She made everything seem light and adventurous. Like we were walking around a zoo while I learned about animals. She was a good mentor. And one thing she taught me was that only a witch who was very grounded should be given ... darker lessons, shall we say? Sera isn't grounded. And, unhappy that I wouldn't oblige her, she tried taking the knowledge from my mind.'

'Did Reena punish her for what she did to you?'

'No. I did that. I turned Sera's braid into a snake.' The memory plucked at one corner of Emberlyn's lips. 'It didn't last longer than an hour, but it scared the piss out of her.'

A glint of what she could have *sworn* was humor briefly appeared in his eyes.

'I'll bet,' he muttered, before taking another sip of his coffee.

'Have you mentioned the curse jar to Reena yet?'

'No. I'm keeping the knowledge of it in my back pocket for now. I want to see if I can catch someone in the act of planting another. They won't dare if they're aware that I know about the jar you dug up.'

'I haven't mentioned it to anyone, and I won't.'

'I know,' he said with total certainty.

He *should* be sure, but his certainty surprised her. 'Do you?'

'Call it a gut feeling. Not saying I trust you. Don't know you well enough for that. But my instincts tell me I can trust your word on this.'

'What else do they tell you?'

'That you're even more powerful than the coven thinks you are.'

Definitely not all brawn. Emberlyn only said, 'Hmm.' She pushed away from the island. 'I'd better head home. I appreciate you giving me a heads-up about what my delightful family is up to now.' He'd made a point of ensuring that she couldn't be taken off-guard with it, which he hadn't *had* to do. 'You know, Ripper . . . you're okay. For a werewolf.'

His mouth twitched. 'You're okay. For a witch.'

Her insides squeezed as he absently edged forward, again sipping from his cup. He stood a little too close, smelled a little too good, and she felt unbearably conscious of him. Of where he stood, how he held himself, the look in his eyes, the muscles in his body, the . . . gah, this needed to stop. Because while she was tempted to make a move, try her luck, it didn't seem wise.

If he wasn't on board, things might then be awkward between them. Just because they were now allies and slowly becoming comfortable with each other didn't automatically mean that he'd be receptive to any advances she made, did it? He was evidently still wary of her to some degree.

If he made his own advances, well, she couldn't say she'd rebuff them. But – and call her a coward, she didn't care – she wasn't going to try to instigate anything. It was *Ripper's* issues in the way, not hers. At the very least, he needed to be given time to power past them . . . if he could or even cared to.

'Later,' Emberlyn said stiffly, her smile a little too wide. She saw herself out and, without allowing herself to peek in the rear-view mirror to see if he'd followed her to the door, she drove off. During the journey home, she gave her lady bits a huge lecture on how they needed to pull their shit together.

By the time she'd parked outside the manor, dusk had officially fallen. Orange, purple and pink smudged the darkening sky. Silhouettes of the house and trees stretched out like fingers.

Emberlyn slid out of the car, purse and laundry bag in hand. Her evening plans were simple and basically involved tea, food, a book and *maybe* also a bath. Possibly also some clit-love during that bath. It might be the only way to make her hormones calm down.

She closed the car door, locked it with the fob—

A long, drawn-out growl grated the air. It was low. Rumbly. Spine-chilling.

And it had come from somewhere on her left.

Her pulse jumping, she froze. But only for a moment. Ever so slowly, she turned toward the sound.

A figure lumbered out from behind the willow tree. A figure that was overly tall, broad, long-limbed – and covered in fur. Not quite man, not quite animal. Its yellow eyes were pinned on her, glowing with malicious intent. It snarled, baring long canines.

A *Rabid*.

Her heart went ahead and skipped a beat.

It wasn't the first time she'd found herself up close and personal with a Rabid, and it likely wouldn't be the last. Her options were always the same – capture it or scare it off, because she wasn't going to kill it.

The Rabid roared in challenge, flexing its thick claw-tipped fingers. Then it rushed her.

Dropping her purse and laundry bag, she lifted her hands and blasted out a force of glittering, electrically charged magick. The Rabid flew backwards, crashing into the tree, causing the branches to shudder and creak.

Emberlyn began chanting beneath her breath, intending to put the creature to sleep, but it recovered fast and came at her again.

Pausing the spell, she hit it with another blow of magick – or *tried* to. It lurched to the side, dodging the glittering ribbons, and then lunged at her.

Emberlyn backpedaled fast but didn't manage to avoid the arm that reached for her. Hissing as its claws sliced into her shoulder like hot knives, she blasted it with magick again, sending it to its knees with a howl of pain. It reached for her once more, clawing her calf—

'The fuck?' a male voice exclaimed behind her as footsteps thundered her way. She recognized the voice instantly – *Logan*.

The Rabid jumped to its feet and quickly but awkwardly scurried away, disappearing into the shadows.

Its retreat wasn't a surprise. On a full moon, it wouldn't care about being outnumbered; would stay and fight. But on a normal day – injured and operating on animal logic – it wouldn't hang around and risk being taken down.

Reaching her, Logan grimaced at her shoulder wound. 'You all right?'

No, her injuries were burning like the fires of hell. 'Fine and dandy.'

He blew out a breath. 'Come on, let's get you inside.'

CHAPTER TEN

❧

Placing his washed cup on the drainer, Ripper gazed out of his kitchen window. He needed to get out of the room. Emberlyn's scent lingered, faint now but still a tease to his senses.

Vanilla. Pink pepper. Power. Warmth. Life. Danger. It was all those things wrapped into one.

It had been clear that he had taken her by surprise when he'd invited her inside. Honestly, Ripper had surprised himself. He hadn't realized until that moment how much of his leeriness of her had drained away.

There were times when he wondered if she'd put some kind of spell on him. He had good reason for preferring not to get entangled with a witch. It should have been enough to override her draw, but it wasn't. Never had been. And since the moment he'd watched her laugh at Reena for thinking to challenge her, Emberlyn's draw had sunk its claws in him deeper.

More and more he found himself staring at her mouth. More and more he had to clench his fists against the urge to reach out and touch her. And the slightest fucking thing – her smile, her laugh, her scent, her walk – could make his cock stir in his jeans.

At this point, he'd stopped merely *imagining* when it came to her. And that was bad. Fantasies could stay stuck in a mental draw. But now he constantly *wondered*.

Wondered how she tasted, how soft her skin was, how her hair would feel in his hands, how her eyes would look when she came apart around him. And all this obsessive wondering made him feel that he was coming a little too close to *doing*.

He couldn't pinpoint what it was about her that had gripped him so tightly. No other woman had snared his attention this way. She was some kind of living, breathing lure to him. A temptation he didn't know if he could fully resist.

What pulsed between them was tireless. Persistent. Stubborn. And a little addictive in its potency; in the way it made endorphins and feel-good chemicals flood his body.

He could do as Kerr often urged and give into it. But … Ripper still wasn't entirely sure of her. He also didn't know if she was still hung up on Michael to any degree. It would be natural enough, but he didn't want to share a bed with someone who also harbored feelings for someone else. He'd had enough of that with CeCe.

The wall-mounted phone rang, splintering his thoughts.

He crossed to it and picked up the receiver. 'Yeah?'

'Rip, it's Logan,' said his brother, a hint of urgency in his voice. 'I'm at Black Willow Manor. I was on patrol; heard roaring and howling and came right over. The witch who lives here just got attacked outside by a Rabid.'

Emotions surged through Ripper – shock, anger, concern, protectiveness – and every muscle in his body locked in position. 'She all right?' The words came out through gritted teeth.

'She's fine, just a little banged up.'

'You didn't need to call him,' he heard Emberlyn say in the background. 'I'm good. There's nothing anyone can do that I'm not already doing.'

The hint of pain lacing her words sliced at Ripper. 'I'll be right there,' he told his brother. 'Stay with her.' He hung up, darted out of the house and jumped into his truck.

He took a shortcut through his territory, arriving at the manor in record time. He quickly stalked up the path, vaulted up the steps and knocked on the door.

Logan answered, tipping his chin. 'Hey.' He opened the door wide. 'She's in the kitchen.'

Agitation in every step, Ripper prowled past him, tracking the sounds coming from what could only be the kitchen. 'Did you capture the Rabid?'

'No,' replied Logan, trailing behind him. 'I would have tracked it, but it had clawed the witch good so I figured it was more important to get her inside. Then you asked me to stay with her.'

Ripper clenched his jaw, annoyed that the Rabid had gotten away even as he conceded that his brother had made the best choice.

As Ripper entered the kitchen, the pleasant scents of herbs, flowers and chamomile wafted over him . . . but they did nothing to hide the smells of pain and blood. The latter two dragged his instincts to protect and shield straight to the surface.

They also made his blood boil.

Protectiveness was hardwired into his nature, amplified by his Alpha status. It chafed everything in him that someone he'd sworn to safeguard had been harmed; grated on his very being, until his skin felt rubbed raw. Emberlyn wasn't one of his wolves, but she was his to keep safe.

Even Millicent's will said so. Sort of.

Emberlyn stood at the cluttered table, her wrist rolling as she ground herbs into a mortar with a pestle. She'd changed into a racerback top and shorts, probably because her clothes were torn. She'd also styled her hair into a side braid that dangled over her shoulder.

Ripper stalked over to her, briefly eyeing the growling black cat who was angrily prowling up and down on the countertop. 'You all right?' The fury-edged words came out curt and gruff.

Emberlyn slid him a quick look, cool and composed. 'Mostly.' She sighed at the pacing feline. 'Lucie, calm down.'

He felt his face harden as he saw the four rake marks creeping over Emberlyn's shoulder. *Motherfucker.* He shifted behind her to properly examine them. They were long and deep, though not so deep they'd require stitches. 'You hurt anywhere else?'

'Only my lower leg. Got clawed there, too. It could have been worse,' she added with a loose shrug.

If it bothered her to have a pissed-off Alpha werewolf at her back, she didn't show it. Didn't tense. Didn't peer at him uneasily.

'You got antivenom?' All non-werewolves were advised to store it.

'I already jabbed myself with some. It was the first thing I did when I got inside. Well, *after* I used magick to make my blood clot.' She calmly sipped from a steaming cup of what appeared to be chamomile tea.

How she could be calm, he didn't know. But he was starting to learn that Emberlyn Vautier only overly reacted to things if she *wanted* to. Her vengeful acts and power displays weren't about a loss of control; they were generally about sending a message.

A chill swept through the room as a cupboard door flapped open and the mugs inside it began tremoring.

His skin prickling in unease, he glanced at Emberlyn. 'Are you doing that?'

She spared the ajar door a quick, disinterested glance. 'Nope. Don't worry, they won't hurt you.'

'They?' he echoed, but she didn't elaborate. He looked at his brother, who puffed out an unnerved breath.

'You really didn't need to come, Ripper,' she said, setting her cup down on the table. A whole array of things were spread across the surface, including a knife, roller, cutting board, mortar and pestle. She also had stoppered jars of various substances, including herbs, salt, leaves, flower petals and what looked to be ... charcoal?

'I *wanted* to.' Ripper rolled his shoulders, trying to rid himself of some of the tension there. He moved so that his front was mere inches from her side. 'What are you making?'

'A healing poultice.' She crushed a leaf between her fingertips. 'It'll disinfect the wounds, ease the pain and speed up the healing process.'

Logan approached. 'Anything we can do to help?'

'Nah, but thanks,' she replied.

Ripper pinned his brother in place with a glare, not wanting him any closer to her while she was injured.

Logan pursed his lips and raised his hands in a placatory gesture.

Still antsy, Ripper edged closer to her and breathed her in. The smell of blood wasn't unpleasant to werewolves. And hers? It was spiced with magick, giving it a real *kick*.

She eyed him, one brow hiking up. 'Getting bold, aren't we?'

Okay, yeah, it *was* pretty audacious to invade her personal space and sniff her that way. But ask him if he gave a fuck.

Logan snickered. 'He's an Alpha. "Bold" comes with the package.'

Emberlyn made a *humph* sound and turned back to the table.

'What exactly happened out there?' Ripper asked her.

She crushed dried herbs in her palm and sprinkled the bits into the mortar. 'I came straight home after leaving your place.'

Ripper sensed more than saw Logan lift his brows.

'I heard growling when I got out of my car. The Rabid came out from behind the willow tree. It attacked. Retaliating sucked – it was a person at one time. I mostly tried to just put it to sleep, but it was a tough son of a bitch, not to mention fast. I only managed to daze it.' She briskly wiped her hands on a cloth. 'Logan yelled as he approached, and the Rabid heard him and fled.'

They didn't often flee, so ... 'You must have hurt it bad enough that it felt too vulnerable to stick around.'

'You don't look at all spooked,' Logan noted. 'I mean, most people are after an encounter with the Rabid.'

She shrugged but then winced as the move pulled at her shoulder wound. 'When I was a kid, I went through a stage of having recurring nightmares. It started after my mom died. Millicent took me down to the basement and summoned the devil.'

'What?' The word burst out of Ripper.

'She thought that if I knew what it was to look into the face of pure evil, nothing would ever scare me again.' Emberlyn added some chamomile tea to her mixture. 'The nightmares did stop, and it is exceedingly difficult to spook me.'

Logan blinked. 'You ... you met the devil?'

'He was pretty low key compared to the deities she regularly chatted to.' Emberlyn's spoon scraped the mortar as she stirred the contents fast, blending it all together.

Ripper exchanged a look with his brother. 'Low key. Right.' The more he heard about her upbringing, the more positive he felt that Millicent should not have been permitted to raise her. Gill and Dez *knew* what their mother was like, but they hadn't offered their niece a home after their sister died. The assholes had left her with Millicent, not caring what it would mean for her.

'Almost finished,' said Emberlyn, tossing some glittering magick dust into her mortar. She gave the paste one last stir and then set down the pestle. 'There. Done.'

Ripper lifted a small wooden spatula from the table. 'I'll put it on for you.'

Her brow pinched. 'No need, I can do it.'

'So can I.' And he wanted to do it. 'Let me.'

'That wasn't even really a request,' she noted, her eyes narrowing. 'It was an order. I don't respond to those, in case you haven't noticed.'

He cocked his head. 'You know, people usually don't argue with me.'

'Yes, I'm sure they mostly roll over, show you their bellies, and give you your way. I'll bet there's even boob-jiggling when it comes to the ladies.'

Logan snorted.

'But I'm no one's idea of a people pleaser,' she added.

'Your shoulder has been clawed at an angle which is going to make it tricky for you to apply the poultice,' Ripper pointed out. 'Let me do that, and you can smear it on your leg wound. All right?'

She rolled her eyes. 'Fucking Alpha werewolves,' she muttered to herself, placing her hands on the surface of the table. 'Always up in someone's business.'

'We're helpful that way.' He planted one hand on her upper back, hooking three fingers around the crook of her neck while resting his thumb and forefinger on her nape. Her skin was warm and soft and it pebbled at his touch. Her reaction made his gut clench.

It seemed only fair that they were both slaves to this damn chemistry that wouldn't shift.

He scooped up some paste with the spatula and sniffed it. 'I half-expected it to smell like feet or something. It smells like old books.'

'I find the scent comforting, so I added it to the paste.'

He carefully applied it to one slice. 'Did you notice any distinguishing marks on the Rabid?' Old scars would show up as white slashes in the fur. It helped identify any Rabid.

'It was missing a finger.'

Ripper blinked. 'I don't know of any wolves-turned-Rabid that only had nine fingers. The injury must have occurred during the time it was in Bloodhill.' He smeared paste over the second claw mark. 'Anything else?'

'It had a long slice down its left arm from shoulder to wrist.'

Logan pointed his finger. 'It's gotta be Duncan,' he said, referring to a wolf from their clan. 'Nice to know he's not dead, though I'm not sure you can call his current existence a life.'

Yeah, it both saddened and relieved a person to discover that a wolf gone Rabid still lived. 'It would be better not to tell Mae,' said Ripper, referring to Duncan's mate. The guy had been gone eleven years – she'd moved on and had two kids to another werewolf since then. To hear that Duncan was still out there and that he'd been so close to Ashwood ... it would just mess with her head.

Logan nodded. 'Learning about it wouldn't do her or her family any good.'

'I won't say anything,' Emberlyn assured them, her gaze going inward.

Coating the third claw mark in poultice, Ripper wondered if she was thinking on how she'd feel in Mae's shoes; if she'd want to know if Michael had been seen.

Logan rubbed at his nape. 'I don't think Duncan incidentally made his way here.'

Ripper went still. 'Why not?'

'I was only so close to the manor because I'd followed the scent of blood while on patrol. A dead goat was left not far from here.' Logan pointed in the direction of the rear of the house. 'It wasn't killed by an animal, and it didn't die of natural causes. Its throat was slit.'

Emberlyn tensed. 'So someone had hoped to lure a Rabid or two out here,' she mused, a dark note in her voice.

'Seems that way.'

A blast of cold washed over Ripper's nape, and then the can of sugar skidded along the countertop. He went still, as did Logan.

Emberlyn, however, pointed at the can and then flicked her finger to the side. The object grazed the counter as it returned to its original spot.

Okay.

Logan cleared his throat. 'It has to have been one of the coven,' he insisted.

'Or Carver, or one of his clan.' Done applying paste to her wounds, Ripper held out the spatula.

She took it from him with an uttered 'Thanks' and plopped herself on the nearest chair. 'I want to see the goat,' she announced, crossing her injured leg over the other.

Ripper stilled, opposed to the thought of her leaving the safety of the house. 'Me and Logan will move it away from here.'

Dipping the spatula in the mortar, she peered up at him. 'How awesome of you,' she said, her tone dry. 'But I want to see it before you do.'

He dragged his gaze away from her curved lips, mentally crushing the thoughts of just what he could do with that mouth. 'Why?'

'To see if there's any indication that magick was used.' She began expertly lathering her wound in poultice. 'I want to know if a witch was involved.' She shot him a quick look. 'Why do I get the feeling that you don't want me to check it out?'

Because he didn't. 'You're injured. The poultice won't stop the smell of your blood from scenting the air. And if there's a breeze, it'll carry that scent and act as a better lure than any goat.'

'Which is why I intend to use magick to mask the scent,' she said, scooping more paste out of the mortar.

'It's still best for you to remain here,' Ripper insisted.

'Hey, I get that your protective instincts are playing hopscotch right now, but it wasn't a request. And why would I need to stay here when I have two strapping werewolves to keep me safe?'

Ripper clenched his jaw. It galled him that she disregarded his authority. But, he then realized, it was also part of what drew him to her. Emberlyn wasn't at all impressed by his position of Alpha; didn't look at him and *see* an Alpha. She just saw Ripper.

'Finished.' She stood and tossed the spatula on the chopping board. 'Just gotta wash my hands and then we'll go.'

He didn't bother arguing, knowing it wouldn't do him any good. He waited while she cleaned up and then used magick to scrape the scent of blood from her skin. His need to shield her pricking at him like claws, he walked at her side as Logan led them out of the back door and onto the land beyond her yard.

Stopping at a certain spot, Logan frowned down at the patch of crushed long grass that was smeared with blood. 'It's gone.'

'One of the Rabid must have hauled it off.'

'I don't see any signs of magick,' said Emberlyn, glancing around. 'Which isn't to say that one of the coven wasn't involved. They might have avoided using spells just in case the goat was found and I got a good look at it.' She swept a hand over the ground. Magick dust drifted down from her palm and cleaned away the blood.

'Carver was pissed at me when he left my house earlier,' said Ripper. It could have easily been the Alpha.

'They're all pissed. Him. Reena. My family. Anyone who was looking forward to seeing Reena's plans for the land come to fruition.' Emberlyn sighed. 'Bet you regret that Millicent pulled you and your clan into this.'

Ripper felt his brows draw together. 'I regret nothing. And I don't give a shit how many people are pissed or just how pissed they are. Not my problem. The land isn't theirs; never was. Same goes for the manor. *They're* the issue here, not us.'

'I don't think they'll drag this out much longer,' said Logan. 'They'll put up an initial resistance, sure – they feel that they're the victims here. But they'll let this go when the struggle doesn't pay off. There isn't anything else they can do.'

'They'll eventually accept that they're not going to get what they want,' Emberlyn agreed. 'But that doesn't necessarily mean they'll let it go. I'm not the only vengeful witch in town, regardless of what the coven might like everyone to believe.'

Ripper felt his brows dip. 'The rebellious faction that's rumored to exist within the coven, you mean.'

'It's not a rumor,' she asserted. 'I don't know *who* makes up the group, but I know it exists because I've been blamed for many spells they've cast. People just assumed it was me.'

Yeah, Ripper had once been one of the people who made that assumption. He'd failed to realize that, actually, she'd been the faction's scapegoat.

'If they think they can take me on as a group, they might well do it.'

Ripper caught her gaze. 'They won't only have to take you on, Emberlyn. They'll have to also take on my clan. They fuck with you, they fuck with us and vice versa. You think the coven is really dumb enough to do that?'

She twisted her mouth. 'No. But that doesn't mean they won't.'

CHAPTER ELEVEN

❧

Swiping her choice of outfit from the wardrobe two days later, Emberlyn paused on hearing the phone ring. She crossed to the bed, carefully laid her clothes on the mattress, then headed for the phone on the nightstand. She lifted the receiver to her ear. 'Hello?'

'Emberlyn, this is Clarence Robbins.'

She blinked in surprise. The werewolf had not only been her grandmother's lawyer but also the executor of the will. 'What can I do for you, Clarence?'

'I've been contacted by one of the coven's lawyers, Tyra.' He sighed. 'I'm sorry to say that your family is planning to contest Millicent's will.'

She felt her lips tighten. 'Yes, I'd heard that they might.' And she would bet that Tyra was *loving* that she had a hand in this.

'Could you come by my office this morning so that we can discuss it further?'

'I'll be there. What time?'

'My schedule is open until ten a.m. – stop by sometime before then, if you can.'

'Will do.' Ending the call, Emberlyn rubbed at her neck. Her family certainly wasn't wasting any time in putting their plan in motion. She didn't *think* they had a chance of rendering the will invalid, but what if they did? She'd lose her home, lose her connection to it, lose the peace she always found here.

Fuck those assholes.

It would be different if they wanted the manor for the *right* reason; if they gave the first damn about it. But they didn't. It was greed that drove Emberlyn's family to do this. Greed, and the bitterness they felt at the manor choosing her.

As Millicent herself had stated in the letter she'd pinned to the grandfather clock, the manor should be inhabited by someone who adored and treasured it. But if her family did overturn the will and manage to acquire the house, they wouldn't keep or take care of it. They'd relinquish it to Reena, ending the tradition of it being a home to Vautier witches. And *she'd* never love or cherish it. For the High Priestess, it would be a status symbol. A prize.

Emberlyn cursed beneath her breath and then called Paisley.

'Yo?' the witch simply greeted.

'I'm going to be a little late coming in this morning,' Emberlyn informed her. 'Millicent's lawyer has asked to see me.'

Paisley paused. 'That's ... okay.' It was clearly *killing* Paisley not to ask for more information.

Emberlyn's lips twitched. Her friend was upset with her for not calling straight after the Rabid attack – it had meant that Paisley learned of it via Kage, which annoyed her even more. Just yesterday, she'd rather dramatically told Emberlyn to not speak to her for at least a week.

'We can handle things without you,' Paisley sassed. 'Stay gone as long as you want. It's truly fine.'

'I thought you didn't want to talk to me.'

The line went dead.

Chuckling, Emberlyn set down the receiver again. Moving to the bed, she grabbed her forest-green silk blouse. She winced as she slipped it on, the movements pulling at her shoulder wound. The skin around it felt tight.

Thanks to the heavy use of poultice and magick over the past two days, the claw marks were rapidly healing. But since the chafing of any clothing would for sure aggravate them, she applied gauze to both injuries each morning.

It had taken her by surprise when Ripper had asked to tend to her shoulder Saturday night. She'd sensed that his protective instincts were on fire, of course, but still. She didn't think his reaction was so much about *her* as that she was his ally – a person he'd sworn to keep safe. It would have offended his nature that someone under his protection was harmed.

When he'd braced a hand on her back, his fingers curling over her shoulder and resting on her nape, she'd startled. Because the move had been firm, deliberate and held a bold familiarity.

It had also made her nerve-endings sing, and she'd been unable to stop little bumps from sweeping over her flesh.

She'd expected his movements to be swift and all business when he applied the poultice. But his touch had been careful, slow and precise – not at all clinical. And when he'd finished, his hands had briefly lingered. Not in a sexual way. It had seemed more of a protective gesture.

It had still excited her hormones.

Shoving him out of her mind for now, she fastened the buttons of her blouse and stepped into her black pants. They had a slight flare, which meant the lines of her leg bandage wouldn't show through the material. People knew about the attack, yes, but she didn't want to remind them of it – it only prompted the kind of questions and comments she'd been peppered with since the attack . . .

Are you okay?

What exactly happened?

Why was Logan there?

Do you know who the Rabid might have been?

I'll bet you were all shaken up, you poor thing.

She'd meant what she'd told Ripper and Logan – she hadn't been unnerved by the attack. More saddened, in actual fact. Because she'd been forced to hurt a creature who was really a person stuck in that form.

Once dressed, she downed coffee and breakfast in the kitchen before heading out. Arriving at her destination, she parked her car in a space across the street from the lawyer's office. Climbing out, she hooked her purse strap over her shoulder and crossed the road, cursing in her head as she noticed her ex-in laws, the Reeds, stepping out of the nearby dentist's practice.

Both did a double-take as Emberlyn reached the sidewalk, their lips weakly curving.

'We heard about the attack,' said Claris, giving her a head-to-toe scan. 'We'd planned to pop into the hub and see how you were doing.'

Feeling awkward as ever around the couple, Emberlyn gave her a soft smile. 'I'm fine, thanks.'

Colton frowned at that. 'Rumor has it that you were wounded.'

'I was, but not badly. And the injuries are healing well.' She rocked forward slightly. 'Well. Thanks for checking on me.'

'The Rabid . . . it wasn't Michael?' asked Claris.

'No, it definitely wasn't Michael.' Emberlyn knew that for certain, because the Rabid had lacked the three claw scars on his cheek that her ex-mate sported. 'You two take care.'

Bypassing them, she pushed open the lawyer's office door and stepped into the waiting room. Her gaze immediately slid to the male sitting on a plush chair near the reception desk.

Ripper.

She halted in surprise. Her feminine parts responded in a very predictable fashion – waving and smiling seductively.

Would she ever be able to truly prepare herself for the impact of him? Doubtful. One piercing look from those eyes and her thoughts got scrambled.

At the mahogany desk, one of her favorite customers lifted her head and smiled brightly. 'Emberlyn, good morning. Mr Robbins said you'd be stopping by.' Laine stood upright. 'I'll let him know you're here. Take a seat.'

'Thanks, Laine,' said Emberlyn.

As the female werewolf disappeared down a hallway to the left of her desk, Emberlyn returned her attention to Ripper. Her heels clicked along the glossy wooden floor as she made her way to the chair beside his.

'Figured the lawyer probably called you as well,' he said in that gravelly voice that grazed her nerve-endings in the best way.

She sat down. 'He asked to speak with you, too?'

'Makes sense. Your family wants my land, not just your home. How's your shoulder and leg?'

'Healing well.'

'No side effects from the antivenom?'

'None,' she replied, glancing around. The waiting room was all crème paint and mahogany wood. A few framed generic pictures hung on the walls. A water cooler was positioned in the corner while a plant stood in the one opposite.

'You ever had to use it before?' He hooked his arm over the back of her chair.

Her pulse jumped, because it wasn't only a protective display;

he was essentially eating into her personal space like it was nothing. *Ballsy bastard.* 'Only once.'

His face darkened. 'When was that?'

Michael had attacked her before he ran for Bloodhill, but it wasn't something she talked about. 'That's a whole other story. I'll tell you about it sometime.' Maybe. Probably not.

Laine reappeared, smiling. 'Clarence will be with you both very soon – he's just finishing a call.' She returned to her chair and went right back to her computer.

Emberlyn glanced at Ripper. 'On the subject of people being bitten by werewolves, I wanted to ask you something.' She crossed her legs, not failing to notice how his gaze dipped to them. 'One of my best friends, Paisley, is interested in taking the Change.'

His eyes flew back to hers, squinting. 'That's Kage's sister, right?'

'Right. She'd like to join your clan, if possible. I don't know how you go about choosing people, but I was wondering if you could at least speak with her.'

He gave a slow nod. 'I can do that.'

'She has a family thing tonight. Tomorrow sometime after five?'

'I'm free then.'

'Choose a location best for you. She can't meet with you at her house because the coven isn't supportive of her decision.'

'I'll be at the manor around six-thirty.'

Thanks for asking if you can use my home.

A male with slicked-back salt-and-pepper hair materialized, clad in a black suit. He glanced from her to Ripper, a polite smile gracing his jowly face and tugging up his mustache. 'I appreciate you both coming on such short notice. I'm sorry to have kept you waiting.'

She and Ripper rose from their seats and crossed to him. Hands were shaken, and brief greetings were exchanged. Clarence then led them down the hallway and into an office. The décor was very old school, all dark woods and vintage furnishings. Even the brass lamp on his cluttered desktop appeared to be an antique.

Old framed photos of the building hung on the walls, along with some artwork. What appeared to be law books lined the shelves on the wall behind him. Beneath them were filing cabinets and a coffee machine. There were some personal touches. Like family pictures, a cute 'Best Dad' mug, and memorabilia.

He waved a hand toward the seats opposite his desk. 'How are you after Saturday night's attack?' he asked her.

'Pretty good, thanks.' She took a seat. The leather padding was warm from the beams of sunlight that slashed through the windows' Venetian blinds. 'I'd feel a lot better if my family would accept the conditions of the will.'

Ripper sank into the chair beside hers. 'They really mean to render it invalid?'

Faint irritation leaching into his brown eyes, Clarence let out a put-out sigh. 'Yes. One of the coven's lawyers, Tyra Mosby, called me Friday to inform me of it. She claimed it would be best if you released your "false claim" on the land' – his gaze moved to Emberlyn – 'and if you released your similarly false claim on the manor before it came to that.'

Emberlyn hauled in an annoyed breath, inadvertently taking in the scents of coffee, wood polish and leather. 'What did you say to that?'

'I told Tyra that there was nothing false about the claims, and that any attempts to contest the will would result in nothing. I didn't contact either of you about it because I thought she might be bluffing – overturning a will isn't easy, after all. But when I came in early this morning I found an official notice in my mail.' Clarence swiped a letter from a mail tray and held it up.

Emberlyn exchanged a frustrated look with Ripper.

Clarence set the paper on his desk. 'To sum up the letter, Gill is the main challenger of the will. She insists that Millicent lacked the mental capacity to make one; feels that the existing will can't possibly reflect her mother's true last wishes. Gill also asserts that under no circumstances would Millicent want you to have the manor, Emberlyn. She is requesting that you be removed from it until the matter is resolved.' Clarence looked at Ripper. 'She also requests that your clan not set foot on the land in the interim.'

Emberlyn felt her jaw harden. 'She can shove that request up her ass.'

'Yeah, it ain't happening,' Ripper clipped.

'I will be making that clear,' Clarence assured them. 'Don't let it worry you. She has no way or right to enforce these demands.'

'Be honest,' began Emberlyn, 'does she have a shot at winning?'

'She would have to convince the council of her claim. That will be difficult when the will was signed in the presence of both myself and a medical practitioner.'

'Why a medical practitioner?' asked Ripper.

'Because Millicent asked that one talk with her and confirm she had the capacity to write a valid will,' Clarence replied.

Well, damn. 'She anticipated that it would be contested.'

The lawyer nodded. 'Tyra will have surely noticed the practitioner's signature but has proceeded anyway, perhaps thinking it won't be enough to convince anyone that Millicent was stable. What she and your family will not be aware of is that Millicent also left a letter of wishes. Something she wrote separately to explain the stipulations of the will.'

He rose to his feet and headed to the metal drawers. Having slid one open, he pulled out a brown envelope and then shut the drawer. Returning to his seat, he passed the envelope over to Emberlyn.

She took it from him and tore it open. 'Why wasn't this released before now?'

'Because she gave me strict instructions to only release it to you if the validity of the will was challenged.'

Emberlyn pulled the letter out of the envelope and quickly read it. Her brows hiked up. 'My family won't like hearing this.'

Ripper leaned toward her. 'What does it say?'

She angled the paper so he could read it.

His own brows winged up after he'd done so. 'Yeah, they ain't gonna like hearing that.'

Clarence tilted his head. 'Do you understand now why Millicent didn't simply bequeath you the manor, Emberlyn?'

She exhaled heavily. 'Yes. I thought she'd just wanted me to prove I had the right to reside there.'

His chair rocked slightly as he leaned forward. 'Millicent spoke to me about you, you know.'

'Calling me her biggest disappointment, no doubt,' Emberlyn muttered, feeling her lips twitch.

'She did say that. She also said you were a woman to admire. You'd pushed past pain, grief, persecution and prejudice. You didn't let any of it hold you back. You'd carved a place for yourself in this town, started a business she would never have thought of, and chose your own path rather than let her or anyone else dictate what you should do with your life.

'She respected that. Respected *you*. And she cared for you more than I'm sure she would ever have let on.' Clarence paused, looking at her intently. 'Don't let your family ever make you think that Millicent didn't want you to be *exactly* where you are.'

Mentally fumbling after Clarence's little declaration, Emberlyn fiddled with her bracelet. It was hard to imagine her grandmother saying such things, but there was no reason for him to lie. 'I can't blame them for thinking it. She told them she didn't want me to have the manor.'

'Probably to keep them off your back. This letter provides context and background, showing the motivations behind her decisions – and making them seem explainable, not bizarre. In other words, we have what we need to rebut Gill's claim of lack of capacity.'

Ripper planted his hands on the armrests of his chair. 'So, what happens now?'

'A meeting is scheduled for us all next Monday at the town hall,' Clarence replied.

Exactly a week from now, then.

'The only council member who should be on the bench is Shane as he has nothing to gain from the result of Gill's challenge to the will,' Clarence added. 'But both Reena and Carver are claiming that – having now "accepted" the terms of Millicent's will – they will be unbiased.'

Emberlyn snorted. 'Will they *fuck.*'

Ripper grunted.

'All parties, including both of you, would need to agree that they can remain impartial,' said Clarence. 'My guess is that neither of you have that opinion.'

'You guessed right,' Ripper told him.

'If Reena had backed down, she wouldn't have appointed her own daughter to represent my family.'

'Indeed,' said Clarence. 'And if Reena hasn't backed down, Carver will still be under the impression that the project may go ahead.'

After they'd rounded up the conversation, Emberlyn returned

the letter to Clarence for safe-keeping. She and Ripper then left the building, coming to a halt on the sidewalk.

'Millicent really did have all her bases covered,' mused Ripper.

Emberlyn nodded. 'It would appear that way. She wasn't risking that her wishes would be overturned.'

'I don't believe it was just that. From what she wrote in that letter, I think her aim was also to protect your claim on the manor.' Ripper's gaze roamed over her face. 'Regardless of what she may have told you, I don't think you disappointed her, Emberlyn.'

'Why is that?'

'She was right in the things she said to Robbins. It would have been easy for you to stay with her or rejoin the coven – it's normal to want to belong. But you ventured out on your own and planted a flag in neutral territory, asserting your right to be part of Chilgrave. And opening the laundry hub was smart. Real smart.'

It was, even if Emberlyn did say so herself.

'I think, in truth, she was proud of you. She just didn't know how to tell you that.'

CHAPTER TWELVE

❧

Exiting the brewery the following day, Ripper idly scanned his surroundings . . . and noticed Kerr walking along the sidewalk toward him. Something about his sober expression made Ripper tense.

'Heard you were here,' said Kerr. 'I was hoping to catch you before you left.'

Ripper turned to fully face him. 'What's going on?'

Kerr rubbed at his nape. 'I didn't want you to hear this through gossip, and I figured it'd be best to warn you that Logan is probably going to track you down, raging.'

'Raging about what?'

Kerr hesitated, his expression careful. 'Neal's dad mentioned that CeCe has finally agreed to give his son a shot.'

Ripper went very still, his gut clenching. 'That makes no sense. Neal's not her type.' She only ever went for highly dominant males, aware that – being so strong-willed – she bulldozed over others if they didn't push back.

'No, he's not,' Kerr agreed. 'It's why she turned him down time and time again over the years. But apparently something's changed.' He side-eyed Ripper. 'What are you going to do if it is true?'

At his friend's uncertain tone, Ripper felt his brow furrow. 'You ask that as if you think I might beat the shit out of Neal.'

'It wouldn't surprise me.'

Did Ripper *want* to see her cozied up with another guy? No. But ... 'I knew when I turned down the triad suggestion that she'd eventually end up with someone else. What the hell is she supposed to do?'

Kerr narrowed his eyes. 'You're pissed.'

'I'm pissed because she could do better than Neal.'

'You're pissed because you're thinking what I'm thinking,' Kerr contradicted, stepping closer. 'You're thinking this is a stunt; that she's trying to spur you to come around to the triad idea.'

Ripper felt his teeth clench. He *had* been thinking that. Neal had crushed on her since they were teens. If she'd ever wanted him, she could have acted on it way before now. She'd always told Ripper she never would; that she'd only ever see Neal as a friend.

Kerr went on, 'She gave you time. She was patient. She thought you'd come round, but you haven't. So now she feels you slipping away. Alpha werewolves are extremely territorial. What better way to push you into finally claiming her than to show you that you'll be replaced in her affections?'

'No game or stunt or play is going to make me change my mind. She should know me well enough to know that.'

'I think she'll try anything at this point. She's not devious by nature, but that doesn't mean she can't be devious on occasion. Even the nicest person can become a nightmare when they're not getting something they badly want. If she's been imagining a triad for years, she's now being forced to let that dream go. It isn't odd that she won't do it without a fight. And do I think she'd resort to manipulation if it meant being able to have both you and Logan? Yeah, I do. And so do you.'

Ripper wished he could argue, aggrieved that someone he held a lot of affection for would play him this way. He cursed. 'I don't have time for this right now. I've got to get to Emberlyn's place,' he explained, walking toward his truck. 'Her friend wants to go through the Change and join our clan. I said I'd speak to her.'

'Friend?' echoed Kerr, keeping pace with him. 'Has to be Paisley. I don't think Emberlyn really considers anyone other than the twins a friend – just coworkers, customers and allies. Like you, she doesn't easily let people close.' Kerr eyed him. 'You really gonna keep your hands off her?'

That was the plan. But Ripper could feel it steadily crumbling. Which was why he repeatedly reminded himself . . . 'It was only a year ago that she broke the mating tie.'

Kerr shrugged. 'So?'

Ripper pulled open the driver's door of his truck. 'So some part of her might still feel mated.'

'Yeah, but some part of her might not. You could just be making assumptions. Even if she does still have some feelings for Michael, it ain't much different from you having lingering feelings for CeCe. Maybe you can both help the other fully move on, if nothing else. At least *think* about it.'

Like Ripper would be able to do anything else.

He jumped into his truck and closed the door. All things considered, with all that was going on with CeCe, his head should have been too fucked to have room for anyone else. But Emberlyn intrigued him beyond measure.

She also had some hold over his cock. It hadn't been CeCe's

face he saw when he fisted his dick in the shower that morning, it had been Emberlyn's.

She flitted in and out of his mind often throughout the day like a roaming butterfly. He'd push thoughts of her back out ... but they'd return.

Ripper switched on the engine and pulled out onto the road. He didn't drive straight to the manor. He stopped off at the bakery along the way, needing to stock up on a few things.

When he arrived at her house, he noticed an additional car parked there. It had to be her friend's vehicle.

Shortly after he'd knocked on the door, it swung open to reveal Emberlyn. As always, she was the image of class, her peach belted jumpsuit both casual and elegant. She looked entirely too edible.

His body tightened in response, and sexual awareness pulsed between them. He knew she felt it by the way her pupils dilated.

She cleared her throat. 'Hey.' Her eyes dipped to the recyclable cup carrier tray he held and then to the brown paper bag he clasped with his free hand. He'd left his other purchases in the car.

Ripper stepped into the manor. 'Coffee for me. Herbal tea for you.' He gave her the paper bag. 'Custard Danish. The she-wolves at the bakery said it was your favorite.'

She double-blinked. 'Um, thanks. Didn't you bring anything for Paisley?'

'She's not mine to feed.'

'Werewolf logic,' Emberlyn uttered beneath her breath, closing the door.

'Werewolf logic?'

'You all tend to have great manners, but you discount the wants and needs of people who aren't under your protection.'

'Do you go around feeding people who aren't part of your circle?'

'I take your point.' Emberlyn carefully plucked her takeout cup out of the holder, spun on her heel and then walked down the hallway. 'Paisley and Kage are in the living room. Luckily, they already have tea and snickerdoodles, or they'd be feeling left out.'

Trailing behind Emberlyn, he had no way to stop his gaze from dropping to her ass. It was *right there*, high and tight and utter perfection.

Ripper caught movement in his peripheral vision. He glanced to the side ... and did a double-take as the outline of a person faded from view. His muscles went taut as he stopped dead. Either he'd briefly seen a spirit or he'd imagined it. He wasn't sure which scenario would bother him more.

'You coming or not?' asked Emberlyn, pausing at a doorway.

Shoving the little incident aside, he cleared his throat as he walked toward her in answer. Following her into the living room, he saw Paisley sitting on one of the sofas while her brother hung over the back of it. Both straightened as he entered.

'Ripper,' Kage greeted.

'I'm Paisley,' his sister announced. 'Which I'm guessing you already know, since this is a small town.'

Well, yeah, although ... 'We haven't spoken much over the years.'

'I don't run in werewolf circles. I'm hoping that will change, though.'

As Emberlyn lowered herself onto an armchair, Ripper took the sofa opposite her friend.

Paisley scooted forward a little. 'I want you to know that this isn't a snap decision on my part. I've thought about it a lot.'

Ripper removed his coffee cup from the holder. 'So this isn't just because your brother became a werewolf?'

Paisley's lips flattened. 'No. It was my intention way before that rat bastard allowed the Change to take him.'

'Rat bastard?' echoed Kage, his brows flying up in affront.

Paisley cast him a quick glance. 'Hey, I'm just calling the situation as I see it.'

'Why have you got to be so mean?' demanded Kage. 'I'm your brother. You should adore me.'

'And yet ...'

Her eyes dancing, Emberlyn sipped from her drink.

Ripper shifted slightly, bringing Paisley's attention back to him. 'Why is it you'd like to take the Change?'

She rested her hands on her thighs. 'The thought of it always appealed to me, even when I was little. I think maybe it's because clans are so tight and the weak are protected. It doesn't work like that in a coven.'

He frowned. 'You consider yourself weak?'

'Not as a person, no. But my magick isn't strong, so most of the coven consider me a runt. It made me ripe for bullying at school. Of course, they stopped targeting me for their own amusement when Emberlyn became my bestie – she only had to smile at them and they'd slink away like thieves in the night.' Paisley snickered.

He cut his gaze to Emberlyn, who was sipping her herbal tea again. She was a protector just as much as she was an avenger, he thought. Returning his attention to Paisley, he asked, 'Is your family aware that you wish to take the Change?'

'Yes. My parents are not pleased about it. Far from it. But as Emberlyn said, I can't live my life trying to keep other people happy. My mom and dad should want me to put my happiness before their own. It hurts that they don't, but it is what it is. My hope is that they'll eventually come round to the idea.'

'And if they don't? Because this isn't something you could take back. Once done, it can't be undone.'

'If they don't come round, they don't come round. I'll have no regrets,' Paisley stated with such certainty that he believed her.

'I take it you would prefer to join my clan because your twin is part of it.'

Her nose wrinkled. 'No, it's not a factor here. If anything, I'd prefer to be away from him – he's a fucking idiot.'

Kage narrowed his eyes at her. 'I despise you,' he said matter-of-factly.

'Well, that's new,' Paisley deadpanned without looking at him. 'Carver's clan needs shaping up, to be frank,' she said to Ripper. 'Shane's clan is tight and orderly but, let's face it, yours is tighter and more controlled. I'd feel safer in your clan. I never had that in the coven.'

Ripper had never really understood why witches were so obsessed with 'perfection'. Perfection, in their eyes, being strong and in full control of their magick. They looked down on those who didn't meet that standard; targeted them rather than protected them. He didn't get that mentality at all.

'The Change is no easy thing to go through,' he told Paisley. 'It'll take a few days. Aside from the initial bite, it won't hurt. But you'll be tired. Feverish. Drift in and out of consciousness. And there'll be times you'll—'

'Want a lot of sex, I know.'

'Then you know you're gonna need a wolf to fuck you during most of it,' he said bluntly.

She swallowed. 'I'm really not going to have a problem with that.'

Emberlyn choked on her Danish, her shoulders shaking.

Paisley blushed. 'What? They're all hot as hellfire. I'm not gonna lie and act like it'll be a chore.'

Ripper's lips threatened to twitch. 'If you're sure this is what you want, I have no objection to you joining my clan. Are there any unmated wolves in it who you feel comfortable with? If so, I'll ask if they'll put you through the Change. It's not something I do.'

Emberlyn tilted her head. 'How come?'

'As you'll know, a werewolf injects an enzyme into a person's blood to Change them,' he explained. 'Each werewolf has an individual enzyme like they do a fingerprint. She'll always feel a slight platonic connection to the wolf who Changes her due to that enzyme. I'm the Alpha – it's important I'm not more connected to some clan members than others. The only exception is mates and family.'

'Gotcha,' said Emberlyn. 'Makes sense.'

Paisley twisted her mouth. 'I've met quite a few of your clan during my time working at the laundry hub. I can't think of any who I don't feel comfortable with, so I'm not fussed.'

'All right. I'll talk to some of my unmated wolves and get back to you.'

A delighted smile split Paisley's lips. 'Awesome.'

A door slammed upstairs and footsteps marched along the landing, causing the floorboards to creak.

Ripper tensed. 'Who else is here?'

'No one,' said Emberlyn before taking a casual bite of her Danish.

Goosebumps swept over his skin. He looked at the twins, both of whom appeared unnerved. 'Does that kind of thing happen a lot here?'

Emberlyn gave a noncommittal shrug. Not comforting.

After they'd finished their drinks and food, the twins made their excuses and left.

'Thank you,' Emberlyn said to him on returning to the living room after seeing them out. 'I appreciate you being willing to accept her as part of your clan.'

'There's no reason why I wouldn't.'

Sinking back in the armchair, she studied him closely. 'You okay?'

He felt his brow pinch. 'Why wouldn't I be?'

She pulled a face. 'I heard the rumor about CeCe and Neal,' she said, her voice low. 'It can't be easy for you.'

He exhaled heavily. 'It'll be harder for Logan.'

'Why?'

'He cares for her more than I do. He's gonna be exponentially pissed. He would do anything to have her, even enter a triad.'

A line dented her brow. 'So it wouldn't really be his first choice?'

'No. He and I have shared women before, but only ever for a night.' Those females hadn't been girlfriends or bed-buddies, they'd always been women who neither he nor his brother were in any way committed to. Then no jealousy could come into play.

'Is there no way she'd consider committing only to Logan?' Emberlyn asked.

Ripper shook his head. 'I assured them both that I'd be good with it, but she refuses to believe that it wouldn't hurt me to see them together; she says she couldn't do that to me.'

Emberlyn frowned. 'But she can be with *Neal* knowing it would hurt you? That she's fine with?'

'It would seem so.'

'What's the difference?'

Ripper shrugged. 'You'd have to ask her.'

'Am I wrong, or has Neal been trying to win her over for years?'

'You're not wrong.'

'It's a bit strange that she'd suddenly give him a chance,'

Emberlyn casually threw out. 'Could she maybe have done it to—'

'Bring me to heel? Maybe. Makes more sense than her type abruptly changing overnight.' Ripper pushed to his feet. 'I'd better go find my brother and convince him to not beat Neal bloody.'

Side by side, they walked down the hallway toward the front door.

Emberlyn slid him a quick glance. 'Do you think Logan will accept that CeCe has moved on, or do you think he's going to push you harder for a triad?'

Ripper sighed. 'I don't know. Probably the latter.'

'Will it work?'

'No. She wants me to feel that I'm losing her. And I do. But not in the way she's thinking.'

Emberlyn opened the door. 'What you're saying is that she was a close friend for a long time, and this whole thing – the way she's behaved, the way she's pushing, the way she's now playing games – has tainted that friendship. You feel like you might not get it back,' she reasoned.

Ripper pointed at her. 'That's exactly it.' He stepped out onto the porch.

'I hope it doesn't work out that way. I know what it's like to have an . . . absence in your life. A gap where a particular person should be.'

Yeah, she'd know. She'd suffered several losses. Her mother and grandmother had died. Her father had abandoned her. And her mate had turned Rabid and left her. 'You took longer than most people do to declare the mating over,' he noted.

She shrugged. 'I guess taking that extra time made me feel less guilty about forfeiting it.'

'There was nothing else you could have done. Moving on isn't about replacing a person or forgetting them. It's about finding peace. He'd want you to have that.'

She gave him a wan smile. 'Take it easy, Rip.'

Rip. It was the first time she'd abbreviated his name. Few people did it, and he found he liked that she was now one of them. 'You too.'

CHAPTER THIRTEEN

Stalking into his clan's bar Sunday evening, Ripper felt his mouth thin at what he saw. He'd received a call from the bartender to warn him that a fight might potentially break out. It turned out he'd been right, and Ripper hadn't arrived soon enough to prevent it.

Grunts, curses, growls and the sounds of flesh smacking flesh filled the air. One male was very clearly dominating the fight, but he was in no rush to end it – punching, stalking and shoving his opponent into things.

Glasses smashed. Chairs hit the floor with a bang. Table legs scraped the floor as they skidded.

Spectators appealed for the two males to stop, but no one jumped into the fray. He couldn't really blame them. Getting between two fighting werewolves was never a good idea – they could both as easily turn on you.

Hence why the bartender had called Ripper.

It wasn't rare for werewolves to get physical like this – they generally welcomed the rush. As such, he'd shown up here many times in the past to break up fights. Quite often, he would arrive to discover that they were over and the fighters were cleaning up any mess they'd made. They'd often buy each other a drink in apology, and then it would be forgotten.

Tonight, it wasn't going to be that simple. This wasn't a mere drunken brawl or a case of wolves getting into it over something petty. Two people had swanned in here *knowing* that it would set another person off. This had been the result.

Ripper strode over there, shouldered his way through the crowd, and planted himself between the fighters. 'Stop,' he ordered, his voice firm.

They did, their chests heaving, their gazes still locked, their faces set into glowers.

'Pull back. Both of you.'

Each male did as he ordered, neither looking at him.

'Logan, go cool off in the office.'

Swiping at his split lip, his brother angrily stalked off without a word.

Ripper turned to the other male. Given that his face was a mass of bruises and cuts, he was no doubt regretting his decision to rile up Logan.

After leaving Emberlyn's house on Tuesday evening, Ripper had tracked down his brother. The guy had been sitting on his private pier, knocking back beers. He hadn't ranted at or blamed Ripper for CeCe getting together with Neal. Nor had Logan pushed Ripper to finally cave to CeCe's demands.

Quite the opposite.

Logan had claimed that he was 'done'. Knowing she was now sleeping with another guy, that she'd been able to move on so fast so easily, had hit Logan hard. He hadn't been expecting it. The fact that she'd chosen someone she didn't even care about over him had crushed Logan.

'I'm not gonna hunt Neal down and kick his ass,' he'd told Ripper. 'Let him have her. I'm not interested anymore.'

He'd meant it because he'd been positively gutted. And during the days that had followed, he'd made a pointed effort to avoid the couple.

Had tonight been a case of him incidentally seeing CeCe and Neal about town, Logan would have hidden his pain and turned away. But no, nothing about this had been 'incidental', so Logan's reaction was not only understandable but justified.

'Neal, go to the restroom and clean yourself up,' Ripper instructed. 'Then you're gonna clean this mess and get *the fuck* out of here. I'll deal with you tomorrow.' He wanted to talk to his brother.

Neal's back snapped straight. 'Why isn't Logan being forced to help? I didn't throw the first punch—' He cut off as Ripper got right into his face.

'Don't play fucking innocent with me,' Ripper growled.

Neal's gaze dropped to the floor.

'You came here with the sole purpose of setting Logan off. *You* started the fight just by walking through that door. You knew exactly what would happen.' Ripper flicked his gaze to CeCe. 'And so did you.'

Her eyes widened. 'What? No!'

He turned back to Neal. 'Restroom, *now*.'

The werewolf scurried away, a slight hobble in his step.

CeCe crossed to Ripper, wringing her hands. 'I know how this looks, but I swear I didn't—'

'Don't bullshit me,' he bit off. 'You could have gone anywhere with Neal tonight. Any-fucking-where. You chose this bar, *knowing* Logan would be here – he comes here every Sunday night to play darts and shoot the shit with some wolves from our clan. You knew it would hurt him to see you with Neal.

Knew it'd set him off. So the only reason you'd come here is if you wanted that.'

'I didn't!' she protested. 'I would never do anything to hurt Logan!'

'Then why choose this bar?'

'It was a busy week, I had a lot going on, I lost track of the days, thought it was Saturday. I didn't realize my mistake until I walked in and saw people gathered near the dart board. I was about to walk straight back out, I swear. But Logan saw us and rushed over.'

Ripper clenched his jaw. 'Didn't I just tell you not to bullshit me?'

Her eyes flared. 'I'm not lying, I got confused.'

'Did you also get confused when you started dating a guy you only think of as a friend?'

She snapped her mouth shut. 'I could tell that you weren't going to change your mind about the triad. But Logan ... he wasn't giving up hope. I thought that if it looked as if I was moving on, it would force him to let this go and move on himself.'

'So you're using Neal? Does he know that?'

'No.' She averted her gaze, pulling a face. 'I feel bad about it, but I didn't know what else to do. This is my mess. I suggested the triad, I caused all the friction, I needed to put it right.'

'How in the hell was seeing you with Neal *ever* going to put this right for Logan? All you had to do was make it perfectly clear to him that you're not interested in a triad anymore.'

'I did! He could tell I was lying!'

'You really thought that this was the solution?'

She grimaced, adjusting her tee. 'I'm going to go talk to Logan; check he's okay.'

'No, you're not. You're going to help Neal clean this mess, and then you're going to leave with him.'

Her head jerked back slightly. 'Look, I realize you're upset about me and Neal—'

'I'm not, CeCe. I want things to go back to the way they were before, when we were nothing but friends. A natural part of that would be you dating someone. But you're not dating Neal, you're using him. And you're hurting my brother in the doing of it.'

Her lips thinning, she jutted out her chin. 'I love Logan. I love you both.'

'Yeah? You've got a messed-up way of showing it.' Ripper walked off, weaving through the tables until he arrived at the office.

Inside, Logan sat on a chair near the desk, gently probing his jaw. He looked up at Ripper, his eyes dull. 'Neal ain't much of a fighter, but he got a few good shots in.'

Ripper walked over to his brother. 'How did all that play out exactly?'

Sighing, Logan lowered his hand to his lap. 'I meant it when I told you I wouldn't seek him out or confront him. But they walked in here hand in hand, smiling and laughing . . . I didn't see it coming, Rip. It took me off-guard. I didn't think she'd do that to me, and it pissed me off that she did. Before I knew it, I was striding over there.

'I told them both to get out. Told her I thought better of her. Said I wanted them out of my sight. But that mother-fucker went nose to nose with me, saying I needed to accept that CeCe was his; that *he* now gets to come inside her; that I'll never have her again; that he'd one day claim her. Things escalated from there.'

Ripper bit out a curse. Neal had really gone all out to provoke Logan. 'She swore she thought it was Saturday.'

Logan's eyelids lowered. 'Fuck that. Her eyes went wide when she saw me, as if she was shocked. But I know her. That emotion was fake.' He rubbed at his forehead. 'She did this in the hope that I'd find it so hard to see her with Neal that I'd put more pressure on you to give her what she wants, didn't she?'

Ripper gave a weak shrug. 'Probably.'

'I hated the idea of her with him, but I didn't want to think you were right; that she'd do something as cold as use him to play you.' Logan eyed him closely. 'You would never have caved, would you?'

'No. And it wouldn't really have been what you wanted if I had. You and me can't even share a pizza without snarling at each other; how were we ever gonna share a mate?'

Logan's lips quirked a little. 'I told myself we'd make it work.'

'It wouldn't have lasted. It would have fallen apart, and that would have come between *us.*'

'Nothing could do that,' Logan asserted.

'She was already doing it. You've spent months hating me. You talked about switching clans.'

'I was just blowing off steam. I didn't mean it. And I don't hate you. Never did. I hated the situation.' Logan flexed his jaw and winced, probing at a red spot. 'You know, I'm almost glad she did this tonight. It opened my eyes; made me realize you were right.'

'I'd have preferred it if I wasn't right.'

Logan sighed again, his gaze turning inward. 'She isn't someone I ever thought would deliberately gut me open like that.'

'She's still the CeCe you know. People do out-of-character shit sometimes. She'll be regretting it now. And I'm thinking Neal will be getting dumped tonight on top of everything else. She admitted she's using him. She said it was her attempt to make you get the message that a triad isn't going to happen and we should all just let it go and move on.'

Logan scowled. 'Bullshit. I've been a dick to you; even

threatened to leave the clan. She didn't ever try to calm me down. She wanted me to keep nagging you and making threats. I didn't see it.' He paused, his expression pensive. 'But you did.'

'You always think the best of the people you love. I'm too jaded and cynical.'

'*And* half your mind is on the Black Willow Witch.'

Ripper went rigid.

'You think I didn't pick up on the zing between you two? Last Saturday night, Emberlyn brought out your protective streak in full force. She's probably the last person on this planet who needs you to shield her, but that didn't stop your entire being from reacting when she was hurt. You're into her. There's no other reason you'd react that intensely.'

'We're not talking about Emberlyn right now.'

Ignoring that, Logan went on, 'She's nothing like I expected. I'd heard so much crap about her that I thought she'd be an uptight, spiteful bitch. She's not.'

Eager to change the subject, Ripper said, 'Back to what we were talking about before . . . what do we do about CeCe?'

'I don't plan to do anything. I'm not the one in the wrong.' Logan stretched out his legs. 'When she apologizes, I'll accept her apology and hope we can go back to being friends.'

Ripper held that same hope. 'Things won't be the same, though.'

'No, they won't. She took a dump over everything I feel for her. Exploited it. Pushed the right buttons so I'd push *you*. I'll always care about her, but I'll never look at her the same way after this. Not ever.'

The front door swung open, and there was Emberlyn – clad in a skin-tight white dress that highlighted every sensual curve. Just *looking* at her made Ripper feel he could breathe easier. Which made no real sense – especially when his body had a habit of igniting around her, just as it did right then.

'I keep forgetting to ask you to make more of those elixirs for me,' he blurted out. 'You got time?'

Those pale-hazel eyes narrowed, seeing right through him. Truth was . . . after that messed-up scene at the bar, after seeing his brother so cut up, Ripper needed to be with the one person who took his thoughts away from everything else. A person so grounded that she was steadying to be around.

He thought she might call him on his shit; demand to know why he'd really come. It wasn't as if he'd need the elixirs soon – there wouldn't be a full moon for another few weeks.

She didn't challenge his claim, though. Instead, she opened the door wider. 'I have time.'

Some of his pent-up tension slipping from his shoulders, he accepted her silent invitation and walked inside. The energy of the house – all interwoven with her own – put him further at ease, soothing the sharp edges of his mood.

'Follow me,' she said.

He didn't even try not to admire her ass as they walked. He'd given up on that – it was a waste of energy.

Entering the consultation room, Ripper watched as she lit an incense burner, filling the air with the scent of sandalwood. He glanced around, noticing the many changes. Millicent's possessions and presence had given the space a dank and creepy feel. There'd been pockets of shadow all over. He'd always felt cautious on entering. That off-putting vibe was gone.

There was color in the form of gemstones, rock quartz, golden goblets and candles. The air was fresh and smelled of the bunches of dry flowers and herbs dangling from the ceiling. Everything seemed to glimmer – the shelves, the altar, the stools, the cast-iron cauldron, the soft-cream walls, the wooden floor.

The room put you at ease. Drew you in. Tempted you to come closer.

Just like the witch currently bustling around it, collecting this or that.

He claimed the stool near the stone fireplace just as she began laying things out on the altar. An athame, jars, a clay pot, a bottle, a few petals and a weirdly shaped leaf that had been left on the windowsill near small potted plants.

But no book of shadows.

'You already checked the formula for the elixir?'

At the sink, she filled a large chalice with water. 'No need. I make these all the time.' Returning to the altar, she poured the water into the cauldron and set down the chalice. 'I just need to ensure yours is stronger.'

She chanted, magick dust drifting from her palms and into the water. Water that began to simmer. Bubble. Steam.

She was boiling it without fire, he realized. He'd seen Millicent do the same.

'The best way to do that would be to use a drop of your blood.' She winged up a brow. 'Any objections?'

'I'll be drinking my own blood?'

'Not exactly. It's not like with cooking. These ingredients will make a potion. Magick converts the potion into liquid power.'

'Millicent never explained it that way.'

Emberlyn gave a small shrug. 'She preferred to be mysterious. I, on the other hand, like to be transparent where magick is concerned. So, you gonna let me use your blood or not? I don't *need* to. It'll just be quicker this way. But if you wanna be a pussy . . .'

He felt his brows hike up. 'A pussy?'

Humor swam in her eyes. 'Don't tell me the big, bad Alpha werewolf can't deal with having his finger pricked.'

'I wasn't actually going to object,' he said, holding out his hand toward her.

A dart of magick burst out of her finger and touched his. A bead of blood surfaced on his skin, and that same bead flowed on a glittering current of magick right into the cauldron.

'That didn't hurt,' he noted, surprised he hadn't felt a thing.

'Because I didn't want it to hurt you.' She pulled a stopper from a small bottle and peppered some black powder into the bubbling water.

He folded his arms. 'So, Millicent taught you how to make this elixir?'

'No, it was my creation originally. She tweaked it to give it more of a punch, though.'

A line tugged at his brow. 'She told me she created it accidentally.'

Emberlyn smiled, crushing a leaf in her palm. 'She liked her stories. Don't be so sure she always told you the truth.'

'Why do I get the feeling it was more that she didn't think it good for people to know how strong you were?'

'I don't know. Why do you?' With one hand, she used her athame to stir the potion as she added magick with the other. The water hissed, and more steam rose.

He silently watched as she went about adding this and that. Bark shavings. Lavender. Seed pods. A crushed petal. A dab of honey.

Every now and then, she'd sprinkle more magick into the mix as she again stirred it with her athame.

In some ways, she moved just like Millicent as she performed magick. There was no hesitating, no wasted motions. She was brisk, efficient and focused.

But in some ways, Emberlyn differed from her grandmother. Millicent had always worn a little smirk as she worked, always looked up to no good. There'd been some theater with her – dramatic flicks of her hand, speaking in tongues, letting her eyes roll back as she dumped this and that in the cauldron.

Emberlyn was poise and serenity, her movements so fluid they were almost sensual. She was totally in command, the sheer strength of her will spilling from her. Her magick came to her easy, obeyed her every whim as if it adored and would never question her.

And right then, he saw the fundamental difference between how she and her mentor had operated. Millicent had directed her magick with arrogance and entitlement, like a tyrannical boss. Emberlyn brandished hers with confidence and care, ever respectful of this force she channeled as naturally as she moved her arms and legs.

She hadn't only learned from Millicent's successes, he thought. She'd learned from the woman's mistakes as well.

It galled him that he hadn't seen Emberlyn clearly until recently. Maybe it had been a case of self-preservation – if he considered her no better than Rosemary, he could fight wanting her. Because it was precisely the time she'd broken the mating tie that he'd started to *really* struggle to observe her in a negative light.

Whatever the case, he no longer had his guard up around her. Emberlyn wasn't an open book by any means, but she was an uncomplicated person to be around. Balanced. Calm. Steady. Not a game player. And so fucking *capable*.

She handled everything with the ease of someone who had total confidence in her ability to get shit done. He'd never before met anybody so self-sufficient and competent. She didn't need anyone – relied on herself. And she hadn't let the assholes in the coven break her. Everything about her screamed that they'd failed with flying fucking colors.

On the subject of the coven ... 'You ready for the meeting tomorrow?'

'Yup. Clarence seems certain that Gill's fighting a losing battle. I agree with him. The question is what my family will try after that little plot fails, because I highly doubt they'll drop the whole thing so soon. Especially when it'll infuriate them that their case went nowhere.'

Pausing, she added two pinches of sea salt into the potion. 'But enough of them – they'll be taking up plenty of our attention tomorrow. Want to tell me why you had a face like thunder when you first arrived?'

Not really. But he heard himself say, 'I just had to break up a fight between Logan and Neal.'

'Ah. Your brother didn't take the relationship well, then,' she assumed, sympathy washing over her face.

'It made him decide that he was done pining for CeCe. He would have let her and Neal be. But tonight, they both went to our clan's bar knowing that Logan would be there. Things devolved fast. My brother is pissed that she'd want to hurt him that way. While I'm glad he isn't going to keep pushing for a triad, I don't like seeing him so wrecked.'

'It must be disillusioning to realize someone that you love would resort to those measures to manipulate people into dancing to their tune.' Jamming a stopper back into a bottle, she regarded him carefully. 'You feel guilty. Why?'

Ripper felt his shoulders stiffen.

'You don't have to answer if you don't want to, but don't bother denying that I'm right.'

Ripper grunted. 'The night we shared CeCe ... I was hesitant. I didn't think it'd be a good idea. We only ever shared women we didn't care for. But I let myself get talked into it.'

'And you feel that your brother wouldn't be hurting right now if you'd just stuck to your guns.' Pursing her lips, she placed the bottle back down. 'I don't know if that's true. I mean, she didn't just *run* the idea by you. She nagged you to agree. And when you didn't, she tried some underhanded stuff to get her way. I wouldn't be surprised if she's had the triad idea in her mind for a while. If that's true, this might have happened in any case.'

Ripper licked his front teeth, mentally chewing over that. 'You could be right. She said she's accepted that a triad won't happen. I'm not sure I believe that, though.'

'And you came here hoping I'd cook you up a potion that would make her leave you alone? Well, I could. Though Paisley uses a non-magick method and *swears* by it. She'll hold a photo of an ex tightly while sending a *Leave me alone* vibe at it, and then she sticks it in the freezer.'

'The freezer?'

'Uh-huh. She says it works, so I guess you could try it.'

'I might.' He cocked his head. 'Did Michael share you with anyone?'

She double-blinked, apparently taken off-guard by the question. 'He pushed for it once. He was annoyed that I wouldn't agree to it, but when the effects of the full moon wore off he was glad that it hadn't happened.'

'Who did he have in mind?'

'One of his cousins.' Staring into the cauldron, she waved her hand, and the potion stopped bubbling. She gave it one last stir and then nodded, satisfied. 'All done. I just need to cool it down.' A ribbon of magick swished around the pot, presumably cooling it.

As she grabbed several elixir bottles from a cupboard behind her, he said, 'Generally, potions have a shelf-life. Millicent's never did. Do yours?'

'No. There are magickal hacks.' She turned back to the altar and set down the bottles. 'Anyone can use them if they know what they're doing.'

'Why doesn't the coven use them?'

'They probably could. But how are they going to keep their customers coming back regularly if they sell no-shelf-life potions?'

Huh. He hadn't thought of it that way.

'You can still make theirs effective for longer if you stick them in the freezer, but the coven would never admit as much.' She fell silent as she deftly filled each elixir bottle before placing them all in a carrier box, which she then handed to him.

'You lied.'

Her brows dipped. 'About what?'

'You told Kerr that this process is boring to watch.' He fished the correct amount of cash out of his pocket and held it out. 'You lied.'

She took payment from him. '*Or* you just found it entertaining when others wouldn't.'

Possibly. He sure hadn't been entertained when observing Millicent work. More like uncomfortable.

But Emberlyn? She fascinated him. Bewitched him. He looked at her, and he *wanted*.

And he knew he wasn't going to leave without having her.

Just the idea had lust slamming into his system. *She* had slammed into his system. She'd hit him like a bus fucking years ago, and he'd been an idiot to think he could spend his life ignoring it. Acknowledging that to himself brought him something close to relief.

She pottered around – washing her cauldron, returning her ingredients, tidying her altar, extinguishing the incense burner stick – utterly oblivious to the fact that she was going to get royally fucked very soon.

Determination flooded him. He'd come here tonight for this.

It had been his intention all along. He just hadn't conceded it to himself until that moment.

He wanted to lose himself in her; had the distinct feeling that it would be an unparalleled experience.

A voice in his head cautioned him to be careful; that he wouldn't be able to have her only once.

So be it. 'I have a question,' he said as they filed out of the consultation room.

She tossed him a quick look over her shoulder. 'Then ask.'

'You think about Michael a lot?'

She slowed her pace, surprised. 'A lot? No.'

'And when you do?'

Halting in the living room, she turned to face him and shrugged. 'I wonder if he's still alive. And then I hope he's not. Which sounds evil, but he wouldn't want to live in a Rabid state if he had the choice. And there'd be no way to bring him fully back at this point. He's gone beyond that.'

'It doesn't make you evil.'

Her head tipped to the side. 'Why did you want to know if I think about him a lot?'

'Because I don't want to fuck a woman who still considers some part of herself mated.'

CHAPTER FOURTEEN

❦

A burst of shock gripped Emberlyn's muscles, making her freeze. A few times tonight Ripper had taken her off-guard with a comment or question. But this? This took the cake and chomped all the way around its edges.

Without removing his eyes from her, he placed the box of elixirs on the sofa. His pose was casual, but there was nothing casual about his expression. The heat there was *too* hot. And so very dangerous, because it'd be so easy to give into the pull between them ... and he might later regret it.

She watched as his gaze coasted down to her lips and stared, hunger and greed pooling there. Need licked a line up her spine as butterflies danced in her belly. 'Witches aren't on your menu,' she reminded him, a slight break in her voice.

His eyes crawled back up to hers. '*You* are.' He stalked to her, every step slow and deliberate ... until there was only mere inches between them.

Her magick reacted as usual to all that Alpha energy, and it was a struggle to rein it back. Seriously, her magick wanted to own the motherfucker.

'You got my attention years ago. And you wouldn't let it go.' His intent gaze didn't move from her face, as if he was set on noting every shift in her expression.

Caught in the spotlight of his absolute focus, she felt stripped right down to her soul.

Crackling sparks of sexual chemistry fluttered around them like invisible fireflies. The atmosphere turned as charged as a live wire, thick with unbearable tension. A tension that just kept rising, twisting, stretching out.

He lowered his mouth toward hers as he said, 'I've never wanted anything the way I want you.' The gravelly quality to his voice turned molten. 'I feel like I'll go a little insane if I don't have you.'

She drew in a sharp gulp of air that was taut with need. Her body heated, buzzed and felt sexually charged – just like the tension between them.

Staring up at him, she felt . . . trapped. Trapped by the hunger, demands and promises she saw in his eyes.

There was something dangerous about him in that moment. Like a wolf poised to pounce. She knew if she moved one muscle – just one – it would act like a trigger.

This would be a bad idea. Probably. Or not. Honestly, she wasn't sure she really cared. She could barely think.

His gaze skated down to her lips again, pure male greed simmering there. 'You said no man would ever own you. I will. For the length of time I have you under me, you'll be mine. And you'll feel it.'

Ho-ho, what a challenge. 'Don't be so sure.'

His eyes fixed on hers again. 'We'll see which one of us is right.'

She had no idea who moved first, but their mouths collided in a brutally hungry kiss. They went at each other like savages driven to mate – tongues tangling, hands grabbing, fingers digging, teeth nipping.

Her body was like, 'Oh God, finally.' At the same time, it screamed for more. She was practically frantic with the need to answer the cravings that had steadily chewed at her resolve for too long.

Ripper sharply peeled up her dress and gripped her ass tight. He jutted his hips forward, pressing his cock against her clit. 'I gotta have you.'

The world tilted. Her back met the rug. Strong fingers caught the waistband of her underwear. Cloth tore. Her thighs were shoved apart.

And then his mouth was on her pussy.

Her head fell back. *Oh God.* She dug her hand into his hair, riding the maddening raspy pumps of his velvet tongue.

From what she'd experienced, male werewolves loved going down on a woman. Ripper seemed to be no different, greedily licking and lapping and sinking his tongue as deep as it could go. He expertly pushed her into an orgasm mega fast, trapping a scream in her throat as pleasure racked her body in shuddering waves.

Her eyes closed, she slumped to the rug, breathing hard. She heard buttons snap open and then a wrapper tear.

Emberlyn had just forced her eyelids to lift when he slid up her body and lowered his weight onto her, yanking down the top of her dress to bare her bra-clad breasts. He deftly flicked open the front catch and latched onto her nipple, sucking *so hard*. He lavished attention on first one nipple then the other, teasing both into tight throbbing buds.

'I want you in me.' She dug her fingers into his back. So much muscle and strength and power there. It was all entirely too drugging. 'Hurry.'

'No, I'm going in slow.'

Emberlyn was about to fervently object, but then she felt the *very* broad head of his cock inch inside her. Her eyes went wide at the sharp burn. 'Oh, fuck.' She hadn't gotten a look at his shaft; hadn't realized he was quite so thick.

'Shh, be still.' He lazily rolled his hips forward, forcing his dick deeper, groaning deep in his throat. 'Your pussy is so tight.' He put his mouth to her ear. 'My pussy tonight.'

The possessive claim should have outraged her, but there was something arousing about the blatant nerve of it. For the majority of her life, people had been wary of her – she'd made sure of it. It had kept her safe, for the most part. But the flip side? It had isolated her slightly. Aside from Millicent, Michael and the twins, people had always been on their guard around Emberlyn to some degree.

No guy had ever dared handle her this way. Not even Michael. But Ripper just *took*.

He grabbed her. Pulled her. Held her down. Positioned her however and wherever he wanted.

And the pressure of his dick filling her to the point of bursting was glorious.

He swept a hand up her thigh, side and cupped her breast, a hint of possession in the hard press of his fingertips, leaving behind a tingling sensation – and she knew what the latter meant.

She hissed, pricking his hips with her nails. 'I didn't say you could scent-mark me.'

Releasing her breast, he delved his hand into her hair. 'It's already done. My scent is sinking into your skin now. It won't wear off for days.' He bit her earlobe. 'You like that I've done it; like that I do what I want with you.'

God damn the bastard for picking up on that. She sent a rush of magick over him. 'Now you smell of me.' So *ha*.

A growl eased out of him as his free hand clutched her ass tight. Then he was moving, his hips violently snapping forward again and again. Every heavy jut of his hips forced his dick excruciatingly deep – it was bliss, it was pain, it was more than she could take.

But she had no intention of asking him to stop.

'Knew you'd feel good,' he said with a thick grunt. 'Fucking perfect.' The hand in her hair kept her head at the angle he wanted it, so he could stare right into her eyes.

She clasped his nape, lost to the feel of his cock dragging over her supersensitive inner walls as he pounded into her like an animal. It was savage. Brutal. A *taking*.

She'd had rough sex before, but this was different. So basic and primitive that there was something depersonalizing about it. It stripped her of every layer. Witch. Woman. *Person*.

She felt overwhelmed and possessed and downright *owned*. It unnerved her, but it didn't stop her from dragging her nails down his back in demand. 'Harder.'

He gave her what she wanted, every slam of his cock making her breasts jiggle. Right then, he was pure sexual aggression – and she reveled in it.

Her moans turned louder and breathier as she took his increasingly brutal thrusts. The friction soon became too much. 'I'm going to come.'

He roughly palmed her breast. 'Do it. Come.'

She arched into his hand, and the sharp *prick* of his claws knocked her over the edge. Her body shook as wave after wave of glorious white-hot pleasure overtook her.

Above her, Ripper lost it – unleashed every bit of strength and control as he chased his own release. Finally, he speared his cock deep and went still, his shaft throbbing as he growled into her neck.

They both went pliant, their bodies tremoring, their breathing all over the place.

Emberlyn pulled herself together enough to say, 'If you regret this, I'd advise you not to say it. Can't promise I won't give you a pig's tail on your forehead or something.'

He didn't lift his face from her throat as he spoke. 'No regrets here.'

Oh. Good. 'Same,' she said on a sated sigh. 'Same.'

Passing the living-room doorway the next morning, Emberlyn did a double-take and slowed to a stop. Because Lucie sat on the spot where Ripper had last night feverishly fucked Emberlyn, and the feline was staring at her haughtily.

Emberlyn notched up her chin. 'I feel you judging me, but I give not one shit.' She swanned into the kitchen, where she went about making breakfast.

Despite having showered, moisturized and spritzed herself with perfume, she could smell Ripper on her – a faint earthy, woodsy scent. She couldn't really complain that he'd marked her, considering she'd temporarily covered him in the scent of her magick. It hadn't seemed to bother him, to her surprise.

He had left shortly after they'd fixed their clothes, wanting to check on Logan one last time – it hadn't been an excuse to leave; she'd heard the honesty and concern in his voice.

Before walking out, Ripper had pinned her with a look that said he wasn't done with her. Good. She wasn't done with him, either.

When she'd found him on the porch last night, she'd known that something was wrong. It had been evident in his dull expression, the tension in his large frame, and the defensive note in his tone.

She hadn't understood why he would come to her of all people –
only the twins had ever sought her out when needing to confide
in someone – but Emberlyn hadn't been about to send him away.

The last thing she'd expected was for them to fuck on her
living-room floor. Which had been positively spectacular.
Something, however, had been niggling at her since she woke;
something that would put a downer on last night, if true ...

Was it possible that he had – perhaps only subconsciously –
fucked her to flip CeCe the finger?

Emberlyn settled at her table with a cup of tea and toasted
bagel. The more she considered the matter, the more she
doubted its accuracy. Particularly since he'd scent-marked
her – werewolves didn't idly do such a thing. Still, the prospect
continued to nibble at her.

Putting it all out of her mind for now, she ate her breakfast,
snatched her purse and drove to the town hall. She spotted a
few other familiar cars parked around, telling her that her family
had already arrived.

Exiting her vehicle, she glanced around. There was no sign of
Ripper or his truck. But as she began to clamber the wide white
steps of the town hall, another werewolf caught up to her. Sadly.

The Alpha gave her a smarmy smile. 'Emberlyn.'

'Carver,' she greeted flatly.

He clasped his hands. 'Ready for the meeting?'

She paused on the top step near a tall column. 'I am.'

'You're not having second thoughts about going through with
this?' He grimaced, a flash of compassion in his eyes. 'I would,
in your shoes. It'll be hard to prove that Millicent was sane at
the end. Or ever.'

'Hmm.'

'You know, you could always drop this here and now,' he ever
so innocently suggested. 'I'm sure your family will agree to not—'

'Save it, Carver. You don't care how I feel, or how they feel, or how this affects anyone but *you*. Don't insult my intelligence by implying I should believe otherwise.'

His expression hardening, he moved closer. 'You won't win this, you—' He stopped dead in his tracks, his nostrils flaring.

Ah, he'd picked up Ripper's scent on her skin. 'You were saying?' she prodded.

A muscle in his jaw flexed. 'He chose not to listen to my warnings about you, then.'

'You warned Ripper to steer clear of me?'

'It would have been for his own good.'

She felt her lips quirk. 'Don't tell me a strong wolf like you is leery of a little witch like me. You sure you're Alpha material?'

His eyes flashing, he walked toward—

'Step back, Carver,' a gravelly voice calmly ordered, a hint of menace there.

She looked to see Ripper coming at them from the side. Her system spluttered like a faulty engine, overwhelmed by all that raw, gritty masculinity. It drummed at her skin, waking and charging her nerve-endings.

He kept his dangerously intent gaze locked on the other were-wolf as he reached her. 'You're standing too close to Emberlyn for my liking.'

Carver took a slow but very notable step away. 'Getting involved with her ... you have balls, Ripper, I'll give you that.' He walked off, his mouth flat.

Ripper's gaze landed on her, the menace rapidly receding. His feral energy swept over her, tugging at her magick like a damn magnet. Tension rose, the air all but molten with memories of last night.

'You look calm,' he observed, 'so I'm guessing he didn't say or do anything that pissed you off.'

'All he did was make himself look stupid – thinking I'd buy he cares if I'm worried that the meeting won't go as I hope.' She briefly relayed the conversation. 'Oh, and he said he warned you about me.'

Ripper grunted, stepping into her. 'He told me it was a mistake to ally myself with you. I disagreed. I disagree with most of the shit that comes out of his mouth.'

'I think the majority of people outside his clan do.'

He parted his lips, his eyes flitting over her face, and she thought he'd bring up what happened last night. But, instead, he bit down on his lower lip.

She rolled back her shoulders. 'Don't know about you, but I'm all for getting this meeting over with.' And getting some space from him so she could get a reprieve from the mess he made of her body.

'I'm with you on that.' He pushed open the door and tipped his chin, indicating for her to enter first, and then took up the rear.

In the foyer, Clarence grinned broadly. 'Ah, there you both are.'

'Morning, Clarence.' She glanced around the empty space. 'I'm guessing the others are already seated.'

He confirmed that with a nod, stepping a little closer. 'I suggest we ...' He paused, his gaze flying to Ripper as his nostrils flared. 'Well, that's a surprise.'

Tell me about it.

Clarence cleared his throat, gestured for them to follow, and began walking.

Plastering on the bright smile that she knew made people nervous, Emberlyn followed the lawyer through the pointed-arch doorway and into the grand hall with Ripper at her back.

The rectangular space had oak-paneled walls and patterned

marble flooring. Two columns of benches were separated by a narrow walkway. One column was taken up by her family, Tyra, Sera, Carver, Reena, Ward and a few other members of the coven. All faced the dark and striking male sitting at a table on the elevated platform.

Normally, Ripper, Carver and Reena would be up there as well. But, being the only impartial member of the council in this case, Shane would be handling it alone.

Though many in the hall turned, Emberlyn didn't meet any gazes as she followed Clarence to the front row of the empty column. He indicated for Emberlyn and Ripper to slide in first and then joined them, which placed her between both were-wolves – a no doubt deliberate move on their part, feeling she would be better protected this way.

Tyra slid Emberlyn a quick look, a smug light in her eyes that said she was sure she'd win this case. Oh, that light wouldn't be there for long.

Though Sera was Tyra's assistant, there was no actual need for her to be present. The little bitch no doubt wanted the pleasure of seeing Emberlyn legally lose the manor.

Shane glanced at his watch. 'The meeting is due to start in a few minutes but, since we're all here, we might as well begin. I'm assuming neither of you needs more time to speak with your clients,' he said, looking from Clarence to Tyra.

Tyra took papers from Sera. 'Actually—'

'We can start, then,' declared Shane. 'We'll hear from the applicant first. As I understand it, Tyra, your client wishes to have her mother's will declared invalid.'

'That is correct,' Tyra confirmed.

'And this is on the grounds that, in her belief, Millicent wasn't sound of mind?'

'It is, yes.'

Shane's gaze slid to Gill. 'Why are you so sure of this?'

Gill squared her shoulders. 'My mother may not have been a good person, but she loved her family in her way. She would never have treated her children and grandchildren so unfairly as to only bequeath them small or petty things. Not if she was of sound mind. The will can't possibly reflect her *true* last wishes.'

Shane let out a pensive hum. 'I have read a copy of it, so I'm aware of what each of the beneficiaries inherited. What exactly is it you believe that it should have stated?'

'That as the eldest I would inherit the manor, my brother would be given the land and her small fortune be distributed amongst her grandchildren – Mari, Ames and Emberlyn.'

Oh, how reasonable Gill sounded. Given that none of the others objected, it had to be a case of them coming up with this together.

Shane skimmed his gaze over Dez, his son and Mari. 'You agree?'

They all responded in the affirmative.

'In truth,' Dez added, 'my mother did not at any point in her life have the testamentary capacity to make a valid will. As we all know, she regularly performed magick that most consider taboo. She was a lone practitioner. A recluse. Always looked haggard and unkempt. She exhibited all the signs of somebody who is mentally disturbed.'

Ames nodded. 'We all attempted to help her, but she didn't want to be helped. The fact that she left land to an Alpha werewolf shows she was not thinking rationally.'

Shane's brow lifted. 'How so?'

It was Gill who responded. 'She wasn't thinking of the consequences. Reena's plans to expand Bellcrest were no secret. My mother approved of them. It makes no sense that she'd then bequeath the land to Ripper.'

'How do you know that she approved of them?' asked Shane.

'She told me so. Carver was there.'

Behind Gill, Carver raised a hand. 'I was. Millicent praised the drawings I showed her of the houses we intended to build.'

Shane's brows winged up. 'Millicent dished out praise? An anomaly, I would think.'

Emberlyn inwardly snorted. It wasn't an anomaly. It was a crock of shit.

'She was softer near the end,' Mari piped up. 'Maybe because she knew her time was almost up. It'd explain why she openly spoke of who would inherit what.'

Shane folded his arms. 'And what did she explicitly state?'

'She told us all at different points that we were either the main or sole beneficiary,' replied Mari. 'If was as if she didn't always know who she was speaking to, or didn't remember what the will stated. But she was always *very* clear that Emberlyn would inherit nothing. That doesn't line up with the wishes in her will.'

Shane twisted his mouth. 'Do you have witnesses outside of your family who can confirm that she made these promises to you and laid out these terms?'

'I was present for most of these conversations,' Tyra claimed, the lying little bitch. 'As was Sera.'

Nodding, Sera said, 'Millicent kept calling me by my mother's name, clearly confused. She would also ask where Avery was, so lost.'

Bullshit. Millicent hadn't been in any way 'confused' or 'lost' near the end.

'At no point did she even hint at leaving the manor to whoever could manage to gain entrance,' Tyra continued. 'That she would use such an extremely outdated tradition seems yet another sign that she wasn't thinking rationally. All my client wants is for her mother's true wishes to be reflected here. As things stand, they are not.'

'Hmm.' Shane cut his gaze to Clarence. 'I understand that your client feels her claim on Black Willow Manor is not false and shouldn't be rendered invalid.'

'That is so,' Clarence confirmed.

Shane looked at Ripper. 'And you, similarly, feel that your claim to the land is fair.'

'I do,' Ripper firmly stated. 'It originally belonged to Lupin. I am his descendant. Had I inherited the manor, the Vautiers would then claim it should be returned to them due to them being descendants of Lilith. I fail to see the difference.'

Shane inclined his head. 'Interesting point.' He returned his focus to Emberlyn. 'Do you feel your grandmother was of sound mind?'

'Millicent was eccentric to a large and varied degree,' Emberlyn allowed, 'but she was very much sane. She couldn't have controlled her magick if that were not the case.'

Ward leaned forward. 'Actually, that is—'

'My question wasn't directed at *you*,' Shane told him. 'I've heard from the applicant and those on her side of the argument. Now I want to hear from Emberlyn and Ripper.'

Ward bristled, looking as though he would argue, but he subsided when Reena rested a hand over his.

'No one here needs to take my word for anything,' said Emberlyn. 'One of the signatures on the will is that of a doctor whom Millicent asked to verify that she had mental capacity. She also wrote a letter that puts the wishes of her will into context.'

'Letter?' echoed Gill.

Shane's attention shifted to her. 'You knew nothing of it?'

Gill shook her head wildly.

'Millicent left it to me in an envelope she instructed to be given to Emberlyn should anyone attempt to overturn the will,' said Clarence, plucking a piece of paper from his leather satchel. 'I have it here and am happy to read it aloud.'

'Go on,' invited Shane.

Clarence cleared his throat.

Emberlyn, if you're reading this letter then my suspicions are just and my children are in fact hoping to have my will declared invalid. Such loving children they are. I don't blame them for not thinking much of me — they have good reason for that. Why should they love a mother who isn't a real mother? But it gives them no excuse to demand that my last wishes be ignored. I could tan their asses for that.

Despite the crap they tell me, I don't believe for a second that either of them want the manor for themselves. They only wish to sell it. Still, I've given them the benefit of the doubt by allowing them to win over the manor themselves. If they're contesting the will, it means they did not; that you now hold it. The house will have sensed what I myself strongly feel — they care nothing for it and have no intention of nurturing it with their own magick. And if that's the case, where's the wrong in it going to the one person who adores it?

You, I know, will cherish the manor. You, I know, will raise children there who will also grow to love it. That's how it should be.

Gill loved the dollhouse as a child, you know. And Dez's father taught him to drive in my truck. Mari is obsessed with the brooch she stole, and Ames was a master chess player as a child. In other words, I have not bequeathed random objects to them. They will inherit things that have meaning to them, they just probably won't find that enough.

As for my leaving the land to Jax Stone, it's only fair. The land should rightfully be with a descendant of Lupin, just as the manor should always home a Vautier. It's as simple as that. I also know he won't let it become a pretty housing estate — the coven doesn't need one. It'll actually be safer for them not to use my land, since someone has made several attempts to poison it.

I have dug up three curse jars in the last six months. I don't yet know who buried them there. What I do know is that my days are numbered, so I'm not sure I'll figure out who did it before I pass. If I don't, I'm relying on you to do it. They need to be exposed and dealt with — I trust that you'll be creatively vengeful about it.

As for my children and other grandchildren, my hope is that they come to understand why I made the decisions I made regarding the will. I don't expect them to like or approve of those decisions, only to respect them. If they cannot, it's unfortunate. But it changes nothing.

Be well, stay safe and live—

'This is bullshit!' Dez burst out, jumping to his feet.

—large. P.S. Tell Dez, it isn't bullshit at all.

Clarence looked at Shane, lowering the letter to his side. 'That's it.'

CHAPTER FIFTEEN

Ripper scanned the faces of Emberlyn's relatives. All were furious, but only Mari appeared somewhat defeated by the letter. The other three seemed ready to burn shit down.

The rest of the coven exchanged flustered looks, aside from Tyra, who stared intently at the paper Clarence held as if her glare alone could set it on fire. Ripper wondered if, for her, this was like being beaten by Emberlyn all over again, because it was perfectly apparent that Tyra had meant to use this legal battle to hurt her.

'The letter makes no difference to anything!' Dez asserted, even as he allowed Ames to urge him back into his seat. 'She still wasn't of sound mind. Period.'

Ignoring him, Shane rubbed at his nape. 'Forgive my ignorance here, but what is a curse jar?'

'Simply speaking,' Emberlyn began, 'it's a glass jar that will contain things such as broken glass and blood; it will be spelled to cause ill-intent to a person, animal, object or place.'

'I see.' Shane's frown deepened. 'Why would someone wish to curse the land?'

'There's no reason anyone in the coven would,' Tyra clipped. 'We all supported Reena's plans to build a new estate. Millicent has to have lied about the curse jars.'

'I highly doubt it,' Ripper cut in. 'Emberlyn found one last week. I was there.'

Ames snorted. 'She's the likeliest person to have tried cursing the land in the first place.'

Ripper bristled on behalf of Emberlyn. But she didn't seem either offended or upset. In fact, she regarded her cousin as if he was simple.

'If I'd wanted to damage the land, I wouldn't have used something as small-time as a curse jar,' said Emberlyn, her tone haughty. 'Whoever it was, they do shoddy spell work.'

It was bait, he sensed. An effort to make the culprit reveal themselves in some way. But none of the witches in the room currently seemed more agitated than any other.

'It has to have been somebody outside the coven,' Tyra insisted. 'We had big plans for that land.'

'Either one of you didn't care too much about that, or they hoped they could push Millicent to sell the acres if it turned barren,' Emberlyn said to her, earning herself a narrow-eyed look from Tyra.

Unscrewing a cap from a bottle of water, Ames threw Emberlyn a dirty look. 'I still say it was you.'

She softly flicked her hand, magick dust briefly peppering the air. That easily, the liquid in Ames's bottle turned black.

As her cousin gawked at it, she smiled wide. 'You still think I need a curse jar?'

A ball of magick appeared in Ames's hand and then – fast as a motherfucker – he pitched it at Emberlyn.

Her hand shot up and caught it.

Gasps flew out of the witches, every one of them going motionless.

Ripper glared at Ames, a growl of fury rumbling in his chest. He was about to rise and cross to the little shit, but she planted a staying palm on his thigh.

The coven watched through wide eyes as Emberlyn casually twisted the ball of magick this way and that. Then, holding Ames's gaze, she snapped her fist closed and crushed the ball to nothing.

Her cousin paled. Gazes zipped away from her. Reena closed her eyes in what seemed to be exasperation.

Ripper didn't get why they'd reacted that way. Didn't care to figure it out right then. His focus was on her piece-of-shit cousin.

He growled again, catching Ames's attention. 'Unless you want me to slice off your fucking tongue and make you eat it, you won't dare try to harm her again.' The threat was low, menacing and laced with protectiveness.

Shane sighed. 'This is why I don't like presiding over witchy matters. Someone always ends up tossing magick around.'

Clarence's lips twitched. 'Is it much different from how a punch always seems to get thrown during werewolf meetings?'

'I suppose not,' mumbled Shane. 'All right, let's circle back to why we're really here. The will.' He paused. 'The letter does shine a very bright light on things.'

Tyra's shoulders went stiff. 'It doesn't change the situation,' she objected. 'Every sentence in it is as invalid as the will – Millicent was incapable of making sound decisions.'

'That isn't the impression I get from that letter,' said Shane. 'Her thought processes seem clear. I hear no indication there that she lacked mental capacity. Her relatives inherited *exactly* what she wanted them to have.'

Ripper sensed some tension slip from Emberlyn's frame.

Gill's face went crimson. 'But the manor—'

'You believe it should go to you, I know,' said Shane. 'But you did have the chance to earn the house's approval. Your mother ensured you had that chance.'

'Emberlyn is the last person who should be living in it,' Dez threw in.

Shane frowned. 'Why? Because you don't like it? That's not reason to remove her from the manor. You talk as if she stole it from under you. As I understand it, she didn't object to you, Gill, Mari or Ames attempting to enter the house first. She stood back and waited.'

Ward spat a curse. 'She should have been driven out of this town years ago, should have—'

'Be very, very careful,' Ripper warned him, quite frankly fed the fuck up with the coven tossing verbal shit at her.

Ward pressed his lips closed, averting his gaze.

'We're not here to discuss Emberlyn,' began Shane, impatient. 'She isn't on trial here. The purpose of this meeting is to establish whether there's reason for Millicent's will to be rendered invalid. The fact that she anticipated this would happen and took measures to prevent Gill's claim from being successful shows two things. One, she was very much aware of what she was doing when she wrote her will. Two, she was equally aware of what the consequences could be. That demonstrates a soundness of mind.'

Gill looked desperately up at Tyra, who gave a helpless shrug.

Mari leaned forward in her seat. 'We should at least be compensated for how the will breaks the promises that Millicent made to us.'

'You cannot prove she made those promises,' Shane pointed out. 'You have no impartial witnesses.'

Sera lifted a hand. 'I was there. So was Tyra.'

'Both of you legally represent the daughter of the woman who wants the manor for herself. You're also both people who loathe the witch who currently occupies it. That makes you far from impartial.'

Dez's lips thinned. 'The land—'

'I see no reason why it should be taken from Ripper,' Shane told him. 'He has more of a rightful claim to it than anyone in this room.'

'Millicent approved of my mother's plans for that land,' Tyra said to Shane, her hands balling up.

'So you all claim,' Clarence cut in. 'But this letter from Millicent contradicts those claims, as does her will. They carry more weight here.'

Shane dipped his chin in agreement. 'Both those documents are in Millicent's very own words. In this case, it is her words that matter most.'

'Carver confirmed that Millicent approved of the plans,' Sera piped up.

Shane waved that away. 'He's no more impartial than any of you.'

Carver's back straightened. 'You calling me a liar, Shane?' he asked, a dangerous note to his tone.

Shane met his gaze evenly, visibly unconcerned. 'I find it easier to believe that you lied here today than that Millicent praised you in any way.' He rose to his feet. 'It's my opinion that the conditions of the will should remain in place. That's all.' With that, he turned away and swanned off the platform.

As shouting broke out among the coven, Clarence glanced from Emberlyn to Ripper and said, 'I think that went well.'

'*This is a fucking injustice!*' Gill ranted.

Emberlyn's lips hitched up. 'Very, *very* well.' She held her hand out to him. 'Thank you for everything.'

Clarence's mouth curved as he shook her hand. 'No thanks necessary.' He then exchanged nods with Ripper.

Meanwhile, Gill and Dez yelled at Tyra to 'do something'. Reena and Ward hurried over and insisted they calm down. The rest of the coven left, very subdued and avoiding Emberlyn's gaze as if their lives depended on it. Carver stalked out, his cheeks flushed, agitation in every step.

'Shall we go?' proposed Emberlyn, standing.

Ripper and Clarence followed suit. Without looking at the coven, the three of them made a slow and dignified exit. Outside, they exchanged a few words before Clarence headed off.

Ripper turned to Emberlyn. 'I'll walk you to your car.'

She blinked. 'Why?'

'Because I want to.'

She gave a shrug and began walking toward her vehicle. 'Thanks, by the way.'

He felt his brows meet in honest confusion. 'For what?'

'It's hardwired into you to jump to the defense of those under your protection. But when I gestured for you to let me handle the situation with Ames, you didn't ignore me. That mattered.'

Ripper bit into the inside of his lower lip. 'Gotta be honest, I can't promise I'll always stand down when you ask. It'll depend on just what kind of threat you're facing and if that threat heeds your warning. If Ames had struck again in there, I wouldn't have sat back while he attacked you.'

'I know. I wouldn't have expected you to. I just—'

'Can't ever look weak around those people,' he finished as they reached her car. 'I get it. I've seen how they are with you. They sling mud at you all the time.' It was starting to *really* piss him off. 'They'd pounce on any display of weakness you showed.' He edged closer to her. 'But, Emberlyn, having backup doesn't detract from your strength, it *adds* to it. Let them see that you have a fucking werewolf clan ready to go to bat for you if needed.'

She watched him for a long moment, her gaze searching his. 'Two-way street. You and your clan have my magick at your disposal.'

'Speaking of magick . . . what happened in there? You caught Ames's magickal blow, and the coven went weird. Why?' Ripper didn't know enough about the mechanics of magick to understand.

'It was the equivalent of me catching a ball of sharp, jagged glass and effortlessly crushing it with only my hand while in no way causing damage to myself.'

Ripper did a slow blink. She'd said it with a casual tone, like it was no big deal. Going by the reactions of those in the grand hall, that wasn't the case at all. 'Did you know in advance that it wouldn't harm you to catch it?'

'I figured it probably wouldn't.'

'You *figured*?'

She chuckled. 'Kidding. Yes, I knew. But they didn't. It spooked them because it isn't easy to hold magick that's not your own – it should be like trying to grab oxygen out of the air. That I destroyed the ball without causing harm to myself only unnerved them more.'

'When you say it isn't easy, you're playing things down, aren't you?'

She only gave him a slow smile. So secretive, this witch. But he sensed that another reason she was stingy with information was that she was so very unused to people being intrigued enough to ask her such questions.

Fishing her keys out of her purse, she tipped her head to the side. 'Not to nag, but have you found a wolf who'll Change Paisley?'

'Crew has offered to do it. If she's happy with that, he can do it as soon as she'd like.'

Emberlyn's eyes lit up. 'She'll be excited. I know your agreement to accept her into your clan had nothing at all to do with me, but thank you. She's wanted this for as long as I can remember.'

As Emberlyn opened her car door, he caught it and said, 'I want you to know . . .'

A slender brow lifted. 'What?'

'I wouldn't have left so fast last night if I hadn't needed to check on my brother. I don't leave a woman the second I'm dressed – I'm not that guy.'

'I know.' She twisted her mouth, a cautious glint in her gaze. 'Tell me honestly, though. How much of what happened was you getting back at CeCe or venting your frustration about the situation?'

Ripper hadn't considered that her mind would go there. An oversight on his part, really, since he'd turned up at the manor all worked up about the shit show at the bar. It was no real surprise that Emberlyn was asking herself – and him – that question.

He pinned her gaze with his. 'What happened with me and you had nothing to do with her. Did it *feel* like anyone else was on my mind?'

'Not in the moment, no. But then this morning, I started to wonder.'

'You want raw honesty? I fucked you because I wanted you so bad I ached with it. That's it. She had not one thing to do with it.'

Emberlyn gave a slow but accepting nod.

'We both ignored this thing between us for years. We've been dancing around it since we became allies. I don't think there's a way we *wouldn't* have acted on it. It was just a matter of when.'

Her wariness having steadily drained away, she hummed. 'You may be right about the latter. I just didn't think you'd get past your reservations about witches. But then you did, and it happened on the same evening you were furious with a woman you deeply care for. So I had to know for sure if that had spurred it.'

'I get it. And I want you to *feel* sure. Do you?'

'Yes. You wouldn't lie about it.'

Mollified by the certainty in her words, he let out a long breath. 'The fact that I scent-marked you should have put that worry to rest.'

Her eyes narrowed. 'You sure don't seem sorry you did it.'

His shoulders lifted and fell in an unapologetic shrug. 'Why would I be? I don't want anyone else touching you. It makes perfect sense that I'd want to make that clear.'

She looked away, sighing. 'Werewolf logic.'

He leaned forward slightly, subtly sniffing her. 'I wasn't the only one who left a mark. I can still smell your magick on me.' He liked that indication that the possessiveness wasn't one-sided.

'You haven't asked when it will fade. Are you interested in knowing?'

'Not really.' Ripper didn't think she'd permanently mark him, or that she'd refuse to remove the scent if he asked, so he wasn't concerned. He backed up a step. 'Don't forget to pass on what I said to Paisley. You can let me know her response later.'

'Later?'

'Yeah, later when I turn up at your place to have you again. You had to know that was coming.' Before she had a chance to say anything, he turned and walked away.

The moment Emberlyn entered the hub's empty reception area, she was greeted with an almighty scowl from Paisley, who was being condescendingly patted on the head by her twin.

Behind the desk, she slammed her hands on her hips. 'Ripper put his scent on you and you didn't tell me? Seriously?' She threw up her arms. 'I find out everything second hand with you.'

'Not everything,' Emberlyn contradicted, approaching the desk. 'And I fully intended to tell you this morning. It just seems that someone else beat me to it. Who?'

'One of Carver's clan. He came in with some laundry five minutes ago; said he heard from his Alpha that you smelled of Ripper. I'm assuming this means you two have been sexing each other up – something else you haven't told me.'

Joining her friends behind the desk, Emberlyn rolled her eyes. 'Enough with the whining. We've only had sex once. It happened last night. What did you want me to do, call you straight after?'

'*Obviously.*'

Kage snorted and then leaned into Emberlyn. 'Oh, yeah. I smell him on you.'

Paisley mimicked his move. 'I can only pick up a faint whiff of a masculine scent. I wouldn't be able to tell whose it was. Considering he marked you, I'm guessing he doesn't intend for last night to be a one-time thing.'

'I got that impression,' said Emberlyn.

Paisley tossed her a playful snarl. 'Lucky bitch. He's *yowzah*.'

'That's one way to put it.'

Kage folded his arms. 'Tell us about the meeting. All I've heard is that it went in the favor of both you and Ripper. Carver's apparently furious about that.'

'He looked it when he left.' Emberlyn gave them a quick run-down of the meeting.

Kage scowled. 'I can't believe that little shit Ames struck out at you.'

'I did contaminate his water.'

'But you didn't hurt him, you were just illustrating how easy it would be for you to contaminate anything.'

'And I think I got my message across, but I suspect they'll still blame me for the curse jar activity.'

'*Another* thing you kept to yourself,' Paisley snarked.

'The land is no longer mine, so it wasn't my business to share,' Emberlyn pointed out. 'Ripper wanted to keep it quiet.'

She only sniffed. 'Well, I'm glad that the will wasn't overturned.'

'I doubted it would happen,' said Kage, 'but I was worried all the same. Mostly because I know you'd burn down Bellcrest before you cowed to any demands for you to give up the manor.'

'Am I that predictable?' asked Emberlyn.

He snickered. 'No, I just know how much you love that house. And since the moment you began fighting back as a kid, you've never let the coven push you around. You wouldn't ever go back to a time when they got to bully you.'

No, Emberlyn wouldn't. If the majority of the coven wished to hate her, they were welcome to do so – it was no skin off her nose. She didn't care about being *liked*, she cared about being left to live her life in peace.

'I hate that they make out like *you're* the problem,' said Paisley. 'The only true problem they have with you is that you're so powerful they can't take you on. You're not a bad person, aside from your habit of not keeping your bestie well informed.'

'We're still on that, huh?'

'We'll *stay* on it until you shape up regarding this matter.'

Hoping to change the subject, Emberlyn pointed at the panda studs in Paisley's ears. 'Cute earrings.'

'Yeah, if you're seven,' Kage playfully sniped. 'Or childish – that fits.'

Paisley bristled. 'I may be in touch with my inner little girl, but I'm not childish.'

'You collect stuffies,' he reminded her.

'Collect, not *play with*. Lots of people collect toys and fig-urines, mongrel.'

He wagged a finger. 'You can't call me a mongrel now that I'm a werewolf.'

'Why? Because it's made you sensitive?'

'No. Because it's considered a very big insult to werewolves.'

'Bro, it's always an insult. And the bigger, *the better*.'

'Anyway,' Emberlyn cut in, 'I have a little something you'll want to hear, Paisley.'

Her gaze gleamed with interest. 'Do go on.'

'Ripper said that Crew has offered to put you through the Change.'

Paisley's eyes went wide. 'Wow. Okay. Right.' She puffed out a breath, cupping the back of her head. 'Damn, this is really gonna happen. Did Ripper say when it'll take place?'

'He said it can be as soon as you like.'

'Tell him I'm happy to do it asap.' Paisley gave a little clap, her smile bright as the sun. 'I'm so excited. It feels a little surreal. I wasn't sure it would ever actually happen.'

'*Always* copying me,' Kage muttered tauntingly.

His sister's eyes narrowed. 'One thing. Name one thing you've done that I've copied.'

'Okay.' He lifted his chin. 'When we were five, you got so jealous I could talk to "invisible people" that you invented an imaginary friend.'

Paisley's head jerked back. 'No, I didn't.'

'Oh, you forgot Echo?'

'He was real.'

'Then how come I couldn't see him?'

'Because you weren't looking hard enough, and he blended with the background – that's what geckos do.'

Kage's brows flitted together. 'Wait, he was a gecko?'

'Yes.'

'Back to what we were talking about just now,' Emberlyn again interjected, 'would you like me to come with you while you break the news to your mom and dad, Paisley?'

She sighed. 'No, I like you too much to put you through that. Speaking of parents … Michael's will hear that Ripper scent-marked you. Since it's not something werewolves do lightly, they'll guess that you two are sleeping together. I don't think they'll react well to it. Just saying.'

Emberlyn sighed, her shoulders dropping. 'I kind of wish you hadn't.'

CHAPTER SIXTEEN

Driving toward the manor after she'd finished her shift at the hub, Emberlyn felt her brow crease. A familiar vehicle was parked outside her home, and an equally familiar couple leaned against it. *Ethel and Thad.*

She doubted they'd been sent here by her family or Reena on some mission to convince her to give up the manor. Emberlyn had never been close to the twins' parents, so she'd have no reason to oblige them in anything. While they weren't rude to her, they weren't pleasant toward her, either.

Pulling up outside the manor, Emberlyn switched off the engine, nabbed her purse and then unfurled from the vehicle. 'Ethel, Thad,' she greeted.

Wearing weak – and somewhat awkward – smiles, they took slow, tentative steps toward her.

As always, Ethel had styled the same russet-brown hair she'd passed down to her children in a severe high bun. Like Paisley, she was short and curvy. *Unlike* her daughter, she had a strident, haughty, off-putting manner.

A single look at Thad was enough for a person to sense that he was positively meticulous. Well dressed and clean shaven, he kept his thick dark hair short and neatly combed. She had no clue where Kage's tall build came from, because Thad was average height.

Emberlyn locked the car with her fob. 'I'd invite you in, but . . .' It would be senseless. They'd never set foot in the manor, too opposed to the crafts that had been practiced there.

Ethel cleared her throat. 'We're fine out here.' She paused. 'I'm sure you know of Paisley's sudden interest in taking the Change.'

Emberlyn wouldn't say it was *sudden*. More that the couple in front of her had dismissed Paisley's 'interest', not taking it seriously – until now.

'I can see why she would wish to do this,' Ethel went on. 'She and Kage may bicker frequently but they are exceedingly close. It is only natural that she may feel left behind now that he has altered his lifestyle.'

Altered his lifestyle? Such a minor term for 'becoming a werewolf'. A process that had changed him on a molecular level.

'It is not surprising that she might feel driven to close the gap between them by following in his footsteps,' said Ethel, 'but it's no true reason to take the Change.'

'It wouldn't be something she could undo,' Thad cut in, a hard glint in his moss-green eyes – the only physical trait that the twins had inherited from him. 'You've seen what happens to witches who turn werewolf and regret it. They miss their connection with their magick so much that they start fighting their new reality – shifting as little as possible, resisting the urge to run with their clan on full moons, isolating themselves from other werewolves.'

Emberlyn had witnessed for herself just how tortured these people could become. Some had turned up on her doorstep, hoping she might know some spell that could reverse the Change. Unfortunately for them, no such spell existed.

'We'd like you to talk to Paisley,' he continued. 'She listens to you. She heeds your advice. Tell her what a terrible idea it would be to give up being a witch.'

Emberlyn inwardly sighed, wondering if maybe she should have seen this coming. Neither Ethel nor Thad ever asked her for anything, but she supposed it wasn't a shocker that they'd beat back their dislike of her if it meant getting what they wanted in this.

'I've spoken to Paisley about this many times,' she told them. 'Since she was a teenager she has talked about taking the Change one day. I suspect it's partly because she doesn't feel properly accepted by the coven – not only for being a twin, but for not being a strong witch. She feels she has nothing to lose here.'

Ethel frowned. 'Of course she does! She would have to live without her connection to her magick. Can you imagine losing yours?'

'No, but I'm not Paisley. What's right for me isn't necessarily what's right for her – and vice versa.'

'If you really care for her, you will convince her not to go through with it,' Thad stated.

'The only thing I'll ever convince her to do is what will make her happy.' She couldn't understand how they couldn't want the same for their daughter.

'And you truly think that becoming a *werewolf* would make anyone happy?' Ethel scoffed.

'It did the trick for Kage,' Emberlyn pointed out.

Thad's face went rock hard. 'We're not talking about him.'

Dear Lord. 'You both take it as a rejection that they chose to take the Change. A rejection of you, your family and their birthright. But this isn't about you. It isn't in any way a rejection of anything, it's just a pursuit of fulfilment.'

Ethel's thinly plucked brows snapped together, incredulity gleaming in her gaze. 'Fulfilment?'

'Yes. And you should want that for them, whatever form it comes in,' Emberlyn insisted. 'If you can't give your stamp of approval then don't, but at least make an effort to sustain a relationship with them. Giving Kage the silent treatment is pointless – he can't undo the Change, and he doesn't want to. All you're doing is pushing him away, and you'll do the same to Paisley if you don't respect her choice either.'

Ethel's expression turned sour. 'You seem mighty supportive of their choices. Did you encourage them to do this?'

'The only thing I encouraged them to do is not live to please others.' But it didn't surprise Emberlyn that they'd look to blame her.

'Well of course you would. You make no attempt to please anyone but yourself,' Thad sniped. 'I should have severed their friendship with you when they were children.'

Emberlyn gave him a hard smile. 'You could have tried. It wouldn't have worked.' Hearing a vehicle approach, she glanced over her shoulder. 'Ah, here's your son now.'

If the couple were tense before, they turned even more rigid and standoffish then.

Emberlyn felt sad for the twins. She didn't have a fondness for either Ethel or Thad, but she wished they'd get over their funk already. They did love their children. They just wanted to micromanage their lives.

As Kage parked his car near Emberlyn's, she half-expected his parents to scamper – if only in another show of disapproval concerning his 'alteration of lifestyle'. But they didn't move a single inch.

Exiting the vehicle with a plastic carrier bag in hand, he flicked his parents a brief glance and then focused on Emberlyn. 'Brought you something.'

She smiled. 'I'm intrigued.' She fell silent, giving his parents a chance to say something; *hoping* they'd make some overture toward him. Instead, they turned without a word and made their way to their car, the assholes.

Kage only rolled his eyes, but she wasn't so sure he was all that blasé about it.

'Let's go inside,' she urged as she walked up the path.

Following her, he said, 'I heard from my cousin that my parents were heading to see you, so I hauled ass here.'

Ah, bless him. 'While I appreciate you being protective, you didn't need to drag yourself here – it wasn't a big deal.' As she reached the porch, the front door opened for her in welcome. 'It's not like they would have hurt me.'

'Not with actions, no, but they're good at lacerating people with words.'

The dude wasn't wrong there.

'My cousin told me they were hoping they could push you into convincing Paisley not to take the Change,' he said as they strolled into the manor, the door closing behind them.

'They gave it their best shot.'

He exhaled heavily. 'They're stubborn, I'll give them that.'

Emberlyn walked down the hall and into the kitchen, where she set her purse on the counter. 'Want anything? Coffee? Tea? Beer?'

Waving away her offer, Kage placed the carrier bag on the table. 'I brought you this.'

She hummed. 'What is it?'

'Your grandmother's Ouija board. I ain't gonna use it, so . . .'

She snickered. 'Can't say I'm surprised that you're giving it away.' Removing it from the bag, she ran her gaze over it, nostalgia heavy on her shoulders. Wooden and classic in design, it featured letters of the Latin alphabet, several numbers and a small selection of various words – hello, goodbye, yes, no.

Emberlyn placed it on the table. 'I can't count the times Millicent had me use this, hoping we could communicate with my mother.' Emberlyn took the planchette from the bag and rested it on the board. 'Avery never came through.'

He sank onto a chair. 'Don't take it personally, Em. Not all spirits are strong enough to reach out like that.'

'I know. I'm not upset with her, just disappointed that we couldn't connect at all.'

'She might have moved on straight away. It would explain why I never saw her near you. Some spirits cross over fast, others . . .' Trailing off, he shook his head. 'Let's not talk about ghosts – I'm done with that. Tell me more about what my parents said to you.'

Emberlyn claimed the seat across from him. 'In sum, they're totally against Paisley taking the Change. They've convinced themselves that this is a new 'interest' for her; that she hasn't thought it through. They truly believe that she'd regret doing it; talked as if she doesn't know her own mind. Annoyed by that, I gave them a reality check.'

His nose wrinkled. 'Oh, they don't like those.'

Emberlyn snorted. 'I noticed.' She reached over and gave his hand a little squeeze. 'I'm sorry that they're being shits to you.'

He shrugged. 'It's nothing I didn't expect when I decided to let the Change take me rather than use antivenom. They don't have anything against werewolves, they just feel that witches are superior to them.'

'It's more than that. They feel rejected by you and Paisley.'

His brow pinched. 'The only people round here rejecting any-one is *them*. They've shut me out, and they'll do the same to her if she doesn't dance to their tune.'

The planchette began to rattle and then slid across the board to hover over the word 'Hello'. Then it moved to K, A, G, and finally E.

Emberlyn stifled a smile. 'Seems like someone wants to talk to you.'

Kage wouldn't even look at the board. 'No. No, they don't.'

'The planchette just spelled your name.'

'No, it didn't.'

A snicker popped out of her, and then a knock came at the front door. 'That's probably Ripper,' she said, her pulse kicking up as a thread of anticipation wove through her blood.

Kage's mouth curved into a wicked smile. 'I'll head off, then.' He pushed out of his chair. 'Wouldn't want to be a cockblocker.'

'*And* you want to get away from the board.'

He looked appropriately confused. 'What board? I don't see no board.'

Rolling her eyes, she walked out of the kitchen and through the manor until she reached the front door. As she opened it wide, her hormones went wild at the delicious sight of the were-wolf on her porch.

'Ripper,' Kage greeted as he shrugged past her.

The Alpha gave him a chin-tip.

'Later, Em,' Kage called out as he jogged down the steps.

'Later,' she said before switching her attention to Ripper. 'I didn't expect to see you until later.'

'I was supposed to hold a clan meeting, but it had to be can-celed,' he explained as he walked inside. He flicked a look at a departing Kage. 'Everything all right?'

Emberlyn closed the door. 'His parents came here to ask me

to pressure Paisley into not taking the Change. Kage's cousin had given him a heads-up about their intentions, so he came to be sure they didn't upset me. Which they didn't.'

He let out a *Good* grunt.

'So, what can I do for you?' It was more of a tease than a question.

Ripper edged closer to her, his eyes heating. 'The same thing you did for me last night.' He swooped down and took her mouth like he owned it, the bold bastard.

Her magick rose up and turned the air static, drawn as ever to this werewolf who hummed with his own power.

She took a shaky breath when he drew back. 'Do you think we'll make it upstairs this time?'

'No. No, I don't.'

It turned out that he was right.

CHAPTER SEVENTEEN

❧

Pulling her garden snips to her chest, Emberlyn sighed at Lucie. 'If you don't want me to accidentally cut off your ear, you need to give me a little space.'

The cat was either bored or in the mood to be a diva, because she'd been a menace for the past hour – batting at the fairy lights, scratching the fence, taking swipes at the gardening basket, climbing the floral arch, sharpening her claws on Emberlyn's ankle rubber boots and trampling over plants as she chased a lizard through the yard.

Lucie flicked up her tail, its tip twitching, and flounced off to sniff at a herb.

'Thank you.' *Snicks* sounded as Emberlyn went back to gardening. She'd spent the past hour pruning back herbs, removing leaves, flowers and parts of stems.

It was a warm April day, but not hot. It was cooler here beneath the shadow of a hawthorn tree. Still, her hands were sweating inside her thick gardening gloves.

If it wasn't for Lucie's antics, it would have been a relaxing way for Emberlyn to spend her Sunday morning. It was relatively quiet here. Birds chirped. Slight *dings* came from the wind chimes. The breeze made the grass *shush* and the leaves rustle. The faint buzzing of a bee came from somewhere behind her.

There were so many scents – spicy herbs, warm earth, mint leaves, ripe berries and fragrant flowers – and all were comforting in their familiarity.

Often she'd gardened here as a child. With her help, Millicent had kept the yard well tended – weed free, plants well shaped, flowers color coded.

Emberlyn didn't plan to stay out here too long. She intended to pay Paisley another visit. On Wednesday, Crew had put her friend through the Change. But as Paisley hadn't been fit to see anyone until yesterday, Emberlyn had had to keep her distance.

Delighted with her new situation, Paisley had been her usual self. But she tired quickly, which was normal for a newbie were-wolf. She'd be fine after a week or so.

Unfortunately for Paisley, the witch side of her family hadn't yet 'come round'. They'd stayed away in silent protest. Which was dumb, really, because there was nothing to be done about the situation now. The Change couldn't be reversed.

Emberlyn hadn't been entirely surprised on hearing that some coven members – mostly Tyra and Sera – blamed *her* for Paisley's decision, saying her friend would not have done it if Emberlyn hadn't been allied with Ripper. As if Paisley wanting to be a werewolf had come out of nowhere.

Still, no one had said as much to Emberlyn's face. In fact, almost the entire coven had stayed clear of her. They were focused on Reena's new plans – she was going to have Carver's construction company convert two whole streets of houses at Bellcrest into bigger and more luxurious homes.

It was a good solution, really. Now Carver would still have a project to work on and Reena could still provide brand spanking new homes to the people she'd promised.

Ripper hadn't heard a whisper out of Carver – or the coven, either. Likewise, he hadn't had to deal with problems from CeCe. She was keeping a low profile, not upset by the rumor that he and Emberlyn were sleeping together. According to gossipers, CeCe didn't believe it was true. In her view, Ripper had only scent-marked Emberlyn to make CeCe jealous, giving her a taste of her own medicine.

'He would never get involved with a witch,' she allegedly insisted to anyone who dared insinuate that she could be wrong.

Well, she *was* wrong.

Each evening, either Emberlyn would go to Ripper's house or he would go to hers. They'd eat, talk, fuck, talk a little more and then part ways.

It was ... nice. Easy. Uncomplicated. And rather thrilling, since it seemed that he'd been blessed by sex gods or something.

Whenever his scent-mark became too faint for his liking, he would renew it. And she'd return the favor just to keep things even.

As Paisley had predicted, Michael's parents didn't seem to like that Emberlyn and Ripper were sharing a metaphorical bed. They hadn't said as much to her, but their recent smiles were forced and their tone was flat whenever they greeted her in passing, making their disapproval obvious. She'd so far ignored it.

A soft breeze whispered over her and stirred the plants, making the leaves flutter and the stalks bend slightly. Thirsty, she eyed the glass she'd propped on the nearby bench after Lucie had almost knocked it over.

Emberlyn pushed to her feet, her stiff knees protesting slightly, and tugged off a stiff glove. Crossing to the bench, she wiped her sweaty hand on her tank-green jumpsuit and picked up the glass. Tart and cool, the lemonade went down nicely.

Noticing that Lucie was sitting on the fence with her back to her, Emberlyn asked, 'What are you looking at, kitty?' She wafted at a floating ball of dandelion fluff as she strained to spot what had caught the feline's attention.

It was only then that Emberlyn realized an eerie hush had fallen. No birds tweeting, no bees buzzing. Even the breeze seemed to have retreated.

Unease crawling up her spine, she set the glass back down on the bench.

A low droning growl of warning came from Lucie.

Emberlyn yanked off her other glove just in case she'd need to call on her magick. It could be that one of Ripper's wolves had accidentally strayed too far, or that someone was knowingly poking around and spying on her. If it was the latter, they were going to get a magickal bitch slap.

'Not sure who's out there,' Emberlyn called out, her voice hard, 'but I have no problem burying you in my little pet cemetery if you don't get the hell off my land.'

Growling again, Lucie stood on all fours, her hackles rising.

Emberlyn tossed her gloves on the ground and approached the cat, scanning the shadowy wooded terrain beyond.

And then she saw them.

A pair of yellow wolf eyes.

Emberlyn felt her lips part. It was very rare for one of the Rabid to be seen during the day. They usually didn't surface until around dusk but, yeah, *that* was a Rabid.

Another growl rang out, and this one *didn't* come from Lucie.

Fuck. Before the cat could do anything ballsy but dumb like rush at the Rabid, Emberlyn scooped her up. Her pulse thudding, she slowly backed away. *Very* slowly, not wanting to trigger its prey drive.

If she ran, it would charge. And, much faster than she could ever be, it might well reach her before she could get within the manor's protective barrier.

Emberlyn kept on inching back, not once moving her attention from the figure creeping through the labyrinth of trees. It moved forward each time she moved back, stalking her.

Lucie let out yet another droning growl.

The Rabid snarled, its eyes seeming aglow with bloodlust, and then it rushed out of the trees.

'Shit.' Emberlyn slammed up her palm and threw out a mound of glittering magick that rapidly shifted into moths. They surrounded the Rabid – flapping at its face, obscuring its vision, distracting it. As it skidded to a stop, she whirled and ran for the house.

A roar split the air. Then heavy footsteps were tromping, branches were snapping and grass was rustling.

Even as she ran, Emberlyn twisted enough to sling a rush of magick at the Rabid just as it cleared her fence. Her blow dealt it an uppercut that made it stumble, its head snapping back.

She kept running, *finally* arriving at the porch. She jogged up the steps and spun, panting.

The Rabid sprinted toward her, teeth bared. It rammed into the manor's defensive barrier and flew backward. It crashed into a tree so hard a hanging lantern tumbled off a branch and fell on its head.

Emberlyn dashed into the house, closed the door and lowered Lucie to the floor. She hurried to the kitchen, lifted the phone receiver and dialed the Watchers' office.

'Hello?' a male answered almost immediately.

She thought the voice belonged to one of Ripper's wolves but wasn't sure. 'This is Emberlyn Vautier calling from Black Willow Manor. One of the Rabid is in my backyard.'

A curse drifted down the line just before she hung up.

She darted back onto the porch, closing the door behind her to stop Lucie from getting outside. Emberlyn needed to put the Rabid asleep before it chose to run off. Although ... it didn't look as though it had any intention of going anywhere. It was bashing at the barrier it couldn't see, jerking backward at each 'blow' the magick dealt it.

She frowned, thrown. The Rabid were animalistic and savage, but they weren't stupid. Their survival instincts were sharp. Like any predator, if their prey proved to be too much trouble they generally moved on. Only on a full moon would they behave senselessly.

This wasn't a full moon. It wasn't even nighttime. It was late morning, the sun was shining ... and, where usually there'd be an animal cunning in a Rabid's gaze, there was a strange sort of glaze. Her nape prickled in suspicion.

Chanting, Emberlyn lifted both hands and sent out ribbons of magick. The Rabid made no attempt to dodge them, which was equally strange. The glittering motes rushed up its nostrils. The Rabid snorted and jerked back. It shook its head fast, blinking hard.

She kept chanting, the creature firmly in her magickal 'hold' now.

Its eyelids grew droopy, its body began to sway and it staggered like a drunk. With a weak snarl, it lost the fight and succumbed to the sleeping spell – falling flat on its back, out cold.

Emberlyn released a long, relieved breath. She descended the steps and cautiously approached the Rabid. Its muscular chest steadily rose and fell, every rough exhale seeming to chafe its throat.

She examined it for scars but only spotted two – neither of which made her think of any werewolf who'd turned Rabid. Eager to confirm her earlier suspicion, she waved a hand over its body – dripping seeking magick over it, making what was hidden come to the light.

Her mouth tightened as a mini web of magick showed on each of the Rabid's eyelids.

Motherfucker.

The air in his lungs hot with rage, Ripper stormed up the path toward the manor. He could hear a vehicle approaching fast; knew it would be the Watchers. One of his wolves had called to say that Emberlyn had reported yet another Rabid incident. Ripper had leaped into his truck and hightailed it here in record time, determined to get to her; having no fucking clue if she was injured or not.

Again. She'd found herself fronting a Rabid *again*. There was something very fucking wrong with this picture. No way was it a coincidence.

He cleared the porch steps with a single leap. The front door opened ... revealing no one. The manor's sentient power had apparently decided to bid him entrance. A thought he shoved aside, his only interest in tracking down the occupant.

He stalked inside. 'Emberlyn?' he called out, his voice unintentionally sharp.

No response.

Knowing she'd reported that the Rabid had entered her backyard, he made his way toward the rear of the house, again calling out her name.

The back door creaked open, and there she was. Her brow creased in a surprised confusion. 'How did you get in?'

Making a beeline for her, he swept his gaze over her body. There was no blood or visible injuries. No indication she was shaken or upset. In fact, she looked her usual calm and steady self. 'The manor let me in,' he replied.

Her brows hiked up. 'Well, that's a – no, you don't want to get close to me right now, Rip, I have dirt on my clothes.'

He kept on forging forward. 'I don't care.' *Finally* reaching her, he curved his arms around her. She stilled in surprise. Okay, so he wasn't much of a hugger – so what?

Relaxing, she settled her hands on the twin columns of his back.

He pulled in a breath through his nose, clenching his teeth so hard a shooting pain lanced through his jaw. Frustration, agitation, fury – the emotions boiled in his gut. 'You hurt?'

'No. I managed to get behind the house's defensive barrier before the Rabid could get to me.'

Relief should have coursed through him at that, but the dark emotions simmering in his system left no room for anything else. He smelled the spot behind her ear, taking her scent inside him. 'You should have called me,' he insisted, his voice roughening with a barely contained growl. They weren't an official couple, no, but she was under his protection.

'I knew one of the Watchers would call you, so I also knew you'd already be on your way here by the time I'd put the Rabid to sleep – assuming you weren't busy with other things.'

Feeling his brows snap together, Ripper pulled back enough to meet her gaze. 'Look at me. It wouldn't matter what was going on around me. If you had even the slightest brush with danger, I would come to you.'

She stared at him, her expression unreadable. 'Even when there'd be nothing you could do?'

'Even then.' He smoothed a hand up her spine. 'Now, where's the Rabid?'

'Outside, asleep. I was pruning herbs in the garden when I saw that Lucie was staring at the woods. Then she started growling. I walked over to see what had unsettled her, and I noticed the

Rabid in the trees. I fended it off with magick as I fled to the porch, knowing it wouldn't manage to bypass the protective barrier.'

'How long will it stay unconscious?'

'Until I or another witch awakens it. Don't worry, it isn't going anywhere.'

A brisk knock came at the front door.

'That'll be the Watchers.' Ripper slowly released her. 'I'll let them in.' He stalked to the door and opened it wide. Kerr, Shane, Logan and a male witch filed inside. The latter was Ward's brother but, unlike Ward himself, Marvin was a decent guy.

'How's Emberlyn, and where's the Rabid?' Logan asked.

'She's fine,' Ripper replied. 'And it's outside.'

Moments later, they were all gathered in a circle around the sleeping Rabid.

'You don't often see any Rabid in town this early,' Shane noted.

Crossing his arms over his chest, Ripper planted his feet wide. 'This is the second time one came at Emberlyn. It happened last month, too.' It was no coincidence. It had likely been lured this way using a dead animal, just like the last Rabid.

'There's a chance this guy is one of my wolves, Lincoln Mathers,' said Shane, his expression grim. 'He turned Rabid two years ago. That scar on his throat? Lincoln had one just like that. What's that crisscross pattern of magick on its head?' he asked Emberlyn. 'The sleeping spell?'

Beside Ripper, she nodded. 'As for the little webs over its eyelids, they had nothing to do with me.'

He regarded her closely. Her tone was cool and controlled, but it held the slightest edge of anger. If Ripper hadn't spent so much time around her, he wasn't sure he would have picked up on the latter.

She went on, 'Somebody else did that. I just unveiled the spell.'

Kerr frowned. 'What's the intent behind it?'

'To haze the Rabid's vision with a killing rage,' Marvin said in astonishment as he held his hand above the Rabid's eyes, reading the spell.

'The fuck?' Logan bit off.

Emberlyn breathed in through her nose. 'As I see it, there'd be no reason to do that unless a person wanted to set the Rabid on somebody. In order to do that, though, they must have first captured it – probably while it slept. Moving it wouldn't have been easy, so they likely knocked it unconscious before bespelling it. I don't think they then released the Rabid in a random spot; that it coincidentally happened upon the manor. I think they placed it some distance from here deliberately before waking it.'

Ripper felt the corners of his eyes tighten. 'In other words, someone sicced it on you?'

'That would be my guess,' she replied.

A scolding lash of anger whipped at Ripper, and he whirled on Marvin with a snarl.

The male witch threw up his hands. 'I knew nothing of this! I swear! Emberlyn, I ... I don't know who would do this, but I can tell you it was *not* a coven-wide effort. I would have heard about it, and I would have put a stop to it. This was one person acting alone or a few people secretly working together.'

'Like who?' demanded Ripper. 'That damn faction your coven likes to claim doesn't exist?'

Marvin hesitated. 'I don't know. It's a simple spell – a witch of any skillset could do it.'

'The effect is only ever temporary,' Emberlyn cut in. 'So this Rabid was bespelled at some point this morning. Would Carver or one of his wolves have captured it if asked?'

Ripper gave his head a stiff shake. 'No wolf would do this. The Rabid are still thinking beings; they're victims of circumstance.'

Shane nodded, the move hard and curt. 'They don't deserve to be used like this, and none of our kind would condone it. It's fucked up.'

'I agree,' Marvin said quickly. 'It's cruel. I can't think of a witch who would do it either.'

'Well, at least *one* of the coven did,' said Kerr, cricking his corded neck. 'And something needs to be done about it.'

Ripper grunted, his muscles tight with anger. 'Twice now Rabid have been used as attack dogs. There needs to not be a third time. Not only for Emberlyn's safety, but because it's utterly inhumane.'

'We should hold a meeting at the town hall for all of Chilgrave and address it there,' Shane declared. 'For witches to hold a grudge against another is one thing. For them to drag the Rabid into it, *bespell* and use them this way is another.'

Logan dipped his chin. 'Whatever culprit or culprits is behind this ... they're fucking cowards. They should have gone at Emberlyn head-on themselves. At which point she'd have made them suffer, yeah, but that's the risk they'd take. If you ain't prepared to be part of a fight, you don't use someone else like a puppet to do it for you.'

Ripper rolled his shoulders, trying to shake off the irritability that raced through his veins, making him feel antsy and on edge. He had no idea who'd done this, which meant he had no one he could punish. The annoyance of that grated his skin.

Shane looked back down at the Rabid. 'Let's take him to the office so we can work on reversing his mental state.'

As a team, the Watchers deftly carried the Rabid through the house and over to their all-terrain vehicle.

From the porch, Ripper and Emberlyn watched them drive off.

He then turned to her and palmed her neck, his hold gentle even as rage beat at him – hit, shoved, kicked, slapped him; pressed his every hot button. 'Come to my place with me.'

'I'm supposed to be stopping off to see Paisley in a little while.'

'I'll go with you. I need to check in with her anyway. You can stay with me until then.'

Her brow lifted at what even he had to admit was a slightly tyrannical tone.

'Emberlyn, any number of things could have happened to you today. You could have failed to notice the Rabid until it was too late. Or you could have fallen while fleeing, enabling it to catch up to you. Or Lucie could have pounced on it, at which point you wouldn't have run because you would have wanted to save her. Those scenarios – and many more – are playing out in my head. I don't want to leave you alone, and I'd rather you were away from here for just a little while.'

Her brow knitted. 'I'm not unsafe here.'

'The house can protect you, I know that, but … just come with me.' His instincts were driving him to take her to his den, a place she was just as safe. He wanted to feed her. Make her tea. Fuss over her. Keep a close watch on her.

Maybe she sensed that, maybe she understood, because the lines in her face fell away and she dipped her chin. 'Okay. But I have to change and put my gardening stuff away. Then we can go.'

CHAPTER EIGHTEEN

❦

Emberlyn side-eyed the wolf in the driver's seat. The atmosphere in the truck was tense. Anger was rising off Ripper like steam, and he was all but overflowing with protective energy.

Oh, she was pissed too. She just hadn't thought *he'd* be equally so. His hackles weren't just up, they were on fire.

Neither of them had said much. But he would occasionally rest his hand on her thigh as he drove, silently checking in touch-wise in that way werewolves did.

Maybe it was silly of her not to have expected him to react quite so fiercely to what had happened earlier. But he hadn't done so on the last occasion she'd had a run-in with a Rabid. They hadn't been enjoying sexytimes back then, true, but it wasn't as if she and Ripper were *together*. He never stayed at her place overnight or invited her to sleep at his – a telling point. Werewolves only slept beside someone they were serious about.

Ripper was a protector, though, wasn't he? That someone who

wore his scent would be targeted was bound to put him in such a furious state.

She flexed her fingers in her lap, feeling ... twitchy. Which was unusual for her. But though she was calm, her hold on her temper was frayed around the edges. Her rage kept trying to claw its way out of the hole she'd buried it in.

No, she wasn't going to give the masterminds of the recent bullshit the satisfaction of getting her all riled up.

Finally arriving at his lake house, he parked his truck and shepherded her up his path, sticking close with every step as if he might need to jump between her and a bullet. Inside the building, he guided her through to the kitchen and urged her to sit at the island. Wordlessly, he retrieved one of her homemade herbal tea balls from a cupboard and began preparing her a hot drink.

Ordinarily, Emberlyn would have offered to take over. Today, though, she said nothing, sensing that he needed this. He needed to feel he was doing *something* for her, angered by the fact that he was unable to avenge the attack on her.

Finally, he set a steaming mug in front of her. It was a week ago that he'd asked her to bring some of her tea balls here for whenever she visited. Each time she'd made a cup, he'd watched closely, intent on learning how she liked it. This incredibly gruff wolf could be sweet at times.

Lifting her cup, she asked, 'Are you any calmer yet?'

His gaze met hers, hard and flinty. 'Well, let's see ... you were attacked by a Rabid. Again. Someone evidently wants you dead. And I don't know if that someone is going to cut their losses or persist in trying to make it happen. So the answer to the question is *hell no*. How can you be so fucking calm?'

'Would you rather I was ranting and raving? Not in my nature.' Emberlyn sipped at her tea. 'Emotions cloud judgement. Case in point – you're not seeing what I see.'

The corners of his mouth dipped down. 'Which is what?'

'This person wouldn't have felt confident that a Rabid would kill me. Injure me, yes – maybe even badly. But not kill me. I'm nothing close to an easy target, which they'll be well aware of. They'll also know that, since my ex-mate turned Rabid, it would infuriate me for a werewolf in such a state to be used like an attack dog.

'They *want* me to be angry, Rip, because they want me off my game. It galls me that they thought I wouldn't see that. It's quite frankly insulting.' She leaned toward him. 'Whoever did this is not worth any of the emotions you're feeling right now. They're a coward, just like Logan said.'

Digesting that, Ripper said nothing for a long moment. 'Who do you think it was?'

Oh, the possibilities were endless. 'A great many people in the coven don't like me. We're not just talking Reena, Tyra and my family. We're talking anyone who felt "wronged" whenever I sought vengeance – that list is *long*. And there'll be witches who aren't happy that I'm sitting pretty in the manor, shitting all over Reena's housing development plans. Then there's the rebel faction to consider.'

'Nothing about the spell itself clued you in to who might have cast it?'

'As Marvin said, it was a simple one. Which doesn't mean that the culprit couldn't have worked a stronger spell – they might have just stuck to something easy so that *any* of the coven could have seemed responsible for it.'

'The suspect pool just got a little smaller, though. They used a goat last time – anyone could have caught and killed one, witch or wolf. This time, by utilizing a spell, they've exposed themselves to be a witch. Why do that?'

Chewing on it, Emberlyn drummed her nails on her cup.

'Maybe they saw no point in trying to implicate werewolves now that you and I are sleeping together and wearing each other's scent – that in and of itself suggests that no werewolf would dare come at me, since it's a hell of a lot more serious than us being allies.'

'Fair point,' he conceded.

'I think Marvin is right; I think that this was one person or a few acting in secret. No way would the entire coven remain silent about this.'

She might not be liked, but there was no prejudice against werewolves. Plus, plenty of witches were connected to them – whether through matings, family lines, business dealings or friendships. Not many of the coven would have agreed to overlook what was done to Lincoln.

Emberlyn took another sip of her tea. 'I also don't think Reena's involved. Having me killed, or even badly injured, isn't her style. She's no coward. She'd want to defeat me in a magickal duel; prove herself to be more powerful.'

Ripper planted his hands on the island. 'She also wants the manor, though. That could have motivated her to go off-script.'

'Maybe. It just doesn't seem likely to me.' Emberlyn sighed. 'Well, one good thing came out of this: Lincoln is now home. He was only Rabid for two years, so his mental state should return to its original one.'

Ripper's expression turned grim. 'He won't ever be the same. Not really. But he won't have lost himself.'

'His family will for sure be elated that they'll have him back.'

'But they'll also be furious that he was bespelled. Every werewolf in town will be. Whoever did that to him seriously fucked up. Before, it was the coven and Carver versus you and my clan. Not anymore. Shane had intended to stay out of the matter, but Lincoln is one of his wolves – that makes it his business now;

he'll side with us. Also, Carver will back down completely, because he won't like this either.'

'You truly think he'll withdraw his support from Reena and my family?' Emberlyn wasn't so sure.

'I know he will. Trust me, the coven are on their own now. They just don't know it yet.'

Dumping a carrier bag on the laundry hub's reception desk the next afternoon, Laine puffed out a breath. 'If you can help me with this, I will adore you forever.'

Emberlyn felt her lips tip up. 'I'll do my best.' She waved at the infant in the stroller, who she knew to be Laine's niece. The curly haired toddler shyly waved back.

'I recently split up from my boyfriend,' Laine explained. 'His scent is all over my bedcovers, and it's driving me nuts. I've washed them, but the smell won't come off.'

'I can get rid of it for you,' Emberlyn assured the werewolf.

Laine's entire body – facial features and all – seemed to sag in relief. *Thank God.* Most of my wardrobe is drenched in his scent, so I'll be bringing it here in dribs and drabs.'

'There's an alternative. I could come to your house and magickly cleanse it of every trace of him. It wouldn't take me long.'

Laine's eyes widened. 'Oh my God, yes, please do it. I don't care what your price is, I'll pay it.'

Paisley materialized at Emberlyn's side. 'Before becoming a werewolf, I wouldn't have understood your desperation, Laine. But now, I *so* get it.' Blowing out a breath, she turned to Emberlyn. 'Imagine a guy's signature cologne being *all over* your home and embedded in every fabric. A guy you want to forget and move on from.'

Emberlyn grimaced. 'I can see why it would be a mindfuck.' Much as it had been to live in the house she used to share with Michael on his clan's territory. The memories of their time together had been all over it, making it impossible for her to stay.

'The sooner you can do your cleansing thing the better,' Laine declared.

'Is tomorrow any good? I can come after work.'

'Tomorrow is *perfect*.' Laine flinched when her niece threw a pacifier at her head. 'Ow. What is your problem, Missy?'

Chuckling, Emberlyn swiped a complimentary sparkler from a tub near the phone. They functioned like handheld fireworks – you ignited them, and they provided a temporary display of crackles and flames and sparks. Only they weren't powered by chemicals, they were fueled by magick alone and were perfectly safe for little ones to use.

'Here.' She 'lit' the fuse with a brief dart of her magick and then handed it to Laine, who gave it to the now-grinning pup.

While the little girl shook and swirled the rod, Emberlyn wrote a tag for Laine's bedcovers and handed them to Paisley.

Hearing the doorbell, Emberlyn looked up. Her pulse jumped in delight as Ripper stalked inside. As usual, her feminine parts did a little jig.

To be fair, what else was a girl's hormones to do in the face of all that masculine supremacy?

He held the door open for Laine, who thanked him with a pretty blush and left the hub.

'Oh, hi, Ripper,' Paisley greeted, chirpy.

He grunted . . . as was his way.

Emberlyn smiled as he approached the desk. 'What brings you here?'

His gaze took a lazy dip down her body – or as much as he could see of it, since she stood behind the desk – and then darted back up to meet her eyes. 'I had a thought.'

'Did it hurt at all?' she teased, earning herself one of his mildly exasperated looks.

He planted his feet. 'I figure we should arrive at the town hall together for the meeting.'

Emberlyn blinked. 'Together?'

'It'd be good for us to present a united front that can't be ignored by the coven.'

Paisley pointed a finger. 'This. I like this.' She looked at Emberlyn. 'Those assholes currently targeting you need to get the message that it's best for their health that they leave you alone.'

'I'm not sure how much of an impact it will have' – the afore-mentioned assholes had ignored that message so far – 'but I have no objections.'

Ripper grunted in satisfaction. 'I'll pick you up from your place around six-thirty.' He tilted his head. 'Have you had a lot of people asking what happened yesterday?'

Feeling her lips thin, Emberlyn nodded. 'Nosy-asses have been waltzing in and out since this morning.' All they'd been told so far was that Lincoln was captured in her backyard. 'I said that all would be revealed at the meeting.' She paused. 'It's good to hear that he's doing well up to now.'

'It'll take another few days for him to be in a fully functional state, but he's getting there.'

Paisley planted a hand on her hip. 'Is it true that Emberlyn didn't call you about the attack?'

His mouth tightened in annoyance. 'Yes, it's true. One of my wolves gave me a heads-up.'

Emberlyn gave her a pointed look. 'See?'

Huffing, Paisley folded her arms and cut her gaze back to him. 'When it comes to big stuff that happens in Emberlyn's world, I always find out from other people. She never calls with deets.'

'So I shouldn't take it personally, then?' he asked.

'No.' Paisley poked her tongue into the inside of her cheek. 'Technically, neither should I. But I do.'

Emberlyn's snort died as she caught sight of the Reeds passing the large window. They peered inside, their eyes hardening on her, before quickly looking away.

'Are they giving you issues?' Ripper asked, apparently not having missed the byplay.

'Nope. I don't talk to them much.'

'They don't like that she broke her mating tie with Michael,' Paisley explained to him. 'They lost their shit over it at first, but then they acted all sweet and understanding while still making comments about how Michael would be here for her if he could. They basically try to make her feel guilty for moving on.'

Ripper swiped his tongue over his upper teeth. 'I see.'

'And they definitely don't like that she's been rolling around the sheets with you,' Paisley added. 'They've been giving her the cold shoulder lately.'

Emberlyn gave her a wide-eyed look. 'Okay, Chatty Charlie, you can hush now.'

Ripper cast Emberlyn an annoyed look. 'You should have told me.'

She lifted her shoulders. 'There's nothing to really tell.' It wasn't as if the Reeds had said or done anything noteworthy.

'And if there was?' he challenged, flicking up a brow.

'I would . . . I would tell you.'

'Ha,' Paisley burst out. 'A total lie.'

Emberlyn gently poked her shoulder. 'Hush, you. You've said quite enough.'

'And *you* don't say enough,' Paisley sassed.

'You're both such whiners.'

Ripper frowned. 'We just want to be kept firmly in the loop about important things that happen in your life.'

'Exactly,' said Paisley, sliding her a haughty look. 'Forgive us for giving a damn.'

'You're forgiven,' Emberlyn deadpanned.

Paisley only rolled her eyes.

'I have to meet with Crew about something, so I'm off,' Ripper announced, backing up a step. 'Six-thirty, Emberlyn.'

'I'll be ready.'

CHAPTER NINETEEN

Emberlyn unclipped her seatbelt and plucked her purse from between her feet. The passenger door was pulled open, and then Ripper held out a hand. He did that now. Opened doors for her. Helped steady her whenever she stepped in or out of his truck.

When it came to werewolves, that stuff wasn't mere courteousness. It was a sign of respect. If someone had told her weeks ago that there'd come a time when the anti-witch Jax 'Ripper' Stone would respect her, she would have laughed.

Emberlyn took his hand and slid out of the vehicle. The evening breeze was cool, but her white long-sleeved shirt and taupe high-waist tailored pants provided a nice buffer.

He released her hand and cupped her elbow. 'You ready for this?'

'Yes. I'm interested in how it's going to play out,' she replied.

As they crossed to the town hall, Kerr, Logan and Crew slipped out from behind the shadowed columns.

'The hall is packed, but our wolves are keeping some space

free on the front row for us,' announced Kerr, opening the glass door. 'The only council member who hasn't yet arrived is Reena.'

'She's usually the first here,' Ripper absently noted, urging Emberlyn into the building.

Then ... it was like they were a bridal party ready to march down the aisle, because the other wolves gathered at his and Emberlyn's backs as, side by side, they walked into the grand hall.

The large space was crowded. Many people sat. Others stood behind the benches or leaned against the walls.

The coven and Carver's clan had taken up one column of benches – among those on the first row were her family, Tyra and Sera. The other two werewolf clans had taken up the second column of benches.

Catching sight of Paisley and Kage on the third row, Emberlyn gave them a quick smile as she walked by.

Ripper guided her straight to the front bench. The wolves there scooched all the way over to make room. Once Logan slipped in, Ripper gestured for Emberlyn to take a seat, after which Kerr and Crew joined them. As such, she ended up safely sandwiched between several wolves – no doubt by design.

Being made to feel 'part' of a group was ... strange. A little too foreign to be comforting just yet. It would take some getting used to.

After giving her a long look, Ripper climbed the steps to the platform and took the empty seat between Shane and Carver.

Kerr bumped his shoulder into hers. 'Your cousin Ames is trying to get your attention.'

'I know,' said Emberlyn, keeping her gaze forward as she placed her purse on the floor. Her peripheral vision had caught him waving his arm from the parallel bench.

'You ignoring him for the fun of it?' asked Kerr. 'Because I get it.'

'There's just no point in giving him my attention. All he'll do is make some silly comment designed to get a reaction. The thing about Ames is that he's average in most respects. Nothing about him stands out, so he uses other people to gain attention and seem relevant. And since he's probably still feeling sour about what happened at the last meeting, he won't have anything nice to say to me.'

Seated on her other side, Logan looked her way. 'You mean that thing where you caught and crushed his magick?'

'For Ames, who links his power to his physical prowess, it was the equivalent of me stomping on his dick,' she explained.

Logan grimaced. 'Gotcha.'

'Out of curiosity, who's trying to burn holes into my back with their eyes?' She could feel *someone* glaring at her.

Logan cast a furtive glance behind her. A sigh rattled his lips slightly. 'That would be CeCe. Ignore her.'

'I intend to. She bores me.'

Kerr snorted in amusement.

'I'm wondering what her issue is, though. From what I've heard, she doesn't believe that I'm actually sleeping with Ripper.'

'She doesn't,' confirmed Logan. 'But it'll still annoy her something fierce that you wear his scent and he walks around smelling of your magick. The longer that goes on, the more worked up she'll get. Don't be surprised if she approaches you about it.' He paused, his expression turning sober. 'If that happens, you call Ripper; he'll deal with it.'

Emberlyn couldn't help but chuckle. 'You're cute. *Call Ripper; he'll deal with it,*' she mimicked before shaking her head. 'It's like you're new around here.'

A snicker popped out of Kerr. 'Yeah, Logan, she's no damsel. Just sit back and enjoy how much it both frustrates and turns on your brother that this woman does not need him.'

Emberlyn felt her lips bow up.

It was minutes later that Reena and Ward arrived. Ward took a seat between Tyra and Sera while the High Priestess headed for the platform. More townspeople filed in a little at a time, until the entire hall was jam-packed.

When seven p.m. hit, Shane cleared his throat and said, 'Let's start, shall we? Firstly, for all those wondering how Lincoln is doing, things are progressing well. His family is delighted to have him home. But they're also furious on his behalf. Why? Someone placed a spell on him that trapped him in a state of bloodlust.'

Gasps and mutters sounded throughout the hall while several voices loudly burst out comments . . .

'What?'

'You must be joking!'

'Bloodlust?'

'That's not possible!'

'You can't be serious!'

Ripper raised a hand for silence, and everyone immediately quieted.

Emberlyn half-turned in her seat, wanting to better observe the room.

'You are sure that Lincoln was bespelled?' Reena asked Shane, seeming genuinely disturbed.

'Positive,' he replied.

Her brow pinched, she shook her head in incredulity. 'But . . . why would *anyone* do that?'

Ripper stretched out his legs beneath the table. 'You can't guess? This is now the second time in a relatively short period that a Rabid found its way to Black Willow Manor. The first time, one was lured out there using a dead goat. On this occasion, it would seem that Lincoln was caught, bespelled, and then placed near the manor – his instinct in that form would have been to hunt the nearest lifeform he could sense. Which he did.'

'If Emberlyn told you that he was bespelled, how do you know she didn't lie?' Ames piped up, the little prick.

'I can confirm it to be true,' said Marvin. 'I was the one who later untangled the spell.'

Carver shook his head, the image of horrified. 'This is ... there aren't words.'

Reena straightened her shoulders. 'I will be launching a full investigation into this matter.' She said it as though everyone else could thereby relax; that there was no need for them to involve themselves.

Ripper raised an unimpressed brow. 'Like you did about the curse jars? How did that work out?'

Reena's lips flattened. 'I have not yet identified who is responsible. It seems probable that it's the same person – or people – who bespelled Lincoln.'

Claris shot her a narrow-eyed glare. 'I thought you don't teach such magick in your coven.'

Ward's head whipped in Claris's direction. 'She does not. It is forbidden. But there are those who secretly practice such spells,' he admitted.

Shane stilled, his gaze bouncing from Reena to Ward. 'Who?'

She licked her lips. 'I do not yet know, but I am working on finding out.'

'You don't know a whole lot, do you?' Colton snarked.

'Or,' began Logan, 'maybe you just don't want us to be aware of who's responsible because you want to punish them yourself, just like with Rosemary.'

Reena inched up her chin. 'The culprits will be found, named, tried and punished. I assure you of that.'

'I don't feel assured,' Logan told her.

'Neither do I,' said Ripper. 'And I'm not leaving this in your maybe-capable hands, Reena. I will be looking into this matter myself.'

'As will I,' Shane announced.

'Same here.' Carver plucked at his collar. 'In the meantime, consider the housing development project canceled.'

'*What?*' Reena burst out.

Carver's expression firmed. 'One of your witches used magick to trap a Rabid into a state of bloodlust and use him as their pet killer. Once they've been identified and punished, I'll reconsider. But for now, the construction plans aren't going ahead.'

'It wasn't one of us,' Sera swore. 'It was *her*. Emberlyn.'

Emberlyn rolled her eyes. *Oh, here we go.*

Ripper glared at the slim blonde who'd shot to her feet and stabbed a finger in Emberlyn's direction. 'I suggest you sit down.' Even he heard the menace in his tone. 'Emberlyn isn't on trial here.'

Sera reluctantly sat, at which point a smirking Tyra whispered something into her ear.

'Though it pains me to say it, since Emberlyn is my niece, I would have to agree with Sera,' said Gill. 'The only witch who'd do something so unethical is Emberlyn.'

Paisley groaned. 'God, Gill, would it kill ya to leave Em alone *just once?*'

Gill glared daggers at Paisley. 'She's an opportunist. She could have bespelled Lincoln into a killing rage herself after putting him to sleep. It enables her to implicate the coven.'

Emberlyn sighed at her aunt. 'That theory doesn't make any sense. Even if I was so cruel as to do something so horrid, I'd see no reason to do it. I want to know who's sending Rabid my way. Implicating the coven would influence the direction of the investigation, which could then lead to the culprit being unidentified if they're not a witch. Seriously, think before you speak.'

Gill's eyes went squinty. 'You're not—'

'Enough,' said Ripper, his tone clipped.

'It makes no sense that it be Emberlyn,' said Reena. 'She has nothing to gain from any of this.'

'Untrue,' Sera contradicted. 'Look at how the clans no longer trust us. That could have been her goal; to isolate us from them.'

'To attempt such a thing would risk her being alienated from her newfound allies, which would mean she then had no one,' Reena pointed out.

Ethel dipped her chin. 'It would be a foolish move, and Emberlyn is hardly foolish.'

Sera's brow hiked up. 'You don't consider calling on deities, demons and other dark beings foolish?'

Emberlyn tossed Sera a bored look. 'If you do, it's astonishing that you came to me asking to be taught how to summon them. And when I refused, you tried invading my mind to steal the information from me.'

Shane went motionless. 'I did not hear of this. People gossip about pretty much everything around here, but not even a whisper of this traveled through the grapevine.'

'The coven as a whole are aware of it,' Emberlyn informed him. 'They're aware of a lot of things that you won't have heard about.'

As Ripper, Shane and Carver looked at the High Priestess, she gave a defensive shrug and said, 'You do not announce *clan* matters to the entire town. Why would you expect me to share coven business with one and all?'

Ripper winged up a brow. 'Is that why you kept what Sera did quiet, or is it because she's your niece?'

Reena looked away. 'We're getting off topic.'

'Not necessarily,' said Shane, folding his arms. 'You say there are some in your coven practicing magick that you don't condone. Going by what Sera did to Emberlyn, she may very well be one of them.'

Reena shook her head. 'I have questioned her over the curse jars; I am satisfied by her answers that she had no involvement in that.'

'I'm not,' Ripper told her.

'Emberlyn's manipulating all of you,' Sera stressed, 'and you're letting her. She has sold every piece of her soul, just like Millicent did.'

Kage threw the witch a hard glance. 'If you really thought that, you wouldn't test her so much.'

Sera's face turned to stone. 'She's your friend, so you have a blind spot where she's concerned. Like it or not, she does the devil's bidding to feed her power, just like Lilith did.'

Gasps tore out of many other witches.

'Sera!' reprimanded Penelope in horror.

Sera scoffed at her mother. 'Oh, come on. Everyone here knows that the most likely explanation for how the first witch and first werewolf came to be is that they made a pact with dark beings.'

None of the coven spoke up in disagreement, but none nodded along either.

'I didn't ask Emberlyn for help conjuring them because I wanted to do it,' said Sera. 'I was trying to gather evidence to prove that *she* did it. That's why I tried punching my way into her mind. Look past the smiles and pretty face and fancy clothes. That woman is hollow.'

Ripper ground his teeth, ready to verbally tear into her ... only to realize that Emberlyn didn't seem at all bothered by her words. She was eyeing Sera curiously.

'It's interesting just how intent you are on keeping the conversation focused on me,' mused Emberlyn. 'It's also interesting how Tyra keeps whispering things into your ear, clearly feeding you things to say.'

Tyra squinted at Emberlyn. 'I am not goading her; I'm attempting to calm her down.'

Ignoring that, Emberlyn added, 'I could almost think that the two of you don't *want* what happened to Lincoln to be discussed in more depth.'

Sera's eyelid twitched. 'No, I just refuse to sit here while you turn three werewolf clans against my coven. They should know the truth about you.'

'The truth as *you* see it, you mean. Not everyone will think as you do.' Emberlyn glanced at the other witches. 'Hands up anyone in the coven who thinks I'm innocent.'

Many arms limply jerked up like they'd been yanked by strings.

The owners of said arms gasped and then held the limb to their chest protectively.

The twins chuckled while Kerr caught Ripper's eye and smirked with a shake of his head.

Emberlyn offered Sera a pleasant smile. 'Did you see that? Such a vote of confidence, wouldn't you say?'

'You made them do it!' Sera accused, her cheeks scarlet.

Emberlyn ran her gaze along the benches of witches. 'Were any of you forced to raise your hand?'

None responded, averting their gazes.

'They're afraid of you,' Sera bit out.

'Because they're smart, unlike you,' Ripper cut in. 'Now pipe down.'

Sera's nostrils flared. 'If you weren't sleeping with her, you wouldn't be so blinded by her. I'm telling you, there's something *wrong* with Emberlyn. Always has been. Her own parents knew it. Look how easily her dad skipped town and left her behind. Her mother didn't even fight her heartbreak to live for her daughter. Michael all but abandoned her. Millicent didn't give much of a crap about her, either, and the twins only befriended her for protection. There's a reason Emberlyn has no one, you're just not seeing it.'

A growl vibrating in his chest, Ripper leaned—

Emberlyn let out a dark, flat, drawn-out laugh that somehow rang with power.

Many witches cringed away from the sound. Those sitting near Sera edged along the bench, creating distance from her – even Tyra.

Cocking her head, Emberlyn raised an index finger. 'Can anyone else hear that? A little tinkling sound?'

Actually, Ripper could. It made him think of a small bell.

Emberlyn lifted her purse onto her lap, opened it up . . . and a ginger tabby feline head popped out. 'Hey, pretty girl,' she cooed as the cat climbed out of the purse, leaning into her strokes. 'You sensed I needed a cuddle, didn't you? Look at her, Logan. Isn't she just adorable?'

His lips twitching, Logan read the tag on the collar. 'Bessie. Nice name.'

Sera pushed to her feet, her brow creased, her eyes narrowed. 'Bessie? My Bessie?' She gawked at Emberlyn. 'You – I – that's – Bessie, get over here!'

The cat spared her owner an aloof glance, rubbing herself against Emberlyn.

Sera fisted her hands. 'What have you done?'

'The same thing I could do to the familiar of every witch in this hall if I so pleased. Familiars aren't mere animals,' Emberlyn told Kerr, her tone conversational. 'They are guardian spirits in

animal form. They come to serve, guide and protect the descendants of the first coven. Descendants of Lilith are their particular
favorites. If called on by who they believe to be her strongest
living progeny, they'll go to that witch's aid.'

In other words, Emberlyn could call every familiar to her
and keep them up in her manor should she so wish. As the
truth of that hit the hall, a hush fell over the coven; their
expressions ranging from shock and alarm to displeasure and
apprehension.

As for Ripper's clan, they were grinning in amusement,
looking quite impressed. Aside from CeCe, her friends and
Neal – they were all stone-faced.

Reena pressed a finger to her temple, clearly stressed. 'Sera,
leave. Do not say anything else, just *leave*.'

Her niece gaped. Spluttered. Scoffed. She looked to Tyra,
as if for backup, but the redhead didn't meet her gaze. None of
the other witches did either, not even Penelope. Realizing she
had no support here, Sera cursed and scooted to the end of the
bench. Sparing Emberlyn a withering look, she then indignantly
marched out of the hall.

Emberlyn carefully placed Bessie in her purse, upon which
point the feline disappeared.

'So many outbursts here tonight, Reena,' Shane remarked.
'No wonder there's a rebellious faction within your coven. You
have little control over your witches.'

'Agreed,' said Ripper. 'I doubt we'd otherwise be having this
meeting.'

Reena shifted in her seat. 'As I said before, I *will* identify and
deal with whoever is responsible for these crimes.'

'And as we made clear before,' Carver put in, 'the clans will
also be looking into this.'

Reena stiffened. 'It is my right to punish my own.'

'Only if you find them first,' said Shane. 'So you had better hope that you do.'

Ripper let his gaze touch on every witch in the crowd. 'No Rabid will again be used, and no further moves will be made against Emberlyn Vautier,' he asserted, menace heavy in his voice once again. 'By all means hold onto whatever grudge you bear, but keep it at that. Or risk my clan coming down on your head. Though I'd imagine that what we do to you will be nothing compared to what she'll do.'

Shane stood. 'This meeting is now over.'

CHAPTER TWENTY

❧

Ripper grunted as she took him deeper, making his cock touch the back of her throat. *Fuck.* He bunched her hair in his hand, the silky feel of it like cool water against his fingers. 'Your mouth was made for this.'

Sitting on the edge of his bed, Emberlyn flicked her fuck-drunk gaze up to his. The sight made molten lust punch him right in the gut, basic and fierce.

He was letting her set the pace *for now*, enjoying the show. She was deliciously naked, every inch of her bared for his view as he sank into the hot wet cavern of her mouth over and over.

Every breath he took felt filled with her. The scent of her need infused the air. It was pure bait, a siren's call. The taste of her was even better – it sat on his tongue, warm and sweet with magick.

Only minutes ago he'd shoved her onto his bed, dropped to his knees at the foot of it and eaten her out until she'd screamed. He'd then stood upright and snapped open his fly . . . at which point she'd knifed up, fisted his cock and taken it into her mouth.

Who was he to object?

As he stared down at her, a wave of ownership washed over him. He loved watching her blow him. There was no artifice with her. No practiced movements. No script she followed. No technique she consistently used.

Emberlyn just did whatever she felt like doing in that moment – always so tuned in to his reactions, always so easily anticipating what he wanted.

She was dangerously addicting, but he didn't care. At all. He only ever wanted more.

His hand flexed in her hair as she tongued the sensitive spot beneath the crown. She closed her mouth around him again, sucked even harder than before . . . and, shit, his witch knew her way around a blowjob.

He did that a lot now. Called her 'his witch' in his head. Which he partly blamed his clan for.

Since the town meeting a few days ago, many of his wolves often referred to her as 'Ripper's witch'. With the exception of the obvious few, they liked Emberlyn. Respected her strength. More, they liked her *for him*.

Nails dragged down his bare chest and navel, leaving prickly trails of heat. She rubbed the flat of her tongue along the underside of his shaft and swallowed more of him. *Fuck.* Okay, he was done with letting her set the pace.

Ripper cupped her jaw. 'Now all you do is suck. Don't otherwise move.' He thrust his cock forward, grinding his teeth as her throat contracted around the head.

He kept a tight grip on her jaw to hold her still while he used her mouth as he pleased. And he *did* use it. With abrupt forward-snaps of his hips, he crammed his cock in her mouth again and again and again. Until it was either stop or blow his load down her throat.

He had other plans for tonight.

Ripper withdrew his dick and swiped his thumb over the outer edge of her swollen lower lip. 'You on birth control?'

Pale-hazel eyes opaque with need narrowed. 'Yes.'

Using his hold on her hair, he tipped her head back and lowered his own. 'I want to come *inside* you.' He filled his hand with her breast and squeezed. 'You good with that?'

She tongued her lower lip and then nodded.

His cock went even harder, throbbing like a motherfucker. A reaction almost vicious in its intensity.

Ripper grasped her hips and tossed her further up the bed. She was lithe. Flexible. Easy to position how he wanted her. He liked that. 'Lay back.'

She did so, parting her legs in an achingly slow, teasing movement.

He shed the rest of his clothes and joined her, kneeling between her thighs. 'I told you earlier that I was gonna fuck you slow.' But as she'd agreed to him coming inside her, 'slow' wasn't going to happen – he was too sexually revved up now. 'I changed my mind.'

He tossed her legs over his shoulders, notched the head of his dick inside her, splayed a palm on the bed either side of her head, and roughly rolled his hips forward – burying every inch of himself in her pussy.

She sucked in a breath, her hands flying up to grip his forearms, her nails stabbing hard. 'Fuck, you're deep.'

'I'm gonna go even deeper.' He pounded into her, his pace nothing short of ferocious. He felt her body strain; knew she'd be rising to meet every thrust if she could have moved. In this position, trapped beneath him, she could only take.

Moans eased out of that carnal mouth still swollen from blowing him. Her breasts bounced prettily with each forceful dig of his cock. Her pussy, so hot and tight ... he didn't think he could ever get enough of it. Enough of *her*.

He curled over her a little more, snarling against her temple. 'I'm gonna fuck you on the next full moon. *Knot* you.' Knotting always – and only ever – occurred during full moons. 'You'll feel my dick swelling inside you. It'll lock deep. So deep my come will stay right where I fucking put it.'

She hissed, stabbing her nails harder into his skin – just shy of drawing blood.

'I'll do it, Emberlyn. Don't fucking doubt it.' He took her harder, sliding his shaft over her clit; feeling her pussy spasm and tighten.

'Ripper,' she rasped. Then her release hit her, dazed her, dragged a scream from her throat as her pussy strangled him.

He hammered into her once, twice, and then erupted inside her – his release amplified by the knowledge that he wasn't filling a condom this time, he was filling *her*.

Shaking with aftershocks, Ripper lowered her legs and settled his body over hers. He nuzzled her neck, breathing her in. She still smelled of him. He wondered if she'd noticed that his scent took longer to fade now – an indication that it had become embedded deeper into her skin. A thought he liked.

Her fingers sifted through his hair. 'I have to say something,' she said, her voice languid but also ... cautious. 'It may or may not spoil the mood, depending on if your personal views line up with mine.'

He lifted his head to meet her gaze, struggling to read it. 'Okay.'

'By scent-marking each other, we silently agreed to exclusivity, right?'

'Right.' If she was considering changing that, he wouldn't be fucking pleased.

'You mentioned the next full moon, and ... Look, I know what they do to your kind. I know they make you seriously hypersexual and it isn't easy to maintain control. Some werewolves have the attitude that what happens on full moons doesn't count; that if they sleep with someone other than their partners or mates, it should be understood and forgiven. I disagree. If that's an issue for you, if you want the freedom to go with the flow on full moons, okay. But if that's the case—'

'It isn't. There are wolves who use full moons as an excuse to fuck around.' And it *was* an excuse. 'I'm not one of them.'

She drew in a subtle breath. 'Okay.'

As a thought entered his mind, he felt his eyes narrow. 'Did Michael consider it an excuse?'

Emberlyn tensed, surprised his mind had gone there. Everybody liked Michael; considered him a 'good man'. One so good he'd never do anything as awful as cheat on his mate. The prospect wouldn't even occur to them. It hadn't occurred to her, either.

So she'd gotten the shock of her life when it happened.

He'd come home one morning with his tail tucked between his legs, struggling to meet her eyes and – after a lot of prodding and pushing from her – finally admitted he'd slept with another woman the previous night. But that wasn't something Emberlyn talked about.

'No,' she replied, her voice coming out unintentionally flat.

Every line in Ripper's trademark stony expression smoothed out as his face softened. 'He did, didn't he?' Not a question, a sure statement.

She looked away, swallowing hard.

'At some point, he had sex with another werewolf and pled that the full moon made him do it,' Ripper surmised.

She snapped her gaze back to his. 'Do you really want to talk about my ex-mate while your cock is still inside me?'

Ignoring that, Ripper stared at her, pensive. 'You're not the kind of woman who'd overlook your mate betraying you, no matter what excuse he came up with. You broke it off. The mating.' It was a guess. And it was correct.

She cursed low and harsh, rubbing at her scalp.

He touched his forehead to hers in a gesture that, for a were-wolf, was as intimate as any kiss. 'Talk to me, baby.'

Baby. The soft, possessive endearment wriggled its way past her defenses, and she heard herself admit, 'I broke it off. I'm not forgiving enough to look past something like that. It's just not in me. It's not like he *asked* for forgiveness. He didn't even apol-ogize. He got defensive and played the whole thing down; made out like I was being dramatic.'

Anger flickered in the depths of Ripper's eyes. 'So you two argued?'

'Big time. It got ugly. When he realized there'd be no changing my mind, that I was seriously done, he lost it.' She licked her lips. 'He was still riding the high of the full moon, so I guess that contributed to why he morphed into his In-between form.'

Ripper's gaze went slitted. 'He attack you?'

'Yes. I scared him off with magick.'

'You said you were hurt by a Rabid before,' he remembered. 'You meant Michael.'

She swallowed. 'Yes. He didn't simply morph, he turned Rabid.'

Ripper slowly shook his head, incredulous. 'Secrets aren't easily kept at Chilgrave. How did I not hear about this?'

'I only told Paisley. Michael said zip about the cheating to others. He wouldn't have even told me if I hadn't pressed him so hard. He was clear that no one else knew and no one else would … as if that made the situation better. He also told me he'd sworn Opal to secrecy.'

'That's who he cheated on you with?'

'Yes.' Part of Carver's clan, Opal was now mated and pregnant. And she pointedly avoided Emberlyn to this very day.

'Did you confront her?'

'Yup. She cried and apologized profusely. Which, to be fair, is more than Michael did. And her tears and remorse were genuine.' Still, Emberlyn hadn't felt all too forgiving; she'd wanted to skin the bitch alive. Instead ... 'I made her a deal.'

'Deal?'

'I wouldn't make her pay if she kept what happened to herself. She was ashamed and didn't want to suffer any consequences, so she was quick to agree.'

Ripper frowned. 'You were protecting his reputation. Why?'

'A lot of werewolves consider betraying mates taboo. I knew there'd be some who'd judge him enough that they wouldn't put their safety on the line to search for him in Bloodhill. I didn't consider him my mate anymore, but I didn't want him stuck in that form. I wouldn't wish that fate on anyone.'

Ripper's frown deepened. 'If you didn't see him as your mate, why did you hold off longer than most would have in your shoes to publicly declare that the mating tie was broken? Why not ...' He trailed off as realization played out over his face. 'You blame yourself for him turning Rabid.'

Damn him for reading her so well. It made her feel far too exposed. 'I knew better than to argue with a werewolf still riding the high of a full moon.'

Ripper's gaze snagged hers, serious. 'It isn't your fault, Emberlyn. There wouldn't have been an argument if the prick hadn't cheated on you.'

'You're pissed,' she noted, hearing the emotion roughen his gravelly voice.

His expression was all *Well, obviously*. 'Yeah, I'm pissed,' he bit off. 'You were his mate. His loyalty to you should have been absolute. It's bad enough that he cheated on you. That weak motherfucker blamed the full moon, expected you to give him a free pass and didn't even apologize.' He touched the tip of his nose to hers. 'You deserved better. If the prick was still around, I'd punch the piss out of him.'

That angry little rant touched her on a level she wouldn't have expected. Very few people had been protective of Emberlyn; few had cared how she felt or what she needed. Somehow, Ripper had become one of them.

Swallowing, she wound her fingers in his hair. 'Kiss me.'

He didn't hesitate. He took her mouth in a sensual, hungry, explicit kiss. And the dick that had earlier slipped out of her began to harden against her clit.

He pulled his lips free, his eyes flaring with heat. 'This time, you get slow.'

CHAPTER TWENTY-ONE

◈

A couple of hours later, Ripper lowered his cutlery to his empty plate and leaned back in his chair. Across from him at the dining table, Emberlyn was almost done with her meal. He'd never seen anyone tackle spaghetti with elegance, but she somehow managed it.

As he watched her, satisfaction rumbled in his belly. He liked feeding her. Liked seeing her enjoy something he'd made for her. But he also just plain liked watching her eat.

She really *tasted* every bite, chewing it slowly. Always sat upright, her posture perfect. There was no slurping, no scraping the dishware with utensils, no splashing sauce or dropping food.

He had the feeling her grace was innate, because it was *not* something she'd gotten from Millicent – that woman had been far from elegant.

Anger still lingered in his system. Fucking Michael had cheated on her. The guy would have known better than most how much Emberlyn had been let down by all those around her. He, her own mate, had become one of them.

Full moons had power over a werewolf's control, yes, but not in a sexual sense. They might feel the drive to mate, but it wasn't all-consuming. Still, some used that bullshit defense for cheating, and there were people who bought it.

If Michael had honestly expected Emberlyn to buy and forgive it, he either hadn't known her well or he'd thought he could manipulate her into letting it go.

Had the guy openly admitted he'd had a moment of weakness and then apologized to Emberlyn, Ripper could have at least respected that Michael had owned his fuckup. Everyone made mistakes. It was part of life. But you couldn't betray your mate and then call them dramatic for being crushed by it.

She could have spread the news of Michael's betrayal far and wide. Could have wrecked his reputation. Could have turned other wolves against him. Could have made Opal suffer in any number of ways for any length of time.

Instead, Emberlyn had kept it quiet to ensure searches would still be launched for Michael. She had more compassion in her than people would guess, but Ripper supposed she preferred that it wasn't common knowledge; never wanting to display what others might perceive as weakness.

He wondered if she would have grown up to be quite so vengeful and ruthless if the coven hadn't targeted her the way they had since she was a small child. Probably not. Even as he wished that she hadn't suffered such persecution, he still wouldn't want her to be any other version of herself than the pitiless witch in front of him.

Having finished her food, she set her cutlery down on her plate and lifted her glass of water. Sipping at it, she eyed him. 'You swore you'd stop being mad if I stayed for dinner. You're not living up to your end of the bargain.'

'It's hard to not be pissed.' He nudged her foot with his own beneath the table. 'You're mine to protect now. He hurt you. I want to beat the shit out of him.'

'His current fate is far worse than anything you or I could have put him through.' She set down her glass, her expression turning ... inscrutable. 'You haven't asked if the rumor is true,' she said, her tone careless.

'What rumor?'

'That I used magick to make him turn Rabid. Knowing he betrayed me, you must be wondering if in fact I did do that to punish him.'

Ripper felt his brow furrow. 'The thought didn't even enter my head.' He leaned forward, planting his lower arms on the table. 'You're many things, Emberlyn, but you're not callous.'

A hint of warmth blotted her eyes. 'Watch it, Rip. I might start thinking you like me.'

He hiked up a brow. 'That's not already obvious?'

Snorting, she carefully slid her plate aside. 'On another note, who taught you to cook?'

'My aunt Yvette.' She ran their clan's diner, and she kept nagging him to take Emberlyn there for dinner.

'That explains why you're good at it.'

'You're not so bad in the kitchen yourself. Millicent gave you lessons?'

'Very early on so I could feed myself. She spent a lot of time refining her craft.'

He felt his lips thin. Honestly, the more he learned about Emberlyn's childhood, the more he disagreed with the general consensus that she was 'raised' by Millicent. Her grandmother had been too self-focused to truly raise anyone. 'What made her so power-hungry?'

Running one finger down the stem of her glass, Emberlyn gave a delicate shrug. 'Kage will tell you it was because she was a sociopath. Maybe that's true. With Millicent, it seemed to be all about the rush. She was always trying to beat the initial high she'd felt on gathering more power the very first time. She kept chasing it, kept telling herself that the next thrill would *finally* be so much better. Only it never was.'

'Like with a serial killer who keeps trying to beat the high of their first murder.'

'Yes. I think she believed that once she beat it, she'd never crave it again; that the empty spots inside her would be filled. Those cold voids ... they allowed her to cross lines others wouldn't, but they denied her any real sense of fulfilment.'

'She cared for you, though.'

'In the only way someone like that can care for another,' Emberlyn conceded with a nod. 'I think she also cared for all three of her children. She just couldn't give anything of herself to them. She didn't know how, and she didn't try to learn.'

Ripper cocked his head. 'How are you ... you? You had no real role model.' Her mother hadn't been in her life long enough to have a true influence on her.

She twisted her mouth. 'I looked up to Lilith.'

'Lilith?'

'I know it's rumored that she had an "in" with Satan – I can't comment on that, as I'm not sure if it's true or not – but she was always real nice to me. Very dignified and stylish.'

His brows drawing together, he leaned further forward. 'You've met Lilith?'

'The spirits of many Vautiers roam the manor. Not my mother, though. I never saw her. Not all spirits are strong enough to cross realms. Avery wasn't strong.'

So he'd heard. 'Your mother really died of heartbreak?'

'In a sense. She loved with her entire being, and she thought that the sperm donor was her forever. When he left, it wrecked her. She checked out. Stopped using magick. A witch who can't or who doesn't use their magick can fade away and die.'

'Like Rosemary did.' He was about to speak again, but then the distant purring of a car engine reached his ears. 'I have a visitor.' Annoyed at the interruption, he pushed to his feet with an aggrieved sigh. 'Don't do that thing again.'

'What thing?'

'Clean up all on your own when I disappear from the room.'

'You cooked. It only seems fair that I clean.'

'You do it even when *you* cook.'

'Those were accidents; I forgot you wanted to help.'

He inwardly snorted. 'Well, don't "forget" this time.'

She raised her hands. 'I'll wait for you before I get started.'

He gave her a look that said she'd better – to which she only regarded him flatly – and then stalked out of the room. He reached the front door before his visitor knocked. When he opened it, he had to bite back a curse. *CeCe*.

Taking tentative steps up the path, she offered him a bright smile that was edged with caution. She wouldn't be smiling if she knew he had company. But as he'd earlier picked Emberlyn up from the manor, her vehicle wasn't parked here.

Stepping onto the porch, he pulled the door closed behind him. Not to hide that Emberlyn was here, but to keep her shielded from any shit CeCe might toss.

Her face fell. 'I'm not welcome inside, I take it.' She sighed, pausing at the base of the stone steps. 'I really am sorry for everything, Rip. I'm trying to make it right.'

So she'd said before, but he'd yet to see her actively attempt it.

She gingerly climbed onto his porch. 'I know I'm not your favorite person right now, but we've been friends *how* long? Definitely too long to throw that friendship away. It's worth saving. I came here to fix things so we could get back on track.'

Maybe she did come here for that reason, and maybe they could in fact do that. This wasn't the time or place to explore this matter further, though. 'We can talk tomorrow. Not here and now.'

Her brow furrowing, she moved closer. 'Why not? It's a Wednesday evening, there's no clan fires to put out, you don't have visitors. I don't see how this could be a bad time.'

The breeze fluttered around them, carrying woodsy scents and stirring up their own. When her face went rock hard, he knew she'd picked up the smell of Emberlyn intertwined with sex.

She staggered back a step as if he'd gone to slap her. 'So, it actually is true. You're fucking the witch.' She put a hand to her mouth, her eyes widening in horror. 'Oh, my God.'

He tipped his chin at her vehicle. 'You need to leave.'

She flicked the front door a glance, her face contorting into a sour look tinged with jealousy. 'Is she in there?'

'CeCe, go.'

Her face sullen, she balled up her hands. 'It makes no sense! You don't trust witches. You keep your dealings with them short and sweet. You don't *fuck* them.'

He shot her a severe look. 'Who I have in my bed is my business, not yours. Never yours.'

Her cheeks reddening, CeCe notched up her chin. 'Is *she* why you won't agree to the triad? Has this been going on for longer than people think?'

'Jesus, are you still going on about that fucking triad?'

She flinched. 'You don't have to speak of it with such disgust. If there's anything you should be so put off by, it's *a witch*. You're out of your mind to be even associating with Emberlyn Vautier! She's a lunatic! She's—'

'Marked as mine,' he finished, the words rough and low, 'so watch what the fuck you say.'

She snapped her mouth shut, shaking her head. 'Something's *wrong* here. You would never roll in the sack with one of her kind. Maybe she bespelled you or something. If a Rabid can be trapped in a state of bloodlust by magick, then a person could also be trapped in a state of sexual lust.'

He couldn't help but pull a face at the ridiculous notion. 'For shit's sake, CeCe, *just go.*'

'I'm trying to help you!'

The door behind him creaked open, and then ... 'Sounds more like you're trying to convince yourself that I'm no threat to your triad dream,' said Emberlyn.

Shit. Ripper glanced over his shoulder. His witch casually propped her hip against the doorjamb, cool and calm, regarding CeCe with a mix of boredom and pity.

He half-turned, about to usher Emberlyn back inside.

'We're having a private conversation here, if you don't mind,' CeCe snarked at her.

'If you wanted to keep it private, you shouldn't have raised your voice. I don't have werewolf hearing but even I heard you just fine.' Emberlyn folded her arms. 'If you have something to accuse me of, you can at least do it to my face. It's only fair.'

CeCe straightened her shoulders. 'You did something to him.'

Emberlyn's lips kicked up. 'I've done quite a few things to Rip.' Her tone was pure sex, and it made CeCe's eyes blaze.

'You put some sort of spell on him! He would never otherwise touch you!'

'You really do believe that,' Emberlyn sensed. 'Only because you *want* to believe it, but still.'

'I know I'm right!'

'I know you're eaten up with jealousy right now. You think of Ripper as yours; think of yourself as *the woman* in his life. The only one he ever let close.'

CeCe's upper lip curled. 'Don't talk like you know me.'

'Why? You talk like you know me.' Emberlyn pushed away from the doorjamb. 'I don't know if this will really sink in – you seem to be a person for whom logic isn't always required – but it's safe to say that Ripper doesn't consider himself yours. He wouldn't have covered me in his scent, let alone sexed me up, if he did.

'I don't point that out to be a bitch, only to highlight that you're both on different pages. I realize that might be hard to accept, I do, but try. Because it can't possibly be worse than living in denial.' She coolly sauntered back inside.

CeCe glowered after her. 'Hey, where are you—'

'No,' Ripper bit out when she went to storm past him.

CeCe's nostrils flared. 'You're fine with her speaking to me that way?'

'All she did was give you a dose of the truth. I'm hoping you'll listen to it. Now go.' He growled when she went to argue. '*Don't* test my patience any more than you already have.'

CeCe dragged in a breath, clamped her lips shut and stormed off.

Only once her car had crossed the boundaries of his land did he return inside. In the kitchen, he found Emberlyn stood at the sink facing the window. 'She's gone,' he said. 'I'd apologize for her behavior—'

'No need.' Emberlyn turned to him. 'You didn't do anything wrong.'

Studying her calm expression, he realized . . . 'You're not even angry at what she said, are you?'

Emberlyn only shrugged.

He stalked to her. 'You're so used to people laying accusations at your feet that you're not even bothered she claimed you're using magick to control me. It pisses me off that you've had reasons to become so used to it.'

'A lot of things are pissing you off tonight.'

'We can add something else to the list.' He gestured at the spotless kitchen. 'You said you'd wait for me before you started cleaning up.'

One slender brow lifted. 'Did I?'

'Yes, you did.' He snapped his teeth, gently grazing her chin. 'You lied.'

'I didn't lie.' A haughty glance. 'I simply changed my mind.'

'You do that a lot.'

Mischief danced in her eyes. 'You're not used to it yet?'

He planted a hand on the counter either side of her, caging her in. 'I'm more used to it than I care to be.'

'You'd be bored if I gave you your own way in everything. Not that you'll ever admit it.'

Truthfully . . . she wasn't wrong on either count.

CHAPTER TWENTY-TWO

❧

'Personally, I think you should go slap her,' Paisley declared with a haughty sniff as they stepped forward in the line.

'There are four "hers" over there,' began Emberlyn, glancing out of the bakery window. 'Which one are you referring to?'

'Any or all of them. CeCe is their girl, I get it, but she's no victim here. They look at you like you're going out of your way to make her miserable.'

They did indeed. It had been like that for the past week.

CeCe hadn't taken Emberlyn's advice to stop living in denial. Nope, she'd been sure to share her 'the devil's witch has magickly mind-fucked Ripper' opinion far and wide – something he'd later reamed her ass for. She now officially loathed Emberlyn.

If the weird woman had hoped to rile up her clan and turn them against Emberlyn, she'd failed. No one outside CeCe's group of friends seemed to agree with her. In fact, many of Emberlyn's customers had snickered or rolled their eyes about it, accurately calling CeCe's theory ridiculous and jealousy-based.

'The only person getting in the way of CeCe's happiness is CeCe herself,' Paisley added. 'It's almost like she's been driving down a road of self-sabotage recently.'

'While blindfolded.'

'And drugged.'

'I don't think things would have gotten so bad if she wasn't quite so stubborn. She just wouldn't accept or respect Ripper's decision. Persistence is a good trait, but you have to know when to quit; that there are times when it's best to let something go. Otherwise, the trait becomes a flaw.'

Paisley dipped her chin. 'There's fighting for what you want, and there's staying in a fight that you just can't win.'

Right then, the person in front of them moved away. *Finally*.

Stepping forward, Emberlyn smiled at the woman behind the counter and then peered down at the tall glass case. She pointed at an egg-salad sandwich. 'I'll have one of those, a bottle of water and a raspberry tart, please.'

Gathering the order together, the baker asked, 'You eating in or out?'

'In.'

'I'll have my usual please,' Paisley piped up.

The baker squinted as she remembered, 'A meatball sub, a chocolate square and a can of soda. Right?'

Paisley grinned. 'Right. I wish my memory was that good.'

They both edged over to the stainless-steel counter and paid for their orders. Emberlyn piled everything on a plastic tray, which she then carried over to the window table that Paisley had selected.

'They're *still* there,' complained Paisley.

Emberlyn glanced out of the window. Yep, CeCe's buds were still there, and still staring. 'But not brave enough to come face me, so they're not worth my notice.' She unloaded the tray, arranged the items on the table and placed the tray on the corner pile.

Once she and Paisley were seated, Emberlyn released a little magick that would keep their conversation private. The effect was like thin, transparent walls slamming up. The sounds around them – dough tumbling in the mixer, plates clattering, the whir of the dishwasher and the conversations of others – promptly faded.

Anyone who tried eavesdropping on Emberlyn and Paisley's chat would hear only muffled voices, no words distinguishable.

'Ooh,' began Paisley, 'Kerr's ushering them away, look.'

Emberlyn tracked her friend's gaze to see Kerr glaring at the group, waving his hand to indicate they get moving. He caught her eye through the window, rolled both his own and then walked off.

'Notice they left fast. They're only bold when they think no one above them in the clan's hierarchy is paying attention.' Paisley removed the cellophane from her sub. 'You know, I'm insulted on your behalf that anyone would imply you'd need magick to snag a man's attention *or* keep it.'

Emberlyn nabbed her plate – which was slightly warm, presumably from the dishwasher – and slid it closer. 'It's CeCe's attempt to explain away Ripper's sudden interest in me.'

'Sudden?' Paisley scoffed. 'There's been zing between you and him for years. She obviously didn't notice.'

Eyeing her friend, Emberlyn unwrapped her sandwich. 'I didn't realize that *you'd* noticed.'

'I didn't bother mentioning it because I didn't think anything would come of it. I'm happy to be mistaken, because you deserve to have something good in your life.'

'You talk as if it'll be permanent.'

'You don't think it's heading in that direction? Because you'd be wrong – it totally is.'

'Not necessarily.' Emberlyn bit into her sandwich, frowning when some egg slipped out of the other end. 'Though CeCe's doing a good job of getting on Rip's last nerve, he still cares for her. Not that I believe he'd choose to build something with her – she screwed that pooch too badly. I just mean that those feelings might get in the way of him building something with someone else.'

Chewing some of her sub, Paisley shook her head. 'I don't think so. Ripper would be a fool to let you slip through his fingers. And he's no fool.' Paisley tilted her head. 'You seeing him tonight?'

'Yup. He's picking me up later. We ate at my place the past couple of evenings, so he declared that it's his turn to cook. He's rather good in the kitchen.' And in the bedroom, but that was off-topic.

'I really do think you should keep him.'

Biting into her sandwich again, Emberlyn frowned. 'Like he's a dollar I found on the floor?'

'Yes. Because you *want* to.'

Conscious of some egg sticking to her cheek, Emberlyn plucked a napkin from the table dispenser and wiped at it. 'Actually—'

'You want to,' Paisley repeated. 'Admit it.'

Sighing, Emberlyn conceded it with a brief tilt of her head. 'I never expected him. I mean, I always knew he was super protective, but I didn't think that trait would ever be centered on me this way.' She crumpled up the napkin and dumped it beside the dispenser. 'He gets so mad when anyone gives me issues. If he thinks something is playing on my mind, he prods and pokes until I talk about it; he wants to fix it, make me feel better. And he's always goddamn feeding me.'

Paisley's eyes gleamed with suppressed laughter. 'It bothers you that he wants to get behind your walls, because it's working very well. It also weirds you out a little as you're not used to people angling to get close to you.'

'It would be annoying if it was in any way patronizing. But it's not.' Emberlyn grabbed her bottle, unscrewed the cap and knocked back some water. 'It's like . . . he knows I can quite easily handle my own shit and take care of myself. He just doesn't want me to have to do it alone.'

'How is that bad?' asked Paisley around a mouthful of food, covering her lips with her hand.

'I didn't say it was bad.' Emberlyn placed her water back down. 'It just makes it hard to be okay with knowing that this might not be something he intends to make permanent. And honestly, the idea of "more" is a little scary. The last time I had a werewolf in my life, it didn't end so well.'

'That was a whole different beast. And the probability of it happening again is super low, as we once already covered.'

'Ripper feels the call of the moon more than most.'

'But he's strong enough, especially with the aid of your elixirs, to fight it. And he'd damn well never use it as an excuse to cheat.'

Emberlyn took another bite of her sandwich. 'I told him what Michael did.'

Paisley's eyes went wide. 'Really?'

'I wasn't going to. But he guessed, and he pushed me to admit it. Then he called me "baby", and apparently I'm a total sucker for that because the next thing I knew I was blurting out the story.'

Her lips twitching, Paisley opened her can of soda. 'Hearing that, I like Ripper more than I already did. What did he say?'

'Something about wanting to punch the piss out of Michael.' Which had been . . . touching. 'He said I deserved better.'

'You do.' Sipping her drink, Paisley watched Emberlyn

carefully. 'You trust Ripper. You've been super secretive about Michael's betrayal – you even kept it from Kage, though we both know it's because I'm your favorite.'

'I kept it from your brother because he wouldn't have agreed to keep it secret,' Emberlyn countered. 'Kage would have been too furious at Michael to protect his reputation. He would have talked everyone into letting Michael rot in Bloodhill.'

'Don't think I wasn't tempted to do the same. The only reason I didn't is that I make a point of never breaking my word, unlike Kage. Anyway, for you to have told Ripper that Michael betrayed you, you must trust him.'

Emberlyn hummed. 'I guess I do.' Which said a lot, because she didn't put her faith in people easily. 'So much so that I didn't even ask him to promise not to repeat what I told him.' She'd automatically known that he never would. 'But I trusted Michael, too.'

'Ripper is *not* him. He's stronger. Has more integrity. He's loyal right down to his soul. Hence why I'm telling you that you really ought to keep him.'

'I could only do that if he was interested in being kept.'

'He is. He may not consciously know it yet but, believe me, he is.'

Walking down her front path later that day, Emberlyn watched as Ripper rounded his truck. Their gazes collided and, quite naturally, her pulse lost its rhythm as their chemistry sparked to waking life. It often felt like said chemistry was electrically powered. Like her body had been plugged into a damn socket. That ever-present pull between them just never eased up.

He looked his fill, like always – his eyes flaring with heat. She'd learned that he liked this dress. Champagne-colored and body-hugging, it had a subtle thigh slit and provided a nice flash of cleavage.

As she reached him, he stepped into her, sucking the oxygen out of the air. Or, at least, that was how it felt – the uncivilized vibe, the rough and gritty deliciousness of him . . . it all stole the breath right out of her lungs.

He dragged the tip of his nose along her cheekbone. 'You've got to stop doing this.'

She blinked. 'What?'

'Tempting me to fuck you out in the open.' He cupped her hip, his warm lips grazing her cheek as they slid to her ear. 'I only have so much restraint.'

'Don't blame me if your cock is hard.'

'Who should I blame? It ain't your fault that you stroll around looking like every man's fantasy, I get that – you would no matter what you were wearing. But you knew if you put on that dress I'd remember what happened the last time you wore it.'

She almost shivered on recalling 'the last time'. Her dress had ended up hiked around her waist as he'd fucked her against the wall – he hadn't even properly closed his front door he'd been on her so fast. 'Maybe I want a repeat.'

Something wicked seeped into his eyes and pooled there. 'Oh, you'll get one.' He opened the passenger door of his truck, lifted her by her hips and set her on the seat.

She batted away his hand when he went to put on her seatbelt. 'We've had this conversation, I can—'

The weight of his lips on hers silenced her. His tongue slipped into her mouth, tangled with her own and swept her into a maelstrom of carnal sensation.

There was a *click*, and he pulled back. Among the heat in his eyes was a pinch of amused satisfaction.

And she realized he'd taken care of the seatbelt situation while she'd been distracted.

'You're an ass,' she told him matter-of-factly.

His massive shoulders gave an uncaring shrug as he closed her door. Moments later, he was beside her.

Using magick, she wrenched at his seatbelt and wrapped it around him until yet another *click* sounded in the small space.

His brows lifted, mirth still a flickering flame in his gaze. 'Thanks, baby.'

There he went with the 'baby' again. It made her belly clench.

He switched on the engine and drove down the dirt road which cut through the land that Millicent had willed to him. 'How did your day play out?'

'Work. Lunch with Paisley. Whipping up more potions. That was pretty much it.' She placed her purse between her feet. 'What about you?'

He shifted gears. 'Me and a bunch of my clan were hunting in Bloodhill until a couple of hours ago. Then it was a matter of delivering the meat and scrubbing myself clean in the shower.' He tossed her a sideways glance. 'I suppose you decided to leave out the part where Kerr had to hurry along CeCe's friends,' he added, his tone hard but casual.

She shrugged. 'It wasn't worth mentioning. They were just staring.'

'You and I know what it means when werewolves stare like that. They're making it known that you're on their shitlist and warning you to watch your back.'

Yes, she *did* know that. However . . . 'I'm not worried.'

'That isn't the point. You're mine. I don't like anyone thinking they can act that way toward you.' His voice roughened with irritation and possession. 'To add to that, I'm their Alpha. They should have too much respect for my claim to you than to behave that way.'

Sensing just how deep his annoyance ran, she guessed . . . 'You had a little talk with them, didn't you?'

'Not because I think you need anyone else fighting your battles for you. In fact, I can't think of a single person who needs that less than you do. But, as I pointed out before, they should show more respect, given who you are to me.'

'I get it.' She nibbled on her lower lip. 'I hope you don't think I should behave "respectfully" toward them if they ignore your warning and come at me.' Because that wouldn't happen.

He shot her a grave look. 'If they ever come at you – which is unlikely – do what you have to do.'

Surprise pricked at Emberlyn. As their Alpha, he'd be instinctively protective of them. For him to basically give her the go-ahead to deal with them as she saw fit, he was essentially prioritizing her welfare over theirs. And damn the bastard for that, because it only made Paisley's suggestion to keep him all the more attractive.

'You watching the game Friday?'

Assuming he meant the high school football game, she nodded. Each clan had their own team, as did the coven. 'Me and the twins always attend together.' She and Paisley would cheer and boo and pretend they knew stuff about football.

'You should come with us. All three of you.'

She felt her brow pinch. 'Who's "us"?'

'Me, Logan, Kerr, Crew and a few others.'

Well, that would be new. Emberlyn and the twins usually straddled the edge of the spectator crowd, never part of any groups. 'I suppose we could meet you there.'

'Or I can pick you up.'

'I usually give the twins a ride.'

'Crew can do that. Then you can ride with me.' It was a pressing suggestion.

'Does it really matter if you and I arrive separately?'

'No, so it'll be easy for you to agree to shake things up,' he cleverly replied. 'It makes sense. Crew lives closer to both Paisley and Kage than you do, and the shortcut I can take through this land to your house makes it a quick drive.'

Very true, but she sensed that that wasn't his sole reason for 'suggesting' this. 'You like driving me places, don't you?'

'Yeah,' he easily confirmed. 'It's one of the ways in which male werewolves like taking care of who belongs to them. You should know that already.'

She *had* known that. She just hadn't thought it would apply to him – they hadn't been involved with each other long, and they hadn't agreed on anything permanent. Yet.

'Plus, it means I know you're safe.'

She felt a brow inch up. 'Are you implying that I'm a bad driver?'

'Not at all,' he assured her. 'I'm protective. You know that. Right now, you have trouble coming at you from several angles. It makes me antsy. I like to have you where I can see you. Also, while I don't anticipate you having a road accident, I prefer driving you places because my truck can better sustain a hard impact than your car.'

'Don't be so sure.'

He cast her a quick frown. 'What does that mean?'

'My car is protected by blood magick. It's tougher than a tank. Maybe I should pick you up instead.'

His shoulders lifted and fell. 'Whatever you want. Makes no odds to me as long as you're not alone.'

A crackle came through his truck's communication radio.

He picked up the walkie talkie, pressed down on the side button and put it to his mouth. 'Problem?' He released the button.

Another crackle. 'Yeah,' Kerr replied. 'Your aunt Yvette called. A fight broke out at her diner. I figured you'd want to deal with it.'

Ripper's face firmed. 'Call her back; tell her I'll be there in two minutes.' He set down the radio and gave Emberlyn a quick look. 'Gotta make a pitstop.'

'No problem.' She wasn't surprised he'd want to deal with the situation himself, given that it involved his aunt.

Ripper took a turn that led to the town's neutral territory and drove straight to the diner. He whipped his truck into a parking space, his alert gaze taking a moment to scan the many other vehicles and the people loitering outside.

As Emberlyn unclicked her seatbelt, he cast her a quick frown. She squinted. 'You're not going to ask me to wait here, are you?'

'I could, but something tells me it'd get me nowhere,' he muttered, exiting the truck.

The man was not wrong. She collected her purse, swung open the door and allowed him to help her slide out of the vehicle.

He curled his fingers around her wrist in a move that felt protective . . . like he didn't want to have to wonder where exactly she physically was at any point.

Planting a hand on the door, he effortlessly shoved it open and tugged her into the diner. Aside from the banging, cursing, yelling and crashing coming from the restrooms, it was relatively quiet – every patron and worker was silent, on their feet and nosily straining to hear what was going on.

The crowd parted to allow them through, nodding at them in respect.

In the men's bathroom, they found one of Carver's sons exchanging blows with a member of Shane's clan. And they'd made a *mess*.

A stall door was hanging on one hinge. The hand towel dispenser was on the floor. The trash can had been knocked over, and litter was strewn across the tiled floor.

Ripper released her wrist, his hard gaze fixed on the wolves. 'Enough.' The word was a harsh, growl-edged whip that sliced through the air, heavy with a pure Alpha power that stirred up her magick.

The brawling males paused, their shoulders drooping ... as if the power in Ripper's voice had crashed down on their shoulders like a heavy and encumbering weight.

'Both of you back up,' he ordered.

They did, panting and a little unsteady. Both sported cuts, swellings and the beginnings of bruises.

'The fuck is going on here?' Ripper demanded, looking from one male to the other.

They glared at the floor, silent.

'I asked a question. Someone had better fucking answer it.'

Carver's son, TJ, raised adrenaline-glazed eyes to Ripper. 'I was about to leave the bathroom when Benny accused my dad of being in on what happened to Lincoln. I told him that was bullshit. He laughed, called my dad the coven's pet dog and said a whole bunch of other crap. I threw the first punch, I'll admit it. But he started in on me for no damn good reason.'

'Oh, come on,' Benny appealed, turning to Ripper, 'we all know that Carver's in league with Reena.'

Ripper glared at him. 'We don't know shit. *You* don't know shit.'

'*She* does,' said Benny, pointing at Emberlyn. 'She'll tell ya I'm right. Carver's part of it, ain't he?'

Emberlyn lifted her shoulders. 'I can't say for sure, so I'm not going to. I don't lay accusations at people's feet unless I have proof of guilt. Do you have proof? I'd love to see it.'

Benny's jaw hardened. 'I don't need evidence—'

'Sure you do,' she contradicted. 'Otherwise, it's just speculation.'

TJ nodded curtly in agreement while Benny flushed.

Ripper advanced on the latter male. 'I don't care what you choose to believe – that's between you and you. And if you want to voice it to Carver or one of his wolves, that's your prerogative.' He lowered his face toward Benny's, his eyes boring into his. 'But you don't air that out *here*, in my aunt's diner.'

'I-I *am* sorry about that p-part,' stammered Benny. 'But I'm not sorry about what I said.'

'Which is why I ain't sorry I punched you,' TJ told him. He refocused on Ripper. 'It wasn't cool of us to throw down here, though – I'm sorry for that. I'll clean up and pay for the damage.'

'You both will,' said Ripper. 'I don't care that he threw the first punch, Benny. You tossed the first verbal hit, and you had to know it would result in a fight.'

The restroom door creaked open, and Shane breezed inside. 'One of my wolves called.' He took in the entire scene. 'Give me a rundown, would you, Rip?'

Ripper relayed everything to the other Alpha, who was quite clearly peeved at his wolf for starting shit here of all places.

Shane scowled at Benny. 'Once you've cleaned up, you'll be leaving with me – and you won't like what's coming next.'

Carver turned up soon after. There was a lot of blustering and cursing from him when he heard what Benny had said to his son. Emberlyn suspected the only reason the Alpha didn't fly at the offending wolf was that Ripper would have flipped.

Once the restroom was set to rights and the brawlers left with their Alphas in tow, Yvette sought out Ripper and gave him an affectionate smile. 'Thanks for stepping in, darlin'. They weren't going to stop any time soon.' She looked at Emberlyn, her smile widening. 'I keep telling my nephew to bring you here for dinner. You might as well stay and eat.'

Ah … but that would be something close to a date, and he might not want to—

'I was gonna say the same thing,' said Ripper, turning to Emberlyn. 'You up for it?'

She felt her lips curve. 'I'm up for it.'

CHAPTER TWENTY-THREE

❦

Raising her hands above the altar Friday morning, Emberlyn stared down at the pocket-sized chunk of bloodstone as—

Scuffling sounds coming from below.

Pressing her lips together, she stomped twice on the floor. 'I'm trying to concentrate.'

Another noise came from the basement. A light crash this time.

'You're not luring me down there, no matter what you do. My answer is still no.' Emberlyn drew in a centering breath and began to chant. Teal, black and silver magick motes slowly drifted down from her palms. Motes that swirled, thickened, pulsed and sparkled.

Then they shot downward into the bloodstone, engraving the protective spell into it. The gem tremored, pulsing with light.

Done reciting the spell, she closed her fists. The bloodstone stilled, the glow fading. She scooped it up – it felt warm in her hand, purring with power. Satisfied, she placed it in the pocket of her black ribbed pants.

She'd agreed to do a healing session this afternoon. Reworking a person's energy involved unblocking clogged pathways and ridding them of negative vibes. It was easy to accidentally take the latter inside you. The bloodstone would deflect any negative energy.

She usually did such sessions after the hub closed for the day, but it wasn't going to be possible this time. Not if she was to attend the football game later. Her client had no issue with an afternoon appointment because they didn't want to miss the game either. Paisley, Chrissie and Clem had already agreed to hold the fort – they could easily manage without Emberlyn for a few hours.

She walked about the study, blowing out the incense burner and putting things away. The door hinges creaked as Lucie swanned inside, meowing loudly in a way that said, *Give me your attention.*

Emberlyn cocked her head. 'What is it, kitty?'

Another meow, this one less whiny.

'I don't know what that means.'

Lucie chirped and glanced outside the room ... and it was a mere moment later that a knock came at the front door.

'Oh, I have a visitor? Well, I appreciate the heads-up. Thank you.' Emberlyn exited the study with Lucie and made her way to the front door. Opening it, she almost froze. Because what the fuck was Reena doing on her porch?

The house had let her get this far, which meant it didn't currently perceive her as a physical threat to Emberlyn. That didn't mean that the High Priestess hadn't come to pester her again.

Reena quickly lifted her hands in a placatory gesture. 'I'm not here about the will or the manor or anything related to those matters. Nor am I here to cause any sort of trouble. I'm here because, well, I don't know who else to consult about this.'

Emberlyn felt her eyes go squinty. 'Expand on "this".'

Reena licked her lips. 'I wanted to talk with you about the rebellious faction in my coven.'

Huh. *Not* what Emberlyn had expected to hear. It could be a ruse, of course; a way to convince Emberlyn to speak with her. But that wasn't really Reena's style.

There was only one way to find out just how genuine the High Priestess was being.

'I have twenty minutes before I need to leave for work,' Emberlyn told her.

'This shouldn't take that long.'

Emberlyn gestured to the porch table, and then she and the other witch sat across from each other much as they had a few weeks ago.

Seeming somewhat hesitant, Reena braced her elbows on the armrests of her chair and interlinked her fingers. 'There has always been a rebellious faction, you know. Probably always will be. Because there will forever be witches who want to explore or at least understand the forbidden. In the past, the faction was never destructive; never caused problems within the coven. *This* time round, however, I cannot say the same.'

Emberlyn frowned as she read between the lines. 'Not-so-nice things have happened to coven members?'

'Yes,' Reena admitted, her voice low with mental fatigue. 'No physical harm came to anyone, but possessions were destroyed. Secrets were exposed. Arguments were caused. It was all rather petty, really, but still damaging.'

'A little like some of the things *I* was accused of doing that I swore was not me.'

Reena exhaled heavily. 'Yes.'

Emberlyn couldn't say she was necessarily *appeased* by the High Priestess's admittance that she'd effectively been used as a scapegoat, but it was a welcome change from having her claims of innocence dismissed. 'Do you know who's part of the faction?'

'No. I've questioned many potential suspects but felt forced to clear them of any wrongdoing – I could find no evidence to support my suspicions. Since hearing about the curse jars, I've redoubled my efforts to identify the faction members, because it seems likely that one or all of them are responsible.' Reena gave a tight, self-deprecating smile. 'And I have been entirely unsuccessful, as have those who I recruited to help.'

'Who were those recruits?'

'My inner circle – Ward, Tyra, my sister Penelope, Getty and a few others. They're as eager to unmask the faction members as I am, and they're equally frustrated by how fruitless our attempts have been.'

Emberlyn tipped her head to the side. 'Why come to me? And why be so forthright about everything?'

'Because' – Reena took in a shaky breath – 'with regards to the curse jars, I think I was the target, not Millicent.'

Emberlyn felt her brows snap together. 'Why?'

'The damage to the land didn't really impact her, did it? She found the jars an annoyance, nothing more. The only person who would be truly affected by the land being poisoned is the person who had great plans for it. Me. I'd been cooking up those plans for several months. I think that someone wanted to sabotage them. So much so that they kept replanting jars, even though they knew what Millicent would do if she caught them – that is a huge risk to take. But they did it anyway.'

Mentally running through it all, Emberlyn nibbled on her lower lip. She hadn't considered this possibility.

'My coven was angry with me due to the promises I was unable to keep. That anger eased when I came up with the alternative of refurbishing existing houses. But then Lincoln was bespelled, and my plans were foiled again because Carver dropped the project. So, once more, anger is rampant in the coven – made worse by how the wolves now all look upon us with suspicion. I'm being pressured by all three Alphas for answers I just don't have.'

Pausing, Reena looked down at her fingers. 'Carver and I were friends. He won't give me the time of day now. He doesn't see how I could not know what's going on within my own coven. He thinks I'm covering up the truth.' Her gaze lifted to meet Emberlyn's. 'I'm not. I'm truly in the dark here.'

Searching her eyes, Emberlyn believed her. 'So you think that though Lincoln was bespelled and placed near here, the witch or witches responsible weren't so much interested in harming me as they were in making your situation worse.'

'Yes. I believe they wanted to turn the clans against the coven, knowing it would leave my hold on my position shaky. I'm supposed to protect my witches. But right now, they feel unsafe.'

Emberlyn drummed her fingers on the armrest. It bothered her that she hadn't considered this theory herself. It made sense. All of it.

'I'd like to know your thoughts on this,' said Reena. 'You have no reason to help me – I've certainly failed you many a time. I wouldn't blame you for throwing me off this porch. But this situation impacts you regardless of whether I'm the focus or not. It benefits us both to be frank here.'

Well, she wasn't wrong there. And while Emberlyn felt zero inclination to aid the woman after their history, she'd be stupid to let it color her perspective and dictate her choice. 'I'd have to agree with you. I think it's highly possible that there's someone in your camp who's put a lot of effort into making trouble for you. And if so, it's probably a woman.'

Reena's brow pinched. 'Why a woman?'

'Unless you've earned yourself an enemy, the only real reason for a person to take such risks and invest so much of themselves into this is that they have something big to gain. Like becoming High Priestess – only a woman could do that. If they can make the coven mad at you, they'd have a shot at replacing you. People could come together to force you to step down.'

Her expression thoughtful, Reena nodded. 'That makes sense. Who would you consider a suspect?'

'Aside from my family, I don't know your witches well enough to say who might have an interest in what you consider "the malevolent path". If you know of any who do, look closely at them. It wouldn't surprise me if Ames is part of the faction – he asked Millicent for lessons in blood magick once; she refused to oblige him.'

'Can you give me names of witches who came to you over the years looking for potions or spells that would be considered unethical?'

'I can do that. But there's no point if you're going to dismiss the names of people who you believe wouldn't ever set you up to deal with all sorts of crap.' Reena liked to blind herself to what the people she cared for were capable of, from what Emberlyn had observed. 'You'd be surprised who showed up at my doorstep over the years.'

Reena looked away, uncomfortable. 'My ex-husband was one of them, I know – he confessed to it years ago.'

'So was your sister, Penelope,' Emberlyn added, causing the High Priestess's gaze to shoot back to hers and widen. 'And her then-partner, Bennet. Your right-hand Getty, too – yeah, even I was shocked she showed here. She always seemed so disapproving of "other" crafts.'

Reena shifted in her seat, cursing beneath her breath. 'That they came to you doesn't necessarily follow that they would betray me.'

'Why? Because they're family and friends?' Emberlyn snorted. 'Gill, Dez and their kids are my family – look how they treat me. If people want something bad enough, things like loyalty, love and honor can fly out the window. Aren't there people *you* trampled over in your effort to rise to the position of High Priestess?'

Reena hesitated. 'I take your point,' she finally mumbled. 'Did your grandmother ever say who she thought might be part of the faction?'

Emberlyn shook her head. 'Millicent didn't care about coven issues unless they impacted her.'

'When I wanted to be voted in as High Priestess, I considered challenging her to prove my worth to the coven. But I knew I would lose. Another idea I had was to drive her out of town. But, again, I knew I'd fail.' Reena paused. 'I tell you this because whoever wants my position may think of doing the same to you. Unlike me, they may be willing to take the risk of losing. They've taken plenty of other risks so far.'

That much was certainly true. 'You like to claim the right to punish your witches yourself. I'm going to be clear to you right now that if any of them take the risks you just mentioned, I'll handle it *my* way. And if I were you, I wouldn't retaliate against me.'

Reena let out a soft snort. 'The warning is not necessary. You think I'm not aware that you're more powerful than I am? Much as it vexes me, I'm unable to deny it.'

'And yet, you thought to take the manor from me the very night it chose me.'

'It was an act born of anger and desperation. Though I didn't realize quite how powerful you are until that night. I knew then that I had no chance of taking the house from you by force, so I tried talking you round. It became clear that you wouldn't part with the manor. And when your family's attempt to invalidate the will failed, I accepted the situation. If I were to challenge you, I would lose – and look weak. A witch of my status can never afford to look weak.'

Emberlyn hadn't thought she'd say it, she really hadn't … but she had the honest feeling that the woman across from her genuinely meant her no further harm. Not that she now thought of Reena as anything close to an ally. This truce was situational, and it wasn't likely to last. But it at least meant that she had one less person coming at her *for now.*

'I'll give you the names of those who came to me looking for the kind of magickal aid that you'd consider unethical. I advise you strongly to look closely at *all* of them. By that, I don't mean question them. I mean watch them. Monitor their activities. Even follow them, if necessary. Feed false information, set traps, don't share your suspicions with others. Trust no one, because they will have infiltrated your inner circle. You'll have at least one spy in your camp for sure.'

Sighing, Reena rubbed her temple. 'It's ironic that, right now, I trust you more than I do my own people.'

'You don't trust me, but you trust that I don't have my eye on your position. That makes me no threat to your status quo. You just sadly can't say the same about those who've sworn fealty to you.' And wasn't that a bitch?

'Are you going to keep glaring at my legs?'

Ripper forced his gaze upward to meet the pale-hazel eyes staring at him in mild exasperation. 'Not your legs, your pants.'

Emberlyn's brow pinched. 'Why?'

'I have an issue with them.'

'What's that?'

'They hide your legs from me.'

She blinked. 'You talk as if it's their motive. Like my pants are purposely inconveniencing you.'

'Feels that way.'

She rolled her eyes and turned back to the football game. Her tongue took a dainty lick of the ice cream he'd nabbed for her at halftime. His dick twitched in envy, so easy for her it was almost embarrassing.

Their sides were all but plastered together, since there wasn't much empty space on the bleachers, but he was perfectly fine with that. The closer she was, the better.

Excitement rolled off the fans. Some waved flags or signs. Others ate or took pictures.

Ripper had never watched a live game on TV – there was no cable here. But he'd watched reruns, as well as movies that featured large events. The football games here might be smaller, but the fans were louder, rowdier and more prone to cause riots – likely because they were so personally invested in the games.

Little specks of magick skipped along Emberlyn's skin, as if the anticipatory energy bounding around acted like a magnet to the power inside her. Throughout the game, his witch had let out the occasional cheer or boo but – as opposed to the screaming fans around them – she was her usual collected self. Not stoic, not uninvested in the game, just composed.

Her muscles were loose, her expression placid, her smile easy. But a fine line of tension – so fine he could have missed it if he hadn't come to be so attuned to her – rode her spine. 'You don't like crowds?' he asked.

She side-eyed him. 'I don't like the friction that's building in the air. Shit's gonna go down at some point.'

'Probably.' Shane's team was up against Carver's. The latter was losing, and the spectators could sense it. A shouting match would break out eventually, but no fights – people typically saved that for the parking lot.

Emberlyn didn't seem to know it, but Ripper had never taken a woman to a game with him before. Not even one he'd dated. But he wanted his witch with him. And this way, he could be sure that she wasn't being crushed by the crowd or forced to deal with more bullshit from her family.

'Would you stop doing that,' Paisley complained from beside Emberlyn, frowning at her twin.

Dusting a dead fly off of his palm with the other hand, Kage asked, 'Doing what?'

'You're always killing flies.' Paisley sniffed at him. 'Insects deserve love, just like any other creature.'

Her brother raised a brow. 'Even spiders?'

'Fuck, no. Don't talk craziness around me.'

Kage snickered. 'Almost forgot to tell you. Mom called.'

Paisley's lips parted. 'Finally? What did she say?'

'"Hello, Kage."'

'And?'

'And nothing. I hung up.'

Emberlyn's brows drew together. 'Why?'

'I don't want the silent treatment to end yet,' Kage explained. 'I'm not ready to have her try to stab holes into my happiness.'

'She hasn't called *me*,' Paisley muttered.

Kage flicked a hand. 'I'm her favorite. You know that. You're a little too childish for her tastes.'

His sister glared daggers at him. 'Childish? I'm not childish!'

'You're wearing sneakers that look like a fairy took a shit all over them.'

Paisley peered down at her glittery footwear. 'It's called fashion.'

'Yeah, for *nine*-year-olds.'

Emberlyn sighed. 'Could you two be nice to each other for five minutes?'

Kage blinked. 'I mean ... no.'

'Sounds complex,' Paisley said to her. 'I prefer the simple things.'

Kage slid his sister a look. 'It's why you like yourself so much.'

At that, the twins began squabbling and bumping each other's shoulder.

Ripper leaned into Emberlyn. 'So they're not close?'

His witch seemed surprised by the question. 'Oh, they're super close. You can't tell?'

'No. No, I can't.' Feeling eyes on him, he looked to his right ... just as CeCe *fast* swerved her head to face the field. He inwardly sighed. He'd caught her staring several times, and it was getting annoying fast.

At least she was staying out of his – and, more importantly for him, Emberlyn's – way. She'd also ceased spreading her stupid little 'Ripper's under a spell' claims. Emberlyn had bewitched him for sure, but not in the literal sense – there was no magick involved.

Just then, he caught sight of Reena walking up the concrete steps. Her gaze clashed with that of Emberlyn, and the two women – what the fuck? – exchanged the most subtle chin tip.

He frowned. 'Did you just greet Reena?'

Her shoulders stiffening, Emberlyn very slowly turned her head toward him. 'You watch me far too closely.' She didn't sound too happy about it.

'Why wouldn't I? You're mine. My scent on your skin says so. Now, what don't I know?' He leaned in, planting his palm on her thigh. 'Talk to me.'

Sighing, she flicked a hand. Suddenly, all the sounds around them became muffled. He realized she'd formed a sort of magickal invisible bubble around them.

'I had an interesting visit from Reena today. Relax,' Emberlyn added when he tensed. 'She didn't harass me to give up the manor again. It wasn't about that.'

'Then what?' he asked, leery.

'She has a theory.' Emberlyn licked at her ice cream just before it dripped onto her finger. 'She believes that whoever buried curse jars on what's now your land did it to foil her plans, *not* impact Millicent. Reena feels that she's the main target. Lincoln may have been sent after me, but what happened to him has turned the clans against the coven, which weakens her standing.'

Ripper twisted his mouth, considering that. 'She could be right. I automatically assumed that this was about *you*, since you have enemies. But maybe that's what someone is counting on.' Reena's theory actually made a lot more sense, because targeting Emberlyn was nothing short of self-destructive.

Emberlyn took another lick of her ice cream. 'Reena wanted a list of the coven members who came to me for the kind of spells and potions she'd deem amoral. She's trying to identify who's part of the faction. It is likely one of them – maybe even all of them – who's behind this. To take so many risks, they must have a substantial goal in mind.'

'Like becoming High Priestess.'

Emberlyn nodded. 'That would be my guess.' She paused as half the crowd erupted into cheers that barely overrode the whines and groans of the rivalling team's fans. 'Our cunning little culprit is pitting others against Reena. Now the coven feels unsafe. It wouldn't be hard for one voice or a few to convince others to put pressure on her to step down. If that doesn't work, they'll try something else.'

'Like what?'

'When aiming to take over the coven, Reena thought of either challenging Millicent or trying to drive her out of Chilgrave to make a statement. She warned me that whoever wants her position could think of doing the same to me.'

Just the thought made anger scratch at his insides. Once, he'd looked at Emberlyn and *wanted*. Now? Oh, there was still plenty of 'want'. But it was different. More.

He wanted to possess, protect, cosset, keep, hog her. And he did *not* fucking want other witches coming at her. She'd dealt with enough of that shit.

It pained him to say it, but ... 'Again, she could be right. Our culprit is cunning, like you said. But they're not wise, or they wouldn't have dragged you into this. They also wouldn't have underestimated Reena's willingness to do what's necessary to keep her position, even if it meant consulting you.' He paused. 'So you two are allies now?'

'Hell, no.' Leaning down, Emberlyn plopped her ice-cream stick into the empty soda can on the floor between her feet. 'I don't trust Reena as far as I can throw her, nor do I have a modicum of respect for her. And I will never forgive her degree of inaction over the years. But I can still be objective here and concede that she made valid points. Plus, it'll be good to let it *seem* as though she and I are on good terms. It'll make any faction members nervous to see me and Reena seeming civil. If they'd aimed to come between us, they'll realize they failed. I do like to highlight when the assholes from the coven fail at anything.'

A smile built in his chest because, yeah, he'd noticed.

Just then, the noise around them turned louder, so she'd evidently dropped the 'bubble'.

Paisley glanced from him to Emberlyn. 'What are you keeping so secret?'

Emberlyn waved her hand. 'I'll tell you tomorrow, it's not important.'

'Speaking of tomorrow,' Ripper cut in, 'you're working, right?'

'Until two p.m.,' Emberlyn told him. 'I'll drop off some clients' laundry on my way home, and then I'll be done for the day.'

'I'll meet you at your place around six.'

She tilted her head. 'You were serious about spending the full moon with me?'

'Very serious.' And equally serious about what he'd promised he'd do to her.

She must have been remembering that promise, because heat seeped into her eyes. 'All right.'

CHAPTER TWENTY-FOUR

❦

Stood just inside the doorway of her apartment, Paisley knocked back the elixir and shuddered a little. 'Tastes like green tea, but super minty.'

Emberlyn took the empty potion bottle from her and jammed the stopper into it. 'You nervous about tonight?'

Paisley let out a quick breath, putting a hand to her stomach. 'Yes. Crew keeps reassuring me that I'll be fine; says he'll be right there and won't leave my side. But even now, the lunar goings-on are affecting me. Like my body knows that a full moon is coming. I'm a little scared to find out just how strong an impact it'll have. I don't want to end up in my In-between form, or wake up smelling of bad sexual decisions.'

'If Crew said he won't leave you, then he won't leave you. Which means the only person you'd be getting down and dirty with is him.'

Paisley's lips hitched up. 'He rocks in bed, so I'd be fine with that.'

Kage pushed away from the wall. 'Wait, you're sleeping with Crew?'

'Why, you gonna be the protective big brother and go order him to treat me right?' Paisley asked, a mocking note to her tone.

Kage blinked. 'And contribute to your happiness?' He paused, humming. 'I don't know. The thought never really crossed my mind.'

Paisley squinted at him. 'You're such an ass. We're *twins*. Doesn't that mean anything to you?'

'Should it?'

Letting out a sound of exasperation, Paisley turned away from him. 'Be thankful that you're an only child, Emberlyn. Siblings are the *worst*.'

Feeling her lips twitch, Emberlyn peeked up at the wall clock. 'We'd better get downstairs. The hub needs to open in, like, two minutes.'

'First, you have to tell me about the secret convo you had with Ripper last night at the game. You told me you'd give up the goods today.' Paisley folded her arms. 'Let's hear it.'

Kage cocked his head, visibly intrigued.

'Reena came to see me yesterday.' Emberlyn relayed the entire conversation to her friends, adding, 'I wouldn't have thought she'd ever seek me out for advice; it still feels weird that she did.'

Kage rubbed at his cheek. 'She could be just trying to make you *think* she means you no harm when, really, she's plotting to take you down. But that doesn't sound like Reena.'

'No, it doesn't,' agreed Paisley. 'She may be right that *she's* the real target. It would actually be kind of smart of whoever's responsible to make it seem that they're after you. It'd mean that people would suspect your enemies, not hers.'

'I think it has to be someone in the faction, or maybe several of them.' Emberlyn looked from Kage to Paisley. 'Do either of you have any inkling as to who might be part of the group?'

Kage pursed his lips. 'There are lots of witches who think the coven should be taught about malevolent practices for informational purposes. I've never heard anyone openly admit that they want to dabble in them, though. Whatever the case, this faction will be tight. Secretive. Maybe even generational.'

Emberlyn nodded. 'And they will have infiltrated Reena's inner circle for certain. They'd need to keep tabs on her and be sure she isn't figuring shit out. It also means they can mislead her and paint people as trustworthy when they're anything but.'

'It's partly her fault that it's gotten this bad,' Paisley claimed. 'She never took the faction seriously. Prior High Priestesses kept an ear to the ground. She ignored any and all rumors of the group, acting as though it didn't exist; too arrogant to consider that it might ever work to undermine or overthrow her.'

'Well, she's considering it now,' Emberlyn muttered.

Paisley plucked at her lower lip. 'I don't believe any of my family are part of it, but I also don't think they'd much care if she was replaced. They don't like having a leader who never holds her close ones accountable for anything. She always makes excuses for them, especially Tyra and Sera, and will even give them false alibis.'

'Speaking of Sera, I wouldn't be surprised if she wants to be part of the faction. I don't think she is, because they seem intent on not drawing attention to themselves. No one can say that about Sera.' A secret organization wasn't likely to trust her.

'She claims to look down on you but, really, she's jealous. You have what she wants – the freedom to practice whatever forms of craft you choose. So yes, she'd definitely be interested in being part of the faction. But I can't see them reaching out to her and inviting her to join. She's too mouthy and dramatic.' Paisley tilted her head. 'Did I tell you that she's been advising my mother to officially disown me?'

Emberlyn felt her brows snap together. 'The fuck?'

'Our cousin gave us a heads-up about it,' said Kage, his jaw tight.

That fucking heifer. 'Why would Sera care either way?'

'Because if I'm upset *you'll* be mad, maybe?' suggested Paisley. 'She can't go at you, but she can irritate you via other people.'

Emberlyn pressed her lips tight together. 'Someone needs to shoot her in the ass.'

'There'll be people who've thought about it. It's not just you she annoys.' A sudden shiver racked Paisley's body, and she let out a shaky breath.

Concerned, Emberlyn studied her closely. 'You all right?'

'I keep getting shivers. Crew said it's normal for a newbie werewolf on the day of their first full moon.'

Ah. 'If at any point today you feel like you need to get out of here because the upcoming full moon is playing havoc with your system, just go.'

Paisley saluted her. 'Will do. Thanks.'

'You have any regrets about taking the Change?'

'Not one. I mean, it's still weird having no connection to my magick. But I don't feel like it's left a hole behind. Being a werewolf is its own form of magick, really. I find it way more fulfilling than I did living as a witch. And it feels really good to not be seen as the weak link, you know?'

'I can imagine.' Emberlyn had worried her friend might later lament her decision, and it was a relief that she didn't. 'I'm glad you're happy.'

'Aw, you're the bestest.' Paisley held out her arms. 'Can I have a hug?'

'No.'

Paisley pouted, her eyes dancing. 'I know you're not a hugger, but I'm a werewolf. We need touch.'

Emberlyn poked her in the forehead. 'There you go.'

'I said touch, not pain.' Paisley rubbed at her forehead. 'I really never got why werewolves were so tactile. But it's a kind of language. A way we communicate. It feels more natural than using words. We do it to comfort, to check in, to reassure, to express affection, to . . . *anything*.' She sniffed at Emberlyn. 'I'll bet you let Ripper cuddle you, yet here you are denying *me* one. It ain't fair.'

'*I'll* hug you, sis.' Kage wrapped his arms around her. 'Love you.'

Paisley smiled, hugging him back. 'I love you, too.'

Emberlyn felt her mouth curve. 'Aw, that's sweet.'

'Not really,' said Kage. 'I'm only holding her here so she has to smell my fart.'

Paisley's brow furrowed. 'What? You can't be – *oh my God, what the fuck have you been eating? That reeks!*' She gagged. 'I'm going to be sick. Really, I'm gonna hurl. Make him let me go! Now, now, now!'

Ripper was shoving clothes into his duffel when his phone rang. He crossed to the nightstand, his muscles tight, his body feeling charged and restless due to the upcoming full moon. He lifted the phone receiver and put it to his ear. 'Yeah?'

'It's Kerr, you want a ride to the clearing?'

Ordinarily, Ripper would have accepted the offer. He needed to shift; to run off the energy invading his system. The pull of the moon tugged at his skin, sang in his blood and hummed in his bones.

But another pull was so much stronger.

'I'm not going to the clearing tonight,' replied Ripper. 'There's somewhere else I want to be.' Someone he wanted to be with.

'Figured as much,' said Kerr, a smile in his voice. 'Say hi to your witch for me.' The line went dead.

Ripper lowered the receiver back to its cradle. *Your witch*. He'd grown to like the sound of that far too much.

Once upon a time, the draw he felt toward her had been powered by sexual chemistry. It was no longer a simple case of that. Emberlyn was his own personal magnet.

Ripper returned to the bed and zipped up his duffel. He'd packed himself some gear because he planned to run to the manor in his wolf form. He'd need clothes for when they ate dinner – which would come *after* he fucked her.

He stripped off his clothes, snatched his duffel and stepped out onto his porch. There, he let the shift take him. Parts of his body shrank, others elongated, bones moved and popped.

Done, he shook his body, settling into his fur. With his teeth, he grabbed his duffel and then took off.

He galloped through the woods, winding his way through weathered trees sporting territorial marks. He kicked up dead leaves, dodged animal droppings, leaped over fallen trees and stomped over clumps of spongy moss.

Branches shuddered with the breeze that raked through and rustled his fur. Brambles and bushes shook as small forest creatures scampered into their burrows. The scents of greenery, animal scat and a hint of ozone laced the air.

Grass slid over his legs as he ran and ran, enjoying the burn in his muscles. He smelled a deer nearby but ignored the temptation to hunt. The temptation of Emberlyn was stronger.

Finally, he arrived at the manor. He nudged open the gate with his head and trotted up the path. His claws scrabbled the porch steps and deck.

He was about to paw at the door, but it swung open. No Emberlyn stood on the other side. He padded into the house, dumped his duffel and then followed her scent, tracking her to the kitchen. She stood near the sink in a silky, mid-length robe ... and quite possibly nothing else.

She blinked as she noticed him. 'The house let you in again, huh. Don't shift just yet.' She squatted in front of him. 'Damn, you're *huge*.'

He stood still as she petted him – weaving her fingers through his fur, lightly rubbing at his ears, stroking his back and flank.

Needing to touch her in return, he began to shift back.

She rose to her feet and edged away slightly, giving him room. And once he was stood before her, she smiled wickedly and dropped her robe.

Fuck, she was naked. A punch of sexual hunger hit his lower stomach and made his body tighten.

His mouth went dry as he looked his fill. She was a fucking vision. Sensual and perfect and his.

Need crawled all over him, elemental and oppressive. It *demanded* satiation. His cock turned so thick and heavy it ached.

Her gaze dropped to his dick, her fingers clenched, her tongue flicked out to touch her lower lip—

And his control splintered into a thousand pieces.

He was on her in an instant, snatching her hips to haul her to him as he closed his mouth over hers. He thrust his tongue inside and lashed her own. She gave as good as she got, her hands grabbing at his shoulders.

Slanting his head, Ripper drove his tongue deeper, took the kiss up several notches. It quickly turned hot and hungry and wild.

He slid his hands over her. She was soft and warm and malleable under his palms, like melted wax. He dug in his fingers, wishing he could leave his prints all over her.

Lust scorched his insides and flowed through his every vein. Hunger and possession. So fucking much possession – a drive to take and dominate and mark. It invigorated him, like a shot of adrenaline.

He let her feel the prick of his claws, knowing she liked it.

Her breath hitched, and she moaned into his mouth. The sound wrapped around his cock and squeezed.

He reached down and rubbed her clit between two of his fingers. Rolled it. Thumbed it. Pressed on it. Circled it with the tip of his finger. Rubbed it again. Lathered her slickness all over it. Kept toying with it until he was sure she was ready for him . . . because he wasn't going to be anything close to gentle.

Grabbing a fistful of her hair, he snatched her head to the side to expose her throat and licked his way up the lifegiving vein there. He put his mouth to her ear and said, 'You're gonna get *so fucked*. I will use you until it hurts, Emberlyn. That's what little playthings are for.'

Emberlyn gasped as – in one swift, unceremonious move – he spun her to face the table and then bent her over it. *Well*.

It would be a lie to say that it annoyed her. In truth, she'd come to crave this. The pulling, the grabbing, the manhandling, the *taking*. It was all done with a frenzied desperation and intoxicating entitlement.

His body curled over hers, heat pouring off him. He always burned hot, but this was different. She'd swear she could toast bread on him.

'Don't move a fucking inch,' he ordered, his pitch low, the gritty quality in his voice at an all-time high. The authority secreted in his tone snatched her focus and seized her compliance.

In general, he treated her as an equal – but not in the bedroom. Here, he demanded control. Knew that she wanted to surrender it.

A calloused hand palmed her pussy from behind, and then two strong fingers drove deep. His rough groan was one of masculine appreciation and it tightened her nipples to hard little points. 'Wet.'

He straightened. His fingers disappeared. A palm pressed down on her back. The broad tip of his cock pushed into her.

And then he slammed home.

Her head shot up at the shock of his abrupt possession – it sent a dart of fire streaking up her inner walls, making her hiss through her teeth. 'Coulda warned me.'

'Could've. Didn't.' His grip on her hip bruising, he railed her hard. Like *really* hard.

Emberlyn clutched the edges of the table, closing her eyes as his cock aggressively stabbed in and out of her. His pace was feral. Merciless. Out of control.

It had to be said that the guy fucked like a boss. He didn't just press her best buttons, he punched them and . . . *jackpot*. Bells dinged, lights blared, winnings showered down. The responses he evoked in her were nothing short of carnal.

His palms smoothed up her back to grip her shoulders. Tingles spread over her skin, telling her she was being scent-marked all over again. The thought made her pussy spasm.

Groaning, he took her harder. Until it hurt, just as he'd promised. But the pain heightened the pleasure, making pure chemical bliss flood her.

She would have tipped her hips back to meet his thrusts if she could have moved. Instead, she remained still; taking what he gave her; needing more and more and more.

'You've got a perfect ass,' he ground out, gripping it tight. 'And right now, it's mine.'

The rough possession in his voice stroked that place inside her he seemed to have woken up. And that only pushed her closer to her orgasm. She was *almost there.*

He switched his angle and thrust even deeper, trapping her breath in her throat, going so deep he was more or less fucking her womb.

The friction inside her tautened, heated and crackled.

Then ... something started to happen.

A thin ring seemed to form at the base of his shaft. A ring that whirled as it slowly made its way up his dick, stroking her inner walls *just perfectly*. At the same time, his cock pulsed and thickened. Thickened to an unbearable level.

She clutched the table tighter. 'Oh, God.'

'Feel it, Emberlyn,' he snarled. 'Feel my dick swelling inside you.'

'Rip, it's—'

'You can take it,' he gritted out.

She shook her head, not so sure he was right.

'You can. You will.' He ruthlessly fucked her harder as his cock kept swelling, pushing against her inner walls, stretching them until it hurt.

The building knot rubbed at her g-spot, winding her tighter. Claws pricked her skin, adding to the pain, spicing the pleasure ... just as Ripper jammed his cock deep, the knot inflating even further.

Game over. A thrashing current of bliss volleyed into her; surged through her so violently it stole her breath. She needed to arch. Buck. *Something.* She couldn't move, locked to him.

Ripper's cock throbbed and twitched over and over as he pumped his come into her – it seemed to be never-ending.

Finally, her orgasm subsided. Which was right about when her brain seemed to short-circuit. She pretty much melted against the table, limp as a noodle, her breathing all over the place. She drifted, her eyes closed, her thoughts blank and fuzzy, a feeling of pure peace stealing over her.

Fingers wove into her hair. 'Quick warning, baby. This is gonna be a long night.'

CHAPTER TWENTY-FIVE

❧

When her eyes fluttered open the next morning, Emberlyn found herself looking at a sleeping Ripper. He lay beside her, one hand resting on her ass, his breathing deep and easy. She froze, snapping to full alertness.

Only let a werewolf sleep in your bed if you don't mind that they might never leave it.

It was a well-known quip. A jokey reminder that they attached; that their social etiquette was different.

For a witch, it could mean little to nothing if they stayed over. For a werewolf, it meant that they saw you as far more than a bed partner. It went beyond them feeling possessive of and comfortable with you. It showed that they also trusted you enough to be in such a vulnerable state around you.

Emberlyn's lungs clutched tight. Few people had given her their trust – understandable, but a little sad. So it meant something to her that Ripper trusted her, because it indicated that he saw past her reputation.

As for the message he was sending by sleeping over ... Wait, *was* he sending a message? Could it be that he'd fallen asleep accidentally? Because it seemed that *she* had, since she had no memory of doing so.

She remembered their sex marathon; remembered they'd come upstairs shortly after dinner and he'd talked her into showering with him. They'd barely dried off before he'd tossed her onto the bed and gone down on her. She'd returned the favor and ... then it was blank, so she'd obviously drifted off after that.

Considering they were under the covers, their heads on the pillows, he'd obviously moved her around some. And he'd either decided to stay or simply conked out. The latter wasn't far-fetched – a night of endless hot sex could steal a person's energy. It had certainly stolen hers.

But if his falling asleep in her bed *hadn't* been accidental ... Emberlyn didn't know how to feel about it. Much as she wanted something lasting with Ripper, the idea of 'more' was a little scary. This wasn't a simple boy-meets-girl situation. Their histories were messy and complicated.

If Ripper had purposely stayed over, it didn't necessarily mean that he wanted *the ultimate* commitment. Werewolf attachments could be temporary, just as they could be platonic – or, for that matter, switch swiftly from romantic to platonic at some point. But the last time she'd been in this situation, the attachment hadn't been temporary or remained platonic. She'd eventually been officially claimed by a wolf who had later betrayed her. So this whole thing was tap-dancing all over her nerves.

She'd never in her life been vital to anyone. Her father had left her without a backward glance. Her mother had withdrawn from her due to heartbreak. Millicent hadn't ever put her first, and the rest of her family had had little to do with her. It should have been different with Michael. He'd been her mate, for

Christ's sake. Yet, he'd cheated on her; acted as if he didn't need to apologize for it. And then he'd disappeared.

After a lifetime of being disappointed by others, she'd become used to being on her own; to only relying on herself. It was her comfort zone, at this point. If Ripper *did* want more, he wouldn't stand for that. Already he pushed for more than he was due.

But he gave so much back, didn't he?

Always supporting her. Always so protective of her. Always trying to take care of her.

He seemed so in tune with her. If her mood changed, he sensed it. If she fidgeted, he noted it. If her body stiffened even slightly, he stilled just the same.

It was strange to have someone so focused on her. Someone for whom she was never an afterthought. Someone who saw and accepted her. She'd come to like it, and she knew it'd hurt like hell to lose it.

Her full bladder nagging her for relief, Emberlyn slipped out of bed, careful not to wake him. Nabbing a long white T-shirt from the futon, she drew it over her head and went into the en suite bathroom. She did her business, freshened up, moisturized and brushed her hair.

Exiting the bathroom a short time later, she halted at the sight of Ripper sitting on the edge of her bed in only his boxers. A searing heat crept through her as his eyes roamed over every inch of her body from head to toe. He could make her feel so very hyperaware of not only herself but also him.

'You practically roll out of bed looking all perfect, don't you?' he grumbled.

She blinked. 'Not really. Though I'd thank you for the compliment all the same if you didn't sound so put out.'

'Not put out,' he said. 'I just don't find it fair that you have that advantage over us mere mortals.'

Emberlyn snorted – a sound that died as he stood upright and stretched. Oh, what a show. Muscles rippled and flexed so deliciously. She cleared her throat, walking further into the room. 'I don't remember falling asleep.'

'I went to use the bathroom after you sucked me dry,' he said bluntly, lowering his arms. 'When I came back, you were out.'

'So you tucked me into bed and, what, decided to stay?'

He slammed an unblinking stare on her, an unwavering determination glimmering there. 'I did.'

So it hadn't been an accident. He'd chosen to stay. And his tone said she could like it or lump it – he gave no fucks.

That was an Alpha werewolf for you. They were all a law unto themselves.

She folded her arms. 'I don't recall inviting you to sleep over.'

'Must have slipped your mind.'

Her pulse did a little skip as he began stalking toward her, sheer intent in every step.

Looming over her, he sniffed at her face and hair. 'I like the strawberry smell of your shampoo. Like it better when it's mingled with my scent.'

He was so damn *casual*. As if nothing had changed. As if it were only natural that he had moments ago woken *in her bed*.

Studying her face, he rested his palms on the sides of her neck. 'Unwind, baby,' he coaxed, his pitch low, his voice soft. 'What's happening is good. Don't fight it. Let it be.'

'You sure you're not still just caught up in the full moon's high?'

'I'm sure.' He held her gaze with a serious stare, his face a mask of intensity. 'I don't know how you made yourself this important to me so fast, but here we are. It's done.'

He said it with such finality. Such acceptance. He clearly wasn't one bit torn over this.

Still cupping her neck, he breezed his thumbs along the underside of her jaw. 'I should have seen it coming, really.' His eyes drifted over her face, aglow with possession. 'You're magick, Vogue, deadly nightshade and pure class all wrapped into one. It's a hell of a package. And there's a hint of cotton candy there.'

She felt her brow fly up. 'Cotton candy?'

'Sweetness,' he expanded. 'You don't let many people see it. I see it.'

There seemed to be little that the perceptive motherfucker didn't see.

He nuzzled her face in a gesture of affection that made her chest pang. 'Don't fight it,' he repeated. 'Let's ride this out; see what does or doesn't come of it. Can you agree to do that?'

She watched him, her gaze hawklike in its predatory intensity. There was a hint of caution there. Always so careful, his witch.

Ripper thought it ironic that many townsfolk believed her to be reckless. In truth, there were no impulsive or ill-thought-out moves with Emberlyn. She did everything with purpose.

That cautiousness stemmed from having no one at her back, he supposed. You could never afford to set a foot wrong when there was nobody to catch you if you fell.

She had him now. Fuck, she'd 'had' him for weeks. He just hadn't seen it.

Now, he could no longer deny or ignore that – to put it simply – he was fucked. Totally fucked. All caught up in his witch's web . . . and completely okay with it.

Ripper had fallen asleep beside her with no idea how she'd react to what it signified. Given that she'd been heavily involved with a werewolf before and things had later gone tits up, he hadn't known what reaction to expect from her. His witch was handling it as calmly as she did everything else. But . . . she was leery.

Of course she was.

Emberlyn had been let down one too many times by one too many people. They were all fuckers, in his opinion. They'd made it so that she was so unused to people wanting to keep her around for good that she now struggled to believe he wasn't going anywhere. He couldn't make her any promises, because he had no idea if they'd work in the long-run. But he didn't foresee it going to shit.

While he had known in the beginning that he wouldn't be able to have her only once, he hadn't anticipated that he'd come to want more. But the pull between them . . . there was no 'getting used to it', no softening its hard edges, no developing an immunity to it. Because it had tied them.

There had been only two other women he'd felt something real for. But it was more intense with Emberlyn. More defined. More *set*. She meant something to him. Held an endless fascination for him.

She had so many layers. Some tough, some vulnerable. And when she allowed him to see flashes of those vulnerabilities – and she really did allow it; there were no accidental slips with Emberlyn – it got to him.

She was his equal in every way. She didn't fear him. Didn't pander to him. Didn't treat him like he was an Alpha. And she made no compunction about speaking her mind around him. Hell, she'd once fucking threatened him.

More, she entrusted him with the part of her who liked being *taken* in bed. She'd trusted him with a secret that few knew. She'd let him in little by little, found her way past his every defense, and now it was too late for them to go back. They could only go forward and let it all play out. 'You had to know we were heading in this direction, baby.'

Unfolding her arms, she set her hands on her hips. 'I wasn't sure you'd want anything serious just yet.'

'Why not?'

'Because of all that crap with CeCe.'

'You don't think I still want her, do you?'

'No. But when a person you care about kills what you feel for them, it doesn't exactly leave you in the mood to begin a full-on relationship with someone else.'

'Maybe that'd be the case for me if the woman standing in front of me was anyone but you.' He slid a hand from the side of her neck around to her nape. He tugged her closer, nuzzling her face again. 'I told you once that I've never wanted anything the way I want you. It was no lie, no exaggeration. With each piece of you I got to know, another piece of CeCe went right out of my head. There's no room for her or anyone else up there now. Only you.'

Emberlyn fell silent, ever watchful. But she didn't stare at him, she stared *into* his eyes – intent, probing, searching. 'You mean that,' she eventually said.

'Yeah, I mean it.' He swept his thumb up the column of her throat. 'You have me. She never did. I shared her. I would *never* share you. If anyone dared touch you, I'd break their fucking fingers.' He wasn't kidding.

Her brows inched up. 'Overboard.'

'Yet true.' He briefly touched the tip of his nose to hers. 'Now let's get off the subject of CeCe and discuss what has you wound tight. It's a bundle of things that are all interlinked. No one ever made you feel that you're enough exactly as you are, which pisses me the fuck off. But you know it isn't the case with me. I make you feel accepted, known, understood – just as I make you feel owned every time I'm inside you. You've never had any of that before. Not fully. And it rattles you that you now do. But it doesn't need to. You're safe with me.

'You weren't safe with the coven; they wouldn't accept you.

You weren't safe with Michael; he let you down. You weren't even completely safe with Millicent; she wasn't there for you emotionally. But, baby, I swear you're safe with me.'

Her throat bobbed, and she dropped her gaze.

'Don't hide from me,' he said, his tone soft. 'Eyes back to mine.'

'No.'

Well, of course she couldn't just do as he'd asked without hesitation. She never did. But it was one of the many things he liked about her. 'Em, look at me.'

She did, though he figured that was more due to her surprise at his abbreviating her name.

He slid both his hands up to cradle her face. 'You trust me?'

'I wouldn't have told you the truth of what happened with Michael if I didn't.'

He'd suspected as much. 'Then trust that I mean everything I've said here.'

Her eyelids drifted down, and a long breath eased out of her. Finally, her eyes met his again – the conflict was now gone, replaced by a hard determination. 'We'll ride this out, then. But, Rip, if you fuck me over—'

'Won't happen,' he stated, relief blowing through him. He'd worried that she might put up roadblocks or demand they slow things down. That wasn't how his kind operated.

Werewolves liked their space and boundaries, and they were careful how much of themselves they gave to another person. But if such an intense attachment formed, they had no limits.

'No threats are necessary.' He skated his hands upward and sank his fingers into her hair. 'Keep trusting me. There'll never be a time when you can't. I swear that to you.'

She swallowed, the last of the cautiousness in her gaze draining away; the stiffness leaching from her frame as she leaned slightly into his touch.

Good girl. He nuzzled her temple. 'Now, let's have breakfast. I'm fucking famished.' He held his breath, half-expecting her to suggest he head downstairs and get started on breakfast while she showered – needing to snatch a little alone-time to process.

Her eyes still holding his, she gave a slow nod. 'Okay.'

His chest clenched. Because that easy and simple agreement – no hesitation, no vying for space, no indication that she had any reservations – showed she really *was* all in this. Good. He truly couldn't have accepted anything else.

CHAPTER TWENTY-SIX

A couple of hours later, Emberlyn pulled up outside the house of Mari's boyfriend. Her brow pinched. Quite a few people stood in his neighbor's front yard, tense and angry.

Weird.

Emberlyn's scalp prickled. Mari had called her, asking if they could talk, saying she had important information to share. *Why* she'd care to share anything at all with Emberlyn was so far a mystery.

It wasn't as if they were at all friendly with each other. But Emberlyn hadn't been able to understand why Mari would call her here on false pretenses, so she'd decided to go see what was so 'important'. Better that than Mari turning up at the manor.

Besides, it would give Emberlyn something to do while Ripper dealt with whatever clan issue had cropped up that demanded his presence. After Kerr had sought him out, he'd left with a promise that he'd be back soon. It was mere minutes later that Mari had called her.

Ripper likely wouldn't be happy that Emberlyn had come here without him, but it wasn't all that different from him addressing clan issues alone. He'd know that. But, protective as he was, he still wouldn't like it.

God, they were actually together now.

For the first time in years, she was in a serious relationship. One that could potentially have a real future. She didn't have to be alone anymore. All of which was good but still ruffled up her nerves.

Emberlyn was no coward, though. She'd repeatedly taken risks throughout her life. There were times when it hadn't paid off, but there were times when it had.

When it came to Ripper, the only regret she'd have would be not taking a chance on him, on *them*; not knowing what *could* have been. So, as she'd told him, she would do as he asked and ride this out.

Had Millicent foreseen that Emberlyn would end up in a relationship with Ripper? Had she 'bequeathed' Emberlyn to him as a way to nudge them together faster? Or would this never have happened if it hadn't been for the stipulations in the will that had led to them becoming allies?

There was no way to know, but it wouldn't be surprising to learn that Millicent had seen it coming.

Mentally putting that aside for now, Emberlyn exited the car and strode up the cobbled path. The witches in the neighboring yard fell quiet, watching her carefully.

Mari's boyfriend's front door opened, and the young woman stepped out. She gave Emberlyn a tremulous, apologetic smile. 'I'm sorry.'

Halting, Emberlyn squinted. 'For what?'

Mari slid the witches in the other yard a quick look. 'They were talking about gathering a large number of people and storming the manor. I thought it'd be better if they could just *talk* to you so things wouldn't escalate that way.'

Confused, Emberlyn frowned. *Storming the manor?* 'Explain.'

'*You!*' a male voice called out, his tone a whip.

Emberlyn's head snapped to the side. A man stormed out of the house next door, his eyes blazing, his face splotchy with anger. Bennet was a schoolteacher, a pillar of the coven's community ... and he was currently carrying a little girl who could be no older than five. His daughter, Emberlyn noted.

'Look,' he hissed at Emberlyn. 'Look what you did!'

It was only then she realized that the child sported several bandages. Concern creased Emberlyn's brow, but the emotion quickly became buried beneath the shock of his accusation. 'What *I* did?'

'You bespelled that Rabid and sent it here; it attacked my daughter!' He hugged the child tight, his hold protective. 'She could be dead now!'

Shocked down to her core, Emberlyn turned to fully face him. 'A Rabid came here?'

'Don't play stupid,' spat Getty. 'We thought we had someone in our coven working against us. Sera's right – it was *you* all along.'

Getty's teenage son nodded. 'You set up our coven to take the fall!'

Bristling, Emberlyn raised a palm to stay their words. 'Back the fuck up. Where did you get the insane idea that *I* was responsible?'

Hank pushed to the front of the crowd, his chest puffed up. 'None of our coven would send Rabid to Bellcrest. We wouldn't risk our own.'

Emberlyn inwardly snorted. 'That's clearly not true, because I had nothing to do with it.'

Scoffs rippled throughout the crowd.

Frustration grating at her nerves, Emberlyn looked away from him with a sigh. Her lips thinned as she noticed that many of Bennet's neighbors were straining to witness the little scene unfolding here. Heads were poking out of windows while some people stood on their doorstep.

'It has to be you,' Hank insisted.

She rolled her eyes at him. '*Think.* If I'd hatched some great plan to make the clans turn against your coven, why would I do something like use magick against you when it would expose me as the guilty party?'

Silence momentarily fell, but it was broken by Bennet. 'Maybe you don't care about the consequences. Maybe you're crazy like Millicent.'

'And maybe you're just so accustomed to using me as a scapegoat that it was all too easy for you to assume I was involved,' Emberlyn shot back.

'We *know* it was you,' Hank upheld.

Emberlyn arched a brow at him. 'Oh, so you have proof?'

Hank spluttered. 'We don't need any. It's obvious that you're behind this.'

'Not obvious,' she contradicted. 'Just your opinion. And you have not one thing to back it up.'

'You won't convince me that you're innocent,' said Bennet. 'You may not have meant for a child to be harmed, but you recklessly let loose a Rabid on Bellcrest.'

Emberlyn cocked her head. 'You're not interested in reason, rationality or truth right now, are you? You just want a target for your anger. Someone you can blame for the harm that came to your daughter.' She looked down at the child and noticed she was trembling. 'You should take her inside. She's already shaken; she doesn't need to be witnessing this as well.'

Bennet shot her a scornful look. 'Don't act like you give a

damn. This is *exactly* where she should be right now. She should have the opportunity to watch as the person responsible for her attack is confronted and held accountable.'

'Perhaps she should, but that person isn't me.' Positively done with this little scene, Emberlyn shook her head. She wasn't going to stand here while they tossed false accusations at her. She'd done enough of that over the years.

She couldn't stop them from being determined to think the worst of her, but she sure didn't have to listen to their crap.

Contempt and resentment roiling in her belly, Emberlyn turned without a word and headed down the path.

Two male witches on the sidewalk slid in front of the yard's gate to block her access to her car. Both were Watchers, and both glared at her with something close to revulsion.

Emberlyn halted, annoyance crawling up her spine and snapping it straight.

'You're coming with us,' declared the taller of the two, who also happened to be Ward's younger brother, Patrick.

If Emberlyn wasn't seething right now, she would have chuckled at the audacity of him. 'No, no, I'm not.' He was a damn fool if he thought she'd allow him to detain her.

His fellow Watcher, Ruben – who was also Getty's nephew – planted his feet. 'You'll do what we say when we say it. And we say you're going to our unit to be questioned.'

'You can *say* whatever you like,' Emberlyn told him, her tone clipped. 'I'm not leaving with you. You want to question me, you can do it right here.'

Ruben's cheeks flushed. 'You don't get to dictate what we do.'

'Right back atcha. You might be Watchers, but you have no grounds to take me away like I'm some criminal.' And going with them, even to avoid a scene for the sake of the little girl who'd been attacked, would have been like an admission of guilt.

'She sent the Rabid here!' Bennet shouted. 'She needs to be detained!'

'Oh, I agree,' Patrick cut in. 'You're coming with us, Vautier.' He flapped his hand, magick crackled . . . and then energy-cuffs appeared on Emberlyn's wrists, yanking them together behind her back.

Motherfucker. Anger fluttered through her blood, wrapped around her bones, charged her magick and quickened her pulse. Emberlyn glared at him, her heartbeat thrashing in her ears. 'You think you can *bind* me?' she demanded, furious. She pulled at the cuffs, and they disappeared. 'You think you can *force* me to go anywhere?'

Patrick swallowed while Ruben flexed his fingers nervously.

Her skin prickled in awareness as she realized that the rest of the crowd had taken advantage of her distraction. With the exception of Mari and Bennet, they now surrounded her; magick dust whirling around their hands.

Emberlyn let out a dark laugh that echoed with power. 'Try it,' she bit out, silently calling up her own magick, bracing it to defend her.

Crackling streams came at her from all angles in a flash.

Her magick slammed up like a shield, causing every stream to pause mere inches from her body.

Emberlyn wagged a finger and *tsk*ed. Then she threw out her arms. Her magick 'wall' bulged outward, shoving the crackling streams back at their 'senders' and knocking them off their feet. The only thing stopping her from doing anything worse was knowing that it would scare a child who was traumatized enough.

As the crowd struggled to their feet, Emberlyn snarled at them. 'You're all pathetic. Only fucking cowards gang up on a person like this.'

'You assaulted us!' shouted Patrick, magick motes swirling around his hand.

'No!' Mari materialized, placing herself between Emberlyn and the Watchers. 'You have to stop. This isn't right!'

Hank gaped at her. 'Mari, *move*.'

She didn't. 'I honestly can't believe you were part of this, Dad.' She looked at him like she didn't know him. 'Imagine it was me. Imagine a bunch of people circled, condemned and attacked me like that. What would you do? No one even asked her about her whereabouts or considered the points she made. You'd all decided she was guilty, and you weren't interested in anything she had to say to defend herself.'

Emberlyn eyed her cousin curiously. Mari was speaking up for her? *This is new.*

'We will question her once we get her to our office,' clipped Patrick.

Emberlyn looked him up and down. 'I'm not going anywhere with you.' He was plain ridiculous for thinking otherwise.

'What's happening here?' a female voice sharply called out. *Reena.* She shouldered her way through the crowd, looking from face to face.

'Oh, nothing unusual,' Emberlyn replied. 'People are accusing me of stuff I didn't do. You know how it goes.'

Reena glared at the other witches. 'I told you I don't believe that Emberlyn is responsible for what happened.'

'And I disagree,' snarked Bennet, coming up behind her.

The High Priestess whirled on him. 'Because you've fallen for a goddamn trick. You'd prefer to believe that an outsider is our culprit. The person who did this was counting on that. If there's one thing Emberlyn never does, it's cover up her actions. I don't see why that would change now, or why she'd do anything to implicate herself if she *was* intent on keeping her participation secret. Who summoned her here?'

'I did,' Mari piped up. 'They were discussing riling up a

huge number of people and storming the manor to "deal" with Emberlyn. I thought if she could just *talk* to them, if they could just hear her out, it wouldn't get that far. But they didn't even ask if she had an alibi or anything. They circled her, attacked her and then got angry because she defended herself. If that had happened to any of us . . .' She shook her head. 'It was just wrong.'

Pausing, Mari looked at Emberlyn, appearing genuinely distressed. 'I'm sorry I called you here. I wouldn't have asked if I'd known they'd react that way.'

Hmm, maybe. Maybe not. Right now, Emberlyn wasn't feeling inclined to take her word for it. She didn't trust a single person in the coven.

'You want us to ask her if she has an alibi, let's do that.' Patrick inched up his chin as he again glared at Emberlyn. 'Where were you this morning?'

'At home,' she replied.

'Can anyone verify that?' he asked.

'Yes. Ripper.'

'What time did he arrive at your house?'

'Yesterday evening. He didn't leave until about ten minutes before I showed up here.' She didn't miss how people exchanged looks, evidently knowing exactly what that meant. 'When did the Rabid turn up?'

Patrick dropped his gaze. 'Approximately half an hour ago,' he mumbled.

Reena addressed the crowd, saying, 'So Emberlyn clearly couldn't possibly have done this. You fell hook, line and sinker for a trick, just as I told you.'

'She should still be detained,' insisted Ruben, whiny. 'She *attacked* us.'

God, they were such babies. 'I defended myself, and you knew I would. You just thought you could overpower me as a group. And you thought wrong. You should all be ashamed of yourselves.'

But they weren't. None of their expressions held a hint of regret. Only anger, scorn and defeat.

Her annoyance building once more, Emberlyn shook her head in disgust. 'So many of you look down your nose at me, but it didn't stop you from seeking me out when you wanted something.' She pointed her finger from person to person as she expanded, 'A seduction spell. A voodoo doll. A pain-inducing potion. A lesson in blood magick. An anti-aging serum. Help with insomnia. A karma spell. A fat-burning potion. Pain-relief sessions. Aid with summoning a deity.'

Each person tensed, embarrassed by what she'd revealed about them while also surprised – and, in some cases, a little unnerved – at hearing why others had sought her out.

'I could go on and on,' said Emberlyn. 'And on and on and on. It's as if you all have the strange idea that you can pick and choose when you'll be nice. Oh, how mistaken you are.' It was time she got that message fully across. Because what happened here was *fucked up*, and she was done being their whipping boy.

Emberlyn sharply slashed out her arm. 'After today, *none* of you need bother to come to me for anything ever again,' she clipped. 'No more serums, spells, sessions or potions. No. More. *Anything.*' A rumble of power echoed in the latter word.

The crowd went completely silent, realizing she'd *literally* bound herself to her word. They couldn't later come crawling to her with apologies and excuses and offer to pay her double for what they wanted. They'd never again get any type of aid from her.

Reena cleared her throat. 'Emberlyn, I apologize for what happened here today. It was completely unacceptable. My coven is better than this. Those involved will be punished.'

Emberlyn met her gaze evenly. 'Yes, they will.' Chanting beneath her breath, she balled her hand up into a tight fist.

Each member of the crowd gasped. At one point or another, she'd used magick to help them with the most superficial shit. And now she'd undone it.

A head went bald. Hair turned gray. Jowls reappeared. Teeth yellowed. Breasts sagged. Acne returned. Lush lips thinned. Cellulite came back. A rash resurfaced. A face lost its uplift.

Bennet looked at Emberlyn, his eyes wide. 'Does this mean ...' He trailed off, apparently not wanting to finish his sentence out loud.

'That you'll need to go back to just buying Viagra like everyone else with your problem?' she asked. 'Yes. Now, everyone get *the absolute fuck* out of my way. Or I start having some *real* fun.'

Folding his arms, Ripper skimmed a hard gaze over the five females sitting on his brother's porch steps – their heads down, their shoulders hunched. Irritation spasmed in his muscles, making his body tense.

This. He'd left his woman's side for *this* bullshit.

He had intended to spend the entire day with Emberlyn. Maybe even convince her to go out for dinner – yeah, he wanted to make it publicly clear very fast that she was well and truly taken. Instead, he was having to verbally tear apart five grown women who were intent on acting like kids.

They had since cleaned up the mess they'd made before he arrived, but that didn't improve Ripper's mood. Especially since one of them in particular seemed set on making herself a problem.

CeCe had had quite the eventful night, according to Kerr. And having heard what she'd done to Ripper's truck in his absence – a slice of news that had *really* pissed Ripper off – he had a pretty good idea of what had inspired her to resort into full-on drama.

CeCe spared him a sheepish look. 'We said we were sorry.'

Ripper flicked up a brow. 'And that makes everything all right, does it?'

She sighed, all fucking forlorn.

He glanced from Kerr to Logan to Crew, sensing that they weren't buying her act either. Her friends were genuinely embarrassed and shamefaced. If there had been a hole they could crawl into, they would have dived into it head first.

'It was just a prank,' she defended.

Logan frowned. 'And, what, you're fourteen years old? Because adult females rarely toilet paper someone's house.'

Her friends cringed, their cheeks reddening.

CeCe weakly shrugged. 'I thought you'd find it funny. We used to prank each other all the time.'

A muscle in Logan's cheek ticked. 'We didn't do anything so juvenile. Besides, things were different back then.'

'And I'm trying to get them back to the way they were,' she stressed, a slight whine in her voice. 'I thought it would make you feel, I don't know, nostalgic; thought we could laugh about it and *talk*. Finally talk.'

'Why in the fuck would I have wanted to laugh and chat with you about anything when you acted like such a bitch last night?'

She stiffened, her face falling. 'That was harsh. And unnecessary.'

Kerr barked a disbelieving laugh. 'Are you fucking kidding? You made a pass at me and then cursed my ass out for rejecting you. You tried to embarrass Paisley for having a little fun with Crew and another clan member. You challenged Clem to a fight while in your wolf form – presumably because she was leaving with Logan. Still in that form, you were caught pissing on one of Ripper's tires. *Then* you had the grand idea to top it all off with this.'

A flare of agitation came and went in her eyes as she struggled to appear remorseful. 'I'm sorry. I really am.'

'No, you're not,' Ripper countered. 'Why would you be? Right now, you have what you wanted: attention.'

Her head jerked. 'What?'

'No one fucks up so spectacularly unless they want the attention of whoever would discipline them.' Ripper gestured at the other women. 'Your friends here helped you toilet paper Logan's house, but the rest was all you, CeCe. What, you got pissed when I didn't show at the clearing? You had a pretty good idea of where I was spending the full moon, of *who* I was with, and you didn't like it?'

A pinch of bitterness glimmered in her eyes.

'Is that what inspired you to piss on my truck?' he pushed, his blood still boiling over it. 'You were marking what you have the goddamn nerve to think is your territory?'

She looked down at her hands. 'It hurt, okay? It hurt that you chose to be with her over *our clan*. Just like it hurt to see Logan leaving with Clem.'

'And Paisley?' Crew challenged, his face hard. 'Why have a go at her? Because she was the next best thing to Emberlyn?'

CeCe didn't respond.

'I don't need to ask why you came onto me,' Kerr said to her. 'It's obvious you thought it'd make Rip jealous to hear you'd made a move on his best friend.'

Her gaze flew to Kerr. 'What? No. I was ... I was lonely and hurting.'

'Don't give me that shit,' Kerr spat. 'There are tons of wolves you could have approached last night. You don't even like me, and you know for a fact that I don't like you. If what you'd really wanted was company of any sort, you would have had no reason to come to me for that.'

CeCe waved his comment off, as if choosing to dismiss it because it didn't suit her defense. She looked at Ripper. 'I'll apologize to Clem and Paisley. I'm sorry about your tire, I'll replace it.'

'Don't bother,' Ripper told her. 'My witch will no doubt have a potion that can clean it.'

CeCe flinched. 'Now you're rubbing salt in the wound.'

'No,' Ripper contradicted, 'I'm just not gonna mind my words to pander to your feelings. Why should I? You don't seem to give a fuck about anyone else's.'

Her brows snapping together, she stood upright. 'That's not true. I've made mistakes recently – okay, a lot of mistakes – but I'm not some cold-hearted bitch. And if I was, it would technically make me your type. *New* type, I should say. Emberlyn Vautier has done way worse than anything I did last night. She's a—' CeCe cut herself off when he advanced on her.

Ripper pinned her with a severe glare. 'You need to be very, very careful,' he warned, his pitch low, anger lacing his every word. 'You're on wafer-thin fucking ice right now. If you insult my woman again, I will temporarily banish you from the clan.'

CeCe's face went slack. 'You ... you wouldn't do that.'

'Oh, I would. I've made it clear already, but you don't seem to be getting it. So I'll spell it out for you. *All* of you,' he added, sweeping his gaze over each female. 'Emberlyn is off-limits.'

'I—'

Ripper slammed up a hand, silencing CeCe. 'You don't insult her, you don't stare at her, you don't go near her, you don't touch her. Breaking any of those rules will fast earn you a temporary banishment. Do not call my bluff on that, because I mean every fucking word. She belongs to me, and I protect what's mine.'

'Belongs?' CeCe echoed, her tone flat.

Intent on getting across just how serious his warning needed to be taken, Ripper expanded: 'I slept in her bed last night. All night. So, yeah. Belongs.'

Logan's brows lifted. Crew whistled low. Kerr gave a pleased smirk. CeCe's friends subtly exchanged looks.

As for CeCe herself? She stared at Ripper in no small amount of dismay. 'No,' she breathed. 'No. That's . . . you wouldn't . . .'

Ripper leaned toward her. 'If you fuck up again, it won't be me who deals with you.' Not when she wanted his attention. 'It'll be Kerr or Crew. They can punish you however they see fit, starting from right now.'

'You head off,' Kerr told him. 'Go back to your witch. We got this.'

Crew nodded with a grunt.

'I'll give you a ride,' said Logan, knowing that Kerr had driven him here.

'Wait.' CeCe snapped out the word, a hint of panic there. 'Rip, you can't honestly be serious about her. Dammit, you love *me*.'

'No, I don't. I thought I did. I was wrong. Did I care about you, though? Yeah. Once. You changed that.'

Her face flamed. 'You're just saying all that to hurt me. You love me. You love me so much you refuse to share me.'

'I *did* share you,' Ripper reminded her. 'And you know something? I'd never share Emberlyn – not even for a single night, not with anyone.'

'Rip, I—'

'*Don't*,' he growled when she reached out to touch him. 'You can give up trying to "get things back to the way they were". It won't happen. Not for you and me. Too much shit has gone down at this point.'

'But—'

'Someone get them out of my sight,' he gritted out.

Crew instantly herded the women away. Her friends went easily – no, eagerly. CeCe moved in a daze, her gaze inward.

Kerr turned to Ripper. 'You were right in what you said. It was all an attempt to get your attention on her part, and it was sparked by you choosing to be with Emberlyn over running with the clan.'

Logan took a step forward. 'You really stayed the night at the witch's place?'

'Yeah,' Ripper confirmed. 'I'll be doing it every night from now on.'

Kerr grinned. 'I knew even at the start that you were fighting a losing battle by trying to keep your distance from Emberlyn. It's why I nagged you to just give in already and try dating her.'

Ripper frowned, correcting, 'You nagged me to bed her. That was it.'

'I knew you wanted more than a one-nighter. But I doubted you'd admit it to yourself until you'd spent an evening balls-deep inside her, so I figured I'd push you in that direction.'

Ripper felt his frown deepen. 'You're an interfering motherfucker.'

'And you've got the woman you've wanted for years, so it's all worked out. You should be thanking me.' Right then, the radio attached to Kerr's belt crackled.

'*Kerr, we got an issue you might want to relay to your Alpha,*' said one of the Watchers.

With a speed that spoke of long-term practice, Kerr grabbed his radio and pressed down on the side button. 'What's going on?'

'*I just heard that some fuckery went down at Bellcrest. Ripper's witch was at the center of it. She left, she's fine—*'

Ripper snatched the radio from his friend and spoke into it. 'Tell me what happened. *Exactly* what happened.'

CHAPTER TWENTY-SEVEN

❦

As had become usual, the front door opened in welcome as Ripper vaulted up the porch steps. He stalked inside, rage firing through his blood. He'd been pissed at CeCe before. But having learned what Emberlyn had gone through in his absence, he was even more furious.

If he hadn't been called away, he would have gone to Bellcrest with Emberlyn. He could have had her back; could have kept those fucking assholes from getting anywhere near her.

'Emberlyn?' he called out, prowling through the manor. 'Emberlyn?'

Footfalls came thundering down the steps. He halted, his gaze on the *empty staircase*. A cold breeze fluttered past his left side, ruffling the sleeve of his tee. Fuck, this house gave him the creeps at times.

A creak came from the direction of the kitchen. He tracked the sound, his pace slowing as Emberlyn stepped out of the door that led to the basement. She closed it behind her and turned to him, her face composed and showing no trace of anger.

His woman was good at hiding her emotions.

Visually taking stock of her, Ripper walked straight to her. 'You all right? I heard what happened at Bellcrest.'

'I'm fine,' she said, her voice as empty of emotion as her expression. 'Just a little agitated.'

Yeah? She didn't *look* agitated. 'You should have called me,' he said, inching closer.

'I did. You weren't home. I figured Kerr would hear of it from one of the Watchers and tell you about it once you were done doing Alpha stuff,' she added with a slight shrug, as if the incident hadn't been noteworthy enough to warrant his immediate attention.

'No "Alpha stuff" is more important to me than anything concerning you,' he firmly stated, not missing the flare of surprise in her eyes. 'I want the names of who circled and attacked you.' The Watcher from the coven who'd relayed what happened had refused to name anyone, not trusting that Ripper wouldn't hunt them all down.

'I already dealt with them.'

'So I heard.' He was proud of how well she'd handled the incident. 'But now it's my turn.'

'It would be playing into the hands of whoever bespelled the Rabid. We've established that our little shit stirrer wants to isolate the coven and make Reena look bad. If you go to Bellcrest on the bounce, she'll have no choice but to defend her people even if she agrees that you have a right to your anger. That'll make things worse, which the shit stirrer will *love*.'

Annoyed he couldn't honestly refute that, Ripper felt his jaw tighten.

'I think they were hoping she'd blame me; that she and I would go head-to-head, and then I'd have done their dirty work for them. Except it didn't pan out that way, so they took it a step further and riled up the crowd – it was clear that somebody had. They seemed sure they could gather enough people to "storm the manor".'

He tensed. 'That was what they were planning?'

'According to Mari, yes.'

Motherfuckers. 'Was Reena there?'

'She showed up after the crowd launched their sad little attack. Apparently, she'd already told them that she didn't believe I was responsible for the Rabid's appearance at Bellcrest. They'd gone against her orders to leave me be. She apologized to me on their behalf and made it clear that they'd be punished.'

As Reena didn't have a great history of dishing out punishments that properly fit the crime, Ripper wasn't mollified by that. 'Why did you even go to Bellcrest?'

'Mari called, telling me she had some info I'd want to hear. I was a little suspicious, but I couldn't think what ulterior motive she could have for asking me to come see her. And I didn't want her showing up here at my home.'

He felt his teeth grind. 'She set you up?'

Emberlyn pulled a face. 'Maybe. She claimed it was to prevent the whole storming the manor thing from occurring. I don't know if that's true. But she did seem genuinely upset about how everything went down. Or it could be that I want to believe that because it bums me out to think my own blood would lure me somewhere to be attacked.'

His chest clenched at that. The urge to comfort an itch beneath his skin, he nuzzled her face and curled both his arms around her shoulders. 'I'll have a little talk with Mari; find out for sure.'

Emberlyn's hands settled on his hips. 'She wouldn't confess to any such thing, so there's no point in questioning her over it.'

'Do you think the people who came at you could be the rebellious faction?'

Thoughtful, she absently touched her tongue to the inside of her lower lip. Just like that, his attention zipped right down to that mouth he was a little obsessed with.

'I would've thought they'd avoid drawing so much attention to themselves, but I could be wrong,' she said.

He forced his eyes to return to hers as he considered her point. 'Their actions will make Reena look at them closely. It doesn't make sense that the faction would want that. Or that they'd officially make themselves enemies of you.'

'But it's very possible that whoever riled them up is part of the faction.'

The best way to confirm that would be to ask the members of the crowd. Placing his nose behind her ear, he breathed deep and gently pressed, 'I want the names of those who confronted you today.'

Impatience flitted over her face. 'As I said before, going after them will only make things worse. I get why you're angling to huff and puff and kick some asses, but you're smarter than that.'

'Right now, I don't care about what's smart. My concern is *you*.'

A little softness leached into her expression. 'And I'm fine.'

'I know you are. I know you're too tough for them to ever break you. But you can't tell me it didn't sting big time that they yet again tried to pin something on you. You can't tell me you were blasé about them surrounding you, coming at you from all sides, and trying to *cuff* you.'

She looked away, exhaling heavily. 'It stung because I'm tired of it. And no, I wasn't blasé about the scene that unfolded. But I don't care about those people, so their actions don't hurt me. They're just irritating.'

Hurt, irritated – it was all the same to him. *Any* negative emotions they caused her would be completely unacceptable to Ripper.

The air chilled abruptly, and then a chair skidded across the floor and clanged against a cupboard. Like it had been angrily shoved by someone he couldn't see.

He couldn't lie, his pulse jumped.

The fine hairs on his nape lifting, he refocused on his witch. 'The entities in this house aren't happy right now, are they?'

'Nope.'

'They can take a ticket and get in fucking line. I want the names of the witches who went at you, Emberlyn.'

'Oh my God, you are beyond obstinate.'

As was she. So he knew he'd have a hard time changing her mind. Unless ... he made a suggestion she'd support; came up with a way of handling things that wouldn't worsen the situation. 'How about you come with me while I talk to each person?'

Her brow pinched. 'Go with you?'

'Yeah. Together, we'll pay them each a quick visit. I'll make my feelings clear to them. In doing so, I'll get the message across to the entire coven that I will *personally* seek out anyone who comes at you.'

Pale-hazel eyes narrowed for the briefest moment. 'How exactly will you make your feelings clear? You can't beat them all up. They weren't all guys, Rip. Some were women. Some were elders. There were even two teens in the group.'

'There'll be no violence. Well, not much. *Providing* they apologize to you.' He swept a hand up the back of her neck and sank it into her hair. 'There needs to be consequences, Emberlyn. I want the coven as a whole to see that. They already know you're under my protection. They ignored that so, yeah, I agree that someone riled them up. Let's make them resent that person.'

She twisted her mouth. 'Intriguing approach.'

'That a yes?'

Her phone rang, snaring her attention.

He reluctantly released her and watched as she walked to the wall-mounted phone. She plucked up the receiver and answered, 'Hello?'

Muffled words came gushing down the line, the voice loaded with anger. *Paisley.*

'I *did* call you, you didn't answer,' said Emberlyn. 'If you had, I would have told you ... I wasn't gonna drive to your place just because you didn't pick up ... I had no reason to assume you were sleeping; I thought you were out.'

It was no surprise to him that Paisley had overslept to such a degree – a werewolf's first full moon tended to massively exhaust them.

'Calm down, it's not really me you're mad at.' Moments later, Emberlyn's body stiffened, her eyes going squinty. 'Already worked up about what, exactly?' Whatever response she received made her gaze snap to Ripper and harden. 'I see. No, I hadn't heard ... He's right here, but we were discussing the Bellcrest incident ... I will ... Yeah, later.'

Emberlyn returned the receiver and then faced him. 'So, it seems that there may be something you'd like to share with the class regarding CeCe.'

He sighed. 'I did intend to tell you. Paisley just beat me to it. How much did she say?'

'Just that CeCe tried embarrassing her for having a threesome. Is there more?'

'A lot more.' He crossed to Emberlyn and cupped her hips. 'Basically, CeCe decided to make a fool of herself last night. She came onto Kerr. Taunted Paisley. Challenged Clem. Toilet papered Logan's house. And ... and she was seen in her wolf form pissing on one of my truck's tires.'

Emberlyn stared at him, her expression turning creepily vacant – a sign of fury, he'd come to learn. Her muscles were

locked in place, tight with tension. 'She took a piss on your tire?'
Each word was soft. Quiet. Dangerous.

Ripper smoothed a soothing palm up her spine. 'She offered
to replace it. I said no.' Had it been anyone else, he would have
allowed it. But he wouldn't accept something from a werewolf
who felt she had a claim to him – it would have been as good
as acknowledging the claim as legit. 'I told her you'd likely have
some potion that would clean it.'

'I do.' A flatly spoken confirmation.

'I also made it clear you belong to me now.'

There was no shift in Emberlyn's expression. 'What did she
have to say to that?'

'She claimed it can't be possible; believes I love her. I disabused her of that mistaken belief *fast*, and I warned her – as well
as the women who'd helped her toilet paper Logan's house – that
you were to be left alone or they'd be temporarily banished from
the clan.'

An almost infinitesimal pinch of softness flickered in
Emberlyn's eyes for the briefest moment. 'You would really do
that?'

'Of fucking course I would, baby.' He burrowed his hand in
her hair. 'While I don't believe she would risk that happening
and so should therefore leave you alone, I'm not so confident
she'll cease being a general pain in the ass. Hence why I'll be
leaving her punishments to Kerr and Crew from now on. Any
direct attempts I make to deal with her would be counterproduc-
tive – she wants the attention.' He caught her face in his hands
and snared her gaze with his. 'Never again will I be called away
from your side to deal with her.'

Still no real change in Emberlyn's expression. 'Hmm.'

'You're scaring me just a little.'

'Why?'

'You look eerily calm. I can't sense any underlying emotions in you at all. If I didn't know you, I'd swear you weren't one bit affected by any of what I just spilled to you.' He nipped at the corner of her mouth. 'But I've come to learn that the calmer you look, the more pissed you generally are.'

'I would like to choke her,' she told him matter-of-factly, completely serious.

He blinked and dipped his chin. 'Understandable.'

'And curse her soul to never be reborn.'

'That's . . . You could do that?'

'Of course not. It was just an idle remark.'

Ripper wasn't so sure he believed that. 'Can we move on from talk of her now?'

'Sure,' she easily agreed, her tone still flat.

Yeah, his baby was nowhere near the realm of 'calm'. In her shoes, he wouldn't be, either. He'd want to skin alive anyone who dared act as if they had rights to her. And after what went down at Bellcrest, Emberlyn wasn't liable to quickly dial back her anger.

Wanting to give her time, he held her close and silently reminded her he was there – nuzzling her face, trailing his fingers down her throat, rubbing at her nape, sweeping his hand over her hair, dabbing a featherlight kiss on her temple, stroking his palm up and down her back.

The tension began easing out of her muscles in such tiny increments he wouldn't have noticed if he wasn't so wholly focused on her.

A line briefly dented her brow as he once more petted her nape. 'You're scent-marking me again. And you're being all touchy-feely. I'm not a werewolf; these things don't soothe me.'

'Sure they do,' he said, tracking the path of his fingers as they weaved into her hair. He fucking loved her hair. It was soft and sleek and stunning with its iridescent tint. 'Everyone needs touch sometimes, even you.' He caught her chin with his hand, dipping his face to hers. 'Kiss me.'

'No.'

Ripper almost smiled at the grouchy response. He tugged at her lower lip with his teeth. 'Kiss me.'

'No.'

He pinched her nipple, making her lips part on a gasp. He sank his tongue into her mouth. Kissed. Nipped. Licked. Sipped. Until finally she relaxed against him and kissed him back. 'Now, let's go deal with those fucking assholes who thought to dare harm you.'

As she turned the corner onto Bennet's street, Emberlyn noticed his yard was now empty of people. In fact, the street itself was quiet. His nosy neighbors were nowhere to be seen – their doors closed, their windows shut.

She couldn't claim to have wrestled back all of her anger just yet, though that was partly because CeCe's little stunt had fueled said anger. That bitch had thought to mark Ripper's possession like she had every right; like *he* was *her* possession.

And Ripper ... he'd threatened to temporarily banish CeCe and her friends from his clan if they didn't leave Emberlyn be. And he'd *meant* it. He would honestly do that. It touched her on a level he probably hadn't anticipated.

So many times she'd dealt with bullshit from the coven. None had ever truly been punished by Reena. Emberlyn had become far too used to having to dish out her own brand of justice – no one else was going to do it for her.

But Ripper would.

He would place her feelings before those of his wolves. He would never expect her to let things *slide* for his sake. And now here he was, determined to 'talk' with every witch that had been part of the earlier scene, despite the fact that she'd already handled it.

She understood his need to make his own point. It wasn't even solely a personal need; wasn't only born of his protectiveness toward Emberlyn. It was a political necessity. Like her, he could never afford to look weak or be seen to not deal with any offenses.

Still, she would have preferred that he'd stayed out of it. Not merely because confronting the assholes could worsen the overall situation, but because she didn't want him to be further dragged into this mess.

Too many times lately he'd felt compelled to 'step in' on Emberlyn's behalf. Would he not eventually reach a point where he tired of it? He was an Alpha. He had a clan to manage, businesses to oversee and any related issues to address. He didn't need to be dealing with *her* messes on top of that.

It was Sunday. A day of rest, for the most part. And if it wasn't for his involvement with Emberlyn, he *could* be resting. Instead, he was here.

Things weren't normally *this* bad – both Millicent's will and the rebellious faction had triggered a lot of the recent problems. But Emberlyn would never truly be left in peace by the coven as a whole.

Maybe she could convince him to let her handle things from here on out . . .

Doubtful.

He was an Alpha. They were freaking renowned for swooping in, taking over and fixing the problems of those they felt an attachment to.

As she parked outside Bennet's house, Ripper looked at her. 'Want to play "bad cop, worse cop"?'

She might have smiled at that if she wasn't still wound so tight. 'Should be fun. Which one of us is "worse cop"?'

'This time round, me. It's only fair. You've already had your fun with these assholes.'

True.

They exited the car and, with Ripper in the lead, advanced up Bennet's path. As this was mostly her wolf's show, she hung back slightly when he knocked on the front door.

Bennet answered after only a few moments – his recently shiny-black hair now a dull gray, since she'd undone her spell. His gaze darted from Ripper to Emberlyn, a frantic glint flickering to life in its depths.

He swallowed hard, inching back a little. 'I . . .' And that was all that came out.

Ripper watched him, his stare unblinking and flinty; menace cloaking his large frame. 'I have a question for you,' he said, his voice low, danger looped through each word.

Bennet jammed his hands in his pockets. 'If it's about the Rabid, it ran off before—'

'The Watchers filled me in on the details,' Ripper told him. 'I just need to know why you thought you could get away with what you did to Emberlyn.' A query laced with ire.

Bennet, well, it turned out that he was dumb enough to raise his chin defensively. 'I wasn't one of the people who circled her,' he proclaimed, as if that meant no anger should be directed his way.

Unbelievable.

Ripper moved fast. So fast he was almost a blur. He fisted Bennet's long-sleeved tee, yanked him outside and then slammed him against the wall beside the front door.

Bennet expelled a pained cry, his eyes wide with shock. He flinched as Ripper went nose to nose with him.

'You yelled at her.' Ripper's words were low. Ultra-soft. Coated in rage. 'You insulted her. Laid unfounded accusations at her door. Insisted that the Watchers should detain her. And you did *nothing* when the others came at her.'

Bennet shrank in on himself, his face ashen, breathing so fast he was close to hyperventilating.

Snarling, Ripper sliced out his claws and held the tips against Bennet's chest. 'Tell me how that makes you innocent.'

'It-it doesn't,' Bennet stammered.

'You have a woman of your own. What would you do to a man who put her through that shit?'

Bennet squeezed his eyes shut and turned his face away. 'I-I don't know.'

'Probably nothing,' Emberlyn hedged. 'He's only brave when he has backup, Rip. I'm pretty sure the only reason he held onto his daughter earlier was because he figured I wouldn't hurt him.'

Bennet's eyes popped open and landed on her. 'That's not tr—' He made a choking sound as her wolf snapped a hand tight around his throat.

Ripper's upper lip quivered. 'I didn't say you could talk to her, did I?'

His face going redder and redder, Bennet flapped his hands near the large palm still squeezing his neck.

'You might want to let him breathe, Rip,' she said.

'Why?' A careless question.

She pursed her lips. 'I actually can't think of a reason.'

'You didn't answer my question before,' Ripper said to him. 'What made you think you could get away with it?' He loosened his hold on Bennet's throat.

The witch coughed and heaved in mounds of air. 'I-I wasn't thinking anything,' he eventually replied. 'Not really. M-my emotions were running high – my daughter had been attacked, my whole family was a wreck over it and all I could think was that she could be dead. At the time, it just felt like only Emberlyn could be the culprit.'

Ripper squinted. 'At the time? Not now?'

Bennet hesitated, dropping his gaze. 'Having had a chance to reflect on things, no, I don't now believe she was involved,' he begrudgingly admitted. 'Reena was right in all she said. Besides, Emberlyn has an alibi. You. It couldn't possibly have been her.' He slid his gaze briefly to her. 'I apologize for my behavior earlier,' he said, stiff. 'I ... I was not myself.'

'No, I think you were,' said Ripper. 'I think you felt bold enough to be that person to the fullest extent because the woman you'd targeted was all alone.'

Bennet shook his head. 'It wasn't like that.'

Emberlyn personally didn't agree. 'Who was the first to suggest that I must have sent the Rabid?'

'It was ...' He trailed off, his expression turning shifty. 'I don't recall.'

A growl rumbled out of Ripper.

'Actually, come to think of it' – Bennet cleared his throat – 'it was Hank.'

That fit. He'd pushed to the front of the crowd earlier, hadn't he?

'Reena disagreed, and we all conceded that she'd made valid points,' Bennet told Ripper. 'But after she left, Hank insisted it could only be Emberlyn. The things he was saying made so much sense at the time. Looking back, I don't understand.' His brow furrowing, he gave his head a little shake. 'It was like ... like someone used magick to manipulate me – maybe even *all* of us.' His eyes went wide at the idea. 'That must have been what happened.'

Hmm, it was possible that a spell had been cast that put the angry crowd into a suggestible frame of mind so that 'seeds' could be planted. But it wouldn't have *forced* them to blame Emberlyn for the crime, or forced them to circle and attack her.

'Yes, we were bespelled,' Bennet proclaimed, eagerly latching onto the explanation to evade her wolf's wrath. 'Taking her on, even as a group, isn't something we'd normally do. Especially when she has your protection. This explains it.'

Ripper cocked his head. 'So what you're saying is that it wasn't your fault?'

'Yes, yes. I'm not to blame. There was magickal interference.'

'I should excuse what you did, then? I should let you go?'

'Yes, you—' Bennet choked again as Ripper went back to strangling him one-handed. Fear lived and breathed in the witch's eyes, his face again turning splotchy and red.

'You might want to ease up on the scare factor,' Emberlyn advised Ripper. 'I heard he has a weak bladder.'

'You care if he pisses himself?' Ripper asked her.

Not at all. 'I figured you wouldn't want to deal with the smell.'

'Let me be clear,' Ripper growled at him. 'There are no excuses for harming Emberlyn by word or deed. Not a single. Fucking. One.' A few moments later, he released the guy and stepped back.

His knees buckling, Bennet coughed and spluttered and hacked.

Ripper stared at him dispassionately. 'I think you get the message I'm sending here, don't you?'

Bennet nodded hard. 'I get it,' he wheezed out. 'I really am sorry.'

He was sorry he'd found himself on the wrong side of Ripper's attention. But just maybe it would be enough to cause him to curb his behavior in future. Time would tell.

Side by side, Emberlyn and Ripper strolled down the path. Only once they were back in her car did he say, 'Either the prick was telling the truth about there being magickal interference, or he *wants* to believe it's true because then he can escape the consequences.'

She nodded, not leaning toward any particular theory.

Ripper clicked on her belt. Just the mere graze of his fingers against her hip made her belly clench. But she didn't have to curse her body for reacting to him so fervently anymore. He was hers now.

'He said your uncle-in-law put your name forward,' Ripper went on. 'Could Hank have been the one who bespelled the crowd?'

Considering it, Emberlyn gunned the engine. 'His magick is strong offensive-wise. But I don't see him being powerful enough to take mental hold of an entire crowd.'

Ripper hummed. 'I say we go talk to him next.'

Hank only lived a few blocks away, so the journey there was a short one. At Ripper's knock on the front door, Gill peeked out the living room window. She did a double-take at the sight of them, apprehension washing over her face.

She came to the door, her shoulders stiff, and folded her arms. 'What do you want?' she asked, her nerves clearly rattled.

'To speak with Hank,' Ripper replied, his entire demeanor once more frightening as fuck.

Gill licked her lips. 'He isn't here.'

'Sure he is. I can smell him. He's standing just behind the door.' Ripper shoved it open so hard it flew back, and a loud male cry pierced the air. Ignoring her indignant squawk, Ripper pushed past Gill and yanked her husband out from his hidey hole.

Emberlyn supposed she shouldn't be too surprised that Hank would take cover and expect his wife to protect him. He'd always been a little weasel who expected others to fight his battles for him.

Ripper shoved him against the hallway wall, baring his teeth.
'You really thought you could fucking hide from me? It's like you
asked yourself, "Hey, how can I piss Ripper off even more than
I already have?"'

'You can't hurt him!' Gill protested.

Emberlyn shot her a look. 'Back off. He's a big boy. He can
take his lumps all on his own. Oh, and I'm fine, by the way.
Thanks for asking.'

Plastering his back fully against the wall as if it might help
him escape Ripper, Hank spluttered. 'You can't barge into our
home.' It wasn't a complaint, it was a full-on whine.

'Just did,' Ripper clipped. '*Make* me leave.' It was a taunt . . .
because they all knew that the odds of Hank manning up like
that were slim to none.

And predictably, he did *jack*.

'No, you wouldn't dare, would you? A woman, yes, you'll
attack a woman – especially if you have company. But not
someone who could beat the holy hell out of you.' Ripper held a
hand up near Hank's face and unsheathed his claws. 'Give me a
reason why I shouldn't. It'll need to be a good one.'

Hank stared at the claws through bulging eyes, a sheen of
sweat building on his forehead.

'There is no good reason for what he did,' uttered Gill, defeat
coloring her tone.

Ripper lifted a brow at Hank. 'Hear that? *She* knows. And
here she is, standing up for you. Speaking for you. Taking your
side over that of her niece, which makes me as pissed off with
her as I am with you.'

Gill's eyes widened. 'It isn't a matter of taking sides. He was
wrong. I told him that he was wrong.'

'Did you call Emberlyn to check on her? Did you apologize to
her on his behalf?'

'I've been busy trying to figure out who used magick to sway him.' Gill thrust a hand into her hair. 'You'll think I'm just making up excuses here, but I'm not. *Someone* wove a spell to stir up that crowd. No way would anyone have genuinely thought it a good idea to march to the manor and burn Emberlyn at the stake.'

The fuck? Emberlyn gawked, fury tearing through her once more.

Ripper went deathly still, a growl rumbling in his chest. 'Burn her at the stake?' he echoed, refocusing on his captive. 'That was the plan?'

Hank whimpered. 'S-someone tossed out the idea. I don't know who.'

'You don't know? Baby, he doesn't know.'

'Of course he does,' said Emberlyn.

'Oh, he definitely does.' Ripper edged forward. '*Who*, Hank?'

Cowering, Hank scrunched his eyes shut.

'Tell them, for God's sake,' Gill barked.

His chin trembling, Hank opened only one eye. 'Patrick. It was Patrick.'

So, once Ripper felt satisfied that Hank understood he was to stay away from her, they went to Patrick's house.

He wasn't home, though. According to his girlfriend, he was with a coven member who specialized in mental cleansing – apparently, he was feeling 'dirty' from the manipulative magick that he'd allegedly earlier been gripped by.

Yes, like Bennet and Hank, he claimed to have been magickly coerced.

The girlfriend also stated she was convinced that the coven's rebellious faction was behind what happened.

'Making this claim could just be the crowd's way of covering their asses,' said Ripper as they headed back to her car, 'but it would make sense that they'd been bespelled. Nothing they did earlier could be called wise. These people are dicks, but they're not brave enough to really risk your wrath or mine. They're weak.'

'Which makes them easy to magickly manipulate,' Emberlyn added.

They decided to pay Ruben a visit next. Nobody answered the door. Just the same, no one opened up when they went to the homes of Getty or the others involved. It was likely that they'd been warned Ripper was on the warpath and so they were pretending they weren't home.

Returning to her car yet again, Emberlyn paused at the driver's door. 'Are we stopping off at CeCe's place now?'

Meeting her gaze over the hood, Ripper frowned. 'Why would we do that? She won't know anything.'

'No, but she *does* need dealing with after that shit she pulled last night. You had a little chat with her. Now it's my turn.' Emberlyn jumped into the car and closed the door.

Sliding onto the passenger seat, Ripper said, 'I already handled it.'

'So I should leave the situation be? That's quite a double standard you have, considering you insisted on confronting every person who crowded me.'

Ripper's lips tightened. 'Baby, it's not that I think you should let it go because I dealt with it. You really want to go confront her, I'll give you directions to her house; we'll go there right now. But she'd love for you to turn up there. Love the attention and the drama. Like I said earlier, I'm done giving her attention.'

Emberlyn sighed, understanding where he was coming from. To track her down would be to play into her hands … just as Ripper raging at the coven would have played into the faction's hands. He'd agreed to handle the latter situation differently. She'd be a hypocrite if she didn't do the same regarding CeCe.

'Believe me when I say that she'll be sitting by her window, waiting in anticipation for you to arrive,' he added. 'I'd prefer that we disappoint her.'

Emberlyn inhaled deeply. 'Okay.'

'Okay?'

'Okay.'

His brows dipped, not looking reassured. 'Why do I get the feeling you're going to handle this however you see fit, regardless of what I say?'

'I don't know, why do you?'

'Because you're not a person who's ever made a habit of letting anyone escape the consequences for things they've done to offend you.'

'I've made exceptions.'

'Really?'

'No.' She switched on the engine. 'Seatbelt.'

'What are you going to do?'

'Drive back to the manor.'

'I mean, what are you going to do about CeCe?' he asked, clicking on his seatbelt.

She pulled out onto the road. 'I don't need to do anything. You handled it.'

'You don't *need* to, no, but you're going to anyway. Aren't you?'

She smiled. 'I just love how paranoid I make you.'

'That's not an answer, Emberlyn.'

It was the only one he was getting.

CHAPTER TWENTY-EIGHT

❧

Admiring the skirt on a fashionably dressed mannequin, Emberlyn spared her friend a quick look. 'You're muttering to yourself again.'

Paisley huffed. 'I can't help it. I love my mom, I do, but how hard can it be to respect a "Thanks for the dinner invite but I have plans" response? I already had dinner with her twice in the past week. The damn woman seems to hear the word "no" and feel compelled to change a person's mind.'

'Kind of like Ripper.'

Paisley waved that away. 'No, as a member of his clan, I can confirm he respects boundaries. He just doesn't acknowledge that *you* have any.'

Emberlyn snorted. Ripper was someone who kept a relative distance between himself and others; someone who liked personal space and alone time. But it seemed that once he attached to a person, that changed in a very big way. And over the past six days, it had become apparent that he now thought himself exempt from her boundaries.

All of which should technically irritate her but didn't.

The guy might have *barged* into her life and planted himself firmly in it, but she wouldn't want him to be anywhere else.

'Retail therapy usually improves my mood,' added Paisley, 'but it's not working today.'

Yes, Emberlyn had noticed. They'd been to two other stores before this one, and Paisley had had a face like a smacked ass the entire time.

A few clothing stores could be found in Chilgrave. This particular one was run by, and catered to, werewolves. The lighting was gentle and the background music was low, accommodating their enhanced senses. Also, every material was softer than normal so as not to aggravate their slight skin sensitivity.

Street sounds drifted through the door that had been propped open, as did the magnetic scents coming from the neighboring coffeehouse. A few other shoppers were browsing the store. Salespeople wandered about, doing this and that. Clothes of all material were spread around – some clothed mannequins, others hung on racks, the rest could be seen on shelves and tables.

'At least she wants to see you,' said Emberlyn, her heels clicking on the faux oak floor as they ambled further into the shop. 'It's good that she's over her snit.'

'Totally, but I can't sit through another awkward family meal this week wherein she sporadically cries and my dad fails to look me in the eye. Besides, I don't want to miss our double date.'

'Ripper still isn't impressed that you and Crew invited yourselves along to *our* date.' Emberlyn edged her way through a narrow gap between racks, frowning as a hanger got caught on her sleeve. 'He'll probably chase you away.'

'No, he won't. Though he likes having you to himself, he also likes seeing you surrounded by his clan. It eases his protective instincts. He wants you to have that circle of safety.'

Emberlyn felt her brow pinch. 'Says who?'

'Crew, Kerr and Logan. They talk about you two a lot.'

'Saying what, exactly?'

'They're just pleased that their Alpha is content. He's been alone a long time, and he gives so much of himself to the clan. Neither of which is healthy for any werewolf, but particularly not for an Alpha. Werewolves aren't built to be alone.'

'Is it affecting you now that the Change has fully settled into your cells?'

Paisley placed a hand to her stomach. 'There's like this urge to belong. To stay close to our clan. To watch over each other. So I can totally get why Ripper eats up your time and pokes his nose into every aspect of your business – it's, like, encoded in his DNA. He *has* to know you're safe and well. Crew is the same with me, but I don't at all mind. To be honest, it's a two-way street.'

Emberlyn felt her lips hitch up. 'I've noticed that you seem to be getting along *very* well.' They spent a lot of time together.

'I can't say for sure that anything serious will come of it. I've learned that he typically tends to avoid "serious". But then, so does Ripper. And you, for that matter. Now look at you both – you make a true power couple.'

'Power couple?'

'Yeah. You both scare most of the townsfolk. That makes you both socially powerful. Put the two of you together and *bam.*' Paisley's eyes widened in interest. 'Ooh, nice purse.' She plucked it off a peg and turned it this way and that.

Emberlyn snickered at how easily Paisley was distracted by something shiny.

'*Not* a nice price tag, though. Ugh.' Paisley returned the purse to its peg. 'So what were we talking about? Ah, how scary you and Ripper are. I'll bet the coven's idiotic faction is quailing in its boots. They *massively* fucked up last weekend by setting you up like that.'

They had indeed. The day after Emberlyn and Ripper had paid a visit to those who'd attacked, Reena had turned up at the manor. She hadn't been too happy that some of her coven had had the fear of God instilled in them by Ripper, but she *did* understand why he and Emberlyn had confronted those members – or so she'd claimed.

Emberlyn still didn't trust her. Never would. But she'd keep up the temporary truce for as long as necessary.

Reena was unfortunately no closer to identifying the witches of the faction. It was driving her nuts. She also worried that divisions would form in the coven. While it was good that all were now intent on unmasking the faction members, considering them traitors for bespelling their own, it meant that many were also looking at others with distrust.

Often people came to Reena claiming that this person or that person 'had' to be part of the faction. But they had no evidence, so she could only promise to 'look into it'. That was never enough for her witches, meaning they weren't happy about her inaction.

Basically, the coven was ripe with issues right now.

Gasping, Paisley plucked a tee from a rack. 'This is so cute.'

'It has a werewolf with devilish horns printed on it.'

'Yeah. Cute.' Metal scraped metal as Paisley flicked through the hangers on the rack. 'Please have my size, please have my – aha.' She grabbed a particular tee, grinning broadly. A grin that faltered ever so slightly as her eyes slid to something behind Emberlyn.

'What?' Peering over her shoulder, Emberlyn tracked her friend's gaze to the glass-front window. CeCe's friends were passing the store – *fast*. And totally avoiding looking at Emberlyn.

'Are they still keeping their distance from you?' Paisley checked.

Emberlyn turned back to her. 'Yes. Which is good, because I'm rather tired of Ripper having to butt into situations on my behalf.'

'You're tired of it, or you're worried *he'll* tire of it?'

'A little of both. Anyway, it seems to be working, because I haven't heard a peep from them or CeCe.'

'They have been keeping a low profile lately.'

'Wise of them. Because I don't think Ripper was bluffing when he warned them what the consequences would be if they kept coming at me.'

'He wasn't bluffing. A temporary ban is no joke. You'd lose that feeling of belonging. You'd have no one to run with on a full moon. And not one clan member would lift a finger for you.' Paisley exchanged a brief smile with a worker tidying shelves. 'Joining another clan wouldn't be an option for them – no other Alpha would accept a temporarily banned wolf, because they'd be interfering with a punishment.'

'Kerr told me he wouldn't be all too shocked if CeCe switched clans.'

'She might. I mean, she has to know at this point that neither Ripper nor Logan will ever be hers. Right now, she has a front seat to the Emberlyn and Ripper show. Getting some distance would be healthy. But she may have the feeling that it's *her* clan, so why should she have to leave?'

'I suppose we'll see.' Emberlyn glanced down at the items draped over Paisley's arm. 'You gonna buy those or what?'

'Yes.' Paisley patted them. 'Checkout counter here we come.'

They left the shop moments later ... just as Dez and Ward were heading into the nearby grocery store. Both clocked Emberlyn, averted their gazes and hurried along.

Paisley hummed. 'It's a nice change that they didn't snarl at you or anything.'

'I suppose neither of them want Ripper to come knocking on their door.'

'He would, too. He's in hyper-protective mode right now. Woe betide any who attempt to harm you. If he doesn't fuck up their shit, *you* will ... and you'll do a much more dramatic job of it than he would.'

Oh, totally.

Stood on his doorstep, Ripper folded his arms. 'What part of "It's not a double date" are you failing to understand?'

Crew gave him an easy smile. 'Don't be a grouch, it'll be fun.'

'No. No, it won't.' Ripper tilted his head. 'What is it, you want some sort of buffer between you and Paisley? You're thinking of calling things off?'

'No, nothing like that.' Sighing, Crew scratched the back of his scalp. 'Look, her parents are being a problem, okay? They say they accept the twins' new situation and that they want to fix things, but then their mom will cry and their dad will act all weird around them.' He lowered his arm back to his side. 'Kage isn't all that bothered by it, but Paisley is. Emberlyn is family to her, and she's the only person outside our clan who supports Paisley.'

'So, because you want Paisley to have people around her who make her happy, I should share Emberlyn tonight and let you horn in on our date?'

'Yeah.'

'No.'

Crew exhaled heavily, his eyes dancing. 'You know, you're a little too greedy with your witch's time and attention.'

'As are you with Paisley's. What of it?'

A snort popped out of Crew. 'Okay, you got me there. But at least make an exception for tonight. Paisley's mom has been bugging her all day. She needs cheering up.'

'No one has ever claimed that I have any way of lifting their mood.' Ripper didn't even do well at lifting his own.

'Maybe *you* don't, but Paisley thinks of Emberlyn as a sister – having her company will help. And you know something? You have a better chance of making your witch feel comfortable with our clan if she has familiar people around her, such as one of her lifelong best friends.'

Ripper heaved a sigh. 'An hour. That's all you're getting. Then I want my . . .' He trailed off on hearing the rumble of a car engine. Looking to his left, he saw a vehicle approaching. It wasn't until the car came close that he recognized it as belonging to the parents of Michael Reed.

Crew frowned. 'What could they want? Because, somehow, I don't think they're here to wish you and Emberlyn the best.'

Catching sight of their somber expressions through the driver's window, Ripper would have to agree. His arms still folded, he stalked to the bottom of his path with Crew at his side.

The Reeds parked up and then cautiously approached, their expressions unfriendly, their body language standoffish.

Colton briefly inclined his head in greeting. 'Ripper, Crew.' He cleared his throat. 'We'd like to talk to you, Ripper, if you can spare us the time. In private, I mean.'

Actually, Ripper was planning to go pick up Emberlyn in a few minutes. But he figured this wouldn't take long. 'I have a little time before I'm heading out.'

'I'll wait in the truck.' Crew strolled over to the vehicle and hopped into the front passenger seat. He also lowered the window, the eavesdropping bastard.

Claris clasped her hands in front of her. 'We've known

for a few weeks now that you've been … spending time with
Emberlyn.'

An unusual way of saying 'sleeping with her'. It was almost as
if Claris couldn't bring herself to speak the words aloud.

'I suppose it shouldn't have been too much of a surprise to
us, regardless of your reservations about witches.' Claris gave a
tight smile, adding, 'Our Emberlyn is a fascinating girl, after all.'

The amount of possession loaded into the words 'Our
Emberlyn' rankled Ripper something fierce, but he didn't let
it show.

'You appear to be serious about her.'

'I am,' Ripper confirmed.

Her lips tightening, Claris exchanged a grave look with her
mate. 'We never expected it to reach this point or we would have
spoken to you sooner.'

Ripper winged up a brow. 'About what?'

'About how utterly inappropriate it is for you to become
seriously involved with a woman who belongs to another man.'

The fuck? Feeling his brows snap together, Ripper echoed,
'Belongs?'

'You know she's mated,' Colton cut in, impatience rippling
across his face.

'I know she *had* a mate. That's not the case anymore.'

Claris bristled. 'Emberlyn dragged her heels when it came to
breaking the mating tie. She didn't want to do it. She loves my
boy. Loves him with her whole heart.'

A heart Michael had broken. But as Ripper couldn't share
their son's betrayal with them, he said, 'Maybe so. Matters nothing, though. He's not here. And if he were, it would make no
difference – she renounced him as her mate.'

'That would change if he came back,' Claris insisted.

Ripper shook his head. 'She made her choice. She wouldn't

go back on it. If he returned, he wouldn't be the same Michael anyway. Parts of him would be lost, and he'd never get them back.'

Claris leaned toward him slightly. 'They said that about you when you were Rabid; said you'd be a shadow of your true self if you ever came back. But that's not the case.'

'He's been Rabid longer than I was.'

'But you were just a child. Even a year in that state should have broken parts of your spirit. It didn't.'

Colton nodded. 'Like you, Ripper, our Michael is strong. Unbelievably strong. He would come back to himself if he returned, and he would want his mate. She would go to him; she'd reclaim him in an instant.'

'And you'd be tossed aside like trash,' Claris added. 'That can't be what you want. Do what's best for all involved and step aside.'

Ripper felt his face go rock hard. 'That isn't going to happen.' They were fucking high to think it would.

Annoyance sparked to life in Colton's eyes. 'You'd truly want a woman who was once claimed by another werewolf? You can't tell me it doesn't bother you.'

In truth, the knowledge of it made jealousy score its nails down Ripper's back. He hated that she'd once been another wolf's mate – especially since the son of a bitch hadn't deserved her – but it didn't make Ripper want her any less.

He took a step toward the couple. 'What bothers me is that you'd rather she walked through life alone than find happiness with anyone other than Michael.' It was cruel and selfish. 'You don't like the idea of her moving on because it shows she's accepted that he isn't coming back. You can't handle that because *you* don't want to accept he's gone.'

Colton's jaw went tight. 'He's our son.'

'But not Emberlyn's mate,' said Ripper.

Claris shook her head wildly. 'She belongs to him.'

Anger flared in Ripper's gut and shot through his blood. 'She did *once*. Now she's mine. And it pisses me off that you'd question my rights to her.'

'You can't have rights to someone who already gave them away,' said Claris. 'She broke the mating tie rather than live in a state of limbo, but she never really gave herself permission to move on. She's held back from every man she dated – none of them lasted long. You won't, either. She took things a step further with you, but this is as far as she'll go. Don't you see that?'

'No,' Ripper replied. 'And what *you* see is quite simply what you want to see. You barely talk to Emberlyn; you couldn't possibly know what's going on in her head. Feel free to believe whatever you want to believe, but do not again question my claim to her. We're going to have big fucking problems if you do.'

Twin flags of heat stained Colton's cheekbones. Moments of tense silence slipped by, and then he took his mate's elbow. 'Come, Claris. He's not going to see sense.'

Even as she allowed herself to be led away, Claris looked at Ripper. 'Ask her. Ask her what she'd do if Michael returned; if she'd reclaim him. Then you'll see that we're right.'

Ripper didn't respond; just watched as they got into their car and drove away.

A creak filled the air as Crew shoved open the truck's passenger door. He puffed out a breath. 'That was intense.' He slipped out of the vehicle. 'I was surprised they dared ask you to walk away from Emberlyn. They can't have honestly thought you would, or that anyone considers her to still be Michael's mate – other than them, that is.'

Ripper would have felt sorry for them – it couldn't be easy to lose your child to Bloodhill, knowing what could become of them – if they weren't being such selfish assholes. 'It pisses me off that they expect Emberlyn not to move on with her life just because they've put their own on pause while waiting for their boy to come back.'

Crew eyed him closely. 'You don't think they're right, do you? That she'd go back to him?' It was evident by his tone that *he* held no such opinion.

'No, I don't. They need to believe that, so they do.'

'If you're not worried they're right, why are you looking so grim?'

'Because if they're not prepared to let this go, their next move won't be to come back here – they know I won't change my mind.'

'So they'll go to her,' Crew reasoned before spitting out a curse.

'Yeah. And that I really don't want.'

CHAPTER TWENTY-NINE

❧

As a large, calloused hand snatched one of her nachos, Emberlyn frowned at Ripper. 'You're *still* hungry?' The dude had just de-molished a large platter of chicken wings.

Dunking the nacho into her cheesy dip, he replied, 'Nope.'

'Then why ...' Emberlyn trailed off with a sigh as he held it up to her mouth. *Werewolves and their need to feed those under their care.* 'You don't have to go this far to ensure I eat.' She bit into the nacho.

'I know that.' He dunked what was left of the nacho into the dip and then offered it to her. 'Humor me.'

She chewed on it, inwardly rolling her eyes.

Satisfaction leaked into his gaze – it was easy to see even in the bar's dim lighting because he sat so damn close, his thigh pressed against hers beneath the table, his arm slung over the back of her chair in a gesture both protective and possessive. Occasionally, the hand attached to that arm played with her hair or doodled circles on her shoulder.

'I said bye-bye to my personal space the moment I agreed to "serious", didn't I?'

Mirth warmed his eyes. 'Pretty much, yeah.' The reply was utterly unapologetic.

Honestly, she wasn't that bothered by it. Having him swallow up her space this way made her hormones giddy and tipsy. They were all but throwing themselves at him.

A delicious sexual awareness steamed the air, humming with the promise he'd earlier made: '*When we go back to your place, I'm going to eat your pussy until you beg me to stop. You think you won't beg. Wrong. You'll be so wrecked by then you'll do whatever I want.*'

She was honestly curious as to whether he was right. It wouldn't embarrass her to beg – her pride wasn't so fragile. And 'wrecked' sounded somewhat intriguing.

Hearing a familiar feminine laugh, she looked to where Paisley and Crew were going hell for leather on the dance floor. They both had some serious moves.

Not far from the clan's brewery restaurant, the bar was very old-timey, comfortable and invitingly lively. The décor was neutral and warm, and wooden veneer paneling adorned the bar's walls. The upbeat vibe appealed to her magick, and little motes of it dusted her skin.

There were no dress codes or fancy drinks. A wide selection of beers were served, as well as hearty foods. Classic cocktails, various liqueurs and even coffee were also offered.

She and Ripper had picked a circular table that had a good view of the stage, where the live band played. Consisting of werewolves from all three clans, they were pretty good.

The music didn't override the rest of the noise – the place was far too crowded for that. As such, there was a whole lot of chatter, laughter, clinking of glasses, sizzling of hot food and the cheers or disappointed groans coming from the pool table.

The patrons tonight were all werewolves, and most were from Ripper's clan. Those not sitting around were amusing themselves using the dartboard, pool table or gambling machines, while others danced to the live music.

Emberlyn had done enough dancing for the evening. Ripper hadn't at any point joined her on the dance floor. But he'd watched her like a hawk from their table, a dangerous heat flooding his gaze.

Feeling the velvet rasp of his tongue against her throat, she asked, 'What are you doing?'

'Your magick is dusting your skin, and I like the taste of it,' he rumbled. 'It's sweet and warm with a distinct tang. Makes me ... hungry.'

Her belly clenched at the sexual undertone to his words. 'Maybe don't lick me too much in public. I'd rather not get wet in a room full of people who have an enhanced sense of smell.' She carefully picked up her beer, conscious of how it had become slippery from condensation. It was her third drink of the night and, at this point, she was almost as tipsy as her hormones.

Ripper seemed to have a hollow leg. He'd downed beers, a whisky and two tequila shots. Yet, he seemed sober as a judge.

His lips grazed her ear. 'I never would have guessed you'd order beer.'

'Why?'

'You're all class and elegance. I figured you would have ordered cocktails.'

'It's fun to keep you on your toes.' She tipped back her bottle, and the cool liquid went down easy. No sooner had she set her beer back on the damp coaster than he held yet another nacho to her mouth. 'Thank you.' She ate it, the tastes of salt and cheese bursting on her tongue.

The arm hooked over her chair stiffened, so she wasn't

surprised to see that some wolves were on their way over. People occasionally stopped by their table to say hello to their Alpha. Ripper handled it graciously, but she sensed he'd prefer if they were left alone.

As Kerr and Logan boldly took the seats opposite, she nabbed a napkin from the dispenser and wiped her wet hand.

'Hey,' Kerr greeted with a chin lift.

Ripper gave him a flat stare. 'What do you want?'

'To win your heart,' he mocked. 'What do you think I want? I came to say hey.'

'Which you've done twice tonight already, so ...' Ripper waved them both away.

Logan smirked. 'I'd give you shit for wanting to have Emberlyn all to yourself, but I totally get it. You serious you'd never share her?'

'Yes,' Ripper stated.

His brother sighed. 'That's a damn shame.'

'No, it ain't.'

Knowing that Logan was only poking at Ripper for fun, Emberlyn balled up the damp napkin and tossed it Logan's way. 'Stop taunting your brother.'

'But it lifts my mood,' Logan quipped.

Kerr grinned at him. 'He'd share her with me.' His attention moved back to Ripper. 'Wouldn't you?'

'No,' Ripper stated.

Kerr's lips parted in mock hurt. 'I thought we were best friends. Sharing is caring.'

His brows drawn tight together, Ripper looked from one male to the other as he said, 'Fuck off, both of you.'

They only chuckled.

There was a screech of wood against wood as a burly guy stumbled into the neighboring table and made it skid along the floor. Bottles tipped over and a burger hit the floor with a *splat*, but the people sitting there only laughed good naturedly.

Sighing, Logan stood. 'We'd better get some coffee down him so he sobers up some.'

Nodding his agreement, Kerr pushed out of his chair and followed Logan to the slurring, staggering male wolf.

Ripper's tension eased, but not quite enough for Emberlyn's liking. The truth was that a fine line of tension had been humming through him all evening, and she couldn't ascertain the source of it. Initially, she'd assumed that he was just annoyed over Crew and Paisley accompanying them on their date. She had thought his tension might therefore disappear after some time chilling at the bar, but she'd been wrong.

Emberlyn gently poked his side. 'What's wrong?'

His gaze snapped to hers. 'Nothing at all.'

'Then explain why you're wound tight, and don't blame it on how many people keep interrupting our date.'

He looked away, a subtle sigh easing out of him. 'I planned to tell you tomorrow so it didn't shit on our evening.'

'Much as I appreciate the sentiment behind that plan, I'm not down with it. I'd rather know now.' Otherwise it would only play on her mind, and he wouldn't be able to properly relax.

He angled his body slightly toward hers, saying nothing for long moments. 'I had a visit from the Reeds earlier.'

Emberlyn felt herself go rigid. 'The Reeds? What did they want?'

He hesitated a beat. 'For me to let you go.'

Annoyance made her jaw clench. 'They actually asked that of you?'

He gave a sharp nod, his own irritation clear in his hard expression. 'They still consider you to be Michael's mate. They believe that you still love him; that you'd reclaim him if he came back. And they don't acknowledge that I have any rights to you.'

'They *seriously* said that?' Ballsy. It wasn't a wise idea to try to come between an Alpha wolf and anything he considered his. To take it a step further and imply he had no claim to what he felt he owned? *She* wouldn't advise it, and there wasn't much that Emberlyn would shy away from doing. 'What did you say?'

'In so many words . . . I told them that they can believe whatever they like, but the reality is that you're mine now, not his.'

Good answer.

The hand that had been tossed over her shoulder shifted to palm her nape. 'They may not let it drop – in their mind, they're doing this for their son. They won't pay me a second visit, though. They'll try their luck with you. If that happens, *you call me.* You could handle it on your own, I get that. But you don't have to, baby.' He nuzzled her face. 'You don't gotta do anything alone anymore – you have me now.'

Swallowing hard, she fisted the bottom of his tee. 'Fine. But *you* have to call *me* if they try again to convince you to let me go. I'm not upset that you didn't do it this time – you had no idea when they turned up at your house that they would ask that of you. But now you do. So if they do it again, you call me. And if they try it with me, I'll call you. Deal?'

He touched the tip of his nose to hers in that way he sometimes did. 'Deal,' he said, hesitant. 'But I won't lie – I'd rather take care of this shit myself so you don't have to.'

'Why should you get to have all the fun?'

Humor flickered in his gaze, but it gradually faded as his expression shifted into something more serious. 'What would you do if Michael came back?'

Emberlyn leaned back slightly. 'You don't think I'd do as his parents said and go reclaim him, do you?'

'Not at all. But I wondered if you'd want to be there for him while he recovered, because I know you unnecessarily feel partly responsible for him losing control and turning Rabid.'

'I feel some guilt, yes, but I wouldn't feel inclined to help him through it. That might sound cold, but it's like with you and CeCe. You cared for her a lot, but she did something that changed things for you. Michael's betrayal, the way he blew it off like it was nothing and expected me to just let it go ... I couldn't see him the same way after that. It felt like he was this completely different person to me. So no, I wouldn't want to be at his side during his recovery. My place isn't *at* his side.' It was that simple.

Staring into her eyes, Ripper breezed his thumb down her throat. 'All right.'

'Now, can we move onto a lighter subject?' Because she didn't want thoughts of Michael zipping around his head.

'I was actually gonna suggest we get the fuck out of here. You game?'

Her body lit up because she knew what was coming. 'Totally game.'

Two steps. They got two steps into the manor before he was on her.

Ripper yanked her close and brought his mouth down hard on hers. The sexual *click* was instantaneous. It struck as abruptly and hotly as a bolt of lightning, sending lust roaring through him. A lust that fisted his cock, pumped through his blood and gnawed at his control.

He backed her into the wall, still gorging on her mouth, stroking his hands over her. The kiss was wild – tongues licking, breaths clashing, teeth clicking.

She grabbed onto his shoulders and moaned. He swallowed the sound with a guttural growl, feeling very ... primitive. That two people had questioned his claim to her still grated on his every possessive instinct. A need to reinstate that claim misted his vision; made his touch rougher, his kiss deeper, his nips harder.

The kiss went on and on, until his lips throbbed and his lungs burned for air. Drawing back, he yanked down the side zipper of her dress, shoved its straps over her shoulders and let it puddle at her feet. Her bra went next, and then he caught her nipple with his lips; sucked as much of her breast into his mouth as he could take.

Fingers delved into his hair and tugged as her body arched into his. 'Ripper.' The wealth of need woven through his name made his cock throb.

He grazed the tight bud with his teeth and then rolled it around his mouth. 'What do you want? Be specific.'

'Why? You're gonna do whatever you want anyway.'

His baby wasn't wrong.

Ripper shoved his hand into her underwear and cupped her; felt how warm and damp she was. He spoke into her ear. 'Look what you've done. Your panties are all wet.'

'That's on *you*. I'm just an innocent bystander.'

Withdrawing his hand, he got free of his tee. He shook his head when she went to touch him. 'Palms on the wall. Keep them there.' He put a finger to her lips when it looked like she'd argue. 'Little playthings do as their told.'

Even as she cursed low, she did as he instructed.

'Good girl.' Ripper dropped to his knees, caught the waistband of her underwear and ragged them down. He nuzzled her pussy, hauling the earthy scent of her into his system. He felt like he could survive on that scent. Like it was his own brand of oxygen.

Ripper tossed one of her legs over his shoulder and then dragged his tongue between her folds, groaning his appreciation. Her taste had its hooks in him. Those hooks had been there since he first went down on her, when her taste had wound its way through him and set up a constant hunger in his system.

Again and again, he licked at her slit, feeling her moans right in his dick. He could eat her out all fucking day. Her taste, her smell, her responses, the heat of her, the velvet softness of her sensitive flesh here – he only ever wanted more.

And he took more. Kept on taking it and taking it, ignoring her every demand for him to fuck her already.

The demands soon became threats, which soon became curses, which eventually became whimpers.

And still, he kept taking, though his body all but throbbed with need.

He eased his lips around her clit and suckled, sensing the leg she stood on tremor as her knee buckled.

'Rip, *in me.*'

He swirled his tongue around the tight bundle of nerves. 'You want me to stop?'

'Yes.'

'Then beg me.' Snapping open his fly, he rasped his tongue over her clit. 'Beg me to stop.'

'*Please.*' It was a growl.

Letting the leg over his shoulder slide down to the crook of his elbow, he rose to his feet and slammed his hips upward, shoving his cock deep; claiming her in a hard possessive thrust that made her body jolt in shock.

Her head fell back and hit the wall. '*Fuck.*'

Gritting his teeth as her pussy clamped down on him, he palmed her ass tight and lifted her. 'I'm going to take this ass one day. Maybe even on a full moon.'

She curled her free leg tight around him, grabbing at his nape with one hand while sinking the fingers of her other hand in his hair. 'If you knotted my ass, I'd pass out.'

'I wouldn't stop fucking you if you did.' He took her brutally, swept away by a violent current of lust – the waves so turbulent there was no way to do anything but drown.

Hot and wet, her snug pussy clutched him so tight he felt claimed by it. The rhythmic sounds of flesh smacking slick flesh sliced through the air, loud and abrupt. Her hard nipples dug into his chest, rubbing against him with every rough jolt of her body.

His building release was like a fire in his gut. A fire that hissed. Spat. Crackled. Snapped. Threatened to take him over.

He kneaded her ass, digging in his fingertips. It fit just right in his hands. Everything about her felt 'just right'. The thought caused a wave of possession to wash through him. He snarled. 'So fucking mine.'

She whimpered, her pussy heating and quaking as it began to tighten around him.

'Come with me, Em.'

She did, her eyes going blind, her pussy clasping him *so tight*.

He growled. 'That's my fucking girl.' The fire in his gut turned into a roaring blaze as his release burst over him. He exploded, pumping hot streams of come inside her. He grinded, groaned, shuddered. Then the strength left them both.

CHAPTER THIRTY

Lying flat on her front, Emberlyn shifted her leg slightly on the mattress. 'I won't be able to fall asleep if you keep doing that,' she slurred without opening her eyes.

Positioned on his side next to her, Ripper nuzzled her shoulder – one he'd deliberately bared by tugging her collar aside. 'Why not?'

'Because having someone knead my ass is somewhat distracting.'

He palmed it possessively beneath her long shirt. 'It's mine. I should be able to stroke it whenever I want to.'

Dear Lord. 'It's not a pet, Rip.'

'But it's a part of my toy, and toys are meant to be played with.'

She let out a soft snort. 'Just go to sleep.'

'Answer a question for me first.'

Emberlyn opened her eyes to find his gaze fixed on her. 'Shoot.'

'Why don't you ever ask me anything truly personal? I nose into your business – past and present – all the time.'

She didn't detect any hurt in his voice, only curiosity. Still, she snuck her hand out from under her pillow to brush her fingertips over his chin as she assured him, 'It's not because I'm not interested. I just know that your past has to be extremely hard for you to talk about.' Painful, even. 'I figured that if you ever felt comfortable telling me then you would.'

He traced the dimple on her butt cheek, having apparently memorized its exact location. 'Ask whatever you want to know,' he invited.

Emberlyn bit her lip, conflicted. She had lots of questions. And she wanted him to know, to *feel*, that she hadn't kept them to herself so far out of disinterest. But she was leery of hitting a hot button. 'Okay, but if you don't want to answer then you don't have to – I won't be pissed or anything.' She paused. 'Do you remember the time you spent Rabid?'

He hesitated only briefly. 'Not a single day of it. I can recall flashes of this and that, but they're dreamlike. They don't feel real. What I most remember is the feeling of ... simplicity. Human emotions are absent – there's only primal instincts and urges. You're not you. You're not anyone. You have no past, no future. You just exist.'

'What about what happened ... before?'

His gaze turned a little inward. 'I can vividly remember my father battling another wolf; remember seeing him die. I remember my mother's scream – there was so much grief and fury in that sound. Then she was soon after dead, and a battle broke out around us. I saw Logan on the floor, bloody and still. I thought he was dead as well.'

Pausing, Ripper brushed his lips over her bare shoulder. 'The next thing I remember is waking up in the Watcher's unit with people hanging over me, saying it was good to have me back.'

Emberlyn blew out a breath. 'It had to have felt like you'd skipped four years ahead in a matter of moments.'

Nodding, he snaked his hand further up her shirt and swept it halfway up her spine. 'My body didn't feel like mine. It was older. Different. So was my voice – it had broken by that point.'

'That had to have been so weird.'

He grunted. 'Everyone was smiling, glad I was *me* again. But I didn't feel at all like me, and I was still mentally stuck in that moment where I'd lost my parents.' He smoothed his palm back down to her ass. 'The only thing that stopped me from being overwhelmed by the grief, discomfort and rage was seeing Logan alive.'

'But then you also felt guilty,' she surmised.

His eyelids lowered slightly. 'What makes you think that?'

It was an obvious assumption to make. 'You're super-duper protective. He's your younger brother. You'd just learned you'd been gone four years and he'd been relatively alone all that time.'

After a few moments, Ripper closed his eyes. 'Yeah, I felt guilty as shit.' Sighing, he rubbed the back of his head. 'Logan sensed it. Told me it was fucking stupid. He didn't hold it against me that I left him.'

'Because you *didn't* leave him, Rip. You thought he was dead. Nobody chooses to turn Rabid—'

'I almost did,' said Ripper, opening his eyes.

Emberlyn felt her brow crease. 'What?'

'I felt the pull to go back to Bloodhill. Like a birdsong. It called day and night. More than once I almost gave into it.'

'So you could go back to feeling nothing again,' she reasoned. 'Makes sense.'

His brows flicked together. 'Does it?'

'Your world had imploded. It had gone to shit with the death of your parents, which for you felt like something that happened two minutes ago . . . and then on top of all that you had to process you'd been missing for *four years*. There was so much you needed to adjust to. It's only to be expected that there were times you wanted to escape it all.

'You didn't escape it, though, Rip. You stayed. You pushed through it. You *thrived*. I mean, you're Alpha of your fucking clan. An Alpha who's massively respected and whose clan is tight. So don't give your fourteen-year-old self a hard time – he doesn't deserve that.'

His gaze softened. 'Maybe not. He died, though, Em. Jax Stone didn't come back from Bloodhill. *This* version of me did. It was why I didn't care when people started calling me Ripper soon after. I didn't feel the same person I was before.'

She stroked his jaw again. 'I like this version of you just fine.'

Swallowing, he ever so gently bumped his nose to hers. 'I never told anyone else that I'd felt tempted to go back to Bloodhill.'

Her chest went tight. 'Thank you for trusting me with it.' It was as humbling as it was touching. 'If someone had told me six months ago that there would come a day you would trust me with anything, I would have snorted and insisted they were high.'

He slipped his hand beneath the curtain of her hair to cover her nape, the warm weight of his palm like a brand. 'Back then, I didn't know you. I also didn't want to want you,' he admitted.

'Oh, I know,' she said, feeling her lips hitch up. 'I wasn't too crazy about the fact that I wanted you, either.'

'Why not?' he asked, clearly offended.

'I didn't believe that anything would ever come of it, so it was just annoying.'

'If we hadn't become allies, I wouldn't have gotten to know you; wouldn't be in your bed right now. That pisses me off. I should have seen before now that a lot of the rumors about you are just that – rumors.'

'You had a blind spot when it came to witches who aren't so well behaved,' she pointed out.

'It's gone now.' His finger lightly tapped her lip. 'I see you.'

'You do.' She felt her nose wrinkle. 'I'm not sure I like it.'

A smile blotted his gaze. 'You'll get used to it.'

Emberlyn only *hmph*ed.

He whispered his lips over hers. 'Sleep, baby.'

She let her eyes fall shut. 'Night.' She groaned when his hand roamed to her butt once more. 'Seriously, give my ass some peace.'

'Tried. Can't.'

'Can't, or won't?' she challenged.

'Both. I mean, it's *right there*.'

She inwardly rolled her eyes. This was what she got for accepting an Alpha in her bed and life. She really only had herself to blame.

Stalking into the consultation room the following afternoon, Ripper found Emberlyn stood at the altar, her gaze on an open old text – a grimoire, maybe? He couldn't tell. And if he was honest, he wasn't trying to figure it out, distracted by the sight of her in a tan, V-neck dress with matching strappy heels.

When he'd declared that he'd make lunch – well, they'd already established that he liked feeding her – she'd told him she'd 'go work on some potions' while she waited. The scents of various herbs were strong in the air, giving him an idea of what she'd so far thrown into her bubbling cauldron.

Casting a quick look at the cat curled up on the stool near the fireplace, Ripper set his hands on his hips. 'The basement door is jammed.'

Emberlyn slowly flipped the page. 'Why are you trying to get into the basement?' she asked without looking at him, her tone a little absent.

'I can hear noise coming from down there.' As if small animals were skittering around and wrestling or something. 'I want to check it out.'

'No need.' An airy response. 'All is fine.'

'I want to check.'

'Don't bother.' Pale-hazel eyes briefly slid his way as she opened a drawer behind her. 'It won't let you in.'

'It?'

'The basement.'

'How can it not—' Cutting himself off, he shook his head. 'I don't understand this house sometimes.' It seemed alive to some degree. And it was definitely haunted.

Honest to God, he'd opened a particular door upstairs when taking a wrong turn looking for the bathroom a few weeks back and that door had slammed in his face while someone – or something – inside the room had hissed in warning.

When he'd told Emberlyn, she'd simply said, 'Yeah, you don't want to go in that room. Best to pretend it's not even there.' Then she'd gone back to sipping her tea while reading a book . . . like it was no biggie that not only was she clearly not alone in this house, but the entities weren't all harmless.

Right then, having fished a pair of snips out of the drawer, she began making her way to the window.

That easily, his irritation leached away because . . . 'I swear, watching you walk is straight-up porn.'

Emberlyn blinked, stilling. 'That's one I haven't heard before.'

'Only because no guy has dared say it out loud.' They'd all been thinking it – he'd put money on it.

She shot him a playfully prim look and snipped a leaf of a potted plant on the windowsill. 'You do a lot of things other men haven't dared do when it comes to me.'

'You like that, though.'

She huffed but didn't deny it. As she returned to the altar, she held her hands above the cauldron and rubbed her palms together, letting tiny bits of crushed leaf fall into the brew.

He walked to the altar and sniffed. 'What are you making?'

'Potions for insomnia.'

'You making them for the Founders' Fair?' The event took place the last weekend of May every year to celebrate the anniversary of the date Chilgrave was founded. 'You usually have a market stall, don't you?'

'I do. And yes, I'll be selling these at the market – along with a dozen other kinds of potions.' She peered down at the old text again and then chanted low. Magick dust in colors of teal blue, black and silver coasted down into the cauldron. The water there fizzed and gurgled for a few seconds.

'Are you going to let any of the witches who attacked you buy anything from you?'

'Nope.' She stirred the brewing potion with her athame. 'I meant what I said to them. I'll never lift a magickal finger for any of them again.' She set her blade down on the altar. 'They can go swivel.'

A smile warmed his chest. 'So ruthless and unforgiving.'

'You say that as if it pleases you.'

'It does. I like that you take no one's shit. Fact is you shouldn't have to.' He wouldn't want her to be any different.

A knock came at the front door.

She pulled a face, clearly annoyed by the interruption.

'I'll get it.' He left the room and walked to the front door. Opening it, he found Kerr standing on the porch wearing a *We gotta talk* look. Ripper sighed, his hand clenching the edge of the door. 'We need to make it a law in the clan that no shit is permitted to happen on a Sunday. It isn't unreasonable to want at least one day per week where there's pure peace.'

'I hear you,' Kerr muttered.

'Whatever this is can't wait until tomorrow?'

'Depends. I'm not sure how much worse it will get in the hours between now and then, so I thought it best to check. Also, it could be that CeCe's wrong anyway.'

Feeling his jaw harden, Ripper stepped aside and waved his friend into the manor. 'Wrong about what?'

'She came to me with a . . . complaint. She would have gone straight to you, but she knows you're pissed at her.'

'What kind of complaint?' Ripper released the door, and it closed by itself.

Kerr grimaced. 'She believes that Emberlyn has used magick on her somehow.'

'What? Why?'

Humor glimmered in Kerr's eyes. 'Because her hair has turned lime green, and there are tiny bits of mold in it.'

Ripper went still. 'You're joking.'

'Nope,' said Kerr, the word coming out on a barely suppressed chuckle. 'I mean, it could be that *another* witch is responsible . . .'

But it was unlikely. Very unlikely.

When Emberlyn hadn't explicitly stated that she wouldn't retaliate over CeCe territorially marking his tire, he'd expected *something*. But then days of nothing had gone by, so he'd assumed that she'd chosen to let it be, to just be content with the fact that *he* had dealt with it. And it now seemed more than probable that he'd assumed wrong.

Ripper returned to the consultation room with Kerr close behind him.

Emberlyn didn't look their way, seeming absorbed in what she was reading as she skimmed her finger along a page of the open book. Her nose wrinkled at whatever she'd read.

'Em?'

'Hm?' An absent response.

'Em?' Ripper pressed.

'Yeah?' she asked distractedly, still not looking at him.

'Remember when CeCe marked my tire?'

'Um-hm.'

'Did you retaliate?'

'You said you'd handled it,' she said, her tone flat and inattentive, her gaze still locked on the book in front of her.

'I did, but she's recently developed a strange little problem.'

His witch blindly reached out and grabbed a small bottle from the collection she'd plonked on the altar. 'Misfortunes often befall those who cause issues for others.'

'Misfortunes. Right.' Ripper folded his arms. 'Her hair is green and moldy.'

Emberlyn pulled the topper off the small bottle. 'Oh. Yeah. That was me.'

Kerr barked a chuckle, his shoulders shaking.

Figuring he should have expected that she'd do something like this, Ripper rubbed at his nape. 'You haven't been anywhere near her. How could you have done it?'

'Proximity doesn't make a difference with all spells,' she replied, sprinkling some sort of white powder into the cauldron.

'Her hair is her crowning glory,' Kerr cut in, grinning. 'But of course you knew that.'

'Of course.' Her eyes cut to Ripper. 'At least I didn't make her smell of urine the way she did your tire.'

He felt his head twitch to the side. 'You considered that?'

'Among other things, yes. I like to plot. You know that.'

Yeah, he did. 'Can you undo the spell you cast?'

'I *could*,' she said, jamming the cork back on the bottle.

'Are you going to?'

No response.

Ripper inwardly sighed. 'Baby.'

'Yeah?'

'Much as I appreciate the creativity behind your revenge – and admittedly find it amusing – I need you to undo the spell.'

'Why?' Adding more magick dust into the brew, she stirred it with her athame again. 'To placate her itty-bitty feelings?'

'No, because I don't want the rest of my clan to fear you. They *should* fear you, I know that, but I'd rather they didn't.' He wanted them to be perfectly comfortable around her. 'Help me out here.'

She let out a long-suffering sigh and then looked at Kerr. 'Tell her that her hair will go back to its normal color if she says the following words out loud: "*Ripper belongs to Emberlyn, not me.*" She'll also have to write lines.'

'Lines?' Kerr echoed, his lips twitching.

Emberlyn nodded. 'If she wants rid of the mold, she needs to write "*I must not piss on people's tires*" twenty times.'

Kerr laughed, spinning to face Ripper. 'This is extra. I love it. CeCe, however, is gonna *hate* it.'

Anyone would hate having to concede a difficult truth aloud. But for them to then have to write lines like a child – a silent message that a person saw them as child*ish* – would add insult to injury. So yeah, it was 'extra'.

Ripper took a step toward her. 'When time passed without anything happening to her, I thought you'd decided to let my punishment be enough.'

Opening a jar of honey, Emberlyn again briefly flicked her gaze his way. 'I was just lulling her into a false sense of security. It makes things more fun.'

'Agreed,' said Kerr. 'You need to keep this witch, Rip, because she's awesome.'

'Thank you, Kerr.' Emberlyn dropped a little honey into the cauldron. 'So, she reported it you, huh?'

'She did,' Kerr confirmed with a nod.

'Did she cry? I was hoping she's a sobber.'

'There were tears.'

Smiling, Emberlyn closed the honey jar. 'Excellent.'

Kerr chuckled again. 'I'll see you guys later.' With that, he left.

Ripper remained in the consultation room, watching as his witch added lavender to her potion. Green and moldy. She'd turned CeCe's hair green and moldy while also providing a way to reverse it that would *gall* the female wolf.

God, she was mean. Seriously mean, but in the best way. It was one of the many, many things that he liked about her. 'Why didn't you tell me about the spell?'

She waved her hand at the cauldron, and the brew ceased bubbling. 'You would have done what you did just then – asked me to undo it. I would have said no. You would have nagged me. We would have gone round and round in circles with neither of us willing to back down.'

'So? There's a lot to be said for angry sex.'

She chuckled. 'I suppose we *would* have worked it off in bed.'

Ripper crossed to her. 'Like I said last night, I see you. But you still often manage to surprise me.'

She searched his gaze. 'You're not mad at me?'

'No. I'd have done a fuck of a lot worse to anyone who territorially marked something of yours and professed to love you.' They would have been pissing blood for at least a week. 'I'm kind of scared of what you'll do to me if I ever upset you.'

'Aw, you don't need to be afraid of me.'

'Oh yes, I do.'

Her lips curved. 'Definitely not all brawn.'

CHAPTER THIRTY-ONE

❧

Traipsing through a shallow, trickling creek, Ripper glanced around Bloodhill Forest, ever vigilant. His boots stopped his feet from getting wet, but the water's icy coldness seeped through.

Several of his clan were hunting game with him, including his brother – who currently walked alongside him. Others were scattered around, but none were too far away.

Adjusting his hold on his bow, Ripper stepped onto dry land. Typically, they didn't wander too far into the forest when hunting. It wasn't necessary. The Rabid tended to hole up near the mountains, so the wildlife found a home closer to the town where they were safer.

Though it was unlikely that they'd stumble upon any Rabid while hunting, it was best to be cautious. The Rabid slept during the day, but they would wake if you came too close to their lair and attempt to scare you away. Those occasions were few and far between, but they did happen. Which was why every hunter took handguns.

Arrows wouldn't take down Rabid. A silver bullet? Different story.

A fatal shot wasn't necessary – the silver would weaken the Rabid enough that they couldn't fight as they were dragged back to town, where they could be helped.

At one time, people used to regularly go to Bloodhill to capture Rabid so they could return them to their natural state. But the creatures were hard to track, and it meant roaming *deep* into Bloodhill. That was risky, especially when Rabid tended to travel in packs and would attack without a qualm. Too often people had been badly injured and forced to kill Rabid in their own defense, which no one wanted on their conscience.

Nowadays, people generally only attempted to search for newly turned Rabid. They were easier to find and usually traveled alone because they didn't instantly join packs. Once upon a time, they'd searched for Ripper, too.

It was strange for him to think that this forest had once been his home. For four damn years he'd lived out here. Yet, he felt no sense of comfort.

He was better at traversing it than most, his sense of direction spot on. As if he'd retained memories of the typography. But he didn't look at any landmarks and feel nostalgia or experience any flashbacks.

The hazy memories of his time here were vague and short. He could see flashes of a cave in his mind. Of fights with other Rabid. Of stalking a fox. Of splashing in a stream. But there was no 'story' to follow and piece together.

The forest was like many others in the world. There were miles upon miles of trees that seemed tall enough to scrape the sky. Sporadic bursts of wildflowers and shrubbery could be seen. There were creeks, rivers, waterfalls and even hot springs. The air was fresh and scented of tree sap, warm earth and moss.

But Bloodhill differed in one respect. It had a gloomy, ominous feel. A vibe made worse by the number of dead, crooked trees.

It was quiet. Too quiet. As if every bit of wildlife had adapted to be silent so as to avoid the Rabid's detection. There were rarely tweets or chirps, rarely any deer grazing in plain sight, hardly any glimpses of squirrels hurrying up trunks or even lizards zipping through the underbrush.

All he could hear right then was the creak of branches, the skitter of fallen leaves, the trickle of the creek, the sound of their boots scuffing ground ... and the yawn that at that moment cracked Logan's jaw.

Ripper spared his brother a glance. 'That's the fifth time you've yawned in the space of an hour.'

Logan shrugged the shoulder that wasn't weighed down by his backpack's strap. They all took supplies such as food, water and first aid necessities. 'What can I say? Clem knows how to exhaust a guy in bed.'

'You two seeing each other now?'

Logan wrinkled his nose. 'Sort of. We're keeping it light. At least for the time being.'

'Light?' Ripper snorted. 'You've spent so much time with her lately I've barely seen you.'

'That's partly because you're always with your witch.' Logan plucked a berry off a nearby bush. 'Things still seem to be going good with you two.' There was a questioning note in his tone.

'They are.' It had been a little over two weeks since the 'green and moldy hair' incident. Ripper still saw Emberlyn every day, and they never spent a night apart. Which, as a guy who liked his space, he would have thought he'd struggle with – attachment

or no attachment. But being around her steadied him. Relaxed
him. Made him feel recharged.

Logan tossed the berry into his mouth. 'When are you gonna
claim her, then?'

Ripper's step faltered in surprise.

'Don't tell me you haven't at least considered it.'

His hand flexing around his bow, Ripper walked onward as he
admitted, 'I actually didn't let my mind go there.'

Logan's brows flew together. 'Why not? You're totally gone
for her. Lost.'

Ripper didn't feel lost – that implied a sense of drifting, of
disorientation, of struggling to find his way. He knew that from
personal experience. Emberlyn was solid ground. An anchor.
One he held tight to.

But gone for her? Yeah, that was accurate. It was just that . . .
'I never imagined I'd take anyone as a mate.'

Logan watched him so closely he almost tripped over a
tree root. 'Has this got something to do with what Mom went
through when Dad died in front of her?'

Ripper swallowed, his gut twisting. 'I can still hear that
scream. The agony in it, the mindless rage . . .' It had been the
cry of a broken soul.

'There's a very big difference between our mom and Emberlyn,'
said Logan, his voice soft.

'What's that?'

'If something happened to you, Emberlyn wouldn't lose all
control and throw herself into a fight she couldn't win. She'd
fucking destroy everyone she held accountable – and she'd do it
right there right then with a minimal amount of struggle.'

Ripper felt his lips almost twitch. Yeah, his witch would do
exactly that. She was no slave to her emotions, even when they
were running high.

'You never envisioned yourself claiming CeCe?'

'Not once.' Ripper inadvertently kicked a pebble, sending it skipping along the ground. 'You?'

'Too many times,' Logan mumbled.

'You were right in what you said. You care for her far more than I ever did.'

'You meant what you told her, didn't you? You never actually loved her.'

'I meant it,' Ripper verified.

'She's kept her head down since the whole hair-turning-green thing a fortnight ago. I think she's still shaken over it,' Logan added, a hint of humor in his voice. 'Much as she will have known that Emberlyn's a vengeful creature, I don't think she was prepared for your witch to do *anything* like that.'

His brother wasn't the only one who'd found it amusing. Ripper had been wrong to worry that his clan would be so unnerved by Emberlyn's actions that they wouldn't want her around. On the contrary, they respected that demonstration of strength and pitilessness.

'It was a genius punishment on Emberlyn's part – she forced CeCe to have to own up to her actions and admit to a difficult truth.' Halting, Logan turned to him. 'And now you've gotta admit to your own difficult truth.'

Stopping at his brother's side, Ripper frowned. 'Which is what?'

Logan regarded him with a serious expression. 'You have some decisions to make regarding Emberlyn. You might be okay *now* with how things currently are between you, but that won't last. We're werewolves. It's in us to claim what we intend to keep. You won't be able to fight it unless you break away from her before it gets too late.'

'Break away?' Ripper all but snarled.

'Walk, or get over your reservations about mating – one or the other. To *not* claim her wouldn't spare her pain if she lost you, it would just mean you weren't mated.'

Ripper ground his teeth, his thoughts—

'*Fuck.*' The barked curse made them both tense. It had come from Crew. A birdcall came next – a *Get over here* message from the werewolf in question.

Ripper and Logan tracked the sound, finding Crew staring at a tree. Their other clan members materialized, coming from various directions.

'What is it?' asked Ripper.

He pointed at the tree. 'That.'

Ripper did a double-take. A pile of skulls and other bones – most covered in stringy flesh and blood – rested against the large tree.

'Jesus,' Kerr breathed.

'What could have done that?' asked Crew. 'I mean, I can smell Rabid piss – you can't mistake it for anything else; it's too distinctive. But they don't collect the remains of their kills and stack them like this.'

Ripper glanced around, noticing there were deep grooves in the nearby trees. But some claw marks were smaller than others, as if not all were made by the same creature.

'They do now,' said Logan. 'Because there's nothing else out here that would. You ask me, it's a *Stay away from my territory* message.'

Crew frowned. 'Rabid mark their slice of territory, but they don't use scare tactics to keep other packs away. Why would one suddenly do this?'

'Maybe because this has somehow become a public area,' said Ripper. 'Generally, the leader of the pack will do the marking, but there's more than one urine marker here. I can smell several.

And not all the rake marks were done by the same Rabid. More than one pack has come here, and it's like they *keep* coming; feel compelled to claim it.'

Logan scratched his nape. 'Why, though? Sure, there's plenty of wildlife to hunt in these parts. But no Rabid needs to settle in this particular spot. What could be drawing them here?'

'Maybe *they* have something to do with it,' said Crew.

Following the path of his friend's gaze, Ripper noticed that two small symbols had been carved into the same tree against which the bones were piled.

'What the hell are they?' asked Logan.

Ripper squatted down to look at the symbols, feeling his face tighten. 'I don't know. But I know someone who will.'

Laying out the small pair of torn jeans on the hub's counter, Emberlyn hummed as she took in the entire row of ripped clothes. 'Let me guess,' she said to the female werewolf in front of her. 'He still keeps shifting before he's finished undressing.' 'He' being the nine-year-old boy at his mother's side, who blushed furiously.

The she-wolf gave a sharp nod. 'He and his friends are always racing and seeing who can strip and shift first. But more often than not, they're so determined to win that they don't *fully* strip first. Which is cheating,' she told her son.

Refusing to meet his mother's gaze, he stared right at the counter.

It was not at all unusual for Emberlyn's customers to be parents who were aggravated by their child's habit of tearing their clothes during shifts. But this poor she-wolf was here more than most. 'I can use magick to make his clothing more resistant to tearing, but . . .'

'It won't make him learn not to cheat, which is why I'm not

paying for such a service. In fact, I won't be dishing out any cash at all. From now on, he's going to use his allowance to pay for repairs.'

He gawked. 'What?'

'Is it so outrageous that you'd pay the *literal* price for your deliberate carelessness?' his mother questioned.

His shoulders slumping, the boy sighed at the wall, his face all scrunched up. 'Ah, man.'

Hiding a smile, Emberlyn swiped a tag and nabbed a pen. 'I can have them ready by tomorrow.' She scribbled the relevant details onto the tag.

'Thanks, I'll see you then.'

'See you, then. Bye,' Emberlyn said to the little boy.

'Bye.' It was the mumble of a long-suffering martyr.

As mother and son then left, Emberlyn attached the tag to the pair of jeans.

Footfalls preceded the sound of Paisley yawning loudly. Sidling up to Emberlyn with a mug of coffee in hand, she peered down at the newly dropped-off laundry. 'Another repair job?'

'Yup. Kid still keeps damaging his gear during his shifts. It's a werewolf-child thing, I know, but it has to be irritating. You'll learn that for yourself eventually, since you have this to look forward to.'

Paisley tensed, a pinch of panic in her eyes. 'What?'

'Easy, I'm not saying that you and Crew are destined to shack up and breed.' They were an item, and they were still going strong. But life provided no guarantees. 'I'm just saying that any children you bear will go through this stage.'

Paisley pulled a face. 'I don't think I'd make a good parent.'

'Because your own are crap?'

'Yes.' Looking tired, Paisley chugged back some of her drink. 'This conversation is much too deep for a Monday morning.'

'It's afternoon.'

'Doesn't feel like it.' She scratched her head. 'I saw your old in-laws last night. I fear I may have given away how pissed I am at them for the stuff they said to Ripper. Because whatever they saw on my face made them wince.'

'At least they've chosen to take note of his warning.' The Reeds had kept their distance from both Ripper and Emberlyn since their appearance at his lake house.

Paisley raised her mug as if to honor the gods or something. 'May the idiots continue to heed it.'

'We can but hope.'

'Ah, here comes your dude now.'

Flicking her gaze to the window, Emberlyn noticed Ripper striding toward the hub. Her scalp prickled at the hardness in his expression. Something wasn't right. So the moment he stalked inside, she immediately asked, 'What is it?'

There were times she'd catch him with a hard look on his face, but then he'd see her and it would soften. Today, it didn't. His gaze was flinty and unreadable.

'I need your input on something,' he told her, very little inflection in his voice. 'Can the others cover for you?'

'We'll hold the fort, no problem,' Paisley assured him.

Emberlyn grabbed her purse from under the counter, hung the strap over her shoulder and crossed to him. 'I thought you were hunting in Bloodhill. Did something happen? Is someone hurt?'

'Nothing like that.' Taking possession of her hand, he led her outside. 'I want to show you something, and then I want to know if you can tell me what exactly it is.'

An oddly phrased request, but . . . 'Okay.'

He gave her hand an appreciative squeeze. 'We'll stop off at your place on the way. You're going to need different shoes.'

She felt her brow furrow. 'Why?'

'Because you'll end up with blisters upon blisters if you walk through Bloodhill in high heels.'

She stiffened. 'We're going to Bloodhill?'

He nodded, the set of his mouth grim. 'I wouldn't take you into that level of danger if I didn't need you there, baby. Some magick-related advice is much needed, and you're the only witch I trust. Nothing will happen to you there – I wouldn't allow it.'

'I'm not afraid to go to Bloodhill; I'm just surprised.' And mighty curious as to what he wanted her to take a look at.

They drove to the manor in his truck. Inside the house, she pulled on clothes fit for hiking in this weather – a tee, pants, boots – and nabbed her sunglasses. Then they were on the move again.

After he'd parked at a spot near the fringe of the woods, he led her into the forest. There was a lot of skirting trees, dodging mossy rocks, wading through shrubbery and ducking to avoid low-hanging branches before they finally reached his clan members.

Emberlyn was about to say a quick hey to them, but then a macabre display snagged her attention. 'Well, hell.'

'Ignore the pile, if you can,' said Ripper, ushering her toward it with a hand on her back. 'I need to know what these are.' He pointed at two markings on the tree.

Moving in for a closer look, Emberlyn pushed her sunglasses upward and settled them in her hair. 'These are sigils.' Hovering a hand over each one, she read the magick there ... and felt her mouth tighten.

'What are sigils?' asked Logan as the others gathered around.

'They're basically a written intent.' Seeing the looks of blank incomprehension sent her way, she went on: 'Generally, they're positive – it's about manifesting goals, protecting yourself, stuff like that. To condense the intent, the sentence is simplified, vowels and repeated consonants are dropped and the remaining letters are scattered and overlapped until they form a single symbol. Magick is then embedded in it, thereby activating it.'

Ripper folded his arms. 'You said sigils are typically positive. Does that apply to these?'

'No. Each has a different intent. One is to attract Rabid. The other is to make them sleep. Basically . . . they together make a trap.'

Ripper's eyes darkened and went slitted. 'So a witch is drawing them here and then making them vulnerable so they'll be easily captured.'

She dipped her chin. 'Seems that way.'

Logan spat a curse. 'At least now we know how they're doing it. I couldn't picture a witch hiking through Bloodhill to seek out Rabid. Using these sigils, they pretty much cast out a net.'

'And in doing so, they've risked Rabid packs coming across others,' Kerr pointed out. 'You know what often happens in those circumstances.'

'They fight,' Ripper clipped, the veins in his neck corded. 'Which means that the scent of death here might not only be coming from the animal remains over there.'

'Fuck,' Crew bit off. 'The witch behind this needs killing. Reena . . . she won't issue a fatal punishment. We need to ID the culprit before she does.' He looked at Emberlyn. 'How long have the sigils been there?'

She pursed her lips. 'At least two and a half months. I can remove them, but you should take photos first, or have a Watcher who's also a witch examine them. Not everyone will take my word on things.' They'd insinuate a conspiracy was at work or something.

A muscle in Ripper's cheek ticked. 'Yeah, and that pisses me off.' He turned to a clan member. 'Go get Marvin. Tell him there's something he needs to see.'

The wolf gave a curt nod and melted away.

'A town meeting needs to be held,' Ripper declared. 'Everyone should be made aware of this.'

'And we should closely monitor the reactions of the coven,' Logan threw in. 'Reena *has* to have suspects, but she isn't sharing names. And yeah, okay, that's not a surprise. *You* wouldn't give up the names of people in our clan who'd so royally fucked up,' he said to Ripper. 'But you would act. She hasn't. Which means we need to, because this can't go on.'

Emberlyn sighed. 'I do love town meetings.'

Ripper walked toward her. 'I swear to Christ, no one had better give you shit this time – I'm fucking done with it.'

CHAPTER THIRTY-TWO

❧

From his chair on the platform, Ripper eyed the townsfolk closely. Fifteen minutes ago he'd revealed his clan's findings at Bloodhill. Faces had stared at him, awash with varying emotions such as shock, disbelief, anger and horror. Then the yelling had begun.

And it hadn't yet stopped.

For once, nobody was accusing Emberlyn of anything. The clans were shouting at the coven, and the witches were either defending themselves or pointing fingers at each other while demanding people 'fess up' to being part of the faction. Emberlyn was literally the only witch in town who couldn't be part of it, so not one person suspected her.

Normally, Ripper would have demanded that they calm the hell down. But he was interested in hearing just where everybody's suspicions lay; in what names were most often thrown out as potential culprits. It must have been the same for Shane, Carver and Reena – none of them had asked for silence, either. Like him, they simply observed.

So far, though, no subtle looks were being exchanged among the coven. No expressions harbored any guilt or smugness. But then, the faction had been flying under the radar a long time – they weren't suddenly going to give themselves away.

Ripper glanced at his witch. She sat in the front row between Kerr and Logan. To look at her, you would assume she had no interest in the current proceedings. She was calmly reading a magazine, one leg crossed over the other, one ankle idly doing the occasional twirl. Like someone passing the time in a waiting area.

Ripper didn't doubt that she was listening to every word. And he would bet she'd chosen purposely to appear indifferent to rub the faction up the wrong way.

Well . . . if you were part of an inclusive group and considered yourself High Priestess material, it would gall you that the most powerful witch in town seemed to feel she had better things to do than discuss your existence.

A red-faced Dez leaped to his feet, glaring at Getty. 'Would you stop pointing fingers at me! I have nothing to do with this!'

'Ignore her, Dad,' Ames advised as he tugged on his father's arm, pulling him back to his seat.

'Come on, Gill, you have to admit that Dez makes a good suspect,' said Getty, batting at her graying bob.

Gill sighed, throwing her head back. 'Why would he want to be part of some secret society that's too scared to admit it exists? He has more self-respect.'

'*Thank* you,' said Dez. 'Sera, *you're* a member for certain.'

Bristling on her daughter's behalf, Penelope frowned. 'What secret society would welcome someone who can't keep a damn secret?'

Sera gaped at her. 'Mom!'

'Well, I'm not wrong,' Penelope defended. 'Everyone here

knows you're a blabber. Personally, I'm thinking Hank is involved. Maybe also Patrick.'

The spines of both males snapped straight.

'And *I'm* thinking you're all playing dumb.' Colton twisted in his seat to face the coven. 'You can't expect us to believe that none of you have a clue who's part of the faction. You're just trying to protect them from us, which makes you as bad as they are.'

Crew nodded, his eyes blazing. 'We deserve to know the truth. Several Rabid might have died in that little spot near the sigils. Those werewolves will now never be brought back to themselves and to their families – their chance at getting their life back is gone.'

'Which is heartbreaking,' said Ward, his expression sympathetic, 'but we can't tell you what we don't know. All we have is conjecture.'

'You have to understand,' began Patrick, 'this faction has existed for a long time. It is accustomed to keeping itself secret. We think that members might even be magickly bound to withhold names of their co-members.'

'Well, *I* have no problem revealing names of obvious suspects,' Getty piped up.

'Names of people who *you* find obvious suspects,' Gill emphasized. 'You have no proof of their involvement. In fact, you had no interest in spouting names at all until others started throwing suspicion your way. Suddenly, you're full of opinions. Deflecting, are we?'

Getty narrowed her eyes. 'Where's Mari, Gill? I don't see her anywhere.'

Gill's back went ramrod straight. 'At home. She's unwell.'

Getty winged up a brow. 'Unwell, or uncaring what happens to those in this town? Anyone so uncaring probably has something to hide.'

'It's not enough that you accused both my husband and brother? Now you want to accuse my daughter as well?'

'They were both involved in what happened to Emberlyn not so long ago,' Penelope cut in, glaring at Gill. 'She's their family, but they didn't care.'

'Mari didn't mean for Emberlyn to get' – Gill paused and shook her head fast in exasperation – 'Why are we even talking about that? It has nothing to do with the faction.'

Ethel folded her arms. 'I want to know what Emberlyn thinks.'

Everyone went quiet, the entire room sliding their attention her way.

Emberlyn appeared entirely engrossed in her magazine, but Ripper knew that his woman had heard Ethel just fine. She was simply fucking with the faction.

Kerr exchanged a knowing amused look with Ripper and then gently nudged her.

Emberlyn blinked at him. 'Hmm?'

'Ethel wants to know what you think,' Kerr told her.

A fine line appeared between Emberlyn's brows. 'About what?'

'Surely you have some idea of who makes up the faction,' said Ethel.

'How can she have any real clue who it could be?' Ward demanded. 'She doesn't know us all well enough to be able to weigh in on this.'

'Let's leave Emberlyn out of it,' said Hank. 'Lord knows we've dragged her into our messes far too often over the years.'

'True,' Ethel allowed, 'but you're only saying that because you're in Ripper's bad books and don't much like it. Emberlyn, really, who do you think it is?'

Emberlyn gave a delicate shrug. 'Can't say I've put much thought into it. The faction doesn't interest me.'

An almost unified gasp came from the coven.

Thad spluttered. 'They're causing mayhem.'

'They're causing pain. Anyone can do that.' Emberlyn flicked a dismissive hand. 'The faction isn't worth your fear. They're just a bunch of mediocre witches dabbling in things they don't fully understand – they've proven that with how sloppy their spells are.'

Ouch, baby. That had to have stabbed some egos.

Some mouths tightened. A few heads lowered fast. A person shifted stiffly in their seat, their nostrils flaring. Offended because they were part of the faction, or annoyed that they'd allowed themselves to fear a group of people who in truth weren't at all scary?

Ames blinked. 'How can you say they're mediocre? Look at all they've done.'

Emberlyn's brow pinched. 'They've "done" plenty. They've accomplished nothing. Reena is still High Priestess, I'm still alive, and the faction is now considered a stain upon the town that needs to be eradicated – *everyone* is out for their blood.' She sniffed, an element of condescension in her tone as she added, 'In their shoes, I'd be embarrassed.'

Oh, and now she was sinking the knife even deeper.

Paisley snickered around the lollipop in her mouth, her eyes dancing. 'Agreed,' she mumbled, to which many wolves nodded. That only seemed to annoy the coven more.

Ripper's aunt leaned forward in her seat to touch his witch's shoulder. 'You're truly not worried about them?'

Emberlyn glanced at Yvette. 'I worry that they'll keep harming Rabid and innocent people, but I don't feel that these witches are at all noteworthy. They can't be very powerful or they would confidently step out into the light and establish themselves as a separate coven. I proclaimed myself a lone witch and set up shop. It isn't hard.'

A silence hit the room again, short and pensive.

Dez rubbed at his jaw. 'You know, I never thought I'd say this at any point regarding anything at all, but I agree with Emberlyn.'

Getty looked at him, her brow hiking up in challenge. 'Why? Because you think it makes you look less guilty?'

Dez clenched his jaw tight. 'I'm not part of the faction, Getty. But I agree with every person here who's swearing that *you* are.'

Tyra threw up both hands. 'Can we all stop accusing each other already! It isn't helping. Are we sure there's even a faction at large? How do we know it isn't just one witch working alone? A witch powerful enough and shrewd enough to do all this and get away with it, enabling her to cause divides within the coven and turn the clans against us? Does that not make more sense than for an *entire* faction to remain unmasked for so long?'

Picking up on the insinuation that the witch in question could only be Emberlyn, Ripper didn't bother biting back a low growl of warning. 'What witch would you be referring to?' he asked, his voice *daring* her to be so fucking stupid as to finger his witch – who'd gone back to reading her magazine, ignoring Tyra completely.

Her eyes flickering, Tyra licked her lips. 'I'm not naming names. I just think it's a theory we should consider. Some witches in this town are creatively vengeful and don't much care about how much destruction they cause.'

'Name them,' said Shane. 'I'll look into them.'

Tyra dropped her gaze. 'I'm not comfortable doing so when I have no proof.'

Kage snorted derisively. 'You mean you're not comfortable admitting that you're referring to Emberlyn, because you know what the consequences will be and you don't want to face them.'

Carver grunted his agreement. 'She's the ideal person for you to blame because it would shift the anger from the coven onto her, that's all. And let's face it, Tyra, you have personal grievances with her.'

Considering Carver had months ago referred to Emberlyn as 'the devil's witch', Ripper was more than a little surprised by the Alpha's vote of confidence.

'I won't buy for a second that it's Ripper's woman,' said Shane. 'Emberlyn has a reputation for being vengeful, but she's *specific* about who she targets. There's never collateral damage – you all know that. So, let's discuss who could *really* be behind this.'

Tyra wisely snapped her mouth shut, not looking happy about it.

'I personally don't believe that it's only one person,' said Bennet. 'But I do think the number of witches involved is small. The things that have been done ... Very few in our coven would condone it, and even fewer would be part of it.'

Nods and murmurs of agreement came from most of the coven.

'I think it's worth looking at witches who've mated with werewolves,' Ruben cut in. 'They're still in our coven, yes, but maybe their loyalties have shifted.'

Carver sat up straighter. 'No werewolf would *ever* ask a witch to target the Rabid.'

'In *your* opinion,' said Ruben, crossing his arms over his chest. 'I'm entitled to *my* opinion.'

The two fast fell into an argument.

Shane leaned a little toward Ripper, saying, 'The names I heard most often repeated were Dez, Hank, Sera, Getty, Ames and Ruben.'

Ripper gave a short nod. 'I'll be taking a closer look at them.'

'How many members do you think the group has?' Shane asked him.

'Probably not very many. Maybe twenty or so. The only way to keep an inclusive club secret for so long in such a small town is to keep its numbers low.'

Chewing on that, Shane dipped his chin. 'You have a point there.' He paused. 'They all need to die, Rip. They have blood on their hands. That can't be overlooked.'

'It won't be.'

Just then, Carver slammed a hand on the table. 'Enough,' he barked at Ruben. 'Your theory is pure bullshit. You're just trying to turn the attention away from yourself – anyone can sense that. I've seen a lot of that happening here tonight.'

Shane leaned forward in his seat as he addressed the townsfolk. 'I'm gonna make something clear to the faction members – you know who you are. Your time on this Earth is limited. I don't care who IDs you first, Reena or the clans, you *will* die. All of you.'

Almost as a whole, the coven uncomfortably shifted their attention to their High Priestess, clearly waiting for her to object.

Instead, Reena shrugged one shoulder. 'Why should I fight for the right to punish those traitors? They are not worth the trouble it would cause. They skulk around practicing immoral magick, implicate and bespell others, and here tonight remained silent when others pointed fingers at innocent people. They are not one of us, they are *against* us.'

'Hear, hear,' said Ward.

Other members echoed his sentiment.

Reena fluidly rose to her feet. 'I declare the meeting over – there's nothing else that can be said.'

With that, the townsfolk stood and talked amongst themselves as they made to leave.

When Reena went to step down from the platform, Carver spoke. 'Reena ... I hadn't expected that of you. It can't have been an easy concession to make. Know that it is appreciated.'

'This isn't a coven issue, or a clan issue, it's a *town* issue,' she stated. 'We should be working together, not apart, or the faction will win. So if I have to leave the punishments in this case to you and the other Alphas, it's exactly what I'll do.' She then walked off.

'She isn't wrong,' said Ripper, rising to his feet.

'No, she isn't,' agreed Shane as he also stood. 'It's a shame she didn't do this years ago, though, isn't it?'

Knowing the Alpha was referring to what had happened with Rosemary, Ripper shrugged. 'No sense in me forever being bitter about it. What's done is done.'

Shane spared Emberlyn a slight look. 'I wouldn't have ever thought you'd end up so entangled with a witch, but I can see how it's happened. She's ... extraordinary.'

Ripper narrowed his eyes. 'Not sure I like the amount of admiration in your voice as you speak of her. In fact, I definitely don't fucking like it.'

Shane laughed. 'You're gone, Rip. Completely gone.'

Yeah, so he'd heard.

Ripper descended the platform and stalked straight to his witch, who was chatting with his aunt. He looked down at the magazine she still held. 'Interesting read?'

'Oh yeah, riveting,' Emberlyn deadpanned.

'It proved to be an effective prop.'

'It did indeed.' She twisted her mouth. 'Do you think Reena really won't demand the right to punish the faction herself?'

'I think she'd be a fool to do anything but, and Reena's no fool.'

CHAPTER THIRTY-THREE

❧

'Why are you pouting?'

'No reason.'

Emberlyn sighed at her friend, easily guessing . . . 'You wanted a pony ride but were told you're too old. Am I right?'

Paisley sniffed. 'Perhaps.'

Logan snorted from his seat beside Emberlyn – one that Ripper had recently vacated, needing to relieve his bladder. He'd asked his brother to stay with her, not wanting her to work her market stall alone, even though she needed no help.

All stalls were narrow, only featuring a table to display your for-sale items. Emberlyn offered things such as potions, home-made candles, herbal tea balls, healing salves and packs of oracle cards.

'What happened?' Logan asked Paisley, tipping his chin at the Band-Aid on the back of her hand.

She only pulled a face.

Beside his sister, Kage sighed. 'She got bit by a goat.'

Emberlyn lifted a brow. 'She went to the kids' petting zoo, I take it?'

Paisley inched up her chin, belligerent. 'I reserve the right to regress during county fairs.'

Well, she certainly *looked* as though she'd regressed. She'd had her face painted like a tiger, was cuddling a stuffed frog she'd likely won, and had the string of a pink balloon tied to her wrist.

Each time the annual county fair rolled around, Paisley turned into a seven-year-old child trapped in a woman's body. Emberlyn shrugged. 'So long as you're enjoying yourself . . .'

'Oh, I am,' Paisley assured her.

Everybody appeared to be. The grassy stretch of land had been completely transformed. Carnival games were set up. Food carts were parked in various spots. Market stalls were clustered together selling everything from fruit and honey to purses and art.

Folk music played, not quite overriding the laughter and shouting and ringing carnival-game bells.

There were craft workshops, baking contests, blacksmithing demonstrations and live painting. Canvas tents had been put up to shelter healers, who invited people inside for treatment or consultation.

The kids were in their element. Inflatables were available, including a giant slide, a bouncy castle and an assault course. Many children went back and forth from the petting zoo.

Paisley plucked a particular candle from the table and sniffed it. 'Ooh, I like. How much?'

'You can have it for free if you buy me some funnel cake.' Emberlyn was *famished*, her stomach haunted by the mouth-watering scents of caramel popcorn, corn dogs, fried chicken and cotton candy. But it was the smell of the cake that really tugged at her appetite.

'Deal.' Paisley allowed Emberlyn to wrap the candle and then plopped it in her purse. Her attention zipped to a passing she-wolf who sent Kage an unfriendly look. 'What was that about?' she asked her twin.

He scratched at his temple. 'We fucked during the last full moon. I only meant for it to be a one-time thing. It turns out that she thought there'd be a repeat. When I gently disabused her of that theory, she lost it with me and called me a total asshole.'

Paisley gasped in a mix of horror and anger. 'The bitch *dared* say that to you?'

He blinked. 'You say it to me all the time.'

'I'm your sister. It's my right and privilege to fuck with your self-esteem. *She* doesn't get to do that.'

'I'm sensing you think I should feel warmed by that comment.'

'You can't feel the love and protectiveness rolling off me?'

'No.'

Letting out a *pfft* sound, Paisley turned back to Emberlyn. 'Where's Ripper?'

'You just missed him,' Emberlyn replied. 'He went to answer a call of nature.'

Paisley looked at Logan. 'You sticking with her?'

'I am,' he confirmed.

'Good. I'll return with cake soon.' With that, Paisley skipped away.

Kage gave Emberlyn and Logan a quick raise of his eyebrows and then followed his sister.

Reaching into a box beneath the table, Emberlyn grabbed a candle identical to the one she'd just given to Paisley and set it in the now-empty spot. 'You don't have to stay with me,' she told Logan.

'I know. But you see those two wolves over there?' He subtly indicated where the Reeds were eyeing jam jars at another stall.

'They've been very slowly making their way around the market, sliding you brief glances. They're waiting for the right moment to come over here. It's best to make sure that they have a reason not to do it.'

Emberlyn had noticed that they kept sparing her too-quick looks. She momentarily cut her gaze to someone on their far right. 'The Reeds aren't the only ones lingering.' CeCe had been hovering by nearby tents ever since Logan had made his way over.

His lips thinned. 'Everywhere I turn today she seems to be right there.'

'It could be that she has something she wants to say to you.'

'There's nothing I want to hear,' he said, his voice grim. 'Not right now. Maybe some time in the future.'

Emberlyn gently bumped his shoulder with her own. 'I'm sorry that she hurt you.'

'It's like Yvette said – someone can be a close friend, but they won't necessarily suit you as a partner. In the past, I never had cause to see the sides of CeCe I've seen lately, because we'd only been friends. I recently spoke to a couple of her exes – they said they weren't at all surprised by how she's acted recently toward me and Ripper. They claimed that she's pretty demanding in a relationship. It's her way or no way at all. She expects to come before everything and everyone, including your kids from previous relationships.'

'She has to be the center of her partner's world and feel in control of the relationship,' Emberlyn reasoned.

'She wouldn't have had that control with me. We wouldn't have gone the distance – there'd have been too much push and pull, we'd have found no balance. Me and CeCe worked as friends. She *makes* a good friend. But that was all we were ever meant to be,' he added with a shrug, seeming to have made his peace with that.

It still had to suck that things had played out the way they had.

Right then, a werewolf couple arrived. They smiled, idly browsed the selection of items for sale and settled on potions that aided with joint relief.

As they left, Emberlyn leaned forward in her seat to idly rearrange the potion display. Catching sight of Clem off in the distance, she nudged Logan and casually tossed out, 'I hear you and Clem see a lot of each other.'

He gave her a sideways glance. 'You're not gonna do that thing, are you?'

'Thing?'

'People who are loved up often start matchmaking.'

A potion bottle somehow slipped out of her grasp. 'L-loved up?'

He laughed. 'Emberlyn, I've seen the way you look at my brother. I've seen the way he looks at you. I've seen how you two are with each other. Maybe you haven't admitted it to yourselves yet, but you've been hit by the big L.'

Feeling a little too exposed, Emberlyn moodily righted the bottle she'd knocked over. 'Maybe *you're* the one who's loved up and so you're seeing love everywhere.'

He grinned. 'Nope. I like Clem. She's what I need right now – someone fun who isn't looking for anything complicated. What we have ain't serious, or moving in that direction. You and Ripper? Different story.'

'That's . . . well . . . You're enjoying my discomfort, aren't you?'

His shoulders shaking with a silent laugh, he unrepentantly inclined his head. 'As you once told me, you ain't daunted by much. Seeing you all rattled just feels like further proof that I'm right.'

He *was* right, dammit. Or, at least, he was right about where Emberlyn emotionally stood. She didn't know if she could say the same regarding Ripper.

He leaned into her, his expression soft but serious. 'He never once looked at a woman the way he does you. I've honestly never before seen him so open, relaxed and tactile with anyone. That's how I know this is the real deal for him. So make an honest man of him already.'

Her gut twisted so sharply it hurt. 'You can't be certain he wants to take things that far.'

'Oh, I can. I know my brother better than he knows—'

'Well, don't you two look cozy,' a voice cut in, its tone ugly.

Emberlyn looked up, inwardly sighing as she noticed CeCe approaching.

Coming to stand in front of the table, the woman glared down at Emberlyn, her expression sour. 'Have your eye on both brothers, do you? Watch out. They might share you for a night, but trying to keep them both is a fast way to end up alone.'

'*CeCe*,' Logan rumbled in warning.

The bitterness in the werewolf's face drained away. 'That was uncalled for, I'm sorry.'

'Are you?' *Doubtful.*

'Yes.' CeCe's gaze zipped to Logan. 'Can we talk? Alone?'

'If you have something to say, you can say it in front of Emberlyn,' he replied. 'She's practically family at this point.'

Ouch.

The dart hit its mark, making a hint of pain crease CeCe's face. 'I suppose you're right. Ripper is certainly serious about her. Now that I see it wouldn't hurt him if you and I were together, I don't see why we can't make a go of things.'

Oh. Wow. Emberlyn stared up at her, her lips parted in sheer astonishment. Because CeCe spoke as if Logan should be *thrilled*; should trip all over himself to agree.

'I know I've been something of a bitch lately – I'll make up for that. The person I've been . . . that's not who I am, Logan.'

'It's who you are when you're not getting your way; when the people you consider yours aren't dancing to your tune,' he accused.

CeCe frowned. 'No. No, I just—'

'I'm not interested in dragging this conversation out, so I'm gonna be straight with you.' He leaned forward slightly. 'The days where I wanted us to be together are gone. That ship has sailed. It will not make a U-turn and come back. Friendship is all we were ever meant to have. I just didn't see that until recently.'

Her face tightened. 'That isn't true. You only feel that way because I hurt you. Which I'm so sorry for, Logan. Sorrier than you'll ever know.'

He cocked his head, staring at her curiously. 'Are you thinking that if we were together it'd make Ripper jealous? Spur him to dump Emberlyn?'

CeCe's eyes widened. 'What? Of course not. All I want when it comes to Ripper is for he and I to rebuild our friendship.'

'But only so he'll stop avoiding you,' Logan claimed. 'You want to get close to him again. How else can you push the triad agenda?'

'I dropped that idea,' CeCe clipped. 'I know it isn't ever going to happen.'

'No, it isn't. Because even if Rip changed his mind, I wouldn't. He won't, though. And neither will I.'

CeCe pressed her lips tight together. 'You love me.'

'And you shit all over that. You took advantage of it. Used it. Used me to try to manipulate my brother.'

'I'll make up for hurting you—'

'That's great. Won't make any difference.' Logan gave a blasé shrug. 'Like I said, that ship has sailed.'

Pain and spite washing over her face, CeCe refocused on Emberlyn. 'I suppose you're feeling rather smug.'

Emberlyn blinked. 'About what?'

'You managed to turn both brothers against me.'

Logan gaped at the woman. 'Honest to God, CeCe?'

CeCe clenched her fists. 'You have loved me all your life. That doesn't just switch off. But it would with a little magick.'

This bitch was extra. 'It's pretty sad that you need to feel there's an outside reason why Logan turned you down. Join us in reality, sweetie, and take in the view – he doesn't want you because *he doesn't want you*. And that is on you. You're right that strong feelings don't just switch off,' Emberlyn allowed. 'But they do if a whole lot of buttons are pressed. And let's face it, you did just that, didn't you?'

The female werewolf didn't speak for long moments, resentment tightening her jaw. 'You know, I really do loathe you.'

Emberlyn sniffed dismissively. 'Join the line of haters. Despising me doesn't make you special around here.' Picking up movement in her peripheral vision, she looked to see Ripper fast approaching, a potato spiral stick in hand. His steely gaze bounced from her to Logan to CeCe and back again.

He halted at Emberlyn's side, offering her the potato stick. Oh, he knew her so well. She gratefully took it, saying, 'Thank you.' She wasted no time biting into it.

He didn't respond, busy glaring at CeCe. 'I don't know why the fuck you'd even think to come over here when I told you to stay away from Emberlyn.'

CeCe jutted out her chin. 'I actually came to talk to Logan. Which I wanted to do alone, but he wouldn't move from this spot, so I had no choice but to be near her. But if you want to temporarily banish me, fine. Go for it.' It was a dare.

Ripper's shoulders lifted and fell. 'Consider it done.'

CeCe sucked in a breath, staring at him in complete shock. Her eyes welled up, but anger carved lines into her face. 'Like

I give a damn. The two men I love don't want anything to do with me. No punishment you dish out could hurt worse than that.' She stiffly walked away, her head down, her shoulders bowed.

If Emberlyn was a more forgiving person, she would have felt sorry for the girl. Maybe.

'Get this,' Logan said to Ripper. 'She actually came over to offer me a relationship – and in a way that made it clear she thought I'd pounce on it.' He shook his head, a sigh easing out of him. 'A couple of months ago, I would have.'

'So you told her no, then?' Ripper asked him, threading his fingers through the back of Emberlyn's hair.

'I did,' Logan replied. 'She didn't much like it. She suggested that Emberlyn had used magick to make you and me turn on her – like she hadn't managed that all by herself.'

'*What?*' Ripper growled, his gaze snapping down to Emberlyn. 'What else did she say to you?'

Nibbling at a slice of potato, Emberlyn flicked a hand. 'Nothing notable.'

'She told you she loathed you,' Logan reminded her.

'And I don't care, so it isn't notable.'

Ripper tugged at her hair to tilt back her head so their gazes met once more. '*I* care that she'd dare speak to you that way.'

'Well, you've already issued the temporary banishment, so it's handled.' Emberlyn shrugged. 'If you chase after her to pull her on it, you're just giving her the attention that she craves. You said you were done doing that.'

'Your witch is right, Rip, don't go give CeCe what she wants.' Logan rose from his seat. 'I gotta talk to Kerr about something real quick. Stick close to your woman, brother. The Reeds are still hovering.'

Heaving a sigh, Ripper nodded.

As Logan strode off, Emberlyn said, 'I don't think she thought you were serious about issuing a temporary banishment.'

Ripper's brows flicked together as he sank onto the chair. 'I don't make idle threats. And I'd never undermine my own authority by not living up to my word.'

'I know, but it's a super serious punishment.'

'Which she all but dared me to issue.'

'Daring an Alpha is never wise.' Emberlyn bit into a piece of potato and then angled the stick toward Ripper. 'Want some?'

His honeydew-green eyes warming, he swiped a full slice of potato right off the stick with his teeth. 'So *you're* feeding *me* now?'

'Fuck, no. You're only getting one slice. This is mine.'

He chuckled, low and throaty. It was a rusty sound, and it had her mesmerized.

'I don't think I've ever heard you laugh before.'

He shrugged. 'Never really had much to laugh about. Then came you.'

Warmth blossomed in her belly. 'Dude, you're making me want to jump you right here in front of everyone.'

His eyes lit up. 'I'm good with that, it's ...' He trailed off, his brow furrowing as his gaze shifted to something over her shoulder.

Tracking his gaze, Emberlyn saw that Paisley was on her way back to the table. There was no Kage with her this time.

She held out a brown paper bag. 'Funnel cake, as ordered,' she said around the lollipop in her mouth.

Emberlyn smiled brightly and took the bag. 'Thank you.'

Just then, Logan reappeared. And he was eyeing Paisley like he'd never met her before. 'You're wearing a pink tiara.'

'I know,' said Paisley, adjusting its position.

'And your hair is covered in glitter,' he added.

'Stating the obvious, but yes.'

'You also have unicorn tattoos all over your neck and arms.'

'They'll wash off. Sadly.'

Logan frowned at the smeared face paint. 'Why a tiger?'

'What is it with all the questions?'

'I only asked one.'

'One is one too many.' Putting a hand to her stomach, she looked at Emberlyn. 'I think I've eaten too much candy. I don't feel so good. The tractor ride didn't help.'

Logan cocked his head. 'Isn't that for kids?'

'*Again* with the questions,' Paisley huffed.

Standing upright, Emberlyn waved her over. 'Come sit.'

As Paisley went to skirt around the table, Logan reared back and threw up his hands. She frowned. 'Why are you backing away?'

'I'm not good with children,' he replied.

Paisley gasped in offense. 'You shithead.'

Emberlyn started to laugh.

Logan gave Paisley an appeasing look. 'Oh, come on, you can't walk around like that and expect not to be the butt of somebody's joke.' He glanced at the male approaching the table. 'Crew, control your woman.'

Crew frowned. 'My w—*what the fuck?*'

Paisley set a hand on her hip. 'Why are you gawping at me?'

'How can I not? It looks like a kids' classroom puked on you,' Crew marveled in sheer dismay.

Paisley notched up her chin. 'I'm happy. Isn't that what's important?'

'I – well – I mean – not right now.'

Paisley growled. 'You're all dicks. Emberlyn, *stop laughing!*'

CHAPTER THIRTY-FOUR

〜

'That was quite a day,' said Emberlyn.

Oh, she wasn't wrong. Sinking into the sofa of the manor's living room, Ripper patted the spot beside him and draped an arm over the back of the couch. 'And a profitable one for you.' There had been barely any stock left on her table when the fair came to an end.

She slumped onto the sofa. 'It usually is,' she said, listing into him with a yawn.

He nuzzled her hair, inhaling. She smelled good. Smelled of her, him, magick, strawberry shampoo and her signature floral perfume. 'Tired?'

'A little.' She slung an arm around his waist. 'Thank you for hanging with me at the stall today. I know it had to have been pretty boring.'

'Being with you is never boring.'

A door slammed shut upstairs.

'You know, I'm getting used to that.' The banging, the

whispering, the furniture moving, the eerie noises. 'I didn't even freak this morning when my empty mug slid across the table.'

'It's just life at the manor.' She tipped her head back to meet his eyes. 'Your house isn't free of spirits, you know.'

Ripper felt his brows draw together. 'What?'

'I only saw two—'

'You *saw* two?'

'Nothing malevolent,' she assured him. 'They both used to live there, though not at the same time. That's all I picked up from them.'

'How come you never mentioned it before?'

'I didn't want you feeling uncomfortable in your home. But you said you're getting used to ghostly stuff now, so ...' She let her eyes close, giving him a little more of her weight.

Ripper stared down at her, playing his fingers through her hair. She was so fucking beautiful it made his chest ache. There was a time she'd watched him carefully, not quite sure of his intentions or nature. Now she could sit beside him, relaxed and pliant with her eyes closed. A sign of pure trust.

Emberlyn wasn't a creature who easily put her faith in people. That he'd earned her trust was something he prized and would never take for granted.

'You're staring,' she accused without opening her eyes.

'It's my right. You're my mine.'

She let out a soft snort of amusement. 'Possessive much?'

'If I could, I'd stamp my fingerprints all over you. And I mean *all over you*. Someone would be able to play dot-to-dot on your skin. Of course ... if they tried that, I'd have to kill them. Because a lot of the places that would bear my prints would be parts of you no one else gets to touch.'

'Hmm, well, I bear plenty of other marks – be satisfied with those.'

She *did* bear plenty. He liked to leave little score marks and bites on her flesh. There was just so much pretty skin to mark, what else was he supposed to do?

'Also, I don't think there's a part of me that doesn't wear your scent.'

Probably not. Honestly, at this point, his scent perfumed her skin as distinctly as her magick and sheer strength of will. A strength that appealed to him as much as her looks and, well, everything else about her.

He'd spent every day of his life at Chilgrave, but he didn't need to have encountered more of the world to know that Emberlyn was singular. As soft and sweet as she was shrewd and merciless, his witch was a living contradiction.

He coveted every layer – the classy Alpha, the warm under-belly, the cunning avenger, the uniquely talented witch, the protective friend, the sexual sort-of-submissive who demanded you earn that submission.

He couldn't imagine no longer wearing the scent of her magick – it felt too much a part of him now. Like another layer of skin. 'I want to claim you,' he found himself stating.

Her eyes snapped open, her muscles tensing.

Ripper almost grimaced. 'I never meant to blurt it out like that. I was going to broach the topic at some point tonight, though.' Usually when he'd say something serious like that, she would watch him closely, monitoring his expression ... as if searching for signs of uncertainty on his part.

This time, she looked away, sitting up straight. Trying to process his words, he knew. Attuned to her, he felt no rejection of his statement, only a surprise tinted with disbelief that had caused her to mentally fumble. And now the pulse in her neck beat as hard and fast.

Understanding why his declaration had taken her off-guard,

his heart hurt for her. This wasn't a person who'd ever felt truly indispensable to anyone. It always rattled her a little when he only ever wanted to get closer rather than break away from her.

Deciding to give her a few moments, he stayed quiet while she found her mental footing. If she said she needed more time, he'd give it to her. But he wasn't going to back off completely. Not from this woman who – as unwavering as any tank – had knocked down and trampled over his every mental wall, every doubt, every reservation.

His sexual hunger for her had always been an elemental, relentless force. Something that never faltered, always intense and oppressive. Nothing had ever eased it. Almost as if that need for her had been imprinted on him somehow.

And now *she* felt imprinted on him.

The sensory memories of her softness, her scent, her warmth, the pinch of smoke in her voice – it was all rooted in his brain, vivid and distinct.

In hindsight, it seemed laughable that he'd once thought that he could be satisfied with just spending a little time in her bed; that he could later walk away without a qualm. But he hadn't known her back then. Hadn't had any clue that she had the potential to carve her name into his bones.

Logan was right that he'd needed either to take the jump or let her go. There was no way Ripper could do the latter. Ever. This woman was it for him.

Every cell in his body and instinct in his system insisted that she was his. Deep inside himself, he'd already claimed her. He just hadn't made it official.

She sank a hand into her hair. 'I don't know what to say.'

At the break in her voice, something in the vicinity of his chest melted. 'Let me have a guess at what thoughts are running through your head. You're thinking how you've done the mating thing before and it didn't go so well.'

She gave a sheepish shrug. 'Kinda.'

'You're thinking the best way to ensure that history doesn't repeat itself is just to avoid taking another mate.'

She inclined her head slightly.

'And you're reflecting on how we haven't been together long, so you're thinking that maybe I can't be so sure of us this soon anyway. That about cover it?'

'Yes. And I'm sorry if it hurts your feelings—'

'Don't apologize for how you feel. Baby, I'll be honest, I had my own reservations about mating. I saw firsthand what can happen to a woman who loses her mate. But Logan gave me a reality check, and now I'm gonna do the same for you.'

Her snort was weak. 'How benevolent you are.'

His lips almost drew up at that. 'I know.' His humor faded as he went on. 'I can only imagine what your last hour with Michael was like. As if it wasn't bad enough that he gutted you so deeply you wanted out of the mating, he changed into his In-between form, goddamn attacked you and then disappeared from your life. But I'm not him, Em.'

She frowned. 'Of course you're not. It's just . . .' She trailed off, sighing.

'Colton said that Michael is strong. Bullshit. He's fucking weak. Weak for cheating on you, for not having the guts to immediately admit it, for trivializing your pain and for not even bothering to apologize. Do you think I'd do any of that to you?'

'No, never,' she replied instantly. 'But you feel the pull of the full moon more than most. You turned Rabid once before—'

'And the odds of it happening to me again are seriously low.' He palmed the back of her head. 'Especially now that I have you. You're my very own homing beacon. You call to me more strongly than any full moon. How could I ever leave you?'

*

Those words hit Emberlyn right in the feels. Hard. Her chest clenched painfully.

She'd had a weakness for Ripper from the start – it had been hormonal at first, yes, but still he'd drawn her like nothing else. When she'd given in to the escalating sexual chemistry that seemed to know no bounds, she could never have imagined that, over time, they'd become more and more intertwined until she couldn't imagine him not being part of her life.

Ripper wasn't merely under her skin, he'd become as vital to her as the blood in her veins. To lose him would gut her more than any other loss she'd endured.

For the first time, she could understand why her mother had broken when the sperm donor left her without a backward glance. Emberlyn wouldn't allow herself to fade away if Ripper left, but she would be completely lost.

'Don't let what happened with Michael make you hold back from me,' Ripper insisted. 'You weren't meant for him. You were meant to be mine. We just didn't get that until now.'

Her feels yet again got slammed.

'As for you thinking that maybe I can't be sure this is really what I want ... I don't need to have spent years at your side to know that I don't want to be anywhere else. As we've already established, I see you. I know you. I'm sure of my decision. I don't need more time and – heads-up, baby – I don't have it in me to give you space while you think it over. I can give you time, not space.'

Like she'd ever *want* him to stay away.

'You're not a person who lets their fears dictate what they do. You never have been. Don't let that be different now.'

She exhaled heavily. 'Ames once said that I was a walking curse. That I drove away or destroyed the people around me.'

Ripper's expression hardened. 'That motherfucker is not someone you should ever listen to about anything.'

'I didn't listen. I rolled my eyes. I'm not responsible for the choices that the people around me make. But I am *so tired* of having people fuck me over or leave me. The only people in my life who've been permanent, reliable fixtures are the twins.'

'And now me. I'm not going to join that list of people who let you down. Not ever. I told you before, you're safe with me. Always will be.' He leaned toward her, pinning her with a serious gaze. 'Hear me, Em. I'm not going anywhere. Not even if you tell me you don't want me to claim you, though we both know you'd be lying.'

She couldn't stop her lips from hitching up. 'Oh, we do?'

'You want this. You wouldn't be so rattled if you didn't.'

He knew her too well, really. 'It's just—'

'Love you, Em. Another heads-up – it ain't a one-way street.'

Her chest squeezed painfully, but not in a bad way. Far from it. 'It's a good thing I have you here to tell me what I'm thinking and feeling.'

'Can you honestly claim I'm wrong?'

'No,' she confessed. 'Much as I hate to be soppy, I'll admit I love you more than I've ever loved anyone.'

Pure male satisfaction lit his eyes.

'This isn't just about us, though. You're an Alpha. If we claimed each other, I'd be Alpha female of your clan. They might not be too pleased about that.'

'You're wrong there. With the exception of CeCe and her crowd, they like and respect you. They see your strength of character, how powerful you are. They know you could protect them if necessary. It would comfort them, not put them off.'

She hummed, a little dubious.

'Did you know they all refer to you to others as "Ripper's witch"?'

Surprise fluttered through her. 'No.'

'It's an indication that they acknowledge and support my claim to you; that they understand this is serious for me. If any of them had reservations, I would have sensed it.'

Probably. And the twins would have surely told her.

'You're used to being alone. It'd be pretty normal for you to feel at least a little leery about adopting an entire clan of werewolves. I'd be surprised if you weren't. In your position, I probably would have felt that way. But I'd have considered you worth it.'

She gaped. 'Oh, now that was sly. You worded that in a way that insinuates *I* won't consider *you* worth all that comes with mating you if I don't agree.'

His eyes lit with an unrepentant smile. 'I'm not going to play fair here. Fact is I wouldn't have the first clue how to give you up, and I'm not going to. You belong to me, *with* me – and you know it. I'm yours just the same.'

'Stop making me feel gooey inside, I don't like it.'

The smile lighting his eyes kicked up a notch, his affection clear in the warmth in his expression. He made no attempt to hide it from her. 'Just to note, I wouldn't ask that you move to Ashwood. I got no problem moving in here.'

'But what about *your* home?'

'It's just a building, Em. This place . . . it's special in ways that are freaky as fuck, but I know how much it means to you.'

'You love your house, though.'

'I love you more.'

Oh, she was gonna cry.

Right then, the phone on the side table rang.

It was almost a relief to get a break from the gooeyness. 'It's for you,' she told him.

He frowned. 'How do you know?'

'I just know.'

Squinting, Ripper scooted along the sofa and lifted the

receiver from the phone. 'Hello?' His eyes narrowed further. 'Kerr,' he greeted, sliding her a quick glance.

She smiled at the unnerved look on his face. But her smile faded when his expression tightened.

'You are shitting me.' A curse sputtered out of him. 'I'll be right there.'

'What's wrong?' she asked when he set the receiver down.

'A fight broke out at Yvette's diner,' he replied, pushing off the sofa. 'Again. Fuckers should know better.' He swooped down and claimed her mouth in a brief but possessive kiss. 'I'll be back after I've dealt with it. We have more talking to do.'

That they did, she conceded as he left the room.

Hearing the front door swing shut behind him, she rubbed at her cheek, still a little thrown. Maybe his declaration of intent shouldn't have caught her so off-guard, but she'd thought he might suggest they claim each other *in the future*. Not so soon. And not out of nowhere when she was tired and her defenses were down.

He'd said he'd give her time, but she didn't want to spend weeks chewing on it. Leaving the matter unresolved would eat at her. As would knowing that – though he'd never let her see it – her *needing* such time would hurt him. He was just so damn sure of her, of *them*.

Had she never mated Michael, she probably wouldn't be so knotted up inside right now. Which meant that Ripper was right: she *was* letting her past impact her decision. Emberlyn didn't want to do that.

Ripper would never do what Michael had done. Would never betray her, never hide any fuckups from her, never refuse to apologize if he hurt her. He was too loyal, had too much integrity. And he loved her. Loved her as she did him.

'*You weren't meant for him. You were meant to be mine. We just didn't get that until now.*'

It sure did feel that way. Everything she felt toward Ripper had come to her so easily, so naturally . . . as if it had been inevitable.

She supposed it didn't make much of a difference if they claimed each other now rather than later. Because she *would* say yes in the future. Why insist on more time now? Especially when a sense of such sheer *rightness* thundered through her at the thought of saying yes. She could—

The curtain fluttered. The lamp bulb flickered. The flames in the hearth *puffed* out.

Cold washed over, eerie and otherworldly and filled with a thousand frantic whispers.

Emberlyn sat up straight, instantly alert.

Well, well, well, it would seem that she had company.

Emberlyn pushed off the sofa, walked purposefully out of the room and headed into the kitchen. She stopped at the door to the basement, turned the knob and opened it wide. She didn't clamber down the wooden steps that disappeared into thick pockets of shadow. She merely called out, 'It's time.'

CHAPTER THIRTY-FIVE

❧

Every part of her body aching, Reena weakly lifted her head from the cold, hard ground. A ground she'd pitilessly been dumped on by one of the people now lined up in front of the manor. Her ears ringing, she blinked to clear her blurred vision and focused on the scene playing out in front of her.

Eight robed witches stood with their feet planted and their hands extended. All bloated with power that didn't belong to them, they were chanting fast beneath their breath as they worked to take down the manor's shield.

The taut air crackled with magick, hot and sticky and very *other*. A force not of this world. Not meant *for* this world.

They'd 'borrowed' it, she thought. Borrowed it from some creature or deity they'd summoned, and probably in exchange for a sliver of their soul.

They had to be members of the rebel faction. She couldn't tell who *exactly* they were because each wore an animal mask. Going by the length of their hair and how slender their hands were, she felt sure that the goat, cat, rabbit and blackbird were female. The rest – a fox, wolf, deer and owl – appeared to be male.

Though the power they wielded only danced along the manor's shield, dread licked through her. It wasn't so much these assholes who worried her. It was that they each had a Rabid on a magickal leash that currently kept them docile.

Currently.

They likely wouldn't remain that way for long. Reena was in no state to fight them. She could barely move.

The witches had come at her from behind, the little cowardly bastards. They'd not only attacked her with magick and sapped her of virtually all strength, they had also managed to suppress her own magick, leaving her weak and defenseless.

She had no idea how they'd managed to draw Ripper away from the manor, though she'd heard them gloating about it. Heard enough to understand they'd come here because the rest of the coven now wanted their heads on a silver platter. Only earning respect and fear would make the coven accept the faction as worthy. In these witches' view, defeating Emberlyn Vautier would earn them both.

Reena inwardly snorted. They were underestimating just how powerful the lone witch truly was. Eight witches, twenty witches, forty witches – it would make no difference. Not even while they were tanked up on borrowed magick. They were fools if they thought differently. It was just as foolish of them to think that getting her alone would turn things in their favor. Emberlyn didn't need werewolf muscle at her back.

Trying to sit up a little straighter, Reena winced as pain bloomed through her head again. Her belly churned and beads of sweat broke out on her forehead. Closing her eyes, she tried accessing her magick again. *Failed.* It was still buried too deep.

Hearing a flutter of wings, she looked upward. Three crows had gathered on the roof of the manor. Another soared down and settled on the porch rail. A fourth circled the building before landing on a turret.

If the faction noticed, they didn't show it. They were focused on lowering the shield – their chanting growing louder, faster, more intense.

Reena's gaze slipped down . . . and stopped as she did a double-take. Several partly transparent people stood in the manor's windows, staring out at the scene below. Women and men dressed in clothes from varying eras.

Two in particular caught her attention – Lilith and Millicent side by side, shooting daggers at the faction.

Well, hell.

Magick hissed. Popped. Crackled. Sparked and spluttered in the air. Then the front door swung open . . . just as the manor's shield fell.

And there stood Emberlyn. She took in everything with a glance – the masked witches, the leashed Rabid, Reena on the ground.

Did Emberlyn tense? No. Did she curse? No? Did she look in the least bit bothered or even remotely interested? No.

Her expression remained neutral. No surprise. No fear. No anger. Not even a hint of unease. 'Well, that was rude,' she remarked.

'We couldn't have exactly knocked on your front door,' said the 'goat', her voice carrying a deep, almost mechanical echo that made it hard to identify her – a sure sign that she was struggling to 'digest' the power she'd borrowed. 'Until now, that is.'

'What do you want?' Emberlyn asked them, appearing bored. 'I'm busy.'

'We mean you no harm,' the wolf said, the same echo in his voice that made it as indistinguishable as that of the goat.

Emberlyn shot him an incredulous glance. 'You attacked the shield around my home, which is no different than battering my front door.'

'We merely meant to get your attention,' the wolf assured her.

'Right,' drawled Emberlyn, all skepticism.

The goat lifted her chin as she spoke. 'We came here to invite you to join us.'

Emberlyn's brow pinched. 'Excuse me?'

'As of this night onward, I will lead the coven. Join it. Be part of my inner circle. You will find belonging to the coven more palatable without Reena at its helm. We will have killed her before the night is over. Her time has passed. The old ways are dead.'

Oh, they planned to kill Reena? Good to know. She supposed the only reason they'd brought her here alive was so that Emberlyn would see what these people could do; that they collectively had the power to take down a powerful witch. It was a subtle threat, really.

'So many in town have scorned you for the types of magick you practice,' the goat said to Emberlyn. 'Not us. We understand you. Applaud you. Relate to you. *Join us*,' she pressed. 'You need not be alone anymore. You can work magick alongside likeminded witches who accept you.'

'You think I'm like you?' Emberlyn chuckled. 'That's . . . that's funny. Not in a million years would I show up at a person's house wearing a goat mask, bloated on loaned power. It'll leach from your system soon enough, but you won't regain whatever parts of your soul you gave up in payment. And if you had to borrow power just to subdue Reena, well, can't say I'm impressed.'

Reena almost smiled. Emberlyn sure knew how to deliver an insult in a way that put a true dent in a person's ego.

There were more flutters of wings just before three more crows appeared, all settling on the porch roof, their beady eyes focused on the faction.

'If you are not with us, you are against us,' said the wolf, his tone clipped.

'And *you're* against *me*, in truth,' began Emberlyn. 'You don't *really* want me to join your little cabal. You think to get me on side so that I don't interfere with your plans. What you all truly want is me out of the picture. You'd turn on me the first chance you got, but you'd wait until you thought I'd never expect it.'

Agreed, thought Reena. The faction would likely seek to learn from Emberlyn first, but they would eventually get rid of her.

'Our overture is sincere,' the wolf argued.

'If you do not join us, you will leave us no choice but to ensure that you meet the same fate *she* will meet,' the goat threatened, gesturing at Reena.

'Thanks, but I'll pass ... *Penelope*,' Emberlyn added, her voice hardening. She flapped her hand and – that easily – masks began *flicking* off, revealing surprised face after surprised face.

Penelope. Ames. Bennet. Ethel. Thad. Getty. Ruben. And lastly—

Reena gasped. '*Ward?*'

Her husband glared at her, his expression sour. 'Betrayal is like a hot blade to the heart, isn't it? I felt it knife through me when I heard about you and Carver. A year you spent in his bed. A *year*.'

Reena stared at him, shocked. No, *beyond* shocked. He'd given her not the faintest clue that he'd learned about her ... indiscretion.

'You were so good at hiding it that I might never have known if it hadn't been for Penny,' he said.

The look he and her sister exchanged, the sheer intimacy in

it, was indication enough that ... 'So you had your own affair. But that was not enough payback for you, it would seem.'

'The position of High Priestess is the only thing that ever *really* mattered to you,' Ward spat. 'So now I'm going to make sure that you lose it.'

'No,' Emberlyn casually contradicted, 'that's not how things are going to play out.'

'You're outnumbered eight to one,' Ames taunted. 'Reena can't help you – she can't even access her magick right now.' He cocked his head. 'It's funny. Grams mentored *you* but not *me* because she said that I had no real potential. Look at me now; look at what I can do.'

Emberlyn snorted. 'You can only do it because you're filled with borrowed power. That's nothing to brag about.' She swept her gaze along the line of witches. 'You're not scary. You're not powerful. You're not even a real threat. And if you had any sense, you would have let me be.' Her expression hardened. 'But you didn't. That was a grave mistake, and it's one that you'll pay for.'

Shadows moved behind her as wicked little giggles sounded. Giggles that gave Reena the honest to God's chills.

Those shadows trickled out of the house, at which point Reena could make out several short, skeletal, grotesque creatures. The security lights poured down on them, illuminating their deep-red skin, black twisting horns, yellow eyes, bulbous noses, oversized ears, stinger-topped tails and bat-like wings.

Reena gaped, weakly scrambling backwards. *What in the fresh hell?*

'Just so you know,' Emberlyn added, again casual, 'you didn't hammer the shield down. *I* lowered it. This seemed a good a time as any to finally get rid of you all. I have to say, I'm going to enjoy it.'

Penelope spat a curse. '*Now!*'

The Rabid were released.

The crows swooped down.

The creatures shot through the air like bullets.

The faction released streams of borrowed magick.

Emberlyn threw up her palms, slamming up an invisible shield that *swallowed* the power, causing every faction member to gasp in alarm. Smiling, she thrust her palms forward, emitting glittering rivulets of magick that turned into hundreds of black and silver and teal-blue locusts. 'Now let's have some fun, shall we?'

Stood inside his aunt's diner, Ripper swept a glare over the ten bloody and bruised werewolves lined up in front of him. The last thing he'd expected to find was that the disturbance was caused by members *of his own clan*; people who would normally respect and protect Yvette and her property. Yet, they'd been practically piled on top of each other as fists swung and feet kicked.

More, they hadn't paid any attention to Crew or Logan when ordered to break up the fight. No amount of shouting at them or trying to pull them away from the pile-on had been successful. As if the wolves had been caught up in some kind of bloodthirsty frenzy.

Ripper's command for them to stop had sliced through it, causing the wolves to back off. But they hadn't said a single word since, too busy panting and blinking, seeming confused and disoriented.

'What in the fuck possessed you to do this?' he demanded.

The wolves exchanged sheepish looks, shuffling their feet or holding themselves unnaturally still.

Ripper felt his jaw tighten. 'Somebody needs to answer my question,' he bit off.

Neal snapped up his head and pointed at Caspian. '*He* started it,' he proclaimed in a whiny tattle-tale voice. 'He shoved me.'

Ripper cut his gaze to Caspian, surprised. This particular werewolf could fight, but he wasn't the type to *cause* trouble, only to end it. 'Why?'

Rubbing at his nape, Caspian raised his shoulders. 'Someone told me that I should shove him. And I thought ... "Yeah, yeah, I really should."' He frowned, blinking hard. 'Which makes no sense now, but it did *then*.'

'Who told you that?' Ripper asked him, narrowing his eyes.

Caspian's frown deepened. 'I don't know. I can't remember. I don't remember what their voice sounded like, either. I just remember what they said.'

Kerr looked from Neal to Caspian. 'When you two started brawling, someone told me that I should join in. At that moment, it honestly felt like a natural thing to do. So I did. I can't recall if the voice was male or female.'

The other wolves also claimed to have heard a voice.

Logan sidled up to Ripper. 'I'm thinking a witch – or more than one – sparked this off somehow.'

Ripper's thoughts exactly. 'There aren't any witches here, though.'

'They could have left fast,' said Logan. 'Why would they want to cause a scene, though?'

'And why do it at Yvette's diner, of all places?' asked Crew, stood on Ripper's other side. 'It's a surefire way to piss you off and ensure that you find out who is responsible.'

'I suppose it could be revenge for how you went knocking on the doors of the witches who confronted Emberlyn,' Kerr mused.

Ripper stiffened. 'Emberlyn,' he said under his breath, his scalp prickling with suspicion. He stalked straight to the counter and slapped his palms on it. 'I need to use your phone,' he told Yvette, his stomach hardening as a sense of urgency began to ride him.

His aunt hurried off and quickly returned with the cordless phone.

He punched in Emberlyn's number and held the phone to his ear. It rang. And rang. And rang. And rang. *Nothing*. He hung up. Tried again. Still nothing.

Ripper swore. 'She's not answering.' He set the phone down on the counter as he realized. 'Bait. This scene here was bait to draw me away from her. *Fuck*.'

He rushed out of the diner, aware of Kerr and Logan hot on his heels, and practically jumped into his truck.

Yvette appeared at Ripper's open window just as he switched on the engine. 'Don't panic, your witch is strong. I've heard about a lot of the things she's been able to do. Only one other witch had that ease with magick.'

'Millicent.'

Yvette shook her head. 'Lilith.'

CHAPTER THIRTY-SIX

❧

With a roar worthy of a highlander, Ward batted at the locusts surrounding him and pinned Emberlyn with a glare. He thrust out his palm and a gleaming wave of magick came sailing toward her at super speed. It slapped her face like a hot hand, making her flesh sting and throb.

Not bad, she begrudgingly allowed.

Remaining on the top step of her porch, Emberlyn slammed up a hand and sent out a forceful blow of glittering magick that knocked him clean off his feet. *And that's how it's done.*

Just then, a Rabid rushed up the path, making a beeline for her. She sent out a heavy blow of power that caused it to fly backward, plunging it into the fray. Giggling goblins and squawking crows quickly descended on it.

Just to make things more interesting, she sent a gust of magick upward, letting it circle in the sky. Thunder cracked. Lightning flashed. Crimson rain came pouring down. A whistling wind built up.

Well, if the faction wanted destruction, she'd give them destruction.

'*Bitch!*' cursed Ames, lobbing a ball of power her way too fast for her to dodge. It was like taking a punch to the thigh, the impact so hard it almost numbed her leg.

Snarling, she slashed out her palm, emitting a hot blade of magick that carved at and singed his skin, drawing blood, leaving scorch marks, dragging cries of pain from him.

Two goblins crashed into his back, knocking him down flat. Others grabbed his legs and hauled him backwards.

The faction had no doubt intended to attack Emberlyn as a group – an intention they couldn't follow through with, since the goblins kept them preoccupied. Several had swarmed each witch, attacking hard while laughing like little maniacs.

She really liked their style.

Catching movement on the ground, she looked to see Reena army-crawling away from the scene, clearly weak and shaky, and likely devastated at the participation of her husband and sister. The High Priestess wasn't a woman to flee like that, so she had to be feeling awful to—

A cursing Penelope hurled a clump of magick that quickly morphed into a cobra as it came sailing toward Emberlyn.

Emberlyn caught it by the throat and sharply snapped her hand to the side, breaking its neck. As it crumbled to magick 'dust', she glared at Penelope. 'Like snakes, do you?'

Emberlyn sent out a wave of power that bounded along the ground in front of the faction, forming small crack after small crack. Chanting, she thrust her fists upward slightly ... and snakes came slithering out of the fissures in the earth. Then toads, rats, scarab beetles and huge spiders.

Squealing like a little girl, Penelope backpedaled fast.

Emberlyn laughed – okay, cackled. Whatever.

Penelope's gaze snapped back to her, narrowing with fury. She lifted her hands to retaliate, but then several goblins descended on her. All dragged her backward even as they attacked the now screaming woman.

Marvelous.

Really, Emberlyn could throw up the manor's shield and simply stand back to enjoy the show. But that wouldn't be even half so much fun as drawing out the faction's downfall.

Again, a Rabid charged up the path. Again, it was quickly surrounded by crows and goblins that herded it away. She'd made it clear to her helpers that she didn't want the Rabid to be killed, only kept at bay.

Hearing Ames yell, she looked his way. Oh, it was a total pleasure to see him stumbling everywhere while crying out in pain. One goblin had latched onto his back, stabbing at his throat with the stinger of its tail. Another was wrapped around his thigh, its sharp, filthy fangs biting deep into flesh. A third flew around him uber fast, its horns stabbing him; its bony fingers clawing at him. As such, he was *covered* in bites, scratches and puncture wounds.

All the witches were, to be fair, thanks especially to the contributions of the serpents, rats and insects.

'*I'm going to kill you, bitch!*' Penelope screeched at her, clumsily stumbling up the path with a goblin attached to each leg by their teeth and limbs.

Oh, she was back. Lovely.

A flying goblin grabbed Penelope's hair from behind and heaved with an evil giggle, wrenching back her head and making her spine arch. She cried out, earning herself another giggle. It pulled her hair harder, causing her to clumsily backpedal as she shrieked in pain. Still, Penelope blindly hurled a gust of magick at Emberlyn.

Emberlyn dodged it, twisted her hand, and *snap* went the witch's throat . . . right as Ethel and Thad pressed up against the fence, lashing out with a power that sliced at Emberlyn's arms like jagged knives.

Her heart sank. Killing the twins' parents would bring her no pleasure, despite the crimes that the couple had committed. But they didn't deserve to live. They just didn't.

She slammed a gust of magick at their skulls, wrenching unholy screams out of the pair. Sadness chewed at her conscience until, at the last moment, she eased back the force of her magick, plopping them into a coma. She just couldn't bring herself to be responsible for their demise; the Watchers could deal with them instead.

The couple dropped to the ground like stones, deeply unconscious. She formed a small dome of magick around them, stopping the goblins and other creatures from touching them. It was the most she was prepared to do for the couple.

A Rabid cleared them with a fluid leap as it made a beeline for Emberlyn. Once more, goblins and crows blocked its path and ushered it away. Considering the Rabid only seemed to have eyes for her, it was obvious that they'd been spelled to target her. Collectively, the goblins and birds were doing a fine job at protecting her from them.

They were doing just as fine a job as protecting her from the faction. Admittedly, it was somewhat amusing to watch these asshole witches – who'd caused drama, hurt and damage not only to the town and its inhabitants but also to the Rabid – stagger around, yelling, cursing and letting out pained cries while goblins and animals crawled all over them.

Emberlyn took a quick moment to check on Reena. The woman must have still been unable to access her magick, because she was huddled in a tremoring ball on the grass just beyond the yard.

Emberlyn's peripheral vision screamed a warning.

She tracked the movement, but she did it too late. Magick rammed into her head so hard that her vision went dark around the edges. *Motherfucker.*

Getty laughed, delighted – until a black cat appeared out of nowhere and flung herself right at the witch. Lucie hissed and growled as she clawed at Getty's face, leaving deep, bleeding grooves.

Shaking off the effects of the blow, Emberlyn yelled, 'Lucie, move!' As soon as the feline backed off, she lobbed a lethal wave of magick Getty's way. It rammed into the witch's chest, going right for her heart.

Getty jolted. Wheezed. Slapped a hand to her chest.

And promptly died.

'*No!*' Ruben shouted, grief coloring the sound. He made a mad dash for the gate, shooting magick 'bullets' at Emberlyn.

Hissing as one pinged off her shoulder, Emberlyn called down a lightning strike, directing it right at him. The bolt hit its target, causing Ruben to shake and seize, his eyes rolling back. Then he hit the ground. *Dead.*

Five down, three to go.

Speaking of the other three ... She quickly scanned the scene. Ames was still covered in goblins. Ward was kicking at rats while tugging at the snake curled around his throat. And Bennet—

Was coming right for her.

Before he could attack, she threw out a fluid beam of magick that snapped around his whole body like a vice.

He snarled, struggling against its grip, unable to move. 'You were right. We would have killed you once we no longer had use for you.'

'Oh, you might have *tried*. This would have been the result.'

She flicked a finger and the vice tightened its grip, crushing every bone in his body.

More than ready to end this shit now, Emberlyn switched her focus to Ames. She threw out a 'loop' of magick and used it to snatch his ankle. Then she yanked, pulling him right off his feet and dragging him up the path. The goblins released him and backed off with ghoulish squeaks.

His ravaged face set into a snarl. 'Why couldn't you just die!' he demanded of her, a ball of magick in hand.

Chanting, she yanked her fists toward her, wrenching at his arms and dislocating both shoulders.

Ames cried out, the orb of magick in his palm disintegrating. He tried knifing upright, so she slammed her hands together, shattering his kneecaps this time.

He screamed a very non-manly scream. 'You whore! You fucking whore!'

'I warned you that it was a mistake for you to come here to-night. You didn't listen. So sad. For you, anyway.' She broke his neck with a mere twist of her hand. 'And so eight becomes one,' she drawled, flicking her attention to Ward.

'Get her!' he screeched, shoving a covered-in-goblins Rabid toward Emberlyn. He then struck fast, but she tossed out a wave of glittering magick from her palm that 'shoved' his blow right back at him. He hit the ground hard ... which was right when she heard a rumble of engines.

Emberlyn looked up to see several vehicles fast approaching, including Ripper's truck. Feeling her lips curve, she shifted her gaze back to Ward, whose expression had turned from enraged to outright *terrified* as he noticed the newcomers. 'Hmm, I think I'll let Ripper have you. It's not fair of me to have *all* the fun.'

Ward's eyes sliced to her, gleaming with horror.

She let out two sweeps of magic. One shot upward, easing the storm; calling off the rain and wind. The other healed the fissures in the ground and made the rats, snakes, toads and insects disappear as if they had never been.

Tires screeched as the vehicles pulled up. Werewolves jumped out of their cars only to halt in shock at the sight of the goblins.

Who wouldn't?

Emberlyn chanted, communicating directly with the goblins; redirecting their attention solely to the Rabid so that Ripper could have his fun.

Ward struggled to his feet, looking as though he'd make a run for it, but Ripper had recovered fast from his shocked state and was stripping at lightning-fast speed. He ran right at Ward, shifting shape as he lunged. Then a huge mass of dark-furred muscle landed on the male witch.

Ward fell to the ground, smacking his head hard. His limbs flailing, he screamed. And screamed and screamed and *screamed* – the sounds joined the growls, snarls and roars of the wolf savaging his body with teeth and claws.

Emberlyn felt her lips tip up. Maybe she should have felt disturbed rather than satisfied, but Ward had it coming. Not just for what he'd done to her, but for all he was guilty of as part of the faction.

She looked at Reena, finding the woman's face a hard mask. There was grief there, but also a sense of . . . not quite satisfaction, but a cold justice.

Ripper kept on brutalizing Ward. He tore off strips of his skin. Bit out chunks of flesh. Raked his claws deep into Ward's stomach. Hauled out his intestines. Closed his jaws around Ward's nose and ripped it clean off his face.

Well, fuck.

Ward's cries grew weaker and weaker, until they turned into

whimpers and gurgles. Then finally his body slumped, the sounds cutting off altogether.

Emberlyn glanced up to see the other werewolves hanging back, hesitant to get close. Not fearful of their Alpha, just conscious that coming near her could be misinterpreted as a threat while he was in that enraged state.

Ripper raced to her, still in his wolf form.

Squatting, she stroked his fur, carefully avoiding his bloodied muzzle. As his body started reshaping itself, she rose to her feet. Moments later, she had a naked Ripper wrapped tight around her, drinking in her scent.

'Fuck, baby,' he said, his voice guttural with worry, relief and anger. 'What the hell happened here?'

She licked her lips. 'I'll give you the rundown in a moment. First, I need to do something real quick so the Rabid can be subdued.' She chanted, letting out a rope of magick that turned into hundreds of moths. The moths zoomed around and zigzagged between the goblins, distracting them.

Trying to grab at the flying insects, the creatures followed them up the path.

She released another wave of magick, putting the Rabid to sleep. Once they'd slumped to the ground, the crows flew up to the sky and scattered. The other werewolves wasted no time subduing the Rabid with zip ties.

Frowning at the goblins, Ripper jerked his head back. 'What the fuck are they?'

'My friends,' she prevaricated.

His brows flew up. 'Your *what*?'

Ignoring that, Emberlyn led the way as she directed the moths through the manor. Giggling, goblins either skipped or skittered or flew as they followed. She walked into the kitchen, where she opened the door to the basement. 'Your aid was appreciated.'

Once they'd pursued the moths down the steps, descending into the shadows, she closed the door and turned to Ripper. 'Are you all right? Ward didn't hurt you?'

He did a long blink. 'You have *demons* in the basement?'

She almost laughed at the shocking absurdity of his statement. 'They're not demons.'

'No?'

'No,' she assured him with a flap of her hand. 'They're just red goblins. More particularly, they're attendants of the Blood God.'

His brows snapped together. 'Attendants of the *what*?'

'They're creatures from another realm. They feed off malice, revenge, cruelty, pain. They worship and serve the Blood God, a pure evil deity who – in terms of appearance – is a much bigger version of them.' She paused as she took in his expression. 'This isn't making you feel better, is it?'

'No. Not at all.' He planted his fists on his hips. 'How did they even end up in your basement?'

'Millicent opened a portal for them after making a pact with their deity.'

'What kind of pact?'

Emberlyn shrugged. 'She didn't tell me the terms, which means she thought I wouldn't approve and she didn't want to hear me lecture her. I just know that his attendants will come to the aid of her or her descendants if bidden. They – probably because she practiced so much blood magick down there – like to hang in the basement sometimes.'

He shook his head, incredulous. 'And this doesn't bother you? You never worried that they'd harm you? You never thought *to mention it to me*?'

'No need to get hysterical.'

His brows flew up again. 'Hysterical? This isn't me being hysterical, baby. This is me being freaked the fuck out.'

'So, for future reference, when you're freaked the hell out, you turn hysterical?' Because right now, he was *both*.

He scraped a hand down his face. 'That's it. I'm done with this conversation.'

'Good, because we have stuff to do outside.'

CHAPTER THIRTY-SEVEN

Now that Ripper was once more dressed, he and Emberlyn walked from corpse to corpse. Anger thrummed through his blood. Anger and a healthy dose of guilt. If he hadn't taken the faction's bait, if he hadn't allowed himself to be pulled away from her, she wouldn't have been alone when these motherfuckers came for her.

Not that it seemed to bother her that she'd mostly dealt with the faction on her own – well, if you didn't include the goblins and animals. In fact, he got the feeling that she'd relished it. But it bothered *him* a fuck of a lot.

As did knowing there were goblins in the basement, along with a goddamn portal. But he couldn't be mad about it because they'd been indispensable tonight.

Around them, his wolves were keeping watch on the Rabid they'd detained. The creatures were still sleeping, but after all the bullshit that had gone on tonight, no one was in the mood to be complacent; they were too on edge.

Pausing near the twins' parents, she flapped a hand. The protective dome around them lowered instantly. 'They're in a coma,' she murmured. 'I couldn't bring myself to kill them.'

He would have been surprised if she had, given how deeply she cared for Paisley and Kage. But if she *had* ended the couple, Ripper wouldn't have blamed her one bit. 'I wouldn't have pegged them for members of the faction.'

'Me neither. The twins are going to be devastated.'

At the break in her voice, Ripper rubbed her nape. 'One of us needs to call them before they find out about this from someone else. Want me to do it? As their Alpha—'

'I'll do it. I *need* to do it.'

Respecting that, he nodded. 'I wouldn't have thought Ward and Penelope were faction members, but seeing Ames and Ruben here isn't surprising.'

'I wasn't shocked to see *any* of them because I don't trust a single person in the coven. In my view, they were all possible suspects.'

'This has to have hit Reena hard.' Ripper looked over to where she leaned against the fence, her strength not yet fully back. Her dull eyes kept bouncing from her sister to her husband.

'Yeah,' Emberlyn softly agreed.

Ripper kept pace with her as she began making her way to the High Priestess.

'I won't ask if you're all right,' Emberlyn said to her. 'It would be a stupid question.'

'He wanted me dead,' Reena murmured in a hollow voice, staring down at Ward. 'As if to steal my position from me wouldn't have been vengeance enough, he wanted me dead.'

Ripper frowned. Vengeance?

Emberlyn tilted her head. 'He was right about you and Carver, then?'

Reena swallowed. 'Yes. And I don't blame him for his anger. But there is such a thing as divorce.'

'Indeed,' Emberlyn muttered. 'Do you think he was always part of the faction or that they recruited him; showed him evidence of your affair so that they could use him?'

Ripper started in surprise. He hadn't known that Carver and the High Priestess had had an affair. But, looking back on some of their interactions over the past year, a few clues had been there.

'I suspect it was the latter, but I cannot be sure.' Reena put a hand to her throat. 'Why didn't he just confront me? Yell at me?'

It was Ripper who replied. 'Most likely because you then wouldn't have trusted him as implicitly as you always have; you might have even considered him part of the faction.'

'He hid his pain and rage well. It never occurred to me for even a moment that he knew. To think how much he influenced who I should and shouldn't suspect were faction members ... He deliberately ensured that I was confused; that I doubted my own judgement; that I turned my attention away from people like Ames and Ruben.'

Pausing, Reena shifted her gaze to her sister. 'Penelope did the same. I trusted her. Just as I did Ethel. So when they supported Ward's opinions on who could be part of the faction, I allowed them to slide my suspicions elsewhere.'

'Penelope made clear that she's the one who wanted to take your role from you,' said Emberlyn. 'Did you know she'd had her eye on it?'

Reena took a shaky breath. 'Growing up, we had both talked of being High Priestess one day. But she wasn't unkind to me when I took on the position.' Reena flashed a self-deprecating smile. 'She claimed to be proud of me, and I thought that she meant it.'

Hearing more vehicles approach, Ripper looked up. 'The Watchers are here.'

The Watchers dashed out of their vans, their jaws dropping even though they'd been warned of the carnage they would find. Recovering fast, they sprang into action. Some took reports, some bagged up corpses, some moved Ethel and Thad, others piled the Rabid into the vehicles.

Ward's brother Marvin, however, joined Reena in her moment of grief – as devastated by the situation as she was.

Meanwhile, Emberlyn went inside to call both Paisley and Kage to deliver the grim news about their parents. She returned a short time later, her expression sad and somber. 'They were crushed,' she told Ripper. 'Also furious, but mostly just crushed.'

He draped an arm around her shoulders and nuzzled her temple.

A Watcher from his clan approached. 'We're heading off now,' he told Ripper.

Marvin stirred. 'I'll give Reena a ride home and then join you all at the unit.'

Once the Watchers and High Priestess were gone, Emberlyn used a little magick to 'clean up' the scene – removing bloodstains and repairing damage to the fence and gate.

Ripper looked from Kerr to Logan. 'I want wolves patrolling the perimeter of the manor overnight. Once the coven finds out that some of their loved ones are dead, they might get the stupid idea to march over here and confront Emberlyn. It's unlikely, but I'm not willing to take chances.'

Kerr gave a curt nod. 'We'll make it happen.'

'You just focus on your witch,' Logan told Ripper. 'We got this.'

Ripper tipped his chin their way and, seeing that Emberlyn was done magickly cleansing the area, ushered her into the manor. Closing the door behind them, he planted a palm on it.

'Now, tell me *exactly* what happened out there. You only told the Watchers a bullet-point version. I want a full rundown.'

'Okay, but let's do this while we shower. I need one in a major way.'

So they headed to her en suite bathroom. As they soaped each other down under the hot spray, she relayed everything. He remained silent, just listening, his anger kicking up the more he heard. Fuck those son of a bitches. And fuck *him* for not considering—

She flicked him on the forehead. 'You're not allowed to be mad at yourself for responding to the emergency call.'

He glowered. 'I *left* you.'

'You wouldn't have if you'd known what was really going on.' She rinsed off the soap. 'Regrettably, I don't think that the entire faction is gone. No way did it have only eight members.'

He let out a grunt of agreement. 'Maybe they decided to act alone because the others didn't back their play. Or maybe they were sent here like sacrificial pawns to "test" you.'

She hummed, thoughtful. 'Well, I'm quite sure the coven will claim that the faction has now been eradicated – believing that will bring them the most comfort. But it will also enable the rest of the faction to operate from the shadows in peace, and I don't know if we can trust that they'll abandon their plans to knock Reena off her metaphorical throne.'

Personally, Ripper considered that Reena's problem ... providing it didn't touch his witch. 'Why didn't you call me when you knew the faction was outside? Why call on those damn goblins instead?'

Her face softening, she turned off the shower now that they were done. 'Powerful though you are, it wasn't a battle of muscle and fangs and claws. It was a battle of *magick*. You wouldn't want me involved in a werewolf skirmish.'

Unable to deny that, he moodily frowned as he followed her out of the stall. 'I might not be able to wield magick, but I could still have helped you.'

'Yes, you and your wolves could have done plenty of damage,' she allowed, passing him a towel before wrapping one around herself. 'But I had two very good reasons for not contacting you.'

'Oh, do tell,' he said as he curled a towel around his waist, his voice dry. 'I'd love to know what you could possibly consider *good* reasons.' In his view, there weren't any.

Rolling her eyes at his tone, she padded out of the bathroom. 'You have to understand, Ripper. I had a *huge* score to settle. I've been blamed for those bastards' deeds for years. They've used me as their fall person for as long as I can remember. *You* would have ensured it was over with fast. That was not in my plans. I wanted them to suffer.'

His cock went ahead and twitched at the bloodthirst in her voice. 'And your second reason?'

At the dresser, she swiped a tee from a drawer. 'I didn't want my first night as your clan's Alpha female to be one in which I dragged them into a fight – a fight during which some of them would *definitely* have been injured and possibly even forced to kill some of the Rabid because, let's face it, the faction would have made them attack you.'

'You don't know that they would have – wait, back the fuck up. Alpha female?'

'Yeah.'

The implications of her words settling in, Ripper slowly crossed to her, his heart starting to beat like crazy. 'You're saying yes? You're going to let me claim you?'

She sighed. 'It'd be easy to let all that's happened through-out my life make me hold back from you, from what you're asking of me. Whenever I've given people a lot of myself in the past, they've thrown it back in my face. But you're not them. I know down to my bones that you wouldn't hurt me that way. And fuck if I'll let those assholes in my past ruin this for me, for us.'

His chest warming and tightening, he brushed the tip of his nose along the side of her own. 'You're sure about this?'

'Positive.'

He took the tee from her and threw it aside. 'This is gonna happen right here, right now. You could have been killed out there tonight. I'm not waiting another fucking second to claim you unless it's what you need from me.'

'I don't need you to wait,' she assured him. 'Do it. Make me yours.'

The wave of sexual hunger that swept Ripper under was like nothing he'd felt before. The sheer intensity of it rocked him. His pulse quickened, his blood heated and his cock went rock hard. Not even on his first full moon had his body felt so fucking *alive*. Because this witch, who'd somehow come to mean everything to him, would from this night onward be officially his.

Her pupils dilated as her breaths came a little faster. Her magick rose up to mist the air, ramping up the tension, almost imprinting itself on him.

Ripper palmed the side of her face. 'Let me at that mouth.'

She parted her lips for him, and he instantly plunged his tongue inside. The kiss was slow but deep and greedy. She made him want to gorge on her. Bite her. Mark her with his come. Take her hard and fast and rough.

The latter wouldn't happen just yet, though. He wasn't going to rush this. He was going to savor every damn moment of making her *his*.

Moaning into his mouth, she threaded her fingers through his damp hair and scratched at his scalp.

He whipped off her towel and backed her into the bed. Breaking the kiss, he lifted her and gently lay her flat on the mattress. The moonlight streaming through the window danced along her iridescent hair and made her dewy skin gleam. 'Perfect.'

Arousal was clearly riding her as hard as it was him. Her eyes were dazed, her nipples were tight and her pussy glistened. The scent of her need gripped his dick tight.

Ripper removed his towel and lowered his body onto hers, giving her most of his weight. Dropping his mouth on those lips already swollen from his kiss, he ate at it once more. He explored her body with his hands, smoothing his scent over her, feeling her arch into his touch. He wanted his scent to sink so deep into her that it became embedded in every cell. A part of her.

He spread kisses down the side of her face, her slim throat, her breast and over to her nipple. He circled the bud with his tongue and then latched onto it tight.

She dug her nails into his shoulders as he went on to lavish the taut bud with sucks, licks and nibbles. All the while, he molded her neglected breast, thumbing the nipple there.

'Ripper,' she breathed.

He rocked his hips forward, rubbing his dick over her clit. His cock was so hard at this point he could knock a wall down with it.

She smoothed a hand down his back, her fingers splayed. Fingers that idly brushed over his scars, tracing them carefully. He loved that she never shied away from touching them to 'spare' his feelings. To her, they were just a part of him.

He slid a palm – one that was more than a little covetous – down her front and slipped two fingers into her pussy, grunting as it clenched them. Yeah, she was wet enough for him.

He replaced his fingers with the thick head of his dick and

then, holding her gaze, pushed his cock into that pussy that fit him perfectly. Her lips parted, her eyes went glassier and glassier the deeper he burrowed.

Finally, he bottomed out, groaning. 'Fuck.'

Clinging tight to his back, she arched into his body, pushing her breasts at him. 'Rip.' A breathy moan laced with a plea.

Ripper started driving into her, slow and easy. She never stopped touching him – she stroked the back of his head, scratched at his nape, slid her hands up and down his back, gripped his ass.

He groaned as she unconsciously tipped her hips up. 'That's it, baby, take me deeper.' His eyes dipped to where their bodies joined as he slid a hand down to grip her thigh. 'I swear, it's like your pussy was goddamn tailor made for me.' He hiked up her leg and curved it around him as he scraped his teeth down her cheek. '*Only* for me.'

The more he fucked her, the more she melted. The more she melted, the more glazed her eyes became ... until she looked totally out of it.

He hummed low in his throat. 'Fuck drunk. Aren't you?' She wasn't the only one. He was all wrapped up in her taste, her heat, her scent, the tight clasp of her pussy. He couldn't have pulled out of her body to save his life.

He felt the warmth of her magick flow over him like a roll of steam that sank into his skin. 'Scent-marking me again?'

She stared at him, looking rather pleased with herself. 'It'll be permanent this time. Even if we part ways, you'll still smell of my magick ... unless I agree to undo it. Which I won't. So ha.'

Emberlyn wasn't sure what exact reaction she'd expected to that declaration. A chuckle. A bite. A brow flick. Maybe even a nipple pinch.

Instead, satisfaction bloomed in his dilated pupils as his expression turned nothing short of carnal – his eyes hot, his mouth a cold slash, his jaw a hard blade. That look went right to her nipples. Nipples that were tight and pulsing.

Her body was a *mess*. The need to come slashed at her insides and made her core and breasts ache. 'You're not mad?'

He started rolling his hips fast, slamming hard. She'd take that as a no.

Slapping sounds mingled with their grunts, groans and rough exhales as his hips kept bounding forward heavily, shoving his thick shaft deep enough to hurt a little.

Arching into the drives of his cock, she delved a hand into his hair and scratched at his scalp. He lowered his face to hers, and their lips met in a savage kiss that was all tongue and teeth. He freaking devoured her mouth with such intensity her lungs burned for air.

Finally, he broke the kiss. 'You're mine in every way now, Emberlyn,' he snarled, roughly plowing his dick into her. 'I'll never give you up. Not ever.'

She wouldn't let him if he tried.

The tips of his claws lightly scraped her arms, sides, thighs, outer breasts – wherever he could reach, could *mark*. Loving the sheer primitiveness of it, she arched into the sensations, eager for more.

She dug her fingers deeper into his ass, moaning louder and louder and louder as he insistently jackhammered into her like he was caught in a frenzy. 'Rip,' she gasped.

'Jax. Say it,' he bit off. 'I want to hear you say it while I claim you.'

'Jax.'

Growling, he shifted his angle so he rubbed his shaft over her clit . . . and bit down hard on the crook of her neck.

She came with a scream, her head falling back, her spine bowing, her pussy clamping and clenching.

Ripper fucked her harder, faster, *fiercer*. Then he jammed his cock deep and exploded, filling her with his come.

Almost every muscle in her body losing their tone, she more or less flopped to the mattress. He remained over her like a blanket as they panted, shaking with aftershocks.

Unlatching his teeth from her throat, he hummed against the bite. It didn't sting, since the skin hadn't broken – to do that would have been to put her through the Change – but it certainly throbbed. 'Love you, baby.'

Her chest squeezed. 'Love you, too,' she rasped.

They had some stuff to figure out. Like when exactly he wanted to move into the manor. Like who the rest of the faction members were. Like how best to reveal to his clan that, hey, they had an Alpha female now – one who was also a witch. Maybe he was right in believing that his wolves would take it well, but maybe he wasn't.

Time would tell.

A door creaked open somewhere inside the manor, and then there was the distant sound of footfalls.

Ripper slowly lifted his head. 'Tell me that isn't one of those damn goblins.'

'They don't leave the basement.' Well, not unless she bid them to do so.

He squinted. 'Is there anything else ... otherworldly living in this house?'

She only smiled.

'Fuck,' he muttered.

'Are you sure you want to move in?'

'Well, I'm not living separately from my mate.' He touched the tip of his nose to hers. 'Never thought I'd claim one.'

'Never thought I'd go down this route a second time.'

'There won't be a third,' he half vowed, half warned. 'You belong to me now. There'll never be a time when you don't.'

She felt her lips curve again. 'Sounds good to me.'

ACKNOWLEDGMENTS

Thank you so much to my family for all your love and support – it means everything.

Big shout out to my social media manager, Bev. You hopped on board with no hesitation exactly when I most needed you, thank you.

Mega thanks to the people behind the scenes who make the magic work – Donna Hillyer and the Piatkus team are one in a million.

Last but never in the slightest bit least, HUMUNGOUS thank you to every reader who takes this new series for a spin. You're all the bestest!